"GRANT, MEET McCALEB"

When the door swung open, a Union soldier stepped out. McCaleb got an arm around his throat, cut off his wind, and with the muzzle of his Colt, hit him just hard enough.

"There'll be another one," McCaleb called to Cody.

Again he positioned himself by the door. Again, it opened and a second soldier appeared.

McCaleb caught him around the throat and silenced him with a swift blow of the Colt's muzzle. McCaleb dragged the two unconscious men into the presidential coach. He closed the door behind him and advanced to the door ahead. He drew his Colt, turned the knob, and confronted the President of the United States. . . .

THE WESTERN TRAIL

Ralph Compton

St. Martin's Paperbacks

This is a work of fiction, based on actual trail drives of the Old West. Many of the characters appearing in the Trail Drive Series were very real, and some of the trail drives actually took place. But the reader should be aware that, in the developing of characters and events, some fictional literary license has been employed. While some of the characters and events herein are purely the creation of the author, every effort has been made to portray them with accuracy. However, the inherent dangers of the trail are real, sufficient unto themselves, and seldom has it been necessary to enhance their reality.

THE WESTERN TRAIL

Copyright © 1992 by Ralph Compton.

For information address St. Martin's Press, 175 Fifth Avenue, New York, NY 10010.

EAN: 978-0-312-92901-5

Printed in the United States of America

St. Martin's Paperbacks edition / December 1992

Respectfully dedicated to:
Miss Lena Goodnight, Quanah, Texas
Ms. Pat Sikes, Claude, Texas
Ms. Sue McClure, Nashville, Tennessee

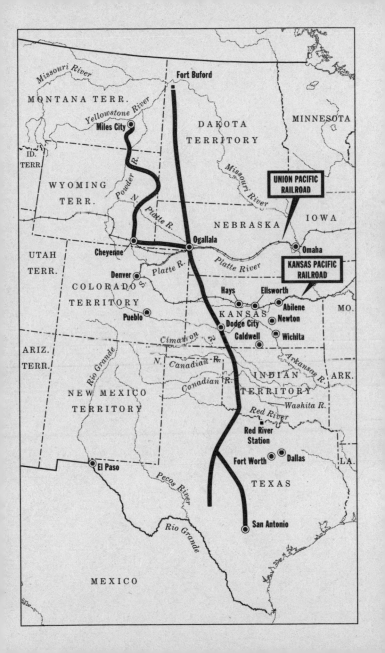

AUTHOR'S FOREWORD

*I*n the aftermath of the Civil War, cash-starved Texans turned to the only resource they possessed in abundance: longhorn cows. Five million of them, wild or nearly so. Much of the western part of the nation was still designated as "territories," including New Mexico, Colorado, Wyoming, Dakota, Idaho, Utah, and Oklahoma. The rails reached Abilene, Kansas, in 1867. Despite the hazards of trailing longhorns across some three hundred miles of Indian Territory, it was the Texas trail driver's only access to the railroad.

Charles Goodnight was the first Texas cattleman to see the advantages of blazing a new trail, to winter his herd on virgin range in New Mexico and Colorado, to seek more lucrative markets. While Goodnight needed money, he saw beyond that immediate need. In these sparsely inhabited, isolated "territories," he saw the need for breeding stock, and the potential for a cattle empire.

The opening of the Western trail finished what Goodnight had started. It ran northerly from San Antonio, across south-central Texas, skirted the border of Indian Territory, and, bearing a bit to the west at Fort Dodge, struck out for Ogallala, Nebraska. The northern leg continued across Dakota Territory to Fort Buford, located on the south bank of the Missouri, at the extreme western border of what would become North Dakota. The western leg of the trail veered from Ogallala to Cheyenne, where it swung north to Fort Laramie, and from there snaked its way across Wyoming Territory. It crossed the Powder River at Montana Territory's southern border, ending at Miles City, at the confluence of the Powder and the Yellowstone rivers.

While the Western trail barely touched the western boundary of Indian Territory, there were Indians in Wyoming, Montana, and Dakota territories. But despite the hazards, it was "seed" cattle from Texas that heralded the beginning of these uncharted territories as cattle country.

In November 1867 the first Union Pacific train rolled into Cheyenne. By the end of 1868, end-of-track had reached the Utah line. May 10, 1869, the Union Pacific and Central Pacific tracks joined at Promontory Summit, Utah. The first transcontinental railroad was completed. Following the Fetterman massacre in 1866, and the Wagon Box fight in 1867, the Bozeman trail was closed. In April 1868 one of the most famous of Indian treaties was signed at Fort Laramie. The Indians would be moved north, away from the railroad. A popular consensus was that the railroad had eliminated the need for the Bozeman trail and its protective forts, thus solving the Indian problem. But these historic moves made little difference in the territories. Just as emigrants following the Bozeman trail hadn't stayed, neither did most of those riding the Union Pacific trains. Despite the treaty, Indians—most notably the Arapaho and Shoshoni—still fought the white man and each other.

The high plains, with their sage brush, mesquite, and buffalo grass, were unsuited to anything except grazing cattle or sheep. Prairie towns provided water tanks where thirsty locomotives drank, and a stop for bored passengers to eat and stretch their legs. But only Texas cowboys found the plains appealing enough to stay, and some of them did. Insofar as Texas trail drives were concerned, the coming of the railroad to the territories changed nothing. It was only a means of getting the cattle to market—if the new rancher survived long enough to have cattle to sell. The Indians continued to be a threat until 1874, the same year that Joseph F. Glidden received a patent for barbed wire. The days of the Texas trail drive were numbered.

Paradoxically, the great war that drove Texans to their knees put them on their feet. Forced from the land of their birth, they settled the territories and built cow country empires along the Western trail.

PROLOGUE

$\mathcal{B}$enton McCaleb was from Red River County, Texas. He was but thirty years old, with straw-yellow hair and blue eyes. In his Texas boots he stood just four inches shy of seven feet. He wore a Colt .44 on his left hip, butt forward for a cross-hand draw. McCaleb had joined the Rangers in 1861. During his four-year enlistment he had met and become friends with Charles Goodnight, Brazos Gifford, and Will Elliot. It had been Goodnight's dream to blaze a new trail from Texas to Colorado Territory, driving a herd of Texas longhorns through eastern New Mexico. The four friends left the Rangers in 1865. The Civil War had left Texas bankrupt, disenfranchised, and occupied by carpetbaggers and Union soldiers. Texas cattle, including Goodnight's, had run wild during the war. With the trail drive in mind, Goodnight set out to recover the remnant of his original herd, along with the natural increase. He invited McCaleb, Brazos, and Will to gather a herd and trail with him. Short on money but long on ambition, the trio headed for the Trinity River brakes to rope wild longhorns. Once they reached southern Colorado, Goodnight chose to settle there and establish a ranch. But McCaleb's outfit moved on, with plans to start a ranch in Wyoming, and from there, to take trail drives into Montana and Dakota territories.

McCaleb's herd of trailwise Texas longhorns was 2,400

strong. There were 1,950 big steers, while the rest was she-stuff and less-than-two-year-olds. Including McCaleb, the 6 outfit consisted of nine riders and a cook. There were his longtime friends and partners, Brazos Gifford and Will Elliot, young Monte Nance and his sister Rebecca, and a Lipan Apache known only as "Goose." The newest riders were Jed and Stoney Vandiver, and Pen Rhodes, whom McCaleb had hired in Denver. Finally, there was Salty Reynolds, the cook.

Now they were nearing Cheyenne, a town established by the Union Pacific as a division point for the railroad.

"We'll take them west of town," shouted McCaleb, "and then back to the northeast. First decent graze and water, let's bed them down."

Goose, the Lipan Apache, trotted his horse alongside McCaleb's.

"Iron horse come," said Goose, proud of his newly acquired English.

McCaleb grinned at the Indian, then waved his hat to halt the oncoming herd. There was as yet no sign of a train, or even the railroad, but if Goose said a train was coming, there would be a train. There was no point in risking a stampede by taking the herd any nearer the track. Then, diminished by distance but distinct, there was the low moan of a whistle, as the engineer signaled for the stop at Cheyenne. McCaleb and Goose trotted their horses toward the slow-moving herd. The flankers, Will and Brazos, had already moved to the point, and the longhorns were beginning to mill. The chuck wagon caught up to them and Salty reined his mules to a halt.

"Want me t' go ahead an' git a head start on supper?"

"No," said McCaleb, "wait for the train to pass. Mules will stampede as quick as cows. Two of those jugheads hitched to the wagon like to have been the death of us. One night when we were crossing the Guadalupes, on our way back to Texas, they went crazy."

The train departed Cheyenne, heading west, and Mc-

Caleb feared they might already be too near the track. They were downwind, and as the train came closer, they could hear the wheels clacking over the coupling joints. There was a bellow from the locomotive's whistle, and some of the cattle bellowed in response, almost as though they were answering it. From opposite directions the riders trotted their horses around the nervous cattle, until the great iron beast was swallowed by distance. When they reached the Union Pacific track, McCaleb trotted his horse across and waited for the herd. But as soon as they were close enough to see the unfamiliar track, the lead steers began to mill. Those behind bawled in confusion, and then decided to hightail it back the way they had come. Mc-Caleb kicked his horse into a gallop, but there was no way he could head them. Monte and Rebecca were at drag, as were Pen, Jed, and Stoney. They rode like demons, swinging their lariats against dusty flanks and shouting their rebel yells.

Finally the resistance took hold and the herd began to turn, but the pursuing drag riders didn't let up. McCaleb thought he knew what they were trying to do. He wheeled his horse and pounded back toward the railroad. Goose, Will, and Brazos were right behind him. They galloped across the track well ahead of the herd and fanned out, facing the oncoming cattle. If they wanted to run, then let the momentum of the stampede take them across the railroad! If there was any reluctance on the part of the lead steers, it was wasted, because the rest of the herd kept coming. McCaleb, Will, Brazos, and Goose advanced, swinging their lariats. Seeing the riders, the herd began to slow and then to mill. The drag riders continued swatting the stragglers, lest they pause, balking at the unfamiliar rails and ties. McCaleb circled the herd, grinning at his riders who had turned it.

"I saw that happen once before," said Pen Rhodes. "Took two days to get them danged cows across the railroad. Ain't often an outfit gets any good out of a stampede, like we just did."

They drove past Cheyenne and headed northeast, putting them just north of the town. They soon found excellent graze, and bedded down the herd along a bank-full stream that someday would be called Lodge Pole Creek.

"I purely like this country," McCaleb told them. "Eventually, we'll take trail drives into Montana and Dakota territories, but we'll have to winter somewhere. We'll need a place to call home. Why can't we do here what Goodnight did in southern Colorado? We'll have it all to ourselves."

He should have known better.

1

June 2, 1868. Wyoming Territory

*T*he herd grazed peacefully along Lodge Pole Creek. They were still an hour away from sundown, but Salty went ahead with supper.

"I can't wait to see the shops and the town," said Rebecca Nance. "Just imagine how much better everything will be with the railroad here. Can't we stay here a few days?"

"I'd planned to," said McCaleb. "I'll need to visit the bank and the land office, and I expect the chuck wagon's mighty bare. Right, Salty?"

"Dang right," said the garrulous old cook. "After th' feed we just had, they ain't no bacon t' go with th' beans we ain't got, an' no coffee t' drink with th' dried apple pie, even if'n we had th' apples t' make 'em."

"In the morning, then," said McCaleb, "we'll see what Cheyenne has to offer."

They gathered around the chuck wagon, enjoying their coffee. They were a good outfit, McCaleb reflected. It was a time for remembering, and he let his thoughts touch on each of them and the trails they'd ridden together. First, there was Brazos Gifford and Will Elliot. They were closer to McCaleb than brothers. They would have given their lives for McCaleb, and he'd have done no less for them.

Brazos Gifford was a redheaded, quick-tempered, Spanish-speaking cowboy from south Texas. He wore a gray, flat-crowned hat, tilted low over his green eyes. The rest of his garb consisted of denim shirt, Levi's pants, and rough-out, high-heeled boots. Will Elliot had curly black hair, gray eyes, and a quick sense of humor. Will was educated. His father had been a lawyer before the war, and Will could hold his own in a frontier courtroom. Will was from Waco, and except for a wide-brim, pinch-crease black Stetson, he wore the same range clothes as Brazos. Each man carried a tied-down .44 Colt low on his right hip, and like Benton McCaleb, each carried a sixteen-shot Henry repeating rifle in his saddle boot. Brazos was twenty-nine, just a year younger than McCaleb, while Will was a year older.

If Benton McCaleb lived to be a hundred, he'd never forget the volatile situation he, Brazos, and Will had ridden into three years ago, when they'd gone to the Trinity River brakes to gather a herd of wild longhorns. While the Comanche Indians were the scourge of East Texas and would have been trouble enough, that hadn't been the worst of it. York Nance, a shameless old reprobate run out of Missouri for mule rustling, had a shack on the Trinity. He also had a son, a daughter, and a shaky alliance with the Comanches. Not only had he been selling them rotgut whiskey, he'd devised a nefarious scheme to supply them with new Spencer rifles! Worse, he had half promised his daughter to Blue Feather, a Comanche chief. McCaleb had an immediate falling out with York Nance, and the old man's dishonest ways had eventually driven Monte and Rebecca away.

Monte, the old man's twenty-one-year-old son, was a swaggering, hot-tempered kid who fancied himself a fast gun. He challenged McCaleb, went for his gun, and was wounded. Rebecca, Nance's twenty-eight-year-old daughter, had been a mother to Monte since his birth, and went after McCaleb. Thus their first meeting resulted in a kicking, scratching, clawing fight that ended with McCaleb dunking the furious Rebecca in the river. Despite instant hostility between the temperamental girl and McCaleb, a relationship developed. Rebecca Nance had green eyes, dark hair, callused hands, and not the foggiest notion of how to be a lady. Motherless since she was five, she could ride, rope, and shoot like a cowboy. And she swore like a bull whacker. But she was as charming as she was beautiful. McCaleb's outfit yielded to her plea; she and Monte had added their small herd to McCaleb's gather. From Texas to Colorado, McCaleb had endured Rebecca's stormy moods and the outfit's bullyragging, only to have the girl become infatuated with an unscrupulous Colorado cattleman, Jonathan Wickliffe. McCaleb had found himself facing hired guns on a Denver street, had been wounded, and had ended up in jail. Only when Rebecca had discovered Wickliffe's plan to kill McCaleb had he managed to reclaim her.

While young Monte Nance became faster and more deadly with a Colt, he was also improving his skills at the poker table. It was a volatile mix, which drew McCaleb's outfit into an alliance with gunfighter Clay Allison and led to a shootout with crooked gamblers in Santa Fe. There, they met the stove-up old cook, Salty Reynolds. Salty was trapped behind a lunch counter, longing to return to the range, but unable to ride. McCaleb, tired of pack mules, had bought a chuck wagon and had hired the crippled old rider. Salty had graying hair, watery blue eyes, and a sharp tongue that hid a soft heart.

The most enigmatic of McCaleb's outfit was a Comanche-hating Lipan Apache they knew only as *Ganos.* "Goose," half-starved and near death, was about to be burned at the stake by Comanches. Scouting the Trinity River brakes, McCaleb, Brazos, and Will had gunned down his captors, freeing the Indian. Goose had remained, riding, roping, and scouting. Goose adapted, becoming deadly quick with a Colt and a consummate gambler, but always an Indian. His constant companion was a foot-long bowie knife, razor-keen, for the scalping of his enemies.

Following the gunfight in Denver, McCaleb had spent the night in jail, pending a hearing. While there, he'd lent a sympathetic ear to three young Texas cowboys in an adjoining cell. The oldest was Pendleton Rhodes. Pen was a studious, quick-witted half-breed from Waco. He had jet-black hair, dark eyes, and a sense of humor. His companions were blue-eyed, tow-headed brothers from San Antonio, Jed and Stoney Vandiver. Stoney was youngest, just twenty-two. Jed was twenty-four, a year younger than Pen Rhodes. The trio had come up the trail from Texas, had sold their horses in Ellsworth, and had ridden the train to Denver. They had gone to a whorehouse, had been given doctored drinks, and robbed. They retaliated by wrecking the place. Benton McCaleb had been impressed with them and had paid for their release. In the summer of 1868, when McCaleb rode out of Denver, Jed, Stoney, and Pen rode with him.

Although Cheyenne was only a year old, it had an air of permanence that most railroad towns lacked. Chief engineer Grenville Dodge had chosen it as a division point for the Union Pacific, and already there was a bank, a land office, and a weekly newspaper. There were six saloons, a barbershop and bathhouse, a billiard parlor, several rooming houses, a whorehouse, a combined livery and wagon yard, and a variety of shops and stores.

"I have business at the bank and the land office," said McCaleb. "Near as we are to town, four of you can ride along. When we get back, the rest of you can go. Pen, Jed, Stoney, and Salty, I can advance you some money to buy whatever you need. You won't get a better chance than this."

"I'm about half scairt to go to town," said Stoney, "after what we got into back in Denver."

"Stay out of the whorehouses," said McCaleb. "You're likely to come out of there with more than an aching head and empty pockets."

"We're new to the outfit," said Pen. "We'll stay with the herd, and take our turn when the rest of you get back."

"I just need a couple o' plugs fer chewin'," said Salty, "an' I'll git that when I go t' stock up th' chuck wagon."

"*Ciudad?*" inquired McCaleb, turning to Goose.

Goose shook his head, shuffling an imaginary deck of cards.

"Don't let us have any money until we're ready for town," said Pen, "or this Lipan cardsharp will clean us out while you're gone."

Will, Brazos, Monte, and Rebecca rode with McCaleb into town. He advanced each of them fifty dollars.

"We've tangled with the law and the courts in New Mexico and Colorado," said McCaleb. "Don't do anything that'll put us on the outs with the law here."

They grinned at him and headed for the billiard parlor.

"You never told me why Pen, Jed, and Stoney were in jail in Denver," said Rebecca. "Did that have something to do with you telling them to stay out of whorehouses?"

"Yeah," said McCaleb, "and if they ever find out I've told you, they'll be so embarrassed, they'll never look you in the face again. Come on, we have things to do."

There was a surprising number of Indians in town, apparently seeing nothing, yet seeing everything. McCaleb headed for Bullard's Mercantile, the most imposing store in Cheyenne. It covered half a block, a roofed boardwalk running the length of it.

"If you're going to the bank and to the land office," said Rebecca, "why don't we go there first? I want to spend some time in the store without us having to hurry."

"Because there's something I aim to take care of here before we go anywhere else. Later on, we'll come back here and you can take all the time you want."

Mystified, Rebecca followed him into the vast store. It was prestigious as anything she had seen in Denver or St. Louis. McCaleb headed for the center of the store and the main counter, on which sat a locked glass display case. She caught her breath at the watches and various expensive jewelry items. There were necklaces, lockets, and bracelets. And rings!

The white-haired man who hurried to wait on them might have been Bullard himself. He wore an expensive dark suit, tie, and a professional smile. Rebecca thought the smile became a bit strained as he took in their dusty clothes and runover boots.

"I want a ring for the lady," said McCaleb.

"The rings—the diamonds—are very expensive," said the man who might have been Bullard. He no longer smiled.

"I expected them to be," said McCaleb. "Let her try that one on; the big one."

"The large one is, ah, five hundred dollars. . . ."

"I didn't ask how much it is," said McCaleb, irked. "I asked you to let her try it on. If it fits, or can be made to fit, we'll take it."

Rebecca became so choked up, she could hardly breathe as he slipped the ring on her third finger. The finger on which she had worn Jonathan Wickliffe's ring, not quite a week ago.

". . . a bit loose," the expensive-dressed man was saying.

"She can take it off when she's ropin' cows," said McCaleb, unsmiling. He took a handful of double eagles from the saddlebag he carried, spilling them out on the counter. Bullard—if that's who he was—had regained his professional smile. Rebecca said nothing until they were outside the store, on the boardwalk. She trotted ahead of McCaleb, and when he reached her, she threw her arms around him, half laughing, half crying.

"Benton McCaleb," she cried, "you and your cast-iron Texas pride! Thank God he didn't know you well enough to tell you the price was five thousand dollars!"

While the building housing the bank was no more than adequate, there was an enormous vault with a time lock. Musgrove, the banker, seemed truly happy to see them.

Especially when McCaleb dropped the gold-laden saddle-bags on his desk.

"I appreciate your business, McCaleb," said Musgrove. "God knows, we need somebody to populate this territory besides mountain men and Indians. The railroad brings folks here and then takes them farther west, on to Oregon and California."

"That's part of our reason for coming here," said McCaleb. "The railroad. Why drive cattle a thousand miles to market when there's a couple million acres of buffalo grass within spittin' distance of the track?"

"My very existence hinges on the railroad, McCaleb. The Union Pacific is my bread and butter, so I am not at liberty to discuss some of the, ah, 'irregularities' which have arisen as a result of government land grants along the Union Pacific right-of-way. I would suggest that once you have met with Malcolm Walker at the land office, you actually homestead—secure by patent—the land you have in mind."

McCaleb and Rebecca had said little, allowing Musgrove to do most of the talking. Once they left the bank, Rebecca voiced McCaleb's very thoughts.

"The government's giving the railroads millions of acres along their rights-of-way. What Musgrove is really telling us is something's crooked going on. He's telling us to shy away from railroad lands. Why?"

"The railroad, or somebody involved with it, has plans for those millions of acres," said McCaleb. "I don't aim to squat on railroad lands or use them for free range. We'll find good grazing land with water and settle there. I don't see how that poses a problem for us or the railroad. We can have access to it without settling alongside the tracks."

The huge map on Malcolm Walker's wall was the result of a survey the railroad had done in Wyoming Territory in 1862. The railroad grants—every other section along the right-of-way—had been blue-penciled. Many of the alternate sections had been blocked off in red.

"The sections blocked in red have been homesteaded," said Walker. "As you can see, where the Green River flows south from the Wind River range all the way east to the North Platte, the Sweetwater valley is tied up with homesteading."

"There's the Powder River basin, north of the Sweetwater River," said McCaleb. "Why are there no homesteaded sections there?"

"Shoshoni and Arapaho lands," said Walker. "The government ceded them the Powder River valley and lands north to the Big Horn mountains after the close of the Bozeman trail."

"The Sweetwater range has been boxed in," said McCaleb. "A hundred and fifty miles from west to east, and seventy-five miles north to south, homesteaded strategically along the Sweetwater to secure all water rights, and covered to the south by the Union Pacific tracks and government grants to the railroad. If I had to guess, I'd say that some jaybird has hired himself enough 'homesteaders' to tie up water rights along the Sweetwater to the north. Still guessin', I won't be surprised to find this same hombre already has, or can get, control of the government grants along the Union Pacific right-of-way to the south."

"I can't confirm or deny what you've just said," protested Walker. "I can assure you that the homesteaded sections along the Sweetwater are in the names of individuals. Different people."

"With every one capable of proving up on his patent," said McCaleb, "and then selling out to someone else."

"Mr. McCaleb," said Walker coldly, "it's not my place to discuss with you the possibility—or even the probability—of wrongdoing under the Homestead Act. I'm here to tell you what's available for homesteading and to assist you in filing if you choose to do so."

"We want to file on ten quarter-sections, then," said McCaleb. "On Box Elder Creek, a hundred miles due north of Cheyenne and fifty miles north of the Union Pacific tracks."

"I see," said Walker with a half smile. "Each of your riders will claim a quarter section, and you—the outfit—will control it all. Legal, of course, but I had the impression you didn't approve of such tactics."

"What's sauce for the goose is sauce for the gander," said McCaleb.

"Maybe we should just move on," said Rebecca when they'd left the land office. "We could go to Montana. Somebody with the railroad almost has to be involved in all this, and we can't fight them."

"I don't aim to," said McCaleb. "We're not makin' a bid for their land, and we've got as much right to homestead as they have. What's botherin' you is that people as greedy as that, owning the Sweetwater valley, still won't be satisfied."

"I know they won't," she said. "If they were that easy to satisfy, they wouldn't have taken so much already."

"It purely ain't my nature to run from people like that," said McCaleb. "Let one buffalo you, and you'll end up always on the run. I won't run."

"How well I know that," sighed Rebecca. "Texans are never truly happy until they're down to their last two or three shells, bleeding from their wounds, and surrounded by hostile Indians or outlaws. Can we go to the store?"

"You can," said McCaleb. "I aim to find out who this jaybird is that's makin' such big tracks along the Sweetwater. Like you said," he grinned, "if he gets troublesome, I'll have to know who I'm gunnin' for."

Returning to Bullard's Mercantile, Rebecca found Brazos and Monte testing the lever action on some new Winchester rifles.

"Seventeen-shot," said Monte. "They're replacing the Henry. Seems like we've made enough money that we could afford some of these. But they're almost fifty dollars apiece."

Rebecca giggled. "We can't afford them. McCaleb spent all our money."

Monte whooped at the sight of the ring and lifted her off

the floor. Even the usually bashful Brazos gave her a squeeze.

"You ain't goin' to believe what Will's done," cackled Monte.

"My God, no," said Brazos. "I don't believe it myself, and I saw it happen. He's always said he was going to find a handsome schoolmarm, and danged if he didn't! Never seen a man, even a Texan, move that fast!"

"This place sells books," said Monte, "and this girl—with red hair and big blue eyes—was lookin' at 'em. Will, he goes over there just like he's got good sense and starts talkin' to her."

"Follered her home," said Brazos, "her smilin' at him all the way. Took up with him because he knowed this Shakespeare that wrote the book they was lookin' at. I'm tempted to buy that book and get to know old Shakespeare myself."

"You should," said Rebecca. "Both of you. There's more to life than billiard parlors and saloons."

"There's the whorehouses," said Monte.

He ducked behind the gun case to evade her angry clutches.

The newspaper office wasn't difficult to find. A flat piece of wood had been pegged to the door, and upon it, in big black letters, some uninspired painter had printed NEWSPA-PER. A counter ran the length of the small room, and behind it stood a single handpress, a cabinet to hold the type cases, and an ink-smeared young man with a pencil behind his ear. He reminded McCaleb of Bascom, the nosy news-paperman from Denver. He wore the same seedy attire and had achieved the same nondescript effect, his tie dan-gling loose beneath an unbuttoned collar. The sleeves of his suit coat were too short, making him appear more gawky than he probably was. He had a thin face, long scraggly brown hair, and matching brown eyes. McCaleb guessed he couldn't be more than thirty. He looked up as McCaleb entered.

"Yes," he said, "this is the newspaper office."

McCaleb grinned. "I'd just about figured that out on my own."

"Can't give people too much credit; they'll let you down every time. Had a sign that said *The Ledger—The Cheyenne Ledger,* really—and every livin' soul that came down the boardwalk stuck his head in here to see what *The Ledger* was. Them that come looking for the newspaper didn't know they'd found it until I told 'em 'Yes, this is the newspaper office.' You're new to these parts; maybe you can restore my faith in humanity."

"I doubt it," said McCaleb. "I need information. I'm Benton McCaleb, from Red River County, Texas."

"Sam Colton. I quit a pretty good job in Omaha to come here, so I don't know if I'm smart enough to be of any help to you."

Briefly McCaleb told him of their plans to homestead on Box Elder Creek, to establish a home ranch there from which trail drives could originate, pushing into Montana and Dakota territories along the Western trail.

"According to the land office," continued McCaleb, "most of southern Wyoming is spoken for. To the south, along the Union Pacific right-of-way, it's government grants to the railroad. To the north, along the Sweetwater, it's homesteaded. Kind of unusual, wouldn't you say, that these homesteaders have taken such an almighty strong interest in the Sweetwater valley? Like I was pointin' out to this pilgrim at the land office, wouldn't take a whole lot of money or brains for a man to control every foot of southern Wyoming just by squattin' on the south bank of the Sweetwater and tyin' up all the water rights. Especially if he was in solid enough with the Union Pacific to get his hands on those railroad grants along the right-of-way."

"Nothing I can tell you," said Colton, "that you haven't pretty well figured out on your own."

"Just one thing," said McCaleb. "Who is this jaybird with one foot in Washington and the other in Wyoming, with enough power that he can lead the Union Pacific Railroad to water and force it to drink?"

"Why is it important to you? You'll be well away from the Sweetwater range, to the east, near the confluence of Box Elder Creek and the North Platte River."

"I've never seen a range hog who was satisfied with what he had," said McCaleb. "Now are you goin' to tell me what I need to know, or have you been hog-tied and branded by this same hombre that's got everybody else buffaloed?"

"Nobody's got a brand on me," said Colton hotly. "I was broke when I got here, and I've gone downhill from there. The man you're looking for is George Francis Train. He's the power behind the Union Pacific because he's responsible for the very existence of the railroad. He masterminded the financing through what he calls the Credit Mobilier of America. He's milked the most respected money men in the nation, had them begging for a chance to invest their money. There are rumors that Train cleared more than thirty million dollars just by 'investing' in the right lands in and around Omaha. He's been accused of using his prior knowledge as to the direction the road would take, and acquiring certain portions of right-of-way, which he 'sold' to the Union Pacific through Credit Mobilier. He has holdings here too."

"Yet," said McCaleb, "he's not satisfied. What does he aim to accomplish by gettin' a stranglehold on a third of this territory?"

"He's after power, my friend. He's offered himself as a candidate for the presidency of the United States. He will accept a bid from either party, but he prefers the Democrats."

"That sneaking, thieving coyote? May God have mercy on us!"

"He has," chuckled Colton. "If somebody was taking bets that a snowball stood a better chance in hell than Train does of getting the nomination, I'd put my money on the snowball."

"So he has the Sweetwater valley," said McCaleb.

"Walker at the land office claims there are homesteaders actually there. Who are they? Cattlemen? Sheepmen? Sodbusters?"

"From what I've learned," said Colton, "they're just there, proving up their claims. George Francis Train has enough money, my friend, to keep them there until the Resurrection. Not only that, he has a pair of roaming segundos that's just pure scared hell out of everybody in the territory. One of them, Maury Duke, has a claim at the west end of Sweetwater valley, where the Union Pacific crosses the Green. This Duke dresses like a dandy, wears a tied-down pistol, and he's taken to riding the train into Cheyenne on Friday night and hanging around until Sunday. He's after Susannah Cody, damn him."

"I reckon she's related to Bill somehow," said McCaleb.

"His niece. She's maybe twenty-five, red hair, blue eyes, and built? My God! The town's hired her to teach school in the fall. Mostly out of respect for Bill, I suppose."

"The other segundo," said McCaleb. "Who and where is he?"

"Kingston Henry. Half-breed. Between you and me, I'd figure Maury Duke for a back-shooting bastard, and King Henry's a cut or two below him. All the more reason for you to settle on Box Elder Creek. He'll be your closest neighbor. He's got a claim at the east end of the Sweetwater valley, at the confluence of the Sweetwater and North Platte rivers, where they turn south. King Henry spends some of his weekends in town, drinking, gambling, and just general hell-raising. He's got a handsome woman living with him, and she's got a young daughter, maybe ten or eleven. God only knows why *any* woman would choose to live with a bastard like him, unless she's got nowhere else to go. I feel sorry for the poor kid."

"Colton," said McCaleb, "you've been a help. Put me down for however many subscriptions this will buy. I'll pick them up or have some of the outfit drop by when we're in town."

The double eagle danced on the countertop, settling in front of Colton.

"You got it," said Colton. "Only thing I've got less of than money is pride. Now if I suggest something to you, will you take it in the spirit in which I intend it?"

"I'm listening," said McCaleb.

"This George Francis Train I've told you about has an office in Omaha, and like I told you, he's richer than six feet down a cow's gullet. Every couple of months he comes here to meet with his segundos, Duke and Henry. He's got a private railroad car that's shuttled onto the siding by the depot. Josh, the station agent, tells me Train will be here this Saturday or next. Maury Duke and Kingston Henry will be here. You have cattle to sell, so why don't you ask Train to make you an offer? He's sittin' on the entire Sweetwater valley, with plenty of graze and plenty of water. You can always go to Texas for more cattle, and this might give you an inside track with Train, no joke intended. He can be as powerful a friend as he can an enemy."

"I'm a mite choosy as to who my friends are," said McCaleb. "Would *you* want him for a friend?"

"Frankly, no," said Colton, "but business is business. You have cattle to sell, and God knows, he has money to buy. I suspect he'd pay a premium price just to keep you away from the Sweetwater valley."

"You're suggesting I sell out rather than risk being run out," said McCaleb angrily. "Colton, I ought to gut-shoot you."

"All right," sighed Colton. "All right. Given a choice, most men would prefer not to fight a range war. Maybe you're the exception."

"Maybe I am," said McCaleb grimly. "If you see George Francis Train, tell him he's goin' to have neighbors. Tomorrow I'm ridin' to Box Elder Creek and get our claim markers in place."

McCaleb returned to Bullard's Mercantile and immediately found Brazos and Monte. Rebecca was nowhere in sight. Monte was quick to lead him to the new Winchesters.

"Seventeen-shot," he said. "Why don't we replace our old rifles with some of these? They're replacing the Henry."

"I doubt that," said McCaleb. "I'll stick with my Henry."

"But I don't have a Henry," said Monte. "I have a Spencer."

"Then maybe we'll get you one," said McCaleb. "You and anybody else in the outfit with a Spencer. Where's Will?"

"Took up with a woman," said Brazos with a chuckle, "and left with her. Rebecca asked, and found out she's come here to teach school this fall."

"Her name's Susannah Cody," said McCaleb with a grin. "She's Bill Cody's niece. Red hair, blue eyes, and whooeee. But she's already bein' courted by a gun-throwin' jasper named Maury Duke."

"You wouldn't know it when she left here," said Monte. "She was bein' courted by ol' Will Elliot. Who'd ever of thought he was such a ladies' man? If she lit up them bluebonnet eyes at me and smiled at me like she done him, I'd shoot this Maury Duke at the drop of a hat. And I'd drop the hat myself."

"If we stake some claims here," said McCaleb, "Maury Duke may be one of the jaybirds we'll have to shoot, and Will's courtin' the schoolteacher won't have anything to do with it. We file our claims on Box Elder Creek, I look for trouble with that bunch in Sweetwater valley. I don't aim to tell all this twice, so I'll wait till the outfit's together. I got a gut feelin' we're about to cut the drawstring on a sackful of bobcats."

"This purely is an interestin' place," said Brazos. "I reckon I'm goin' to like it here."

They rode back to the outfit and waited an hour before Will returned. He endured their jibes and suggestive winks with a good-natured grin, offering no explanation. When

McCaleb decided they'd had their fun, he shouted them to silence. He told them what he had learned about the powerful George Francis Train and the land grab in the Sweetwater valley.

"Tomorrow," said McCaleb, "I'm riding to Box Elder Creek and place our claim markers. I'll take Goose with me."

"Poor Will," said Stoney, with as straight a face as he could muster. "He'll be on Box Elder Creek, and that purty gal will be here in town. Two days' ride here, an' two back."

"Stoney," said McCaleb, "you don't know old Will Elliot like I do. In six years I don't reckon he's looked at a woman, until now. Once he's made up his mind, he never lets any grass grow under his feet. When he rides to Box Elder Creek, don't be surprised if this schoolteacher is ridin' alongside him."

The stranger showed up at McCaleb's camp just before dark, riding a livery horse. Except for a boiled-white shirt, he was dressed in black, including a black Stetson. He hooked one leg around his saddle horn and looked at the grazing longhorns. Finally he turned to McCaleb.

"I'm Maury Duke, and I got a message for you. My boss don't want these brutes on Sweetwater range. He'll buy 'em at thirty dollars a head."

"No, he won't," said McCaleb. "They're not for sale."

2

McCaleb was up before daylight, and by the time Salty had breakfast ready, Goose had the horses saddled.

"It's a little over a hundred miles to Box Elder Creek," said McCaleb. "We ought to be back on Sunday. Brazos, you and Will are in charge, and I want one of you with the herd at all times. If you ride into town, go two or three at a time. Nobody goes in alone. Come on, *Ganos*, let's ride."

They paused only to rest and water the horses. They reined up at a clear-running stream in purple twilight. McCaleb estimated they had come fifty miles. Despite governmental assurances that the Indians had been moved north of the Sweetwater, theirs was a cold camp. On the frontier the very danger one sought to avoid might come clothed in the silence and tranquility of the wild. They ate their supper cold, washed it down with snow water from the stream, and rode just far enough to find graze for their horses. They picketed their animals and rolled in their blankets. Steady munching of the horses assured them all was well. When a wary animal lifted its head to listen, there was a break in the rhythm. It was as effective as a shouted warning to a plainsman.

At dawn they risked a small fire to boil coffee and to broil bacon to go with their cold biscuits. The June air was crisp and cold. McCaleb's fingers, toes, and ears were numb. They were saddling their horses when they heard the unmistakable sound of an approaching wagon. McCaleb backed away from his horse, Goose following suit. There was a light breeze from the northwest. The wagon came into view and rattled to a halt, the big man with the reins startled at the sudden appearance of two strange riders. His left hand rested on the butt of a rifle that rode in a boot near his left knee. He wore a reservation hat over shaggy black hair, and wore a red flannel shirt that seemed ready to split, so massive was the chest beneath it. If he had a Colt, it was hidden by his heavy coat. Beside him sat a blanket-wrapped woman and a big-eyed little girl, only their heads visible. In the ensuing silence, McCaleb's eyes went to the mules drawing the wagon. Burned into the left flank of one of the animals was a distinct H, the upper part of it flaring into three points. Like a crown. Could this man be Kingston Henry? The woman and child fit Colton's description. Kingston Henry would have to be in Cheyenne on Saturday, if Colton knew what he was talking about.

"Howdy," said McCaleb.

The man nodded but said nothing. Goose remained as impassive as ever, and McCaleb kept his silence, waiting. Finally the big man flicked the reins and drove away without a backward look. When the bumping and jolting of the wagon had died away, McCaleb and Goose resumed their journey. There was that feeling of unease—a premonition —that came upon McCaleb, warning him of impending trouble. He pushed the big man from his mind, focusing on the woman and the child. The woman was young, probably less than half Kingston Henry's age, and he recalled what Sam Colton had said. Why had she taken her child and gone to live with a brute like Kingston Henry? While he had seen only the woman's face, she had been more than just pretty. A great deal more. These people were obviously on their way to Cheyenne, probably for Kingston Henry's meeting with Train. McCaleb's outfit—some of it —might be in town. Women were scarce on the frontier, attractive ones all the more so. Men had died over a surreptitious smile. Add one pretty girl, a grizzly of a man like Kingston Henry, and a Texas cowboy, and all hell might break loose. McCaleb grinned to himself. He was creating a crisis in his mind. He was already apprehensive about Will's whirlwind courtship of Susannah Cody. Will Elliot had never been a womanizer, all the more reason McCaleb believed he was serious about Susannah. But had she told Will of Maury Duke's interest? McCaleb had seen Duke only once, but he judged the man a killer.

"I'm ridin' into town," said Brazos. "A couple of you can come along if you want. This is Saturday, so I reckon we ought to go in early and leave early."

"I'll go with you," said Rebecca. "Will, you have an important reason for going, don't you?"

"I have," said Will, "but with Brazos going, I'll need to stay with the herd. Anyhow, when I go, I aim to stay late. I'll wait until McCaleb and Goose get back, so I won't be rushed."

Brazos and Rebecca were half-hitching their horses to the rail in front of Bullard's Mercantile when a thin young man in a wrinkled suit came down the boardwalk. He tipped his hat to Rebecca and paused.

"You folks must be part of McCaleb's outfit," he said.

"My God," said Brazos, "is it *that* obvious?"

"Just an educated guess. I'm a newspaperman, or trying to be, and I've been told I'm too nosy for my own good. Sam Colton's the name."

"I've heard about you," said Brazos. "I'm Brazos Gifford, and this is Rebecca Nance. Rebecca, why don't you go on in the store, and I'll look for you there. I reckon I ought to buy Mr. Colton a beer. I've never talked to an honest-to-God newspaperman before."

They stepped into a saloon that advertised cold beer. Brazos ordered.

"I suppose McCaleb's gone to Box Elder Creek," said Colton.

"I reckon it's no secret," said Brazos. "He'll be back late today, or maybe tomorrow."

"He wasn't pleased with some advice I gave him," said Colton. "Part of my nosy disposition is not knowing when to keep my mouth shut."

"I'll have to agree with you on that," said Brazos. "You told him he should sell the herd to this jaybird with the private railroad car, and not two hours later, Maury Duke rides in and makes us an offer."

"I swear I had nothing to do with that," said Colton.

"Time I was gettin' back to Bullard's," said Brazos.

"I'll go with you," said Colton. "That's where I was headed when I saw you. I see Rebecca's spoken for. Are you the lucky man?"

"No," said Brazos, "McCaleb is. My God, you *are* a meddlesome son!"

"Damn," sighed Colton. "The pretty ones always go for the cowboys."

Brazos and Colton returned to Bullard's and found Rebecca at the candy counter. A skinny little girl in a gingham dress stood there looking down at her small bare feet. Rebecca had bought a small sack of hard candy and was offering it to the child.

"Take it," said Rebecca. "I want you to have it."

The child stole a shy look at her, and then returned her gaze to her bare feet. She had shoulder-length black hair and big gray eyes. Brazos hunkered down before the girl so he could see her thin face.

"What's your name?"

The child said nothing, ducking her head still lower. But Brazos, with his Texas grin, wouldn't be ignored. Finally she lifted her eyes to meet his.

"Penelope," she said softly.

"What do folks call you? Penny?"

She shook her head.

"Lots of them around," said Brazos. "Maybe I'll just call you *Centavo*. That means 'penny' in Spanish. Now here;

you take this candy Rebecca wants you to have, and let us see you smile."

Shyly, she took the little sack Rebecca offered, and rewarded them with a half smile. But it was gone in a second. The big man came down on the girl with all the grace of a bull buffalo.

"Kid, you been told not to have nothin' to do with strangers, an' not to take nothin' from strangers."

With one big hand he snatched the little bag of candy and sent it flying. With his other he slapped the child, and she fell, the back of her head striking the floor. It was an ignominious, terrible thing. Penelope wore no undergarments, just the thin gingham dress. For a heartbeat there was only shocked silence. Then Brazos came out of his crouch, bringing his right all the way from the floor. It caught the giant of a man in the throat, sending him crashing against the counter. Assorted jars of candy toppled to the floor with a tinkling crash. The giant got up and, head down, charged like a bull. Brazos stepped aside, caught the man's shirt collar and sent him smashing head first into the log wall. The building shook, and somewhere along the affected wall, a display fell with a clatter. A young woman with Penelope's dark hair and gray eyes knelt by the sobbing child. Brazos waited for the big man to get to his feet, but the sheriff arrived first.

"Gents," he said, "we don't allow brawling."

"But you *do* allow grown men to slap little girls around," said Brazos. Even the big grizzly of a man who had started the whole thing sat with his back against the wall and listened. Spectators had gathered, but it was Sam Colton who spoke to Brazos.

"Well, you've made King Henry's acquaintance. Now you'll have to kill him, or he'll kill you."

"I've never been opposed to killin' any no-account bastard that needed it," said Brazos, "and I ain't seen many that needed it more'n he does. Is he Penelope's daddy?"

"No," said Colton, looking toward the scowling Kingston Henry. "He's no relation. I don't think Mike Donnegal

was really the kid's papa either. He was an Irish track
layer, killed in what was officially called a 'grading accident' near Bridger Pass. There were rumors that King
Henry might have set up the 'accident' that killed Donnegal, so's Henry could move in on Rosalie. He was always
around, taking care of Mike's funeral, sorry as could be
that a man from his crew had been killed."

The sheriff seemed to have regained control of the situation.

"You folks go on about your business," he said. Then he
turned to King Henry, and the big man got to his feet,
glaring at Brazos.

"Get out of here," said the sheriff, "both of you. Next
time you have differences, settle them somewhere else."

Brazos found Rebecca on the boardwalk, outside the
store. She had been talking earnestly with Rosalie, Penelope's mother. Rosalie sat on a wagon seat, a shaken and
still-sobbing Penelope beside her. Brazos stood there listening, taken by the plight of the young woman and her
daughter.

"Ma'am," said Rosalie, "please don't make things worse.
Thank you for your kindness, but he . . . please, just . . .
leave us alone. . . ."

Brazos took Rebecca's arm and led her away before
Kingston Henry could catch them there and cause more
trouble. But try as he might, he was unable to ignore the
dejected little waif on the wagon seat. For a heart-wrench-
ing moment their eyes met, a pair of big tears rolling down
her thin cheeks. Brazos swallowed the lump in his throat
and turned away. Silently they rode out of town, Brazos in
the lead. Suddenly Rebecca was no longer with him, and
when he looked back, she sat slumped in her saddle, her
horse cropping grass. He trotted his mount alongside hers,
and the stricken look in her eyes shook him to his boots.
He swung out of his saddle and helped her out of hers. She
slumped to her knees and then went facedown in the buffalo grass, sobbing and beating the ground. Not knowing
what else to do, he hunkered down, his back to a cotton-

wood, and waited. Finally she sat up, rubbing her tear-reddened eyes.

"You think I'm just a foolish woman, don't you?"

"No," said Brazos. "I've never thought as highly of you as I do right now. I've never seen a woman cry where the tears was better spent."

"Brazos Gifford, McCaleb's always said you're a man with the bark on, but he underestimates you; you're more than that. My heart went out to that skinny little girl leaning on the candy counter, but she wasn't responding to me. Dear God, how long had it been since she'd smiled? But she did it for you. Between the two of us, we've done just about everything McCaleb told us not to do, but at least we didn't end up in jail."

"We ain't done a damn thing McCaleb would disapprove of," said Brazos. "It ain't like that grizzly-brained bastard's the kid's daddy, 'cause he ain't. You remember McCaleb tellin' us about them segundos Train's got at each end of the Sweetwater valley? Well, this brute I just tangled with is Kingston Henry. His claim ain't more'n twenty miles west of Box Elder Creek, where we aim to start our spread."

"Then let's go to Box Elder Creek," said Rebecca. "The way he slaps that poor child around in public, what does he do when there's nobody to stop him? I'll take her away from there!"

"What do you aim to do with her mama?"

"I'll need your help," said Rebecca savagely. "She's a beautiful young woman. Kill that brute she's living with and take her for yourself."

Brazos laughed, but the time would come when he would vividly recall her words. They were more prophetic than either of them realized.

McCaleb found that Box Elder Creek was appropriately named. The trees grew in profusion, and the stream itself, a tributary of the North Platte River, ran bank-full. As was the custom of the day, McCaleb paced off what he judged to be a quarter section, starting at the confluence of Box Elder Creek and the North Platte River. He placed the corner markers and paced off four more adjoining quarter sections on the same side of Box Elder Creek, marking the corners of each. He then returned to the North Platte, stepping off five adjoining quarter sections along the opposite bank of Box Elder Creek. It would give the 6 outfit two and a half sections, with Box Elder Creek right down the middle. While McCaleb stepped off and marked their claims, Goose caught a mess of speckled trout from the creek. It was a fitting end to the day, and with a small concealed fire, they feasted on hot coffee and broiled trout.

McCaleb and Goose rode in just at suppertime on Sunday. When they had eaten, Rebecca led McCaleb to a secluded place on Lodge Pole Creek where they could talk. They sat facing each other as she told him of the incident at Bullard's. Her voice broke when she spoke of Penelope, and she threw her arms around McCaleb. It was a while before she could talk without sobbing.

"What kind of sheriff, what kind of man, would allow a brute like Kingston Henry to run loose, McCaleb? I saw him slap that poor little girl flat on the floor. Brazos, the girl's mother, and that newspaperman saw it."

"This is a railroad town," said McCaleb. "Kingston Henry is Train's man, and Train is the railroad. There won't be any real change until somebody derails George Francis Train."

"Now it'll be worse," said Rebecca, "after the fight in town. But I'm not sorry, damn him! If I'd had my pistol, I'd have shot Kingston Henry dead!"

"His fight with Brazos won't make that much difference," said McCaleb, "except Brazos will have to watch his back trail a mite closer. We'll have them after us soon as we try to prove up those claims on Box Elder Creek. I aim to file on them tomorrow."

* * *

On Monday, June 8, 1868, McCaleb rode into Cheyenne and registered their homestead claims. At the land office, Malcolm Walker was courteous but cool. McCaleb had little doubt that George Francis Train would be aware of the filing before the day was out. He stopped by the newspaper office and found Sam Colton leaning on his desk. He wore the same nondescript suit, and if not the same shirt, one with equally frayed collar and cuffs. He looked at McCaleb with some surprise.

"I didn't think I'd be seeing you again."

"I reckon your intentions are good," said McCalcb. "It's your judgment that's not worth a damn."

"That's what my daddy said when I quit a payin' job to come here. What can I do for you?"

"I need some information. You were there yesterday when Brazos punched Kingston Henry. Where did he go afterward, and where is he now?"

"He went to the telegraph office," said Colton, "and then he left town."

"What did he learn at thc telegraph office?"

"You think I'd stoop to reading people's telegrams?"

"I know you would," said McCaleb, a twinkle in his eyes.

"I didn't actually read it," Colton grinned, "but the agent's a friend of mine. George Francis Train won't be here until next Saturday. I hear King Henry didn't like driving all the way to town for nothing. I doubt he'll make the trip again this week."

McCaleb was ready to move the herd to Box Elder Creek, but Will's courtship of Susannah Cody had turned serious. Box Elder Creek could wait, if need be. He decided to talk to Will, and when he did, Will surprised him.

"I know you're anxious to get to Box Elder Creek," said Will, "but I want you to hold off another week."

"I will," said McCaleb, "if you've got a good reason."

"I think I have." Will grinned. "Next Sunday, Susannah and me are goin' to stand before the preacher. I'm askin' you to be my best man."

"Why, you old mossyhorn," shouted McCaleb, slapping him on the back.

"Not so loud," cautioned Will. "I aim to spring this on the outfit as a surprise. I talked to Salty, and he's plannin' a big barbecue for Thursday evening. Susannah will be here. It's her idea to hold off until Sunday so her uncle Bill Cody can be here. He's the last of her kin on her daddy's side. The government called him to Washington, and he can't get here until next Sunday morning. He'll ride the Union Pacific work train from Omaha."

The outfit knew something was about to happen when Salty began preparing the Thursday afternoon barbecue. When Will rode in with Susannah, McCaleb was as awe-struck as the rest of the outfit. Redheaded, green-eyed, smiling, she was everything Sam Colton had said, and more. Susannah rode bareback like an Indian, hunkered down around the chuck wagon like a cowboy, and ate beef ribs with the best of them. She teased Salty until she had the gruff old cook laughing, and totally intimidated the others. Pen, Jed, and Stoney ate almost nothing, and Monte didn't do much better. They were torn between awe of the girl and envy of Will. Before Will took her back to town, she had won them all, even Rebecca. But the next day their good-natured ribbing of Will ceased and they became concerned. When the Omaha-bound work train rolled in from end-of-track, Maury Duke stepped down from the caboose.

"Will," said McCaleb, "I know you'd tackle hell with a hatful of water, but this Maury Duke is trouble. Would you take it in the spirit in which it's intended if one of us sided you—watched your back—while he's here?"

"You know I can't do that," said Will. "He's just one man, and I figure I'm as good as he is. If you're sidin' me—much as I wish you could—I'd be admittin' to everybody—especially him—that I'm scared, that I need an edge. Thanks, Bent, but no. This is my game and I'll play out the string."

"This Maury Duke's one of Train's men," said Brazos, "and we'll likely have to shoot the bastard before we're done."

"That's something else," said Will. "If we end up gunning for him because we're bucking Train's Sweetwater land grab, then we'll go after him as an outfit. But if he's gunning for *me* because of Susannah, then it's just me. It's my fight."

McCaleb and Rebecca said nothing, waiting for Will to continue.

"I've left word for Duke at the rooming house where he stays. I don't hold with us stalking one another like a pair of lobo wolves. I'll tell him man-to-man what my intentions are, that Susannah's been promised to me, and tell him to back off. If he wants satisfaction with fists, knives, or guns, then so be it."

"I respect your position," said McCaleb, "but when you ride into town tonight, Brazos and me will ride with you. If it comes to a fight, just you and him, then we'll back off."

Will skipped supper, intending to eat with Susannah. It was dark when McCaleb, Brazos, and Will rode into Cheyenne. Most of the stores were open; business was good, even on Friday night. When they reached Malone's boardinghouse, Susannah was waiting on the porch. By the time Will had dismounted, she was beside him. The girl was distraught. McCaleb and Brazos sat their saddles and listened, for her eyes appealed to them even as she spoke to Will.

"Will, Maury Duke was here. He says he'll be waiting for you by the Union Pacific tracks, near the water tank, that you're to come alone. Must you? Isn't there some other way?"

"No," said Will. "Go in the house and wait for me."

Maury Duke liked to dress in black. He wore his black hair collar-length, and a thin gambler's moustache adorned his upper lip. There was a knife scar on his lower lip, causing it to curl outward in what had the appearance of a permanent pout. He had heavy black brows and was as dark-skinned as a Mexican. Not by the stretch of anybody's imagination was he handsome.

A block from the depot Will reined up.

"From here," he said, "I go alone."

McCaleb and Brazos said nothing. It was something Will had to do, and while they couldn't ride with him, they could set their saddles and be ready if he needed them. Will walked his horse slowly alongside the track until he could see the dim outline of the water tank against the starlit sky.

"That's far enough," said a voice. "Have your say."

"Back off," said Will. "I've asked for Susannah's hand, and she's said yes. I'm telling you to leave us be."

"Can you make me?"

"One way or the other," said Will. "Your choice."

"I win, she takes me."

"No," said Will, "win, lose, or draw, you're out. She doesn't want you."

"She don't, huh? She won't have me, then she won't have you neither, 'cause I aim to kill you."

"When you're ready, then," said Will.

"You ain't gittin' off that easy," snarled Duke. "I want you an' her to lay awake nights, wonderin' when it's comin'. I ain't one to fergit. She takes you over me, then you'd jist as well decide on your buryin' place, 'cause you're a dead man."

With that, he faded into the shadows and was gone. Will rode back to where McCaleb and Brazos waited, and they listened gravely while he told them what had happened.

"After Sunday," said Brazos, "you can take Susannah away."

"But there's the rest of tonight and tomorrow night," said McCaleb, "and Sam Colton pegs Duke as a back-shooter. I won't be surprised if he's right."

3

Saturday afternoon, McCaleb and Rebecca rode into town. She was as nervous as she was excited, for she had to buy a dress for Susannah's wedding. McCaleb was seeing yet another side of her, and enjoying the view.

"Finally," she said, "I have an excuse to buy myself a new dress, and I don't know how."

"I didn't know you needed an excuse. We're a long ways from bein' poor."

"What would I do with a dress on a trail drive? If I rode astraddle in a dress, the riders would forget all about the herd. They'd spend all their time watching me mount and dismount."

Before McCaleb could respond to that, there was the not-too-distant whistle of a locomotive.

"The work train came through at dawn," said McCaleb, "and won't leave end-of-track until sometime tonight. Let's mosey by the depot. I can think of only one reason for this. George Francis Train is about to arrive."

They reached the depot and found a fair-sized crowd gathered along the tracks and standing in the shade of the water tank. When the locomotive drew up to take on water, they backed away. Behind the locomotive was a tender, and behind that, Train's maroon and gold private car. When the engine's thirsty boilers had been filled, the fireman climbed down and opened the switch. Once the big locomotive had chugged onto the siding, he closed the switch, backing the siding's rails away from the main tracks. The fireman then swung aboard the tender and began throwing wood into the engine's hungry firebox, keeping up steam. The town was awed. Now, that was impressive. Not only could Train command the personal use of a locomotive, but one that kept up a head of steam and waited for him.

"Come on," said McCaleb, "I don't want anybody seein' me gawking like a digger Injun."

But somebody already had. Sam Colton had seen them.

"I told you," said Colton. "Buck him, and whatever trail you take, it'll be uphill all the way."

McCaleb kicked his horse into a trot and Rebecca followed.

"He was so charming the first time I met him," said Rebecca. "Now, I could just give him a knee somewhere south of his belt buckle."

Rebecca spent most of Saturday afternoon deciding what she was going to wear. She finally bought a pale green gown trimmed in white lace, and a pair of white slippers. The dress was hauntingly similar to the one Jonathan Wickliffe had provided for her in Denver, but McCaleb said nothing. He was so tired of town, he wouldn't have cared if she'd worn her range clothes to Susannah's wedding. They rode by Malone's boardinghouse, and Rebecca left her new finery with Susannah, where she would have privacy to change clothes. When they returned to the herd, McCaleb invited the rest of the outfit to ride into town if they wished.

"Some of you still have Spencer rifles," said McCaleb. "While you're in town, I want you to ride to Bullard's, pick up a new Winchester and a thousand rounds of ammunition."

"I cain't ride," said Salty, "but I can still shoot out a gnat's eye, if'n you'll stake me to one of them long guns."

"You got it," said McCaleb. "Get it when you go in to load up the chuck wagon. Since tomorrow's Sunday, and the stores are open late tonight; why don't you just take the wagon into town and load up now? We'll need axes, picks, shovels, and two or three crosscut saws. There's a pile of work at Box Elder Creek that can't be done from a saddle."

There was a unanimous groan from the outfit.

Will saddled up at sundown, bound for Malone's boardinghouse. Salty was long gone with the chuck wagon. McCaleb, Rebecca, Brazos, and Goose remained with the herd.

McCaleb knew something had happened when they heard the wagon coming at a furious clip, Salty whipping the mules. Monte had gone to help him load, and the kid laid to it as Salty laid back on the lines.

"Will!" shouted Monte. "Will's been shot in the back, hard hit. He's at Malone's. Susannah says hurry. The doc says Will may not last long."

"Brazos, Rebecca," shouted McCaleb, "let's ride. The rest of you stay with the herd. Keep your eyes open and your rifles handy."

They rode hard, nobody talking. Malone's boardinghouse was ablaze with light. Across the street men with lanterns and rifles wandered between saloons and stores. McCaleb hit the porch running, Brazos right behind him. The parlor was jammed with people. Will, belly down and stripped to the waist, lay on a sofa. With Rebecca at their heels, McCaleb and Brazos fought their way through the onlookers. The doctor leaned over Will, and Susannah was on her knees, on the floor. She struggled to her feet, almost fell, and Rebecca caught her.

"Damn it," bawled McCaleb, "you people get out of here!"

Unwillingly, they went. McCaleb turned to the unconscious Will, and a lump rose in his throat. The doctor had bandaged the wound, but it was bad, low down. A man seldom took a slug in his vitals, especially from a rifle, and lived to talk about it. The doctor straightened up and answered the question he saw in McCaleb's eyes.

"I doubt he'll regain consciousness, and I'll be surprised if he lasts the night."

"There must be *somethin'* you can do!" shouted Brazos.

"I'm no surgeon," said the doctor, "and if I was, I wouldn't give him more than a fifty-fifty chance. The lead's near his spine; if the wound doesn't kill him, he still might die under the knife, or end up paralyzed."

"Then he does have a chance," said McCaleb.

"Only if he has immediate surgery, and you won't find a competent surgeon nearer than Omaha. That's five hundred miles; you'll never get him there in time."

"Maybe not," snapped McCaleb, "but by the eternal, I'm going to try. Brazos, spread some blankets and make a stretcher. Doc, you help him. I want him at the depot just as fast as you can get him there. We're going to Omaha."

"I'm going with you," cried Susannah.

"Come on, then," said McCaleb. "You too, Rebecca. We're going to meet George Francis Train, after all. He's going to take us to Omaha."

"That evil man?" cried Rebecca. "He won't help us."

"Oh, but he will," said McCaleb, "if we have to ride from here to Omaha with the business end of this Colt in his belly."

"Bent," said Rebecca, "we'll need some money."

"Good thinking," said McCaleb. "Susannah, do you know where Musgrove, the banker, lives?"

"Yes," said Susannah. "On the next block, behind the bank."

"Let's go," said McCaleb.

Musgrove wasn't enthused with their visit, and even less so when he learned the purpose of it.

"Damn it, McCaleb, it's Saturday night and the bank's closed. This is highly irregular."

"Musgrove," snapped McCaleb, "you're likely to find a lot of things I do are highly irregular. For instance, I'm likely to pull all that gold out of your bank and put it back in my saddlebag, where I can get my hands on it as I need it. I need five thousand in gold, and I need it quick. Hold it at the bank until I pick it up or send for it."

Suddenly there was the bellow of a locomotive whistle.

"He's leaving!" cried Rebecca.

In their haste, McCaleb and Rebecca had left their horses tied to the porch rail at Malone's, and there was no time to return for them. McCaleb ran for the depot, arriving just as the engine with Train's private car chugged off the side track and onto the main line. McCaleb, his Colt in hand, bounded up the iron steps to the observation platform and through a door. The interior of the coach was nothing less than magnificent, but McCaleb barely noticed it. He slammed open a second door and found himself facing a man who could be described as Lincolnesque, but without the kindliness. He was tall, gangling, with deep-set, gray-green eyes. His jet-black hair flowed over his ears at the temple, matched by his heavy brows, moustache, and spade beard. His expensive gray suit was complemented by a ruffle-fronted white shirt and black silk tie.

"I have only a few dollars," he said calmly.

"I'm Benton McCaleb, and I'm not interested in your money. One of your Sweetwater gun-throwers just back-shot one of my men. Without surgery, he's done for, and for that he must get to Omaha. You're going to take us there, and if we need a ticket, this is it."

He cocked the Colt. Ignoring it, Train picked up the glass from the table before him, only to have McCaleb's slug shatter it in his hand.

"Stop this train," snapped McCaleb. "Now!"

Clutching a silk handkerchief to his bloody fingers, Train got up and pulled a bell cord. The train, barely moving, jerked to a stop.

"Put the gun down, cowboy."

The girl had slipped through a door at the opposite end of the chamber. She had golden hair, wore a filmy night-gown that left nothing to the imagination, and in her right hand she held a Colt pocket pistol. Then the door through which McCaleb had entered swung open and Rebecca stepped in, Susannah right behind her. It was the distraction McCaleb needed. He bounded across the narrow compartment, seizing the girl's wrist, forcing her to drop the pistol.

"Now," said McCaleb, "just to show you how considerate and generous we Texans really are, you folks get two choices. You can ride to Omaha sittin' up decent and comfortable, or you can do it hog-tied and belly down. The choice is yours, but make it quick."

"You give me no choice," said Train. "You are obviously in control, and riding to Omaha bound hand and foot would profit me nothing. However, it's only fair to warn you, once we arrive, I'll have the law on you."

"Then I'll have the newspapers on you," said McCaleb. "I'll cook your political goose to a crisp. First, I'll tell them how one of Mr. Union Pacific's hired gun-throwers shot a man in the back. Second, I'll tell 'em how you had to be forced, at gun point, to allow this wounded man a ride to Omaha for surgery that might save his life, even when you were going to Omaha anyway. You control some of the papers, but not all of them."

"You blackmailing bastard," said Train, with a grim chuckle. "Since you're taking advantage of me, is there anything *else* I can do for you?"

"As a matter of fact, there is," said McCaleb. "I want you to go with me to the depot and send a message to Omaha. I want a hack, an ambulance—something—there waiting, when Will arrives. Rebecca, keep an eye on Mr. Train's, ah, secretary, so's she don't get her sticky little hands on something dangerous, like another pistol. She gets too bothersome, put her belly down and hog-tie her."

The depot had closed for the night, but the agent was still there and they could hear the apparatus clacking away. Train rapped on the window, and the gray-haired old man unlocked the door.

"Mr. Train, thank God you're still here! First message

comc through garbled an' it's took 'em this long to repeat it. This concerns you."

He wrote rapidly. The instrument went silent, clicked to signal the transmission was complete, and then was silent again.

"Good thing you hadn't pulled out," said the agent. "Work train's on its way to end-of-track. Load o' ties an' rails got to be there Monday mornin'. You're t' lay over here until this extry passes and th' track's clear."

Train turned to McCaleb and shrugged his shoulders, a triumphant look in his hard eyes.

"Mister," said McCaleb, "I have a wounded man who needs surgery, and I have persuaded Mr. Train to get us to Omaha. A man's life is at stake. Is there any way you can sidetrack that work train somewhere, long enough for us to pass?"

"No, sir. Ain't a siding nowhere from here t' Omaha. Water stops is on th' main line."

The fireman from the waiting locomotive stuck his head in the door.

"Mr. Train, we're blockin' the main line. You want us to run her back on the siding?"

"I suppose you'd better," said Train. "Message just came through; work train just pulled out of Omaha bound for end-of-track. We'll have to lay over until it passes."

"I have a man dying for need of surgery," said McCaleb. "How long must we wait for this damn work train?"

"Tomorrow mornin', likely," said the agent, "dependin' on when it left Omaha. They didn't say."

"Get on that telegraph, then," said McCaleb, "and ask them when it left. It's important."

The old man cut his eyes toward Train, and the railroad man nodded. But the telegraph key was silent. Again and again he tried, without response.

"Line's dead."

"You're going to be dead," said McCaleb, "if you're lying."

"Honest to God, mister," the old agent cried, "I ain't

foolin' you. It goes out sometimes for a day or two. Lightnin' could of struck th' line."

The engineer from Train's locomotive came in.

"Mr. Train, some gents just took what looked like a dead body into your car. What's goin' on? We're blocking the main line."

"A man's been shot," said Train. "McCaleb here, a cow country pirate, has seized control of my coach and your locomotive for the purpose of getting this wounded man to a surgeon in Omaha."

"What's the problem? We're goin' to Omaha anyhow."

"Not in time to be of any help to McCaleb's man," said Train. "Just had a message over the wire holding us over until a westbound work train comes through."

McCaleb ignored Train and turned to the engineer.

"Is there someplace—anyplace—between here and Omaha where you can get off the main line? Someplace where this work train can pass?"

"No siding as such. There's the spur line they've started buildin' from Julesburg to Denver—"

"Then you could back your engine onto the spur and clear the main line," said McCaleb.

"I expect I could," said the engineer, "except there's no switch been installed. Won't be till the spur track's been laid to Denver. Need a prize bar and a man with a strong back. Have to force the connecting rails of the spur alongside the main line tracks, back my engine onto the spur and then force the spur track out of the way, freeing the main line."

"McCaleb," said Train, "this has gone far enough. You're grasping at straws. I know what you're thinking, and it won't work. It's two hundred miles to Julesburg, five hundred to Omaha. If the westbound work train is four or five hours under way, if it gains any time or if we lose any, then we'd collide head on before reaching Julesburg. Demanding a free ride to Omaha is one thing; risking the lives of others is something else."

McCaleb had backed to the door. He drew his Colt and cocked it.

"It's a risk we're going to take, Mr. Train. A man's life is hanging by a thread. I figure he's worth the risk. For his sake, we're going to cover that two hundred miles, get off the main line at Julesburg, and go on to Omaha when the other train's passed. You gents runnin' the locomotive, I'm sorry you got roped into this, but there's no help for it. I'll stand behind you with a cocked pistol from here to Omaha if I have to. The choice is yours."

"If that's our options," sighed the engineer, "then let's do it without the pistol. There'll be pressure enough without that. Since we're fighting the clock from here to Julesburg, we'd best get started. Does that suit you, Mr. Train?"

Train looked at the rock-steady Colt in McCaleb's fist, an enigmatic, half-twisted smile on his lips. His gray-green eyes burned with what might have been a touch of madness.

"McCaleb has the gun," said Train, "and for the time being, he's giving the orders. You've got guts, McCaleb, and if things had worked out differently, I could even like you. I lose an occasional battle, but never the war. This hand's yours; after that, look out."

McCaleb moved away from the door, allowing the three of them to exit. He then turned to the telegrapher.

"Pardner, I believed you when you said the line was dead. If you get it working again before we reach Omaha, don't get any ideas about having the law there waiting. It won't be in Mr. Train's best interests, and definitely not in yours. Savvy?"

The old man nodded. McCaleb stepped out and closed the door. Lifting his eyes to the starlit sky and to a God whom he often neglected, he offered a silent prayer.

$\mathcal{B}$razos waited halfway between Train's private coach and the depot. He handed McCaleb a heavy canvas bag.

"Rebecca said you needed this, so I went to the bank and got it. Will's ready, I reckon. My God, Bent, he looks awful; this could be it."

"Not if surgery can save him," said McCaleb. "I've got to leave you in charge, Brazos. I'm taking Rebecca with me. I don't trust Train, so I aim for her to stay right there in that coach with him, with her pistol handy. Whatever happens, hold the herd here until I return. Somehow, I'll get word to you about Will. The telegraph's out, but I'll reach you, if I have to pay an engineer or fireman to bring you a message. Stay in touch with Sam Colton; he's a friend of the railroad's agent at the depot. I'll be back as soon as I can. There's a debt to pay, and if Will can't pay it himself, we'll pay it for him. In spades."

The fireman and engineer had mounted to the locomotive's cabin. Train had entered his private coach. Brazos paused at the steps of the car.

"The sheriff found a cartridge case, Bent. It was .44 caliber, so it's no real help. I'd like to go in for a minute . . . before you go."

Will had been placed on the leather sofa in the inner chamber, blanket-wrapped to prevent chill. His breathing was ragged and irregular. Silent, Train sat in a chair. His "secretary" was nowhere in sight, but her pistol, he noted with approval, was now in the hands of Susannah Cody. Rebecca's Colt rode under the waistband of her Levi's. For a long moment Brazos stood over Will. When he finally spoke, they barely heard him.

"Vaya con Dios, pard. *Vaya con Dios."*

Head down, he strode out and closed the door behind him. McCaleb turned to Rebecca.

"I'm going to ride the cab with the engineer and maybe give the fireman a hand. If anything goes wrong back here and you need me, pull that bell cord to stop the train."

"There'll be no problem back here, McCaleb; I told you that. You'd best concern yourself with that westbound work train that's coming closer by the minute."

He chuckled, enjoying the fear in the eyes of Rebecca and Susannah. But there was no time for further argument or explanation. McCaleb swung into the engine's cabin. With a blast from the whistle and a spurt of steam, they were under way. The fireman began chunking wood into the firebox, McCaleb helping. He soon stripped off his sweat-soaked shirt, for even in the chill Wyoming night, the heat was unbearable. Finally McCaleb could take no more, and put his head out the off side of the cab, enjoying the rush of cold air.

"Since we know your name," the engineer said finally, "you might as well know ours. I'm Wiggins and my fireman's Parmenter."

"My pleasure, Wiggins and Parmenter," said McCaleb. "Can't this thing go any faster?"

"It can," said Wiggins, "but not with any degree of safety. We're outrunnin' our headlight already. If I spotted a buckled rail or a bridge out, there's no way on God's green earth I could stop in time."

"This is some hell of a railroad," said McCaleb in disgust. "Less than a year old, and you're already worried about bad rails and bridges out?"

"Friend," Parmenter chuckled grimly, "when you lay

rails over green ties without any ballast, you're askin' for it. The ties mire down in places, causin' humps in the track, and it's like ridin' a clipper ship over rough seas. The buckled rail Wiggins was referrin' to is caused by a break in the track. Happens when the tie sinks beneath a coupling joint, causes the rails to buckle where they join."

"Nearly all the bridges," said Wiggins, "was to have concrete abutments, and they ended up bein' wood. Mostly green wood, at that. Some of 'em didn't survive the first high water."

"Somebody," said McCaleb, "ought to start at the top and work his way down, gut-shootin' them that needs it."

"You'd have to start with the Congress," said Parmenter. "Nobody else can stop it. President Lincoln wanted this railroad built. He picked the congressmen he thought was honest and give 'em a blank check. Pick the most honest man that ever drew breath, give him the key to the vault, and he'll steal you blind. The bible says there ain't no good in any of us. I believe that."

"The love of money." Wiggins chuckled. "That's why this spur track from Julesburg, Colorado, to Denver ain't been finished. Not that they didn't have the money; they did. The city of Denver was some put out when the Union Pacific passed them by and picked Cheyenne for a division point. Denver was told if they raised two million dollars and bought railroad bonds, there'd be a spur line built from Julesburg to Denver. Well, they likely figured a spur track was better'n nothin', so they bought the bonds. Well, the spur's just barely started, and the railroad claims they can't afford to finish it. Not until Denver coughs up the money for two more million in railroad bonds."

Just knowing that such high-level thievery existed was enough to turn McCaleb's stomach. Again he leaned out the cab window, allowing the cooling night air to refresh him.

"Bad weather ahead," said McCaleb. "What effect's that going to have? Will we have to slow down?"

"It won't help any," said Wiggins. "You can see how

little use our headlight is now. In a hard, drivin' rain, we'll be runnin' blind."

"But it'll slow the other train too," said McCaleb.

"Some," agreed Wiggins, "but we don't know how much of a start they've got on us. We're a hundred miles nearer Julesburg, but if we hit the storm and they don't, they'll gain the time that we'll lose."

They were less than three hours out of Cheyenne when the storm struck. Lightning split the sky, dancing along the rails ahead of them. McCaleb let go an iron stanchion when a shock passed through his hand and arm. Wiggins slowed the locomotive down to a crawl. He turned to McCaleb apologetically.

"Visibility's dropped to nothin'. Got to slow down and just hope we run out of this pretty soon."

McCaleb chafed at the delay, but there was no help for it. Despite the high-handed method he'd been forced to use, these trainmen seemed sympathetic to his cause, and he believed they were doing their best. Nobody benefited from a collision with the oncoming work train. McCaleb gritted his teeth and kept silent, sighing with relief when they finally were free of the storm and there was starlit sky above them again. They passed a white post with a black number on it.

"Fifty miles to Julesburg," said Wiggins.

McCaleb leaned out the off side of the cab into the rushing wind. He strained his eyes and ears, half expecting to see the faraway glow of an approaching headlight or to hear the ominous moan of a whistle. He wished he knew how Will was, but in that same instant, he was fearful of knowing. He thought of Susannah Cody. Great as was his anguish, how much greater was hers, as she kept her grim vigil at Will's side? Unhindered, they rushed on through the night. He looked up at the faraway glittering stars in silent gratitude, and new strength swept through him. They were going to get to Julesburg in time!

"Keep your eyes sharp, McCaleb," said Wiggins.

"There's a water tank a couple of miles this side of the spur. We'll need to back up to there and take on water, but that can wait until the westbound's passed. Now that we're almost there, I got some doubts about us bein' able to move them spur rails against the main line rails. My God, if that track-layin' bunch ain't put switchin' plates on the ties, them spur rails ain't goin' nowhere. Not with a crowbar, they ain't!"

"Somethin' ahead," said McCaleb. "Maybe the tank."

Wiggins let off on the throttle, slowing the locomotive. Parmenter had a lantern lit. He nudged a long iron bar with his foot.

"Bring that with you, McCaleb. It's our only hope."

They swung down from the engine cab, Parmenter trotting ahead with the lantern. In its dim glow and by the engine's headlight, McCaleb could see two rusty ribbons of steel veering off to the south. Suddenly, far away but distinct, there was the moan of a whistle! Wiggins inched the big engine a little closer, affording them more light.

"Thank God," said Parmenter, "they've added switching plates, but they never been used. Let's give it all we got."

McCaleb could see the broad plates, normally greased to permit easy movement, now rusty from nonuse. Parmenter slid the flat end of the heavy bar under the spur rail, against the heavy metal plate. Getting his beefy shoulder under the bar, he threw his weight on it. Nothing moved. McCaleb lent his weight and they felt the rail give just a little, but not much. There was a crunch of running feet on gravel. Wiggins took handfuls of heavy grease from a bucket and worked it under the rails, across the rusted iron switching plates. Then the whistle moaned again, noticeably closer.

"Get back to your engine," shouted McCaleb, "and set down on the whistle. If we can hear his, he can hear ours. If all else fails, maybe you can stop him short of runnin' us down!"

"We'll have to do it with the whistle," grunted Parmenter. "He'll never see our light in time. He'll come on us out of a hundred-eighty-degree curve and be in our laps before he knows we're here. Let's try it again, now the plates are greased."

Slowly but surely the spur rails moved, connecting the siding with the main line. Parmenter grabbed the lantern and waved it frantically. With a mighty blast from the whistle, Wiggins moved the big engine onto the spur line. The moment the wheels of the passenger coach had cleared the main line, McCaleb and Parmenter leaned on the heavy bar, forcing the spur rails back to their original position. Their train was safely on the spur, and the main line was clear for the oncoming work train! Suddenly the westbound rounded the curve and its headlight was on them. There was the screaming of brakes, iron against iron, as the work train's engineer tried to stop. But his track was clear, and the westbound thundered past. McCaleb found himself soaked with sweat, breathing hard, his hands trembling. Far down the track the work train had begun backing up. The brakeman swung down from the caboose, his lighted lantern bobbing as he approached.

"What'n hell's goin' on here?" he shouted. "Don't you know that spur track ain't in use?"

"It is now," snapped McCaleb. "Why don't you go wake up your engineer?"

"You ain't s'posed to *be* here," he sputtered. "Omaha cleared th' track for us—"

"Parmenter," said McCaleb wearily, "tell him whatever you have to, so's they'll move on. I'm going to check on the folks in the passenger car and then I'll help you get us back on the main line. Get this damn work train past the tank so's we can take on water."

McCaleb trotted back to the private car and found Rebecca on the steps, trying to see what was going on.

"We're all right," said McCaleb, "soon as this other train moves on. We must get to the tank and take on water. How's Will?"

"He's holding on, Bent. I don't know how. He's still breathing hard and his temperature's going up. Train's so-called secretary locked herself in the room at the other end of the coach, and all he's done is sit there and watch me and Susannah. My God, Bent, I can't stand that man! I feel like he's just sitting there thinking of ways to come after us."

"Likely he is," said McCaleb, "but for now, Will takes priority over everything and everybody else. You and Susannah just stay out of his way and keep your pistols handy. I'm goin' to have them push this rig as hard as they can from here on to Omaha."

The westbound work train had taken on water, and with a blast of its whistle began chuffing away. McCaleb trotted down the track to where Parmenter waited, and they again used the heavy iron bar to connect the spur rails to the main line. Parmenter then signaled Wiggins with the lantern and the engineer backed off the spur. For the last time, McCaleb and the fireman pried the spur line's rails out of the way, freeing the main line. Then they swung aboard the engine and Wiggins backed it up to the water tank. In a matter of minutes they were on their way to Omaha.

"Learned one thing we can make use of," said Parmenter. "There's no rails or bridges out between here and Omaha. We can highball it from here on. That bunch really had a mad on. Said they didn't hear our whistle 'cause we wasn't supposed to be here. They're aimin' to file a complaint against me and Wiggins once they get back to Omaha. Maybe get us fired."

"You won't be fired," said McCaleb. "Mr. Train will see to that. When we get to Omaha, stay with the engine until I get back to you."

Wiggins, assured there were no defective rails or bridges out, reached Omaha in record time. Although it was Sunday morning, the town was alive with activity. With daily trains to and from Chicago, it had grown to the extent that it was no longer considered "frontier." Hacks were abundant. McCaleb flagged one down and sent the driver on the run to the biggest hospital in town. Will would have an ambulance and anything else that might ensure his chance of recovery. McCaleb caught George Francis Train just as he and his "secretary" were leaving the private car.

"One thing more, Mr. Train," said McCaleb.

"Why not?" said Train sarcastically. "You've been leaning heavily on my hospitality all the way from Cheyenne."

Train wrote a brief statement for Wiggins and another for Parmenter, stating that the trainmen had followed his orders, and signed his name. McCaleb accepted them without a word and turned to go.

"McCaleb."

McCaleb stopped, turned, waited.

"I almost wish we had met under different circumstances," said Train, "but we could never work together. In your own way, you're as ruthless as I am. Do as I have suggested, McCaleb, and take your cows on to Montana. I don't want you on Box Elder Creek."

Will's breathing seemed more faint and ragged than ever. The ambulance was an old army vehicle, once a macabre black, now a glistening white. They followed the ambulance in a rented hack and spent an agonizing hour in a barren waiting room while doctors examined Will. Susannah and Rebecca looked so tired and distraught, a sympathetic nurse brought them some coffee. Finally their patience was rewarded and a doctor came out to talk to them.

"I'm Dr. Bennett," he said, "and I'll be very blunt. Without question the bullet had to be removed, and I have removed it. This young man is very strong. He will live. That's the good news. The bad news—maybe—is that the slight damage to several of the vertebrae may leave him less than whole."

Susannah began to sob.

"On the other hand," the doctor continued, "he may pull out of it without any ill effects. The spine holds a lot of mysteries. Right now, all we can do is give him medication to minimize the pain and keep down the infection. I'll have the nurse look in on him every hour until his temperature comes down. There is nothing any of you can do here, except to further exhaust yourselves. You may return tonight between six and nine, if you wish, and I'll leave word with the nurse in charge to give you a progress report."

McCaleb had once seen a horse roll on a young rider, breaking his back. The cowboy had been paralyzed from the neck down, and McCaleb again heard his anguished cries as he begged his comrades to shoot him. Was *this* what lay in store for Will Elliot? Had they saved Will's life only to doom him to a living death?

They found a hotel near the hospital. McCaleb took a room for himself, while Rebecca and Susannah shared one. They had asked for the second floor, hoping for peace and quiet, but there was too much going on. McCaleb lay there wide awake, listening to the shouts and laughter from the boardwalks below. Horses nickered, wagons and buckboards clattered along the streets, while the blast of a whistle and the clanging of a bell announced either the departure or the arrival of a train. Wearily McCaleb got up, tugged on his boots and went to the lobby. There were Omaha and Chicago newspapers, so he bought one of each. He returned to his room and found Rebecca sitting on his bed.

"Poor Susannah was dead on her feet. I thought I was. My God, how do people live in all this noise? I got more rest while we were in the Trinity River brakes, fighting the Comanche and roping wild cows."

"Here," said McCaleb, handing her the Chicago paper.

He began with the front page of the Omaha paper, but found little that interested him. The Arapaho and Shoshoni had signed a treaty, and while they weren't bothering the whites, they were still fighting and killing each other in the Powder River basin. Suddenly he sat up.

"Good God Almighty!" he shouted. "Listen to this!"

She put down her newspaper.

"Some jasper from Oregon drove six hundred head of steers into Montana. Sold 'em to the miners at a hundred dollars a head! That's sixty thousand dollars! We've got nearly a quarter of a million dollars worth of cows!"

"Not quite," Rebecca smiled. "We only have 1,950 steers."

"No matter," he cried, undaunted. "We'll go back to Texas for another herd. Charlie Goodnight'll have a fit when he hears about this."

But she wasn't sharing his enthusiasm.

"Damn it," he said, "I'm forgetting why we're here. Will's lyin' there in God knows what kind of shape, and I'm sellin' and buyin' cows. I swear, if he don't come out of this . . . I—"

She rolled over next to him, squashing the Chicago newspaper between them. He dragged it out and threw it on the floor.

"Nothing in there anyway," she said, "except the fight going on in Washington about Train's Credit Mobilier. How can Congress investigate the thing when one of the biggest thieves in it's a member of Congress?"

"I don't know," said McCaleb. "Have we slid down so low that all we got to talk about is Train's Credit Mobilier?"

She giggled and said nothing more. Despite the noise all around them, they slept. McCaleb awoke first. He let Rebecca sleep. Retrieving his Omaha newspaper, he continued reading. There were only eight pages, and he had reached the last one when he found the paragraph about Bill Cody. He nudged Rebecca and she sat up.

"We forgot about Bill Cody. He was supposed to be on that work train that passed us at the Julesburg spur. This paper says he won't be here in Omaha until Monday. That's tomorrow. Should we tell Susannah?"

"Not yet," said Rebecca. "I don't believe she'd want to see him until she knows about . . . until she knows Will's all right. If it was you lying there hurt, I wouldn't want anything or anybody else on my mind."

"Thank you," he said. "I know how to find him when she's ready for him. I know she's worn-out, but why don't you wake her and let's get something to eat. Us starving to death won't help Will."

Susannah, still downcast but refreshed by sleep, was able to eat. It was a few minutes past six o'clock when they reached the hospital. True to his word, the doctor had left a report for them.

"His temperature's down," said the nurse, "and he's resting well. The doctor says he appears able to move his hands and his feet, and that almost rules out any permanent disability. He may be able to talk to you by this time tomorrow evening."

Susannah sank down in one of the hard waiting room chairs and wept until no tears remained. McCaleb tried to swallow the lump in his throat, and Rebecca dried her eyes on her shirtsleeves.

The doctor didn't allow them to see Will until Wednesday morning, and then for just a few minutes. Susannah was allowed to see him first, and by the time McCaleb and Rebecca saw him, he seemed to have all his color. Or, as McCaleb suspected, he was blushing furiously. He listened as they told him of the hectic trip from Cheyenne. Finally McCaleb told him of Train's offer, and upon having that offer refused, his threat.

"Then by the Almighty," said Will, "I'll go to Box Elder Creek if I have to make the trip in a buckboard. Then there's that sneakin' coyote that cut me down from behind. I aim to see just how handy he is with a pistol when I'm facing him and shootin' back."

McCaleb saw the misery in Susannah's eyes, but she wisely kept silent. It was something a man had to do; failing to do it made him less a man. A nurse informed them they had been there too long and must leave.

"Just one more minute," said Will. "I need to talk to Bent. Alone."

When McCaleb left Will's room, he was mysteriously silent. Rebecca wheedled and begged, but he told her nothing. She would know—and so would Susannah—when

they visited Will on Thursday morning. He further infuri-
ated the two of them when he left them at the hotel and
went alone to do some errand Will had requested. The
following morning, he left them in the hall while he visited
Will alone. He then left the two of them with Will. When
he returned, he had with him a little white-haired man who
had a worn bible under his arm. Immediately there was a
knock on the door.

"Susannah, answer the door," said McCaleb with a grin.

"Uncle Bill!" she shrieked. "Buffalo Bill Cody!"

Cody wore a floppy, broad-brimmed plainsman's hat,
moccasins, a buckskin jacket, and buckskin pants. Cody
was a young man. He didn't look much older than Susannah. His blue eyes danced with merriment.

"We'll spend some time with Mr. Cody later," said Mc-
Caleb. "He's here because something's about to happen
that's mighty special to him. In case nobody's figured it
out, this gent with the bible is a preacher, Reverend Mor-
row by name. Now Susannah, you stand over there by Will.
Rebecca, you belong over here next to me. Now, Preacher,
it's your turn."

The little minister began reading the wedding ceremony.
Rebecca clung to McCaleb and wept through it all. Susannah knelt on the floor by Will's bed and he placed the ring
on her finger that McCaleb had brought. McCaleb slipped
the wedding band on Rebecca's finger next to the dia-
mond. Bill Cody blew his nose on a big red handkerchief
and McCaleb gave the little preacher a double eagle.

"First double marryin' I ever been to," said Cody. "I
knowed you wasn't goin' to make it as a schoolmarm, Susannah; too damn pretty. Reckoned you would find you a
man with the bark on, out here on the frontier."

"You're famous," said Rebecca. "Did you really shoot
four thousand buffalos for the railroad?"

"Give or take a few," said Cody. "But I wish folks would
forget this 'Buffalo Bill' monicker and remember all them
years I scouted for the army. Damn near any man with a

sharp eye and a Sharps rifle can kill buffalo. It ain't just ever'body, though, that can be a scout."

Susannah giggled. "Uncle Bill, just be thankful you didn't make a name for yourself shooting coyotes. Things could be worse."

Cody chuckled. "Lookin' at it in that light, I reckon they could. It don't sound half bad, that 'Buffalo Bill' handle."

"Dear God," sighed Rebecca, "I can't believe it. Married. Me!"

"Better concentrate on it," said McCaleb, chuckling, "because I just kept one of the hotel rooms."

"You lucky bastard," said Will. "It's *my* wedding day too, and I don't have the strength to get out of bed."

"Had the same problem on my weddin' day," said Cody with a grin, "and I hadn't been shot."

"I swear, Benton McCaleb, I never thought I'd live long enough to spend my wedding night with you, and I'm even more surprised to be spending it in an honest-to-goodness bed."

"Well, get up and put your britches on and we'll go out and sleep in the brush and buffalo grass."

She giggled. "Shut up, McCaleb, and blow out the lamp."

5

With heavy heart, Brazos Gifford stood on the track until sight and sound of the locomotive had been lost in the chill Wyoming night. Strong on his mind was the pale face of Will and his shallow, labored breathing. Close as Brazos was to Charles Goodnight and Benton McCaleb, he was closer to Will Elliot. They had "learned cow" together while in their teens, and just the thought that he might have seen Will alive for the last time was almost more than he could bear. His one consolation lay in his total confidence in Benton McCaleb. If it took a doctor in Omaha to save Will, then McCaleb would get him there and he would find that doctor! With only that to ease his mind, Brazos mounted his horse and rode slowly through town. Since it was Saturday night and not even nine o'clock, the place was starting to roar. There was a jangle of piano from two different saloons, clashing to the extent that he couldn't discern what either melody was. McCaleb had left him in charge of the outfit, so now he had to ride back and report. Somehow, without quite understanding why, he felt utterly alone; more alone than he had ever been in his life. There was a light in Sam Colton's newspaper office, and Brazos reined up. Impulsively he dismounted and went in. Colton leaned back in an old swivel chair, his feet on the desk, making notes. He looked up, lifted his eyebrows in surprise and greeted Brazos with a question.

"What can you tell me about the shooting?"

"Nothin' you don't already know," said Brazos. "I reckon you know Will's hurt bad enough that McCaleb's takin' him to Omaha."

"My God, yes," said Colton, "and in Train's private car! Pulled a Colt on Train, according to old man Olson, at the depot. Olson says there's a westbound work train on the way from Omaha, headed for end-of-track. He got the message just before the telegraph went dead. The message was for Train, ordering his locomotive to remain here until the work train passed. Olson says there's no place for Train's rig to get off the main line except at Julesburg, Colorado. There's an unfinished spur track being built, and there's not even a switch to get onto it! McCaleb wanted to know when the work train left Omaha, but the telegraph went dead before Olson found out."

It was news to Brazos. Knowing of his concern for Will, McCaleb hadn't even mentioned this additional danger. Brazos leaned across the counter, his eyes boring into Colton's.

"Colton, you *must* know somebody in Omaha. Once the telegraph's working again, find out if they made it . . . if Will's still alive."

"I'm ahead of you," said Colton with a grin. "I've told Olson I need to get a message through to Omaha as soon as the telegraph comes to life. I'm a stringer for the Omaha paper, and I'll have my contact look into your situation. This whole thing has scared hell out of Olson. He's having visions of train wrecks, and he'll sit right there in the depot until that apparatus starts talking to him. Telegraph or not, we'll know by morning if Train's locomotive got off the main line at Julesburg. The work train will have to come through here. I'll be here the rest of the night. Stay if you like."

"Thanks, Colton," said Brazos. "I'm ridin' out to check on our herd and the outfit, but I'll be back."

* * *

Promising to inform the outfit as soon as there was news, Brazos rode back to town. Colton had made a pot of strong coffee, and Brazos accepted a cup of the brew. He straddled a ladder-backed chair and tilted it against the wall. Eventually they dozed, and it was an hour before dawn before they heard the sound they had been listening for. It failed to penetrate their sleep-fogged minds at first, but at the second blast of the work train's whistle, Brazos was on his feet. By the time he and Colton reached the depot, smoke from the stack of the engine was visible to the east, mixing with the first gray of approaching dawn. Old man Olson, the agent, stood on the depot steps. With a hiss of steam and the clanging of its bell, the big locomotive glided up beneath the suspended spout of the water tank. Except for the caboose, the entire train consisted of flat cars loaded with ties and rails. Down the railed steps at the rear of the caboose came the brakeman, curious as to why three men were at the depot before dawn on Sunday morning. Ignoring Brazos and Colton, he directed his question at Olson.

"Didn't Omaha telegraph you to hold that private car until we were past?"

The old man explained as best he could what had taken place.

"I'm takin' this higher up," snarled the brakeman. "I get back to Omaha, I'll get somebody fired."

"That somebody might be you, friend," said Colton. "The telegram from Omaha was received and delivered. George Francis Train—Mr. Union Pacific himself—made the decision to go ahead. I'm with the newspaper here, and I'm writing the story now. I'll need your name—"

"Now wait a minute," stammered the trainman.

"What about the other train," Brazos broke in. "The one with the private coach. Did they . . . make it to the spur track at Julesburg?"

"Yeah," said the brakeman grudgingly. "Scared the bejabbers out of me, but they done it."

Without another word he trudged down the track and swung aboard the caboose. Colton looked at Brazos and grinned. There was a blast from the locomotive as, its thirst quenched, it lumbered off westward, toward end-of-track. Olson headed for the depot, Brazos and Colton following. Before they reached the open door, they could hear the clackety-clack of the telegraph as the instrument demanded acknowledgment.

"Olson," said Colton, "since we've already been up all night, let's take a few more minutes and send this message I need to get through."

The telegram sent, they left the depot.

"Colton," said Brazos, "I appreciate what you've done. Come on. I'll buy your breakfast."

"Much obliged," said Colton, grinning, "but I need sleep more than food. Why don't you see me late tomorrow afternoon? Maybe I'll know something."

Brazos rode back to the outfit and found them waiting expectantly.

"We have a friend in town," he said. "Sam Colton, the newspaperman, is telegraphing a newspaper in Omaha, trying to find out how Will is. Might as well make yourselves comfortable; we'll be here until McCaleb returns."

"Never did git th' chuck wagon loaded," said Salty. "Found out Will was hurt, an' we lit a shuck back t' camp."

"Exactly what you should have done," said Brazos. "In the morning, you and Monte take the wagon to town and load up."

"We wasn't able to get them Winchesters and shells either," said Stoney.

"Then get them tomorrow," said Brazos. "It's only Monday, and McCaleb may be gone a week, but when he returns, we'll be ready to move out."

"These mules ort t' be reshod 'fore we pull out," said Salty.

"Good idea," said Brazos. "Some of the horses need it too. Do I have any volunteers?"

"Me and Stoney never had much love for it," said Jed, "but our daddy's a blacksmith, so we got the experience."

"Rest of us will pitch in and help," said Brazos. "Where's Goose?"

"Follered th' rest of you t' town las' night," said Salty, "when he found out Will was shot. Ain't seen him since."

"I told him about it," said Monte, "and he got that look in his eyes like when we had that fight in Santa Fe. He just saddled up and fogged out for town."

Brazos had little doubt that Goose was tracking the man who had shot Will. Maury Duke had ridden into Cheyenne on Friday on a work train returning from end-of-track. After shooting Will—assuming that he had—there were two ways he could have escaped. The most likely, and altogether too obvious, was by simply getting a horse from the livery. Had he simply remained in town and surreptitiously swung aboard the departing work train? Not with Goose stalking him, because the train hadn't reached Cheyenne until almost daylight. From what McCalcb had said, Dukc's claim lay at the western end of the Sweetwater valley, near where the Union Pacific tracks spanned the Green River. With all the crooks and turns of the tracks, that was nearly two hundred miles. However Duke had gotten his hands on a horse, it still meant five days of hard riding. Suppose he simply followed the tracks and took the train when it showed, abandoning the horse? There were mountain grades to the west that would slow the tie-and-rail-laden train to a crawl. While he was touched by the Indian's loyalty, he hoped Goose was unsuccessful in his pursuit of the elusive Maury Duke. It was a fight and a victory that belonged to Will.

When McCaleb awoke, the sun was streaming through their second-floor hotel window and the room was sweltering hot. He flung back the sheet and, leaning on one elbow, surveyed the totally naked Rebecca. She opened one eye.

"You're not disappointed you bought the cow without trying the milk, are you?"

"Was I *that* bad?" he grinned. "I was just wonderin' how old Will made out in that hospital room."

"Where there's a will, there's a way," said Rebecca, giggling. "I'm starved."

McCaleb and Rebecca found Will much improved, and a smiling Susannah sitting beside him on the bed.

McCaleb chuckled. "Well, how was the wedding night?"

"Not near as exciting as I'd always reckoned it'd be." Will grinned. "We had an unexpected visitor a while ago. Gent named Appleby, from the newspaper. He had a telegram from Sam Colton in Cheyenne, wantin' to know if I was alive or dead. Colton means well, I reckon, but he sure put his foot in the milk bucket. This Appleby was full of questions about the shooting, wantin' to know why I was brought here in Train's private car, and we just about had to throw him out. I told him you'd send Colton a telegram, and we didn't tell him anything else."

"Good," said McCaleb. "Train's already got a personal grudge against me, and while I have no respect for the man, we do owe him something. I'd not want him thinking I'd gone back on my word. He threatened to have the law on us when we arrived here. I countered that with a threat to give the newspapers a full account of his land grab in the Sweetwater valley, and of one of his gun-throwers backshooting you."

"This Appleby," said Will, "was trying to write a story about your race with that work train, but he couldn't do it without gettin' to the reason behind it. He'd already been throwed out of Train's office.

"The doc says I'll be laid up a good two weeks, but I don't have to stay here. Find us a room in a boardinghouse, will you?"

"We'll have to do it today, then," said McCaleb. "There'll be a work train headed for end-of-track tomorrow, and we need to be on it."

"You'll be in Cheyenne early Sunday morning," said Will, "and you can move out for Box Elder Creek on Monday. I just wish I was goin' with you."

"I'll leave you a horse at the livery," said McCaleb, "and your saddle at Colton's place."

"Whoa," said Susannah. "What about a horse for me?"

"Why," said McCaleb innocently, "I reckoned you'd be stayin' in Cheyenne and teaching school."

"Benton McCaleb," she snapped, "for the first two weeks I'm married to this Texas galoot, he's flat on his back in bed and can't get up. Now if you think I'll have him spend the next year on Box Elder Creek while I'm stuck in Cheyenne, then you've been grazing on loco weed!"

McCaleb sent Brazos a telegram in care of Sam Colton. He and Rebecca then found a secluded boardinghouse to which Will and Susannah would move on Monday. Before the westbound left on Saturday morning, McCaleb spent a few minutes alone with Will.

"You'll be released from here Monday," said McCaleb. "The hospital's been paid and they haven't been told where you're going. I doubt you'll be hearing from Train; he'll wait until we reach Box Elder. I'm leavin' enough money for your expenses and train fare to Cheyenne. Don't try to make the trip too soon. You'll be ridin' the caboose. Don't let any grass grow under your feet in Cheyenne; once you're there, head for Box Elder Creek."

"Don't want me gettin' shot again, huh?"

"Not until you're well enough to shoot back," said McCaleb. *"Hasta luega,* pard."

A week, almost to the hour, after leaving Cheyenne, McCaleb and Rebecca stepped down from the caboose of a westbound work train. They found Brazos, Monte, and Sam Colton waiting. Brazos and Monte had brought saddled horses for McCaleb and Rebecca. Sam Colton was grinning.

"You're slipping, McCaleb. All the way from a private car to a caboose."

"I don't like to ride a man's hospitality too hard," said McCaleb.

Rebecca said nothing. She simply held up her left hand.

"McCaleb," shouted Monte, "she's hog-tied and branded. Now I don't have to worry about her; that's your job."

"You?" cackled Rebecca. "You, worrying about me? Why, I've looked after you practically since you were born. I just hope I live long enough to see you find a decent woman!"

"Once we get to Box Elder," said Monte, "me and Goose will ride to Powder River basin and find us a couple of squaws."

McCaleb knew better than to laugh. Before Rebecca responded, Brazos remembered something and cut in.

"Speakin' of Goose, there's something I almost forgot to tell you. You remember how we lit out for town right after we heard Will had been shot? Monte told Goose, and without a word to anybody, he followed us. Once we'd got Will to the train and some of the crowd cleared out, Goose managed to pick up the trail of whoever shot Will. We got no positive proof, Bent, but from what Goose learned, I'd bet my part of the herd it was Maury Duke. The sheriff says somebody swiped a horse right after Will was shot. Goose was able to track that same horse, and he found it wanderin' loose near Bridger Pass. That's where the trail ended. Duke took the horse and rode only as far as it took the work train to catch up to him."

"I reckon the sheriff hasn't done anything, then," said McCaleb.

"He thanked Goose for returning the stolen horse," said Brazos, "and he was quick to point out that we had no real proof against anybody. I was as quick to suggest that he question the crew of that work train when they got back to Cheyenne."

"This is a railroad town," said McCaleb. "We won't get any help from the law where anybody that's involved with the railroad's concerned. We'll have to stomp our own snakes."

"That's why I didn't push it. When Goose rode in, the

boys wanted to raise hell and kick a chunk under it, but I held 'em back."

They had virtually forgotten Sam Colton until he reminded them of his presence.

"Damn, this is hot stuff." He chuckled. "The rest of the country's got a mad on because of Train's Credit Mobilier, but I've got a whole new angle. I can expose this land grab along the Sweetwater and these back-shooters!"

"Colton," said McCaleb, "I'll personally gut-shoot you if you print so much as a word of this until I'm ready for it. However strong our feelings, we can't prove a thing, and neither can you. I've already threatened to expose Train to the newspapers. If you remove that threat by printing anything you can't prove, you'll give him all the ammunition he needs to destroy us. Besides discrediting anything you write, he'll have you shot dead. I can't make it any plainer. *Comprender?*"

"McCaleb," sighed Colton, "you are a most convincing man. If I understand you, you are saying that at some point I can write this story. How am I to keep track of developments once you've left Cheyenne?"

"You know where Box Elder Creek is," said McCaleb. "Besides, we'll be in town at least once a month, for supplies and ammunition. Now if you're bound to print something involving us, print this: Say that on Thursday, June eighteenth, in Omaha, Will Elliot married Susannah Cody. Me and Rebecca were hitched in the same ceremony, if you want to use that. Susannah's uncle, Buffalo Bill Cody, was there. You can say that me and Will are part of the Six Bar outfit and that we're planning a ranch on Box Elder Creek. Dress that up any way you want, as long as you stick to the truth."

"If you can stay alive, McCaleb, you're going to make some big tracks in Wyoming Territory. You're doing the very thing you warned me *not* to do. You're inviting Maury Duke to take another shot at your pardner, and from what I know of George Francis Train and his land grab, your move to Box Elder Creek will have him pawing the ground."

"I'm saying nothing about that, Colton," said McCaleb. "You know enough to get yourself shot graveyard dead. You'd best be careful."

On Monday, June 22, they began the drive to Box Elder Creek. Even with their trailwise herd, they had their hands full. The big Texas steers had to be held back to the slower pace of the she-stuff, the biggest disadvantage to trailing a mixed herd.

"Thank God it's not that far to Box Elder Creek," said Rebecca. "We've been camped for three weeks, and I'd forgotten how hot, dusty, and nearly impossible it is, keeping those stubborn, long-legged steers from running off and leaving the cows."

"If I ain't bein' too nosy," said Stoney, "is they a chance we'll be goin' back to Texas for another herd?"

"Some of us," said McCaleb, "if the market in Montana and Dakota territories is as good as we've heard. Not gettin' homesick, are you?"

Jed chuckled. "He's gal sick. You and Will tyin' the knot done it. He's scairt this Texas gal he's got on his mind will take up with one of them spit-an'-polish Yankee soldiers."

"No sooner'n the one you got on your mind takes up with one of 'em," bawled Stoney.

"I reckon we'll see how good the beef market is in Montana and Dakota territories," said McCaleb. "Soon as we get settled on Box Elder Creek, I aim for us to trail a herd —maybe a couple hundred head—into Miles City. Can't do much here on the High Plains once the snow comes, except wait for spring. But we can look for a break right after the first of the year and head for Texas. That'll give us enough time to get a herd together for a drive in the spring."

"The Goodnight trail again?" Monte asked.

"No," said McCaleb. "It'll be as crowded as the Kansas trails by next summer. I've had enough of the Pecos anyway. We'll take the Western trail from south-central Texas to Fort Dodge, and from there to Ogallala, Nebraska. Once we reach Ogallala, we can follow the western leg of the trail on to Cheyenne, or drive north to Fort Buford."

"Speakin' of Fort Buford," said Brazos, "we'd ought to light a shuck up there before snow flies. That night I spent at Sam Colton's place, waitin' for some word about Will, I kept Sam talking. The Sioux and Arapaho have been moved onto a reservation in southwestern Dakota Territory. The Shoshoni—Chief Washakie's band anyway—are on the Wind River reservation, in Big Horn basin. The quartermaster at Fort Buford will be responsible for letting beef contracts for Dakota, Montana, and Wyoming territories. Indians can hunt buffalo in the Powder River basin as long as there are enough buffalo to justify the hunt. Within another year, the tribes will be starving without government beef. Nowhere—in any of the three territories—will there be anybody in a better position than us. Lookin' at Colton's map, Miles City can't be more'n a hundred and fifty miles southwest of Fort Buford."

"But it's an almighty long drive from our place on Box Elder to Miles City," said Pen. "Why not just follow the Western trail—the northbound leg of it, that is—to Fort Buford, cut out their part of the herd and trail the rest southwest to Miles City?"

McCaleb chuckled. "Spoken like a trail boss. That's an idea that'll be worth looking into."

"I'm as fired up over all this as anybody," said Brazos, "but before we go slopin' off to Texas, Miles City, Fort Buford, or anywhere else, let's lay some plans. We been in the territory just three weeks, and Will's already been shot. There's a better-than-average chance the same bunch responsible for gunnin' him will be after us, because Train, for some reason we still got to figure out, don't want us anywhere close to the Sweetwater valley. What I'm workin' my way around to is this: if we're aimin' to trail another herd from Texas, a couple of us will have to go there, buy the cows, and hire some riders. There just ain't enough of us to defend this ranch we're goin' to have on Box Elder, go back to Texas for another herd, and trail the steers we already got into Miles City and north to Fort Buford. Besides that, we got to put up some ranch buildings. Cold as it is here in June, what'll it be like in September? Am I talking sense?"

"My God, yes!" cried Rebecca. "I wouldn't have just one of you dead or hurt, for every cow from the Panhandle to Galveston Bay. Let's not go after more at the expense of losing what we have."

Despite the sometimes unruliness of the steers and the lagging of the cows, they bedded down on Chugwater Creek. McCaleb estimated they had covered at least twenty miles. Despite the apparent tranquility, they nighthawked as usual, in two-hour watches. Some of the terrain over which they passed was so overgrown, the chuck wagon fell behind. They took turns, one rider at a time, clearing trail for Salty's mules and the wagon. Hands that had been callused and rope-burned were still susceptible to the blistering effects of an axe handle. They were slowed to the extent they traveled no more than ten miles, and for lack of a convenient stream, spent their second night in dry camp. They ate breakfast by the light of Salty's fire and were in the saddle before good daylight. They wore mackinaws, gloves, and woolen scarves tied over their ears. Without water, the herd had spent a restless night. Many of them already milled about, bawling their discontent.

"I'd say we're still twenty miles south of the Laramie River," said McCaleb. "One way or the other, we'll have to get these brutes to water; they're already so dry and cantankerous, they won't graze."

"Th' wagon's slowin' ever'body down," said Salty. "Leave one rider to clear trail fer me, an' take th' herd on to th' next water. I'll come along soon's I can. Supper'll be a mite late."

"He's right," said McCaleb. "The steers are rarin' to go,

anyhow. We'll just have to swat the cows and force them to keep pace. Who wants to be the outrider and brush clearer for Salty?"

"I'll do it," said Monte. "Yesterday's blisters are all busted, and I can get a clean start."

With not quite an hour of daylight remaining, they reached the Laramie. Salty had fallen so far behind, they no longer heard the rattle of the wagon or the occasional sound of Monte's axe.

"Brazos," said McCaleb, "suppose you and Goose ride back and meet Salty? There'll be no supper, late or otherwise, if he can't get the chuck wagon through the brush before dark."

Brazos and Goose were no more than out of sight when, shocking in the evening stillness, there was a rifle shot. Like a reverberating echo of the first, there were two more. Stoney, Jed, and Pen were already in their saddles when McCaleb stopped them.

"It's up to Brazos and Goose. The rest of us are needed here. It just might be a trick to draw us away from the herd. We'll keep our eyes on the herd and keep our rifles handy."

Brazos and Goose had their rifles cocked and ready before the echo of the first shot died away. Goose swung wide, distancing himself from Brazos, lessening the target of a possible marksman. Somewhere ahead there was the agonized braying of a mule. Breaking out of a thicket, they sighted the chuck wagon in a clearing a hundred yards ahead. Monte stepped out from behind the wagon, his Winchester under his arm. Salty leaned on a wagon wheel, staring ruefully at the dead mule.

"The shot come from over there to our left," said Monte. "Didn't have anything to shoot at, but I put a couple into the vicinity, anyhow."

Goose looked questioningly at Brazos, and Brazos nodded. The Indian jogged his horse to a trot and rode toward the concealing brush. Aware of the chore ahead, Monte swiftly felled a young cottonwood. Trimmed and topped, he and Brazos used it as a pry pole, lifting the dead mule enough for Salty to remove the harness. Utilizing the remaining mules as best they could, Monte and Brazos clearing trail, they got the chuck wagon to camp.

6

*G*oose didn't return until after dark. He held up one finger, pointed east, and then lifted his hand to the darkening sky.

"That's one trail we don't have to follow," said Brazos. "It's one of that Sweetwater bunch, I reckon."

"He got his message across," said McCaleb. "He could have killed Monte or Salty as easily as he shot the mule. No more splitting up; we'll hold the herd to the pace of the chuck wagon. We're maybe three days' drive from Box Elder Creek and nearly twenty miles from the north fork of the Laramie River. Ride extra careful when you're nighthawking, and keep your rifles at the ready."

They reached the north fork of the Laramie river without further incident, and McCaleb estimated they were thirty-five miles south of Box Elder. The next morning they moved out in the first gray light of dawn, the only water they were sure of being Box Elder Creek or the North Platte, forty or more miles to the east. In the early afternoon towering thunderheads began building west of the Rockies, shrouding the sun. The bloodred afterglow fanned out to a dusty rose and then gave way to twilight.

"Not more'n fifteen miles to Box Elder," said McCaleb, "but we won't make it today. It'll mean another dry camp, but not for long, by the looks of those clouds."

Goose said something none of them understood and made swimming motions. There would be water in abundance before morning. A chill wind from the southwest brought the smell of rain.

"Don't shuck anything but your saddles and your hats," said McCaleb. "I've heard these High Plains storms are almighty fierce. Best to take one blanket and throw the rest of your rolls in the chuck wagon."

It was good advice. The herd was restless, cows bawling disconsolately for no apparent reason, except for the discomfort of another dry camp. But McCaleb, born and reared in cow country, knew what was bothering them. He could sense the static electricity in the crisp mountain air, and as he lay down, his head on his saddle, he knew he wouldn't rest there for long. Despite his misgivings, he slept. The storm was contrary to anything McCaleb had ever seen or heard tell of. There was very little thunder. Lightning came in dazzling blue and green streaks. Suddenly a cow bawled, and as if on cue, others joined in. As one, the herd rose to its feet and lit out to the south.

"Roll out!" one of the nighthawks bawled. "They're runnin'!"

Seconds counted. Saddles forgotten, they mounted and struck out hell-for-leather through the rainswept, lightning-splintered darkness. McCaleb let go and almost fell when, before his eyes, his horse's mane turned to green fire. Sparks leaped from one of the animal's ears to the other, and it fled as much from fear as from his urging. Somewhere ahead, amid the thunder of the herd and the wind-whipped rain, he could hear gunfire. Some of the riders were trying to turn the herd. He was riding parallel to the herd, accomplishing nothing. A horn raked his horse's flank and the animal screamed in pain, bucking wildly. Saddleless, it was all McCaleb could do just to hang on. By the time he had calmed the horse, he was hopelessly outdistanced by the herd. He rode on, and when he caught up to the stragglers, he knew the leaders had begun to tire or had been headed and were milling. As suddenly as the storm had struck, so did it pass. Overhead, a mass of clouds parted and a timid quarter moon peeked out. Stars twinkled as though nothing out of the ordinary had occurred. The time for urgency was past; the scattered herd couldn't be rounded up until morning. McCaleb slowed his horse, allowing the thirsty animal to drink from a puddle.

"Halloooo," hailed a voice. "Where is everybody?"

"Don't know about everybody," shouted McCaleb. "I'm here. Where are you? Have you seen Rebecca?"

"This is Pen. Jed, Stoney, and the Injun are with me. The herd split. We stopped some of 'em, but the rest is headed lickety-cut for the north fork of the Laramie."

"Ride on back to camp," said McCaleb. "We can't round them up in the dark. One thing in our favor—that storm passed over in a hurry. I reckon they won't run too far."

By the time McCaleb reached the chuck wagon, Monte was there, limping and leading a limping horse. The two of them had gone down in pursuit of the herd. To his relief, he found Rebecca at the chuck wagon with Salty.

"I didn't have a horse," she said sheepishly. "He got caught up with the stampede and I had to get up there with Salty so I didn't get trampled."

Pen, Jed, Stoney, and Goose rode in.

"Brazos isn't here," said Rebecca. "Has anyone seen him?"

As if in answer to her question, there was a pistol shot. They waited. If it was a plea for help, there would be two more, but there was only silence.

"I'm comin' in," shouted Brazos. He was afoot, limping. "My horse put his foot in a hole," said Brazos, "and busted his leg. I had to shoot him. He piled me off in some rocky ground and I got a lump on my head as big as a horse apple."

Disgruntled as McCaleb was with the stampede, he was thankful. They'd been fortunate. A good rider with a good cow horse didn't worry all that much about being thrown and trampled by the stampeding cattle. The gravest danger was one over which neither horse nor rider had any control. Many a good rider had gone headlong into an unseen arroyo and was crushed to death when the horse fell on him. All too vividly McCaleb remembered having been trapped under a dead horse in an arroyo slowly filling with water. He owed his life to the persistence of Rebecca and Charles Goodnight.

The sun rose in a cloudless sky, and after a breakfast with plenty of hot coffee, everybody was in better humor. Except Brazos; he'd had to shoot his favorite horse. They found most of the herd within an hour's ride. It took the rest of the day, however, to find the others. As Pen had jokingly predicted, some of them had run almost to the north fork of the Laramie.

"The only damn advantage to trailin' a mixed herd," said Jed. "The cows don't run near as far as the steers. If the lightning kept up long enough, them long-legged steers would run clean back to Texas."

"We can't afford to lose any of them either," said McCaleb. "From what I saw in an Omaha paper, they could be worth a hundred dollars apiece in the Montana gold camps."

"Viewin' it in that light," said Pen, "it seems downright sensible goin' back to Texas for another bunch."

They had sunny days and clear, cold nights, and on June 27, 1868, they bedded down the herd on Box Elder Creek. They immediately discovered that all McCaleb's claim markers had been torn down and the stones scattered. A cottonwood had been blazed with an axe—head high—and in the whitened gash, in black paint, was a crude numeral one.

"This is all so foolish," said Rebecca. "You've registered our claims at the land office in Cheyenne. So they've torn down the markers and put a number on a tree. What could it mean?"

McCaleb said nothing. He caught Brazos watching him

and suspected they shared the same thoughts. The numeral on the tree was for Will.

"I hope none of you will think I'm getting above my raising," said Rebecca, "because I don't want to live in a bunkhouse with everybody else."

Pen chuckled. "I reckon it'd be a mite unusual if you did."

"I ain't too excited about livin' in a bunkhouse myself," said Monte. "It gets so almighty cold here on the High Plains, we'd need a fireplace in each end."

"Some of us would spend all summer cuttin' firewood," finished Stoney.

"Well," chuckled McCaleb, "nobody wantin' a bunkhouse makes it a mite easier to tell you what I aim for us to do, startin' tomorrow. Now that I got me a nagging wife who insists on a place of her own, with Will soon to be in the same position, here's what I got in mind. First we'll build us a cookhouse, big enough for a dinin' room and living quarters for Salty. We then put up five cabins, with the idea of two of us in each of them. They can be small enough to be warm, even in this high country. If we lay out the cabins kind of back to back, with the cookhouse at the end of the row, we could throw up a roofed-over dog trot sheltering our back doors in heavy snowfall. It'd be a kind of long shed, a dry place for our firewood, and protection to and from the cookhouse in bad weather. Cedar shakes make for the best roof, and there's a blessed plenty of cedar close by."

Brazos chuckled. "This is goin' to be an almighty *ugly* ranch."

"Ugly I can stand," said Rebecca. "Cold, I can't."

"From what I've heard of our neighbors," said Jed, "if they complain, I reckon it won't be 'cause they don't like the looks of our place."

"If somebody goes to Texas and hires more riders," said Monte, "then we won't have enough bunks. Not with five cabins."

"We can always add a couple more," said McCaleb, "but it'll be sometime next spring before this herd arrives. God knows, we got enough work ahead of us, just buildin' what we'll need for the coming winter."

"Amen to that," said Stoney. "Before we're done, our hands are goin' to be blistered all the way to our elbows. Let these Texas rannies bringin' the new herd build their own cabins."

"I want a wood floor in mine," said Rebecca.

"Now you've done it," said McCaleb, chuckling. "Like the gent in Huntsville prison found a lizard in his bowl of turnip greens, and when he complained, all his cellmates wanted one."

"Well," snapped Rebecca, "the extra comfort will be worth the extra work. If there's anybody here that don't mind getting up in the dead of winter and putting his bare feet on frozen ground, then leave his floor dirt. As for me, I'll have a wood floor if I have to flat the logs and lay it myself."

"How 'bout th' cookhouse?" inquired Salty. "Wooden floor?"

"Cookhouse too," said McCaleb.

In typical cowboy fashion, putting good food ahead of everything else, they built the cookhouse first. The fireplace and cooking area filled one end of the room, next to that were two long dining tables, and at the other end Salty's scant living quarters.

"This luxury's goin' to spoil him for the chuck wagon," said Monte, grinning. "He'll end up stayin' here, and on the trail drives, we'll end up eatin' grub off a pack mule."

"Boy," snorted Salty, "if'n I thought you had th' potential—which you don't—I'd teach you t' cook, leave you here, and I'd go on th' drives in your place."

Unable to ride, the old cook was handy with his hands and with tools. Using a hatchet, a drawing knife, and finally a hand plane, he patiently and efficiently "flatted" the logs for all the floors. They had completed the cookhouse and two of the cabins when their "visitor" arrived. He rode one of the mules that had been hitched to the wagon McCaleb and Goose had met on their first visit to Box Elder Creek. Kingston Henry carried a tied-down Colt on his right hip and carried a rifle in a saddle boot. He sat with his left leg crooked around his saddle horn, rolled a left-handed quirly and looked at them in surly silence.

"Step down," said McCaleb, "if you're of a mind to."

But Henry made no move to dismount. He had fixed his malevolent gaze on Brazos, who, stripped to the waist, still wore his Colt. Brazos returned the cold stare, saying nothing.

"Ever' man's due one mistake," said Henry, "an' you made yours. I ain't forgot. Time's comin' when I'll settle with you."

"When you're ready," said Brazos coldly. "Unless you're partial to back-shootin', like your pal, Maury Duke."

It was a deliberate taunt. Henry's face flushed, but he was careful to keep his big hands on his saddle horn. Without another word he kicked the mule into a lope.

"Rememberin' Will," said Monte, "it's a powerful temptation not to put a couple of slugs where they'd do the most good."

"I can't believe he's carrying a grudge over that fight with Brazos in Cheyenne," said Rebecca, "coming here, making threats."

"Just an excuse to take our measure," said Brazos. "He wanted a closer look, to see how much of an outfit we got."

"I expect you're right," said McCaleb, "about him wantin' a closer look at us. But I wouldn't get careless, was I you. I'd say he's not used to bein' knocked down in public. Men have been shot in the back for less; like Will."

By mid-July the cabins had been completed. They snaked down cedar logs for posts and slender cottonwoods for rails and built a corral along Box Elder Creek, beyond the cookhouse. The north end of the enclosure crossed the creek so that their livestock could drink. On the west end, extending the full length of the corral, they build a roofed, three-sided shelter for a barn. A day later Will and Susannah rode in. Will seemed none the worse for his experience, except thinner. Susannah wore range clothes and her eyes sparkled with excitement.

"Lord," groaned Monte, "you've missed all the fun. We'd ought to charge you rent on one of them cabins."

"You do," grinned Will, "and I won't tell you the news we brought from Omaha and Cheyenne."

"If it's bad news," said Rebecca, "I don't want to hear it."

"Some of it's good," said Will, "but I'm not sure about the rest."

"I want to tell the good news," said Susannah, "because it involves my uncle Bill, Buffalo Bill Cody."

"Go on, then," said Will, "and leave me the chore of tellin' about Mr. Train's latest surprise."

"Uncle Bill Cody's going to scout for the army again," said Susannah, "and he'll be at Fort Buford in mid-August. He says let Montana Territory and the gold fields wait awhile and bring a herd to the fort. He not only knows the commanding officer at Buford, but the quartermaster as well. He can help us get the beef contract for Fort Buford at least, and maybe even for all three territories!"

"I can't believe he's got that kind of pull with the army," said Jed. "Is this the same Yankee army that's squattin' in Texas?"

"The same," Will grinned, "but they've got an almighty lot of respect for Bill Cody. Some of the miracles he's performed as an army scout, they think of him as bein' just a step beneath God."

"He's a good man," said McCaleb, "and a powerful friend. We'll talk more about him and his offer, but for now, I'd like to hear what Will's got to tell us about Mr. Train."

"I got this from Colton in Cheyenne," said Will, "and he told me to tell you he had absolutely nothing to do with the story Train's released to the Omaha and Chicago newspapers. That brakeman from the work train got just enough of the story from the old man at the depot in Cheyenne to interest the newspapers. Once Train's office in Omaha saw how it was going, they got behind it and made George Francis Train the hero. This poor cowboy—meanin' me, of course—had been shot. Mr. Train, at the risk of his own life, with the telegraph down and another train comin' at him, used his private car and locomotive, getting me to Omaha just in time. Hell of it is, Train hasn't said a word. Appleby, that damn fool with the Omaha paper, started it. He got kicked out of Train's office, and that made him all the more determined. I had to sneak out of Omaha using my mama's maiden name. Colton wanted to tell what really happened in his paper, but I told him to leave it be."

"I hate George Francis Train," snarled Rebecca. "Given a choice, he'd have let Will die, although he was going to Omaha anyway. I want everybody to know he went strictly against his will, with a gun to his head."

"Come on," chuckled McCaleb, "give the devil his due. The man might be a scoundrel and an opportunist, but you have to admire his moves. Suppose I let Colton print the true story, admitting that I forced Train, at gun point, to take us to Omaha? There has to be some law against taking control of a locomotive, even if you're headed for the same place it is. Train's got us by the short hairs and he knows it. My admittin' to holding a Colt on him from Cheyenne to Omaha could get me locked up. Like the gent who defended himself for havin' shot a man in Austin by swearing, at that particular time, he was killin' another hombre in San Antone."

"It just doesn't seem fair," said Susannah, "that this man should get the credit for saving Will's life, when one of his men, Maury Duke, was responsible for the shooting."

"It's a matter of proof," said McCaleb, "or the lack of it. First, we can't prove that Duke did the shooting, and second, we can't prove that he's in any way connected to Train. Some smart lawyer could claim that Will and Maury

Duke fought over you. It wouldn't be the first time a woman was responsible for a fight and a man bein' shot."

"Thanks," said Susannah.

"Perhaps," said Rebecca, "Train won't bother us now that he's using the trip to Omaha to make him look like everything but the sneaking coyote he is."

"Whatever reason the man has for not wanting us on Box Elder Creek still exists," said McCaleb. "He'd already told us we weren't welcome here, before I pulled a Colt and bought us passage to Omaha."

"That's why he's done nothing to discourage Maury Duke and Kingston Henry," said Brazos. "The answer is somewhere on the Sweetwater. I aim to do some nosing around. We need to know what's so almighty important to him that we can't settle here, even on patented land."

"Unless they push us," said McCaleb, "that'll have to wait. If we aim to take Bill Cody's advice and trail some steers to Fort Buford by mid-August, then we don't have any time to spare."

Their "map" of Wyoming, Montana, and Dakota territories was woefully inadequate. Prepared by the army in the fifties, it concerned itself mostly with locations of forts, major trails, mountains, and rivers. The only other maps—railroad maps—were less than useless, the only identifiable territory being that through which the rails passed. Mc-Caleb had found just one way in which the Union Pacific's survey of 1862 was of any possible use. By taking their mileage figures—"known" distance from one point to another—he devised a scale by which he could determine unknown distance within that same territory. McCaleb sat hunched on the floor, utilizing the light of the fire to total the figures he'd written on a tablet. Rebecca, fully dressed except for her boots, watched.

"So far as an actual 'trail' is concerned," she said, "there isn't any 'Western trail,' is there?"

"There will be someday," said McCaleb. "So far as Texas trail drivin' is concerned, I reckon we're pioneering it."

* * *

"We'll take five hundred head of steers to Fort Buford," said McCaleb, "and we'll pull out next Saturday, July eighteenth. Five of us will be going. I'm taking Rebecca, Will, Susannah, and Goose. Short-handed as we are, Rebecca and Susannah will have to pull their weight as riders. They'll also have to do the cooking; Salty, we'll miss you, but we don't know how accurate these old army maps are, and we just purely don't have time to clear a four-hundred-mile wagon road. We'll take a pack mule."

"I'm near 'bout scairt to ask what the rest of us'll be doin' while you're gone," said Stoney with a grin.

"We're goin' to need an almighty lot of firewood," said McCaleb, "and you're shy a man for nighthawking. I'd like to leave Goose with you, but I'll need him for scouting. The Sioux have been moved to a reservation in western Dakota Territory, and that's where we're going."

"You're goin' to have all the fun," moaned Monte, "while we cut wood."

"Your turn's comin'," chuckled McCaleb. "You'll be cuttin' firewood while we're gone to Buford, but right after Christmas, when the weather permits, you'll be goin' back to Texas for another herd of steers. You'll be eatin' better than we do, because Salty will be taking the chuck wagon. If this drive to Fort Buford works out, all of you will eventually be going. I won't lie to you—I'm taking Rebecca and Susannah on this drive because I'm just not sure what Kingston Henry, Maury Duke, and the rest of these pelicans along the Sweetwater are up to. I want some fast-shootin', whang-leather-tough Texas cowboys here, so's I don't come back and find all this hard work just a pile of ashes. Brazos is in charge, but I'm countin' on every man. *Comprender?*"

"We'll whip this Sweetwater bunch every mornin' before breakfast," said Stoney, "and spend the rest of the day cuttin' firewood."

"Don't go looking for trouble," warned McCaleb, "but if they start anything, you have my permission to finish it in whatever manner you choose."

* * *

With Goose riding point, they moved out their abbreviated herd in the first gray light of dawn. McCaleb held back for a last word with Brazos.

"I figure twenty days," said McCaleb, "and that's if we average twenty miles a day. Cut that in half on the return trip, but when we leave will depend on when Bill Cody shows up. After all the faunching around the army did in New Mexico, refusing to work with rebs, I'll welcome Cody's help in dealing with them. I feel like I'm leaving you short-handed. Take the first watch yourself and let the others finish out the nights in teams of two."

"I still aim to spend some daylight ridin' along the Sweetwater," said Brazos, "but not long enough for anything to bust loose here."

"Just be careful," said McCaleb. "I don't want to come back here and find a blazed cottonwood with a two painted on it."

"You do," said Brazos, "and it'll represent Kingston Henry and Maury Duke."

7

The first day's drive was uneventful. They crossed the North Platte River and bedded down for the night in western Dakota Territory.

"My God," exclaimed Will, looking over the map. "According to this, we won't reach any water until we turn north, somewhere above the Nebraska line."

"There'll be water," said McCaleb. "This is an old army map, and there's no streams the way we're traveling, because the army trailed their supplies to Fort Dodge, to Ogallala, and from there north. They only made note of the water they found. If my figurin' is close to being right, it's maybe a hundred and twenty-five miles from Box Elder Creek to where we'll turn north on the Western trail. From there on to Fort Buford, we can pretty well count on the army's map for rivers and creeks. On the back of their map I've started one of my own. We come this way again, I'll know all the sources of water between Box Elder and the point where we reach the Western trail."

"We've covered twenty miles if not more," said Will. "Some difference, trailin' these big steers. Let these brutes set their own pace, I'd be surprised if they didn't cover thirty miles a day."

"We had to ride hard just to keep up with them," said Susannah. "I had no idea they stirred up so much dust. Do we have to ride drag all the way to Fort Buford?"

McCaleb chuckled. "It's a western tradition. The women always ride drag. I believe the Indians started it."

"It's dusty," said Will, "but it's the safest place on a drive. If both of you got trampled, we'd end up doin' our own cooking."

"You're liable to end up doing your own cooking anyway," warned Rebecca, "if you don't start treating us like cowboys instead of squaws."

"All right, cowboys," said McCaleb cheerfully, "first rule on a trail drive is that nobody bitches about the dust or the weather. Now, one or both of you gents is welcome to cook supper."

Once the herd was on the trail, Brazos turned back to the rest of the outfit. Following McCaleb's promise of a drive from Texas, they were still in high good humor.

"They'll be gone close to a month," said Brazos, "so we'll have plenty of time to cut firewood. Let's put in a good day and take off tomorrow, it bein' Sunday. How about the four of you mannin' a pair of crosscut saws? I'll do the axe work—toppin' and trimmin'—and take my turn on one end of a saw."

Salty had dried apple pie for dinner, and they got through the afternoon with a minimum of complaining. Brazos had high hopes that Kingston Henry and the rest of Train's bought-and-paid-for "homesteaders" were unaware of the drive to Fort Buford. With half the outfit away, it would be an ideal opportunity for any mischief they might have in mind. Before they learned how short-handed he was, Brazos would do some prowling of his own. Right after Sunday breakfast, warning his riders to keep a sharp eye, he rode out. He took his time, following the Sweetwater west, uncertain as to what he was seeking. If nothing else, he would check out Kingston Henry's place, without revealing his own presence.

For a while he watched the house, seeing not a soul. A thin trail of smoke spiraling lazily from the chimney was the only visible evidence there might be someone in the house. Instead of riding far into the woods at the other side of the clearing, he found a shallow place in the Sweetwater and crossed to the north bank. It too was wooded, but afforded him a closer look at the cabin. He rode past it, to the top of the rise, so that he was able to see the front of the barn. The wagon was there, and he felt a keen touch of disappointment. He continued along the ridge, having learned nothing, yet reluctant to turn away. From the west a light breeze had sprung up. Down the ridge, somewhere to his right, there was a snuffling and grunting that marked the unmistakable presence of a bear. It was an animal best left alone, and Brazos was about to ride on when he heard the childish voice.

"Scat, bear! Vamoose!"

The bear did neither, continuing to grunt and shuffle about. Brazos quietly dismounted near some greasewood, half-hitching his reins to it. He crept down the slope, the light breeze in his face, until he was able to see the head of the big brown bear. Thank God it wasn't a grizzly; they were bad-tempered and mean. He found a stone the size of his fist and flung it into the brush beyond the bear. Momentarily the animal turned toward the sound and then resumed its position, hunkering on its hindquarters like an enormous dog.

"Bear," said that small, wheedling voice, "why don't you go home so I can? Please."

Brazos caught a patch of color through the branches of a broad-leafed cottonwood, maybe a third of the way up. He could return to his horse, get his rifle and shoot the bear, but that shot could be heard for miles. Anyhow, the last thing he wished to do was shoot the animal. The meat was tough and stringy, and skinning a bear was a rotten way to spend any day, especially a Sunday. He found some more stones and threw them, seconds apart, where he had thrown the first one. The resulting noise finally aroused the curiosity of the bear, and snuffling and grunting, it lumbered off down the slope, seeking a possibly larger and more attainable prey. Brazos looked up into those same big eyes he'd last seen in Cheyenne, then full of tears.

"Centavo, you'd best come down. Them rocks I chunked into the brush won't keep your friend busy for long."

"He's not my friend," she said hotly. "I had my bucket 'most full of berries, and he ate them all, the big hog."

"Can you climb down without falling?"

"'Course I can; I'm not a baby!"

She wore the same thin dress, and her feet were bare. She swung from limb to limb until she was hanging by her hands from the one nearest the ground. It was still too far to drop. Brazos took hold of her skinny body and eased her down.

"That first limb's twice as far as you can reach," said Brazos. "How'd you get up there?"

"You get a bear scratchin' and clawin' after you," she said laconically, "and I reckon you can jump as far as you have to."

"I reckon," Brazos chuckled. "How long have you been up there?"

"I don't know. Too long, I reckon. Mama's likely to spank me when I go to the house with an empty bucket. Will you go with me and tell her the bear ate all my berries and chased me up a tree?"

"Maybe," said Brazos. "Who's there . . . besides your mama?"

"Just her. He ain't there. He's downriver gettin' drunk, I reckon."

"He'd have to go to Cheyenne for that."

"No, he wouldn't," she said. "One of them no-account homesteaders has a still and has set up a saloon in a tent. Old King, he spends his weekends down there, and we have to put up with him till he sobers up."

"He mistreats you and your mama?"

"Oh, I dasn't tell you. Mama would skin me. Will you tell her about the bear, so's I don't get a switching?"

"I reckon," chuckled Brazos. "Let's go."

He hoisted her up in front of him and jogged his horse

down the slope. He found a shallow place, forded the Sweetwater and ground-hitched his horse before the small cabin. He saw fear in Rosalie's eyes when she opened the door, and he knew why. Hearing the horse, she had believed Kingston Henry had returned. Penelope stood behind Brazos with her empty bucket.

"Ma'am," he said, "I found her up a cottonwood with a bear tryin' to get at her. The brute ate all her berries and she needed a witness."

"Dear God," moaned Rosalie, "how many times have I told her not to go into the woods, not to cross the river—"

"But Mama," protested the child, "the best berries are on the ridge, and the river ain't that deep. . . ."

Brazos laughed. The woman, torn between punishing Penelope and responding to Brazos's good humor, chose the latter course.

"I'm sorry," she said, trying to smile. "Every time you see me, I'm upset and bawling. It . . . it's just that I feel . . . so alone. God knows what might have happened to her if you hadn't come along."

"Centavo," said Brazos seriously, "you listen to your mama. With just a swipe of his paw, that bear could have broken your bones and hurt you somethin' awful. Next time, I might not be there to chase it away. Understand?"

"Yes, sir," she said contritely. "I'm sorry, Mama. I won't go across the river again."

"You have a way with her." Rosalie laughed nervously. "I want to thank you for what you did—tried to do—at the store. . . ."

"I'm sorry I had to hit your husband, ma'am."

"He ain't her husband," bawled Penelope, "and he ain't my daddy. He's a mean, nasty old man and I hate him!"

"Penelope," she said, her voice trembling, "go in the bedroom and stay there until I tell you to come out. Go right this minute!"

Penelope threw Brazos that same piteous look he remembered so well and trudged off into the adjoining room. Brazos, clutching his hat with both hands, could think of nothing to say. The silence grew long and painful, and despite her efforts to control them, the tears came. Slumping down on a bench, she buried her face in her hands and wept. Brazos sat down beside her, timidly resting a consoling arm across her slender shoulders. That was all it took. She threw her arms around his neck, and never had he witnessed such grief. It shook him to his very soul. He looked up, found Penelope standing in the doorway and was touched by the compassion and understanding in her eyes. Slowly Rosalie's tears subsided and she drew away, unable to look at him.

"I'm sorry," she said. "That was disgraceful. But you were so kind, and I . . . I'm not used to . . . that. You'd better go, before I—"

"Not until you promise me I . . . I can come again," he said.

"You can't," she said miserably. "He . . . they . . . they'll kill you."

"Some have tried," said Brazos, "but I'm still around. They ain't."

He got up and put on his hat. Penelope had inched her way back into the room. Without a word she came to him and took one of his big hands in both of hers. He hunkered down and his hat went tumbling as she threw her thin arms around him. When she finally let him go, it was a while before he could see well enough to find his hat. He stopped at the door. Penelope had a wan smile on her tear-streaked face. Rosalie still wasn't looking at him.

"Rosalie," he said, "whatever the rest of your name is, I don't care. I'll see you next Sunday. You too, Centavo, and don't let me find you on a cottonwood limb, talkin' to a bear."

He was about to mount his horse when Rosalie spoke from the doorway.

"I don't even know your name."

He turned to face her. "Brazos. Brazos Gifford."

"Please, Brazos, for your sake, don't . . . come back. But if . . . if you do, look for a white sheet on the clothesline behind the house. It will tell you that I . . . that he's not here."

Brazos rode slowly, allowing the horse to take its time. Smitten as he was by Rosalie, his thoughts were of Penelope. The child was wise beyond her years, displaying a shocking knowledge of Kingston Henry's habits. What had she witnessed, what had she overheard? He was almost afraid to find out.

Seven days away from Box Elder Creek McCaleb's trail drive reached the junction of their eastward route and the northbound Western trail. Turning north, they covered twenty miles, bedding down on what their map identified as Belle Fourche River.

"How in tarnation do they come up with names like that?" wondered Will. "It sounds like somebody's wife's maiden name."

"Maybe it is." McCaleb chuckled. "Virginia City was originally named after Jeff Davis's wife, but the Yankees didn't like 'Varina.' The next unidentified river we come to, we'll call it 'Rebecca.' Or 'Susannah.' "

The following night, on the Sulphur River, their confidence and good humor received a telling blow. Indians spooked the herd, and all efforts to head it were futile. Come first light, with Goose scouting far ahead, the riders set out in pursuit, riding south, back toward the Belle Fourche. But they didn't get far. Goose had given up the chase and had ridden back to meet them. Shaking his head, he fisted both hands and opened them, spreading his fingers. Four times he repeated the sign, then he spoke.

"Sioux. Muchos. Take cow."

McCaleb held up his Henry rifle, pointing it south, a question in his eyes. Again Goose shook his head, drawing a forefinger across his throat. That was enough for McCaleb.

"Let's round up what's left," he said, "and ride. When Goose backs off, that's just too damn many Indians."

They moved out with the remainder of the herd, 490

head. Fearing yet another raid, they spent a sleepless night at Sulphur River. Their map said the next stream would be Moreau Creek, but it didn't say that Moreau was a wet-weather stream that went bone dry in the summer. McCaleb made a decision.

"The map says we're due to cross Antelope Creek ten miles north of here. I can't see a dry camp, when we're that close to water. There'll be a moon tonight, so we'll push on, like we crossed the Llano Estacado."

Reaching Antelope Creek after dark, they found abundant water. They ate jerky and cold biscuits, not lighting a fire, lest it draw more beef-hungry Sioux. Tired as they were, sleep was long in coming. The yipping of distant coyotes was a constant reminder that their two-legged counterparts were out there somewhere.

"From what you told the outfit," said Will, "I reckon you don't plan to boss that drive from Texas. Who's the lucky jaybird you got in mind?"

"You or Brazos," said McCaleb. "I'd trust any man in the outfit, but there'll be a saddlebag full of gold to worry with, and I'll purely feel better with it in the hands of an ex-Ranger."

"How many head?"

"Four thousand," said McCaleb, "granted that the price is right and that there's enough good riders to trail them. With more and more Texas cattlemen taking their herds to market, I expect we'll have to pay more for good steers, but I'm not against that. You get what you pay for."

"I'd kind of like to go to Texas," said Susannah, "and meet Will's mama and daddy. Will, why don't you see how Brazos feels about it? Unless he has a better reason than we do, I'd like for us to go. I'll pull my weight on the trail, riding drag if nothing else."

"All steers this time?" Will asked.

"All steers," said McCaleb. "We've got breeding stock. Natural increase will do the rest, but it'll take time. Whatever need there is now will have to be supplied with Texas steers. Two-year-olds or better."

* * *

Brazos finished his lone watch, leaving the herd to Jed and Stoney. He returned to the cabin, shucked his mackinaw, gloves, and boots, stretching out on his "rawhide" bunk. It consisted of blankets spread over wide rawhide strips, carefully latticed together like the cane bottom of a chair. It was only Wednesday. Three more days. What kind of fool was he, sneaking around to see a woman who lived with that brute, Kingston Henry? Clearly, Rosalie hadn't intended for him to know Kingston Henry wasn't her husband. While he did know, thanks to the honesty of Penelope, was he any better off? Henry was a drunk, a bully, and a probable killer. Rosalie feared him, and Penelope hated him. Where did Brazos Gifford fit in, or did he fit in at all? He tried unsuccessfully to free his mind of Rosalie's dark eyes, her clinging desperation, her hunger for affection. She welcomed his return, yet feared the possible consequences of it. Despite the unanswered questions, and the looming possibility of further violence with Kingston Henry, he would return to that cabin on the Sweetwater.

Brazos was jolted awake by the crash of gunfire, the frenzied bawling of cows and the whooping of riders. He stomped into his boots, buckling his pistol belt as he ran. He flung open the door and a bullet thunked into the logs just above his head. He drew his Colt and fired twice at the muzzle flash. He heard the pound of boots, and Monte and Pen were beside him. Without a word they all sprinted for the corral, all too aware that their efforts were too little and too late. By the time they were saddled, the herd would be scattered from hell to breakfast.

They rode north, following the sound of diminishing gunfire. When even that had died and silence reigned, the three riders drew up, listening. The herd, however scattered, could be recovered. Jed and Stoney were strong on Brazos's mind. Had the two young riders been taken by surprise and cut down? Some of the attackers might lay in wait, and to call out could result in a fusillade of gunfire.

"Fan out," said Brazos, "and advance. Slow. Don't lose sight of one another, and don't shoot until you're sure it's not Jed or Stoney."

They had traveled no more than a mile when Brazos reined up.

"Hold it," he said. "Horse coming."

It came in a slow lope. Brazos drew his Colt.

"That's far enough," he said. "Who are you?"

"It's us," said Stoney. "Ridin' double. They shot Jed's horse."

"Come on, then," said Brazos. "Either of you hit?"

"Not me," said Jed, "but I might croak from humiliation. They killed my Cayuse before I got off a single shot."

"I reckon all of us were a mite unprepared," said Brazos. "Until now, we've had only Kingston Henry's threats, and we didn't take him serious. We won't make that mistake again. Tomorrow night—and every night until the rest of the outfit returns—we'll unroll our blankets next to the herd. When you're nighthawking, keep your eyes and ears open. Sound off at the first sign of trouble. When you sleep, don't shuck anything but your hat. We'll picket the horses and keep them saddled. Have your rifles loaded and handy. This bunch shows up again, we'll counter their surprise with one of our own. Roll in and get what sleep you can. Come first light, we go after the herd."

"I want to line my sights on the jaspers that stampeded it and shot my hoss," said Jed.

"I share that sentiment," said Brazos, "but I doubt we'll find them with the herd. They don't want the cattle; this is harassment."

Riding bareback to the point where his horse had been hit, Jed got his saddle and they continued on the trail of the herd.

"Six of them," said Pen, "from what I can tell. They aim to run the herd north of the Sweetwater, I'd say."

"That's the unceded Indian land McCaleb was talkin' about," said Jed.

"No matter," said Brazos grimly. "If our Six Bar herd's over there, I reckon we'll be goin' after them."

As usual, be it trail drive or stampede, the cows lagged behind. Before they reached the river, they found remnants of the herd—cows and under-two-year-olds—grazing peacefully.

"We'll get them later," said Brazos. "Let's get that nearly fifteen hundred big steers back on our side of the river first."

It was easier said than done. The herd had hit the Sweetwater at one of its shallowest points and it hadn't slowed them in the slightest.

"Nothin' come out on the north side," said Monte, "except cows. So this bunch of coyotes don't aim for us to trail 'em."

"No," said Brazos, "and they're thinkin' straight, because we can't take the time. They'll keep to the water, everybody gettin' out at a different place, every rider goin' his separate way. Besides, we can't ride into a hostile camp and string a man up on suspicion. Let's try and corral those long-legged steers before they run all the way to Powder River."

They found one small bunch of steers after another and drove them to a valley not far from the Sweetwater. They did separate tallies and compared their figures.

"Still two hundred of the big bastards hidin' somewhere," Jed concluded.

"I'd say you're right," Brazos agreed. "Too many to let go. We'll have to fan out until we cut their trail, and we'd best make it quick. There's maybe another four or five hours of daylight."

They drew up on the crest of a ridge, and in the valley below they could see the missing cattle. But that wasn't all. At the farthermost end of the valley there were six Indian tipis. In the midst of them, an almost smokeless fire burned and there were several dozen Indians visible.

"Now what?" said Monte. "They're bound to see us

when we go after the cows. No way we can sneak them out."

"Don't even think about sneaking something past an Indian," said Brazos. "They have no respect for cowardice. They know those cows are there, and they know they didn't just drop out of the sky, so they won't be surprised to see us. We'll ride down there like we've got every right to."

The Indians made no move toward their horses or weapons. The men, with the exception of their buckskinned chief, were near naked. A dozen of them gathered as the white men approached. The braves were prepared for the buffalo hunt, stripped down to breechcloths and moccasins. Each carried a sheath knife at his waist, and those who stood nearest the tipis had either a lance or bow and quiver of arrows near at hand. Looped around the neck of each horse was a trailing rawhide thong. During the excitement of the hunt, a rider might fall; seizing the rawhide, he used the weight of his body to slow the running horse until he could remount.

The five riders reined up. Brazos gave the peace sign and it was returned. Pointing to himself, the chief spoke.

"Washakie," he said. "Shoshoni."

Brazos had heard of him. Washakie and the Shoshoni had befriended the early settlers, one of the few friends the white man found along the Bozeman trail. The Shoshoni had fought, and continued to fight, with other tribes, most notably the Sioux and Arapaho.

In the camp there was all the evidence of a successful hunt. On lines strung between the tipis, meat had been hung to dry. Great hunks had been suspended over the fire on forked sticks, the dripping juices sizzling as they hit the coals. Three hides had been staked out on the ground, flesh side up, and squaws, two for each hide, were using bone knives to scrape the flesh away.

Washakie placed a palm against each side of his head, extending only the forefinger, like horns. The buffalo sign. Brazos nodded, pointing to the remainder of the herd, then pointed to himself. Washakie nodded, saying nothing.

Brazos reined his horse around and rode back the way he had come, the rest of the outfit following. Except for Monte Nance. He had reined up near one of the squaws, and for a matter of seconds she ceased her hide scraping. Her eyes met his and she immediately looked away. Still he waited, but she kept her eyes on her work. Without a backward glance, he kicked his horse into a lope. The others had reined up, waiting for him.

"Kid," said Brazos, "you purely believe in pushing your luck."

"I'd swap my share of the herd for that little chickadee," said Monte.

"You won't have it to swap," said Pen, "if we don't get these steers back across the river. They'll take it. That buff hide your little chickadee was scrapin' had a Six Bar brand on the other side."

"We'd ought to get a copy of that treaty and have a look at it," said Jed. "It 'pears like every four-legged critter north of the Sweetwater is a buffalo."

"They get away with this," said Stoney, "and we're likely to have them stampedin' our stock ever'time they hanker to hunt buffalo."

"I don't think so," said Brazos. "Washakie has long been a friend to the whites. That's why he and the Shoshoni are allowed to hunt buffalo in the Powder River basin. But like everything else the white man has done for the Indian, it's an empty gesture. The buffalo arc gone. Washakie and his people are holding on, pretending nothing has changed, knowing that everything has. Forever. They have nothing left except their pride, and I won't strip them of that for three cows."

They rode on in silence. In a matter of minutes they had the remainder of their herd moving toward the Sweetwater. Monte trotted his horse alongside Brazos's.

"I want three steers," he said. "Now."

"Sure," said Brazos, "but you reckon they'll swap you that little gal for just three steers?"

"It's got nothin' to do with her," said Monte, flushing.

"You meant what you said, didn't you, about them having nothing left but their pride?"

"I did," said Brazos.

Monte kicked his horse into a lope, cut out three steers and began hazing them up the valley, toward the Indian camp. Pen, Jed, and Stoney watched, their eyes full of questions, but Brazos said nothing. The kid would do.

8

"We pay for our mistakes," said McCaleb. "Mine cost us ten steers. If we'd had another two or three riders, we could have held the herd, or at least have had the guns to go after it."

"We couldn't have done any different," said Will, "without leaving the ranch short-handed."

"We need twenty good riders," said Rebecca, "for all we're trying to do. We need ten on this drive, if only to discourage the Sioux."

"We'll have them," said McCaleb, "when we trail another herd from Texas, but that's a year away."

"I'm new to the outfit," said Susannah, "but I have a suggestion."

"We can use it," said McCaleb.

"Abilene's become a cattle town," said Susannah. "When herds come up the trail, what happens to all those riders once the herd is sold? Suppose you rode to Abilene and hired some of those cowboys that are fresh off the trail and have spent all their money?"

"I might have to do that," said McCaleb. "It will depend on what happens at Fort Buford. If they make us an offer involving regular drives, then we can't wait to hire riders out of Texas."

"We don't have much time," said Rebecca. "Cold as the

high country is in the summer, I'd not be surprised to see a blizzard in September. How far are we from Fort Buford?"

"Another two hundred miles," said McCaleb. "Ten more days, without stampedes or Indian trouble."

On August fifth they bedded down the herd on the Little Missouri, fifty-five miles south of Fort Buford. They reached the Missouri three days later and followed it west to the fort. McCaleb had been directed to the post commander's office and was about to knock when a sign on the door caught his eye. It read: CAPT. MARTIN SANDOVAL, COMMANDING OFFICER. Could it possibly be? He knocked, entering when given permission.

Except for the captain's bars on his shirt collar, and having gained a few pounds, Sandoval had changed little. The young man came out from behind the desk, a grin on his face, and McCaleb took it.

"So it's Captain now," McCaleb laughed. "What in tarnation are you doin' up here? Waco too tame for you?"

"This is the army's idea of a promotion." Sandoval chuckled. "I owe you a lot, McCaleb. I was just out of Indiana, a green-as-grass lieutenant, but thanks to you and your cowboys, I got the credit for putting the quietus on some of the Indian trouble in East Texas. You were dead right—dropping that medicine man with a needle gun convinced the Comanches that Waco was bad medicine. Things got downright tame after that."

When federal occupation had begun, Sandoval and five Union soldiers had been assigned to Waco. McCaleb's outfit, moving the herd north along the Brazos to join Charles Goodnight, reached Waco just ahead of an attack by a large band of Comanches. At considerable risk to themselves, they had joined Sandoval's small contingent of soldiers, and the Comanches had been defeated.*

McCaleb spent the next few minutes briefing Sandoval as to their hope of securing a beef contract at Fort Buford.

* Trail Drive Series #1—*The Goodnight Trail*

Sandoval brightened at the mention of Buffalo Bill Cody's name.

"He's here," said Sandoval. "Rode in yesterday. The brass in Washington cut special orders, calling for red carpet treatment. Should I tell them everybody, even the lowest private, calls him 'Bill,' and that he spends his time in the barracks, playing cards with the enlisted men?"

McCaleb chuckled. "I wouldn't. They might send you back to Waco."

Following Brazos's orders, they rolled in their blankets minus only their hats, their rifles and belted Colts close at hand. Their mounts, saddled and picketed, grazed nearby. The rest of the week passed uneventfully. Sunday at breakfast Monte had an announcement to make.

"I aim to take a ride, maybe after dinner."

"I'm ridin' down the Sweetwater a ways," said Brazos.

"He ain't goin' that way," said Stoney. "He's lopin' over to Powder River basin, to help that little Injun gal scrape longhorn buffalo hides."

Monte flushed, and Brazos wondered if they knew something he didn't. He said nothing. Monte was a man. Washakie's band seemed harmless enough, but that might change if a white man began fooling around with one of their women. The girl who had caught Monte's eye couldn't have been much over seventeen. Brazos had misgivings, but he put them aside. On the frontier a man didn't involve himself in another man's problems, even if that man was a friend.

Right after breakfast Brazos saddled up and rode west along the Sweetwater. He crossed to the north bank, keeping to the ridge so that he might see the little cabin without being seen. On the clothesline behind the cabin a white sheet flapped in the early morning breeze. Unaware that he'd been holding his breath, Brazos heaved a sigh of relief and kicked his horse into a lope. He was splashing across the Sweetwater when the door banged open. Penelope bounded across the porch and down the steps. She had been watching for him, and the knowledge brought a deep-down, unaccustomed warmth. He swung out of the saddle and caught her up in his arms.

His first sight of Rosalie gave him a start. Despite having discouraged his return, she had anticipated it, prepared for it. Her waist-length hair, tangled and unkempt when he'd last seen her, had been brushed, and while the dress she wore was far from fancy, he sensed it was the best she had.

"I feared you wouldn't come," she said, "and feared that you would. My mind tells me I don't have the right to see you, but my heart disagrees, so you know which one I'm listening to."

He eased Penelope to the floor, and she didn't want to go.

"Centavo, your mama and me need to talk. I reckon it'll be a little too grown-up for your ears."

"Please," she begged, "can't I stay? She can't tell you anything I don't know, and it's me that's kept him out of her bed."

Rosalie flushed with embarrassment. She swallowed hard before she spoke.

"She's right," said Rosalie. "She's grown up hard and fast, and some of it's my fault. I've had nobody to talk to, nobody to confide in, and I've leaned on her. But for her, I'd have killed myself."

"Tell me about you," said Brazos, "startin' with where you're from and why you're here."

For a while she said nothing, seeming to gather her courage. Finally, with a sigh, she began to talk.

"I was born in western Kentucky—in Muhlenberg County—and daddy died when I was seven. Mama married a Presbyterian preacher, and I . . . I didn't like him. By the time I was twelve or thirteen, he was after me. When I was fifteen, I ran away. When my stepdaddy found me, I was with a man . . . I didn't know. He had been kind to me, and my stepdaddy had him put in the county jail for kidnapping me. He dragged me home and beat me until I couldn't stand on my feet. Just a few days after I was sixteen, I got sick and the doctor said I was . . . that I was going to have a baby. Stepdaddy said I had disgraced myself and the family, and he took me to St. Louis. I was put in a home for wayward girls."

"That's where I was born," said Penelope.

She continued as though Penelope hadn't spoken.

"The home was all right. Anything was better than what I'd left behind. When Penelope was born, I found they were going to take her from me, that she was to be adopted. I cried and I begged, but it did no good. When she was four days old—the day before she was to be taken away—I stole her from the nursery and slipped out. I had only a blanket for her and the dress I was wearing. I didn't know where to go or what to do. When I'd learned they were taking Penelope away, I'd been so sick, so scared, I'd not eaten. I got lost on the back streets of St. Louis, so weak and hungry I could hardly stand. When we got to the river, I . . . I tried to jump, but I was afraid . . . a coward. I followed the river, knowing we had to get away from town, not knowing where I was going. I heard guitar and fiddle music, and I followed the sound of it. There were some wagons, six or seven, and people were dancing by the firelight. I smelled food and I almost fainted. I went to the wagon fartherest from the fire and sat down on a wagon tongue, in the dark. Penelope was crying 'cause she was sick and hungry, and I was because I was alone and scared."

She paused, swallowed hard and continued.

"That's where Mike found us. Mike Donnegal. He was a big, kind Irishman, old enough to be my daddy. He didn't ask any questions. He brought me a bowl of stew and somehow got some milk for Penelope. He was one of a group of immigrants going to Omaha to work on the Chicago and Northwestern railroad. When they left, Mike took us with him. He was kind to us, asking nothing. We took his name; it seemed like the best way to keep people from asking questions. We lived in tents and shotgun shanties, whatever the railroad provided. I kept house and did

the cooking. Penelope was sick most of the time. I was
. . . dry and . . . couldn't feed her. There was nothing
even close to fresh milk at end-of-track. Mike, bless him,
managed a few tins of condensed milk. It was all that kept
Penelope alive. Then . . . that awful day just west of
Omaha, when Mike was killed. He was part of Kingston
Henry's grading crew. The railroad did nothing. Somebody
was always getting hurt or killed. Kingston came to us,
offered to see to Mike's funeral, and when it was over,
took us in. That was two years ago."

"So he went from strawbossing a grading crew to a cabin
on the Sweetwater," said Brazos. "Why?"

"Ugly rumors that . . . that he was negligent, that men
he didn't like had died in . . . accidents. Newspapers in
Omaha began giving the railroad some bad publicity when
families of some of the men who had been killed complained."

"Why would Henry have wanted Mike Donnegal dead?
Because of you?"

"No," she cried, her voice breaking. "It . . . it hasn't
been like . . . that. He hasn't asked anything . . . that
. . . of me."

"I sleep with her," said Penelope. "That's why he hates
me."

"Now you know," cried Rosalie. "My name is Hollister.
I've never been married and don't ever expect to be. I've
lived with two different men, and I don't expect you to
believe I've only been a cook and housekeeper. Now you
can ride away and consider yourself lucky."

"I believe every word you've said," replied Brazos.
"What I don't believe is that Kingston Henry's going to let
you continue being just a cook and housekeeper. You don't
believe it either."

He saw the answer in her eyes. She buried her face in
her hands and silent tears slid through her fingers. Finally
she spoke, her voice breaking.

"He . . . made me promise . . . I'd stay until the rail-

road was finished. We had nowhere to go, nobody to turn
to."

"He's not even with the railroad anymore," said Brazos.
"How can he hold you to such a promise, and why do you
feel honor bound to keep it?"

"I don't know," she sobbed.

"What's he doing, squatting here on the Sweetwater, besides riding off and gettin' drunk? He can't get grub and
booze for nothing; what's he using for money?"

"I don't know!" she cried. "He never tells me anything,
and I don't ask. All I want is for him to leave me alone; I
don't care what he does."

Penelope caught Brazos's eye. The child knew something her mother either didn't know or wasn't telling. Certainly Penelope was wise beyond her nine years, and before
he left he would talk to her. He watched her sidle away
from them and disappear into their bedroom. Rosalie said
no more. He got up and put on his hat.

"I'll see you next Sunday," he said.

"You'd come back . . . after what I've told you, knowing what . . . I am?"

"Do you want me to come back?"

"No, no. I . . . yes, God help me, I want you to. . . ."

"Then I'll be here," said Brazos.

He took his time getting to his horse. Penelope didn't
disappoint him. She skipped the steps, leaping off the
porch, and he caught her up in his arms.

"You will come back, won't you?"

"I'll come back," said Brazos, "if only to see you."

Rosalie stood in the doorway. When he eased Penelope
to her feet, for just a moment her small hand remained in
his. He mounted up and rode away, waving to them before
entering the cottonwoods beyond the clearing. When he
had passed from their view, he paused to examine what
Penelope had passed to him. Gleaming dully in the palm of
his hand was a gold nugget almost as large as the tip of his
little finger.

* * *

Knowing Captain Sandoval and having the support of Buffalo Bill Cody, McCaleb found that quartermaster approval was little more than a formality. They bought the herd and contracted for another five hundred head. Just as quickly as he could deliver them. Once the herd had been officially tallied and turned over to the quartermaster, Sandoval invited them to the post to dine at his table. Two beautiful women would have created excitement enough at the isolated post, but one of these was blood kin to the revered Buffalo Bill Cody! It was an enjoyable interlude, and Sandoval outdid himself. He doubled up some of his officers so that McCaleb's outfit might have beds for the night. Except for Goose. The Indian relented to the extent that he entered the compound and accepted food, but that was all. He rolled in his blankets and slept with the horses.

"We've enjoyed your hospitality, Captain Sandoval," said McCaleb, "and it's been a pleasure meetin' you again, Buffalo Bill, but we must go. We have the calendar against us if we're to trail another herd here before snow flies. Maybe we can lay over a couple more days on the next drive."

"Maybe I'll ride down to your place next spring," said Cody. "They're figurin' the rails will meet the first part of the summer, way the hell out in Utah somewhere. The railroad wants me there for the ceremony. God only knows why. All I done was shoot some buffalo for the Union Pacific, some of which they still ain't paid me for. I can't see goin' all the way to Utah Territory just to watch a pair of locomotives touch noses. If I go, so's the trip ain't a total loss, maybe I'll spend a few days at your place on Box Elder Creek. We could go huntin' in the Big Horn Mountains. I got me a hankerin' for some mountain sheep. While we're up there, I'll show you somethin' not many white men have seen. It's a big stone wheel, maybe seventy-five feet across. It's called the Medicine Wheel, and it's so old, even the Injuns don't know where it come from or who built it."

"We'll look for you, Bill," said McCaleb, "and welcome."

Monte Nance crossed the Sweetwater, following the same trail they had taken in pursuit of their stampeded herd. He hadn't the vaguest idea what he intended to do. He only knew he wanted to see the Indian girl again. The Shoshoni had been moved into western Wyoming Territory, to the Wind River Reservation, and were allowed in Powder River basin only to hunt buffalo. He wasn't even sure he could find the Indian camp again, even if they hadn't returned to the reservation. But he believed they would remain there until the steers had been slaughtered and the meat dried. Washakie was no fool; how could he return to the reservation driving steers with the white man's brand? No, before they broke camp, the hides would be scraped and the meat smoked or dried.

Monte drew up on the ridge overlooking the tipis and found the scene much the same, except the new lines seemed to have been added to accommodate the extra meat. Squaws were scraping hides and cutting meat into strips, and at so great a distance he wasn't sure if the girl he sought was among them.

"Come on, horse," he said, kicking his mount into a lope. "Nothin' for it but to ride down there and see."

The Indians watched him ride in. He gave the peace sign and it was returned. The next move was his. Boldly he turned to the squaws. The girl he was looking for became aware of his eyes on her and bowed her head. She wasn't the only one aware of his interest. Washakie still stood with arms folded across his bare chest, but his eyes were hard on Monte. When Monte pointed to the girl, Washakie shook his head. He spoke a single word.

"Nania."

He pointed to the girl, then to himself, again shaking his head. What was Washakie trying to tell him? Monte was afraid he knew. Had he committed the most colossal of all blunders and made a play for the chief's wife? The girl was

very young, but what did Monte Nance know about Shoshoni tribal custom? The Spanish seemed to have influ-
enced all tribes, and since he didn't know the Shoshoni
language, he had but one alternative. He tried it. First he
pointed to the girl, then to Washakie.

"Esposa?" he questioned.

"Muchacha," said Washakie, again shaking his head.
"Nania *muchacha."* He then pointed to Monte and uttered
a single word: *"Ninguno!"*

Monte heaved a sigh. The good news was that Nania
wasn't Washakie's wife, but his daughter. The bad news
was that Monte's interest in her was not welcome. The
conversation was over. Monte reined his horse to the left,
deliberately jogging past the area where the squaws
worked. For not more than a second did Nania's eyes meet
his, but Monte's heart leaped. But reason soon returned,
and by the time he'd reached the ridge, he was assailed by
doubt. In the face of Washakie's opposition, what chance
did he have with the girl?

Unsatisfied, he picketed his horse so the animal could
graze, and sitting with his back to a cottonwood, fixed his
eyes on the distant Indian camp. Maybe it would be a
wasted vigil, but he had to know. Would the girl adopt
Washakie's negative attitude? Suddenly he wished Goose
had been there. Reason told him the Apache could have
done nothing, but he couldn't help feeling that Goose's
presence would have impressed Washakie. He waited,
aware of the lengthening shadows as the sun dipped toward the Rockies. If he was out until after dark, Brazos
would likely give him hell, and rightly so. Still he waited.
Dusk was creeping over the valley when he saw her running along the foot of the ridge. He waited until she was
close enough and called to her.

"Nania?"

Up the slope she came, and he went to meet her. She
was breathing hard. He caught her hands, trying to pull her
to him, but she resisted. She looked back the way she had
come, toward the camp, as though expecting pursuit. He

let her go and she lifted her hand, showing five fingers. She then closed her hand, except for two fingers. She pointed to the west, where the sun was but a rosy memory.

"*Aqui,*" she said, repeating the "seven" sign and again pointing toward the diminishing rays of the sun.

"Seven suns?" repeated Monte. "Here? *Aqui?*"

"*Aqui,*" she said, and she was gone.

He quickly mounted and kicked his horse into a lope toward the Sweetwater. Once the Rockies had swallowed the sun, darkness came quickly, and first stars twinkled in a purpling sky as he rode into the ranch. Light streamed out the cookhouse door and supper was in progress.

"Boy," snapped the garrulous Salty, "I ain't makin' supper but onct. If'n you git here while they's some left, that's what you git. If'n they ain't none left, then that's what you git."

Without the herd to slow them, McCaleb and the outfit made forty miles a day on the return trip from Fort Buford. The trail drive had taken them twenty-one days. Homeward bound, they would cut that time in half. Their last camp in Dakota Territory, along the Western trail, was at Belle Fourche Creek.

"I'll always have bad memories about this place," said Rebecca, "because it's where the Sioux stampeded our herd."

"Unless we can come up with enough riders to hold our own against the Sioux," said Will, "I reckon we ought to forget this next drive to Fort Buford."

"We're committed," said McCaleb. "We'll make the drive."

McCaleb, Rebecca, Will, Susannah, and Goose rode wearily into Box Elder Ranch on August 19, 1868.

"My God," groaned Rebecca as she swung out of the saddle, "I take back everything I ever said about wanting to be treated like a cowboy. I feel like just one big saddle sore. Anybody that wants my place on the next drive can have it."

"If there's goin' to be another drive," said Brazos, "then I reckon this one was a success."

"In some respects," said McCaleb. "We'll talk after supper."

Salty prepared an especially good supper, and over final cups of coffee they compared notes. First, McCaleb told of their success at Fort Buford, of the trouble with the Sioux, and of the need for a second drive before fall. He then listened while Brazos, aided by occasional comments from the others, covered the raid on the ranch, the resulting stampede, and their meeting with Washakie. Brazos didn't mention the gold nugget given him by Penelope. He still needed to talk to the girl.

"They haven't made any serious attempt to run us out," said McCaleb, "but they will. We need to know why we're so unwelcome here. Did you learn anything about what's going on along the Sweetwater?"

"Nothing I can talk about now," said Brazos. "So far, I haven't found Kingston Henry at home."

"But you have found Rosalie and Penelope there," said Rebecca.

"I have," said Brazos.

Rebecca neither smiled nor spoke, but Brazos saw approval and relief in her green eyes.

"We need ten riders for the next drive to Fort Buford," said McCaleb, "not so much to trail the cattle, as to guard against attack by the Sioux. I want at least ten good men here, to counter the threat of these coyotes along the Sweetwater."

"Why don't we hire some of those Indians who're in Powder River basin looking for buffalo that don't exist?" suggested Susannah. "We could pay them in cows."

"Shoshonis on a trail drive?" Will chuckled. "My God, if they met up with the Sioux, we'd have to send for Federal troops to stop the war."

"That's exactly what I mean," said Susannah, fire in her eyes. "We have enough riders to trail the herd. What we don't have is enough fighting men to prevent the Sioux from stampeding the herd, stealing us blind, and perhaps killing us. Suppose on the drive to Fort Buford you took four or five cowboys to trail the herd and half a dozen of those hungry Shoshoni to keep an eye out for the Sioux?"

For a moment nobody spoke. It was a daring proposal.

"That's such a sensible idea," said McCaleb, grinning, "there's bound to be a passel of Federal laws against it. Me, I'd be just fool enough to try it. How do the rest of you feel?"

"I'd favor it," said Will, "if we can control the Shoshoni. Can we get them to fight if we're attacked, without having them take this as an excuse to go on the warpath against the Sioux? We'll be in Sioux territory; they will be within their rights. The Shoshoni will be off limits, illegally on the Sioux reservation, and we'll be responsible for havin' taken them there."

"That's why we Texans is always on the outs with the law," said Stoney. "They got laws against ever'thing we do."

"We'd need to talk to Washakie," said Brazos, "and that'll take some doing. I don't talk Shoshoni, and I'd bet my hat Washakie won't know three words of English."

"He can say 'no' in Spanish," Monte said.

"Monte tried to swap him fourteen hundred steers for a little Injun gal," said Stoney, with a devilish chuckle.

They all laughed except Rebecca. She didn't like Monte's sheepish grin. It seemed they were no nearer a solution until Goose broke the silence.

"Shos-ho-nay," he said. "Mebbe."

They watched in amazement as he went through a series of hand signs, concluding with a guttural grunt.

"I hope Washakie understands more of that than I did," said Brazos, chuckling.

"Follow cow, mebbe fight Sioux, eat cow," said Goose.

They all laughed and Goose grinned. He had reduced it all to the simplest terms, and for the first time he had spoken of a cow in English.

"Tomorrow, then," said Brazos, "me and Goose will ride north and see if Washakie's band is still in these parts."

"They're still here," said Monte, before he thought.

Pen, Jed, and Stoney chuckled at his discomfiture.

"That will solve only half our problem," said McCaleb. "Granting that Washakie understands what we want of him, we'll still end up splitting our crew and leaving our ranch unprotected. If we're going to gamble on taking some of Washakie's band on a trail drive to Fort Buford, through Sioux territory, why not camp the rest of them on our holding here? They're allowed in Powder River basin, and that's just across the Sweetwater. If Kingston Henry, Maury Duke, and their outfit comes looking for trouble, I reckon we can accommodate them."

"I hope," said Salty, "you ain't aimin' fer me t' feed that bunch of war whoops three times a day."

"Exactly what I had in mind," replied McCaleb, "with dried apple pie every night for supper."

"Bent," said Rebecca, "this is the boldest plan I've ever seen, but do you have *any* idea what's going to happen if these troublemakers along the Sweetwater end up shot full of Indian arrows? It will simply blow the lid off in Washington."

"I reckon you're right," said McCaleb, "but maybe it's time the lid was blown off."

9

*P*enelope watched Brazos disappear into the cottonwoods. With a sigh, she plodded slowly back into the
cabin. Rosalie sat on the bench, staring into the fireplace.

"You like him, don't you, Mama?"

Rosalie studied the child's anxious face a moment before
she replied.

"Yes," she said, "I like him. More than I've any right to.
I just wish . . . I wish things were . . . different."

"Different how? If he wants us, why can't we go with
him? I've tried awful hard to make him like me."

Rosalie said nothing. She drew Penelope into her arms
and fought back the tears.

It was near sundown when Kingston Henry reined up at
the barn, loosed his mule into the corral, and headed for
the house. He had been gone since Friday morning, playing poker and drinking very bad whiskey. He hadn't eaten
since Wednesday—or maybe Tuesday, he wasn't sure—and
his distended belly reminded him. Sour bile rose into his
throat in nauseous waves. His head thumped like an enormous drum, its painful rhythm matching the beating of his
heart. He was in a vile mood; otherwise, he might not have
noticed the tracks in the yard. He paused, made his way
carefully up the steps and stomped into the cabin.

"Tracks," he snarled. "Who's been here?"

"Just a . . . a . . . rider," Rosalie stammered, "look-ing for stray cows."

"They ain't but one cow outfit in th' territory," he shouted, "an' they ain't a cow in twenny miles of here. Look at you—hair all fancied up an' wearin' yer Sunday best, all fer some range-ridin' cowboy. Come mornin', I'll back-track th' bastard an' see who you're shinin' up to."

"I told you," she cried desperately, "it was—"

He lunged at her, caught the collar of her dress and ripped it to the waist. She screamed.

"You leave my mama alone!" shouted Penelope. She grabbed an iron poker that leaned against the fireplace and swung it as hard as she could. It caught him in the small of his back, just above his pistol belt.

Furious, he released Rosalie and turned on Penelope. She dropped the poker and tried to escape, but he was between her and the door. His huge right hand, big as the paw of a grizzly, caught her in the chest and flung her against the wall. She lay there sobbing, and he had his big hands on her throat when Rosalie swung the length of fire-wood. Fear and desperation guided her, and it thunked into the back of his head like an axe striking a cottonwood log. Without a sound he collapsed on Penelope, and it took all Rosalie's strength to drag him off the child.

"He stinks, Mama."

Kingston Henry had vomited all over the front of Penel-ope's dress. With trembling hands, Rosalie began removing the soiled garment. Henry lay facedown, snoring in a drunken stupor. Tomorrow he wouldn't remember any of this. She hoped.

In Omaha, Maury Duke waited in an outer office until it suited George Francis Train to see him. Finally a secretary came out and ushered him into Train's office. He was headed for a big leather-upholstered chair when Train halted him in mid-stride.

"Don't bother!" snapped Train.

Duke stood before the huge mahogany desk, uncomfortable, his hat in his hands. Train let him squirm awhile before he spoke.

"You," said Train, "and that dunce Kingston Henry, were to remove that Texas outfit from Box Elder Creek. Why haven't you?"

"It ain't our fault." Duke gulped. "Colton, that jasper that owns the newspaper in Cheyenne, has stirred up a stink that might point right at you. We got to take it slow. You made yourself out a hero, gettin' that cowboy to Omaha, and ever' newspaper in the country jumped on it. That was bad enough; now Colton's come up with more on this same hombre. He stole *my* woman and married her. When Colton printed that, he played up the part about Susannah bein' blood kin to Buffalo Bill Cody, and that done it."

Train said nothing. Duke swallowed hard and continued.

"Colton's got hold of some government records showin' you're involved with those land grants along the Union Pacific right-of-way to the south of Sweetwater valley. Colton went to the land office in Cheyenne and got the names of ever'body you've staked out along the Sweetwater. Ever' blamed one, to a man, like Colton said, used to work for the Union Pacific, most of 'em as graders and track layers. They couldn't of had much money, but when end-of-track moved west, they stayed here. Colton's been askin' some hard questions. He's wonderin' how them men, no crops, no cattle, without a job, without a peso, can afford to squat there on the Sweetwater."

"I see," said Train ominously. "It's *my* fault you have failed."

"I ain't sayin' that," cried Duke desperately. "The papers done it to us. They played up the story about that Texan goin' to Omaha in your private car, and when he married Cody's niece, they jumped on that. Hell's fire, this fool Texas cowboy's as famous as Cody, and he's part of the outfit on Box Elder Creek. Now the story's goin' around that he was shot to keep the outfit *away* from Box Elder Creek. We go in there and gun them down, do I have to tell you what will happen? Bill Cody will have Federal troops in here, and them newspapers, from Omaha to Chicago, will lynch you."

"There is a certain childish logic to your explanation," said Train, "but you have carefully evaded the real cause of this stupid predicament. You, Maury Duke. You shot a man in the back, a better man than you, out of pure, blind jealousy. Now events have snowballed until this man that you ambushed is bigger than life and I cannot remove this bunch of Texans from Box Elder Creek without every newspaper in the country wanting to know why. I will concede that this Colton, an apparent backwoods crusader, is a problem. But why *is* he a problem, Duke? Dead men don't make waves."

"He didn't start it," said Duke, sweating. "The Omaha papers started it and Colton just played up their stories. It was you made this Will Elliot somebody amongst the newspapers. Then, when he ups and marries Susannah, ever'thing just went to hell in a handcart."

"Duke," said Train coldly, "I'm not accustomed to losing, whatever the odds or the opposition. Come spring, if you haven't accomplished what you were hired to do, then you may find yourself headed for Hell in that handcart."

Establishing communication with Washakie was an important step; McCaleb decided to ride with Brazos and Goose to the Indian camp. Goose took the lead, greeting the Shoshoni chief in a manner Washakie seemed to recognize and appreciate. He responded with signs of his own and there was a light in his somber eyes that might have been pleasure. But his enthusiasm visibly diminished as he acknowledged McCaleb and Brazos. Brazos had an uncomfortable feeling it was a result of Monte's interest in the Indian girl. For the kid's sake he hoped it didn't become an issue in their dealing with the Shoshoni.

Goose found a bare piece of ground beneath a cottonwood, hunkered down, and with a sharp stick began outlining the drive to Fort Buford. Brazos and McCaleb remained in the background, their appreciation for Goose's talent growing. He constantly embellished his drawings with hand signs to which Washakie responded. Finally Goose got up, turned to Brazos and McCaleb and spoke distinctly.

"Follow cow nort', *soldado* tipi, mebbe fight Sioux. Give cow."

He extended three fingers and McCaleb nodded. Three steers for a Shoshoni escort to and from Fort Buford. It was more than fair, and cheap at any price. Goose again talked to Washakie in signs, and the chief replied. Then Goose knelt, erased the first message with his hand and drew a second one. He fleshed it out with signs, and they sensed some hesitation on Washakie's part. His response was slow. When it finally came, Goose got to his feet, nodded to McCaleb and Brazos, then turned to his horse. Resting his hand on the walnut stock of the Winchester in the saddle boot, he pointed to Washakie. They'd have to sweeten the pot, but Brazos was prepared. He drew a new Winchester from his own saddle boot and tossed it to Washakie. The Indian caught it expertly, delight in his eyes. From his saddlebag Brazos took two tins of shells for the weapon, and without a word passed them to Washakie. Carefully he placed the tins of shells on the ground at his feet and shifted the Winchester to the crook of his arm. His hands freed, he spoke to Goose and the Apache grinned. He turned to McCaleb and Brazos.

"Him stay," said Goose. "More cow."

He held up three fingers, and again McCaleb nodded. The conversation was over. Washakie devoted his full attention to his new weapon, while his comrades watched enviously. Goose trotted his horse back the way they had come, Brazos and McCaleb following.

"He gets a number in his head," said McCaleb, "and he stays with it. Thank God he's got three on his mind. If he'd ended up with ten steers the first time around, he'd ruin us."

"Count your blessings," said Brazos, chuckling. "Where

else you goin' to get this many fighting men for six steers and a Winchester?"

"How'd you manage to have the rifle so handy? You readin' that Indian's mind better than Goose."

"You went to Omaha and left me with the money," said Brazos, "so I bought enough to replace all the Spencers. Bought a couple of extras while I could get 'em. There's another in the chuck wagon. Sold as I am on my Henry, I reckoned I'd as well try out this weapon they say's replaced it."

McCaleb decided to begin the second drive to Fort Buford the following Saturday, August 22.

"Since you've finished a drive to Fort Buford," said Brazos, "I can take this one, if you want."

"No," said McCaleb. "I'm responsible for these Shoshoni, and if *anything* goes wrong on this drive, I'll have to answer for it. For that reason, I'll feel better if I see it through from start to finish. You or Will—maybe both of you—may be going back to Texas for another herd."

"I'd like to go to Fort Buford," said Stoney, "if it don't ruin my chance for the Texas drive."

"It won't," said McCaleb. "If all goes well, we'll be back here the last week in September. If you left here early in December, you could maybe spend Christmas with your folks in Texas. You'll have from four to six weeks to buy the steers, trail-brand them, and get them on the trail by mid-February."

They were silent and he continued.

"I'm taking Goose with me on this drive to Fort Buford because I'll need him to control our Shoshoni riders. Now I need three more of you."

"Since we hired on together," said Pen, "and if it won't hurt our chance of taking part in the drive from Texas, take us."

"That's close to what I had in mind," said McCaleb. "Does it suit the rest of you?"

"Not completely," said Rebecca. "I'll miss you. I've got

the heart, mind, and hands of a cowboy, but the behind of a woman. I'm still saddle sore from that last drive."

"Friday, then," said McCaleb, "we'll need to get with Washakie and find out who he aims to send on the drive and who will stay here on Box Elder Creek. Brazos, talk with Goose before we meet with Washakie. I want the men he's sending with me to be able to understand Goose, because I'm depending on him to keep them in line."

"You'd better be almighty certain Washakie knows what he's to do around here," said Brazos. "I didn't understand any of the talk he had with Goose."

"Washakie's orders will be simple," said McCaleb. "Just be sure that Goose gets them across to him. He and his men are to stake out our holdings and the rest of our steers. If that bunch from the Sweetwater comes looking for trouble, see that they find it."

They moved the herd out at dawn on Saturday morning. Goose rode point, and just ahead of him loped three Shoshoni braves. Three more brought up the rear, trailing the drag riders. Jed and Stoney devoted more attention to the Shoshoni behind than to the steers ahead. McCaleb and Pen rode flank position. Will, Susannah, Rebecca, Monte, and Brazos watched them out of sight. The spectacle had drawn even Salty to the cookhouse door.

"Eleven riders," said Rebecca. "I feel better about this drive. Where are the rest of the Shoshoni—those who are staying with us? I haven't seen any of them."

"You won't," said Brazos. "They're camped along the south bank of the Sweetwater, within hollering distance of us. Every night they'll have sentries all around us and around the herd. We went ahead and cut out the six steers we promised them. They'll spend their days scraping and curing the hides and cutting and drying the meat."

"I don't care what the Indian Affairs people in Washington think," said Susannah, "assuming they're capable of thinking. These Indians are helping us and we're helping them. How can the Congress—or anybody else—improve on that?"

"I don't know," said Brazos, "but if they get after us, I want you to go to Washington and plead our case."

Monte Nance lay on his bunk wide awake, his mind in a quandary. He was to meet Nania tomorrow on the ridge overlooking the old Shoshoni camp. Now the camp was on the south bank of the Sweetwater, miles away from their planned rendezvous. How was the girl to travel such a distance without taking a horse, arousing suspicion and inviting pursuit? Even if he could contact her to effect a change in plans, they dared not meet too near his own camp or that of the Shoshoni. Suddenly he realized she might be sharing his dilemma, and despite the language barrier, he felt close to her. Damn it, he would ride to the appointed place and take his chances.

Brazos rode out early Sunday, following the Sweetwater west, traveling only far enough to escape the eagle eyes of the Shoshoni. Concealing himself in a stand of young box elders, he half-hitched the animal to a sapling and settled down to wait. Neither Monte nor Rebecca had eaten breakfast, and Brazos hadn't missed the anxiety in her eyes or the brooding distress in Monte's. He had waited only a few minutes when Monte approached in a fast lope, splashed his horse across the Sweetwater, and was soon lost among the trees on the north bank. Still Brazos waited, stepping out into the open only when Rebecca approached. Startled, she reined up.

"How did you—"

"The kid had it all over his face, and so did you. I reckon Benton wouldn't stop him—he's as much a man as he'll ever be—but he'd purely raise hell and kick a chunk under it if he knew you were ridin' out alone."

"Brazos, he's my brother!" she cried. "The only kin I have."

"He's also a man, and you won't like what he's likely to say and do when he finds out you're trailin' him."

"But I must know. You're not going to stop me . . . are you?"

"I reckon not," said Brazos. "I've made my mistakes and you'll have to make yours. This is one of them."

He returned to his horse, mounted, and without a word continued along the Sweetwater. She watched him out of sight and then slowly, almost reluctantly, she forded the river.

Monte had ridden no more than two or three miles beyond the Sweetwater when his horse shied suddenly and almost threw him. Nania had stepped out of some bushes, having picked up his old trail to the former Shoshoni camp and followed it thus far. Hurriedly calming his horse, he dismounted, leading the animal into the thicket where Nania had concealed herself. He forgot everything except the girl. He drew her to him, and this time she didn't resist.

The buckskin dress she wore reached her ankles, but it fitted loosely and he quickly discovered it was her only garment. He caught the hem of it, and she allowed him to skin it over her head. She stood there wearing only a half smile, and he caught his breath. He fumbled at his pistol belt and succeeded only in loosening the belt to his Levi's. They promptly slid down to his knees. Nania giggled at his awkwardness and eagerness, and he felt his face going scarlet. But the worst was yet to come. His horse nickered and Rebecca's answered. Nania grabbed her buckskin dress and vanished, stark naked, into the brush.

Monte had drawn and cocked his Colt almost without realizing it. There he stood, in his shirttail, still wearing his pistol belt, his hat gone God knew where, and his Levi's down to his boot tops. While his face went scarlet, his eyes never left Rebecca's. The Colt trembled in his hand as he visibly fought the urge to shoot.

"Damn you," snapped Rebecca, "you can't ever see beyond what Monte wants, can you?"

"Who the hell are you, preachin' to me?" snarled Monte. "You come off like a whore in Denver, nearly gettin' McCaleb killed. If you ever trail me again, so help me God, I'll shoot you!"

10

"My God," said Susannah, "I'm glad we have the Shoshoni here. Where *is* everybody?"

"Brazos rode out first," said Will, "and whatever's takin' him along the Sweetwater involves this Kingston Henry, I reckon. Rebecca barely waited for Monte to get out of sight before she lit out after him. I wish I'd figured some way to get her to go with Bent on this second drive to Buford."

"So Monte can have a foolish affair with some Indian squaw without his big sister knowing?"

"No," said Will hotly, "so the kid can make his own damn mistakes without his mother-hen big sister compounding them. Let a woman go faunching around with a man's pride, and he's likely to get himself killed trying to prove he *is* a man."

"Out here in the territories—with millions and millions of acres of uncharted wilderness—how can a man get himself in trouble with a woman he can't even talk to?"

"It's the nature of the beast," said Will, chuckling. "Lose one man and one woman anywhere in the world, however deep the wilderness, and they'll find each other."

"I can understand how Rebecca feels; he's all the blood kin she has."

"There's more at stake than Rebecca's feelings," said Will. "Remember, we're surrounded by Shoshoni, and they could change their minds about being our protectors and turn on us."

"Monte's sneaking around with a Shoshoni woman is bothering me for that very reason. Why is it such a mistake for Rebecca to stop it if she can?"

"Because she can't stop it," said Will, "and Monte's enough of a headstrong young fool that anything she says or does will make him all the more determined."

"Why don't you talk to Bent," said Susannah, "as soon as he returns, and be sure that he sends Monte to Texas for the drive in the spring?"

"I'd thought of that, but whatever's going to happen will be history by then. When we next see Monte and Rebecca, I expect we'll get some idea as to how serious all this is."

Brazos felt better about leaving the ranch with the Shoshoni there, but he had some misgivings as to the Indian attitude resulting from Monte's questionable conduct. Suppose it reached the point where, to enjoy the continued friendship of the Shoshoni, they were forced to expel Monte from the Six Bar outfit? How many white men had successfully married Indian women? There had been many, but tribal custom varied and each case was different.

So immersed was he in thought, he almost rode into Kingston Henry's clearing without his usual precautions. He hurriedly crossed the river, concealing himself in the timber that lined the ridge. To his relief, that all-important sheet hung on the line behind the cabin. Suppose he rode in one Sunday and it wasn't there? What then? He had finally admitted to himself that he was becoming increasingly jealous of Kingston Henry, although he believed Rosalie was scared to death of him. He was becoming more and more irritated with a situation that forced him to sneak around like a coyote to see a woman who wished to see him yet continued to live in the same house with a drunken, uncouth bastard like Kingston Henry. It didn't help his mood when Penelope stopped him before he had even crossed to the south bank of the Sweetwater.

"Mama says please don't ride into the yard, Brazos. Last Sunday, he . . . he found your horse's tracks."

She said no more, but it was enough. He could imagine the aftermath of the discovery, and made up his mind to resolve this sorry situation, whatever it took. He picketed his horse where it could graze, yet far enough from the cabin to avoid leaving evidence of his visit. He couldn't penalize Penelope for his irritation with Rosalie, so he knelt and she ran to him. It was an opportunity to delay his entry into the cabin and to question her about the nugget.

"The nugget—the big pebble—you gave me, Centavo," he whispered. "Where did you get it?"

"From him," she said softly. "Once, when he was drunk, asleep, I saw a little leather sack poking out of his pocket. I pulled it out just enough to see what was in it. He had so many of them, I didn't think he'd miss just one, so I . . . I took the one I gave you. Will I go to Hell . . . for that?"

"No," said Brazos. "Did you tell your mama?"

"Oh, Lord no," hissed Penelope. "She's scared to death of him. You won't tell on me, will you?"

"It will be our secret," said Brazos. "Do you have any idea where he goes, other than to the saloon downriver?"

"No," said Penelope. "He never talks to us. Sometimes —when he ain't drunk—he comes in wet to his middle, like he's been wadin' the river."

She could tell him nothing more. He gathered her into his arms and went on to the house. To his surprise, Rosalie's hair was as tangled and unkempt as the first time he'd seen her, and the old dress she wore could have been the most nondescript she owned. It further fueled his suspicions as to the furor that must have taken place the previous Sunday. He came right to the point.

"Rosalie, I'll take you away from here, if you'll go."

"I'd go," she said in a small voice, "if it was far away . . . where he . . . couldn't find us."

"It *always* comes back to him," said Brazos angrily. "Don't you reckon I'm man enough to take care of you?"

"You're a good man, Brazos. Too good a man to be shot

in the back for the likes of me. He . . . he'd stalk you like an animal, because he is an animal. Each time you rode away, I'd be afraid . . . afraid I wouldn't see you again. You're offering me something I've dreamed of, prayed for, but I . . . I can't take it. Don't you see? Sooner or later— somehow—he'd kill you, or have it done. It would be more . . . than I could bear . . . losing you. It's for you . . . for your sake."

There was no doubting her sincerity, and he gathered her trembling body in his arms and stretched her out on what he suspected was Kingston Henry's crude bunk. He drew up a three-legged stool and sat beside her. He had, in his compassion for Rosalie, momentarily forgotten Penelope, and when her eyes met his, he was shocked at the sick despair in them. Something had shaken her mightily since his last visit, and the look of her renewed his determination to rescue her from this sordid existence.

A plan began to form in his mind. McCaleb and the rest of the outfit would return to Box Elder Creek in a month. The entire outfit would be at the ranch until early December, when some of them would return to Texas for another herd. There, they could hire more riders. Until then, providing Monte didn't destroy their relationship with the Shoshoni, why couldn't they simply keep the Indians near the ranch for added protection? The question was, could he—Brazos Gifford—save Rosalie and Penelope without forsaking his outfit and violating his own conscience? Even if McCaleb agreed, did he have the right to draw money from their poke and run away from Kingston Henry? But he had the cart before the horse. Before he even considered such a move or spoke to McCaleb, he must determine Rosalie's feelings. It was the moment of truth. If she refused the offer—the sacrifice—he was about to make, then it would be over. When he rode away from the cabin, it would be for the last time. He swallowed hard and began.

"I'm not rich, but the outfit can advance me enough money to take us away for a while; maybe to Omaha. One of my pardners is away on a cattle drive and won't be back until the last week in September. That's when we'll go. For your sake and Penelope's will you go?"

"Yes!" she shouted, throwing her arms around him. *"Oh, my God, yes!"*

Rebecca's heart was heavy as she rode slowly back to the ranch. Brazos had been right. She dismounted before her cabin and walked down to the cookhouse, where Salty had dinner well under way. She slumped down on a bench, and without a word Salty brought her coffee. Rebecca wasn't surprised when Susannah straddled a stool on the other side of the table. Susannah waited until Salty brought her coffee before she spoke.

"Bad, huh?"

"My God," sighed Rebecca, "it's worse than bad. What do you say to your kid brother when you find him in the bushes, his britches down, with a naked Indian girl?"

"You knew where he was going; what did you plan to do?"

"Lord, Susannah, I don't know. I just wanted to stop him. Brazos waited for me, told me I was making a mistake, and he was right. I've made matters worse. Monte will do it now, just to prove that he can. Isn't that always the way of a man?"

Having made the trip to Fort Buford once, McCaleb was familiar with all the creeks and rivers. They averaged twenty miles a day, and sometimes more. There were no dry camps, once McCaleb knew where there was sure water. When the distance to the next creek or river was more than a normal day's drive, they started early and traveled late. By the third day the drive had settled down. Pen, Jed, and Stoney had become comfortable with their Shoshoni escort. There were certain advantages to having Indians around. They were fishermen, and there was an abundance of fish in the creeks and rivers. One evening after the herd was bedded down, Goose and two of the Shoshoni went hunting, returning with a gutted and dressed antelope.

"Mighty lot of meat," said Jed, "for so few of us."

"There won't be any wasted," said McCaleb.

Indians had prodigious appetites. It wasn't unusual for them to fully devour a kill, leaving only the bones. Much of their time was spent hunting, and after a successful hunt they gorged themselves. The next hunt might be unproductive and it would be many days before they again had meat. It seemed almost festive, gathering around the fire, roasting hunks of antelope.

"I like mine a mite rare," said Jed, "but these Injuns beat all. How do they stomach the stuff with blood drippin' off'n it?"

"It's a habit you develop," said McCaleb, chuckling, "when your scalp's at stake. Cooking calls for fire, and that means smoke. It's a dead giveaway in enemy territory. That's why our fires are always small, hidden, and put out before dark. Without the added protection of the Shoshoni, we'd be eatin' cold biscuits and drinkin' creek water."

"I'm startin' to feel powerful safe with 'em around," said Stoney. "If'n I can just keep 'em from scalpin' *me*. I got up last night to go to the bushes, and I ain't took ten steps till one of 'em's got me by the hair with a knife at my throat."

"That's why you're not nighthawking," said McCaleb, "and they're watching the herd. Us bein' up and about in the dark would only hinder them. Once they're in position and we're quiet, *anything* else that moves has to be an enemy. It's the most effective and deadly defense there is —restrain and conceal your own force and then kill anything that moves."

Monte Nance rode in at sundown without a word to anybody. Supper was a silent, strained meal, and Monte was the first to quit the table. With half the outfit away, he had a cabin to himself, and he retreated to it. Susannah was the first to speak.

"I can't believe this is happening. What are we going to do?"

"For now," said Brazos, "nothing."

"My sentiments," said Will.

"He'll do something really terrible," said Rebecca, "to get back at me."

"It won't be easy," said Brazos, "but back off. He's a man, and he'll have to take his own whipping. When an hombre's hell-bent on buyin' trouble, the best cure is to sell him a good dose of it."

Irv Vonnecker's place was a poor excuse for a saloon, but for the time and place, it was adequate. The old tent, faded gray-white, had long since been discarded by the railroad. It had been patched—often and poorly—and leaked like a sieve during a decent rain. The "bar" consisted of a rough board, each end resting on a barrel. Men were seated on crude stools and upended sections of logs cut for firewood. There were no glasses. Patrons brought tin cups, and the whiskey was dispensed from a wooden bucket with a gourd dipper. Including Maury Duke and Kingston Henry, there were eight men. Five of them hunched over an upended barrel, using its bottom for a card table.

"Damn it, King," snapped Duke, "you're too drunk to play. Fold!"

Vonnecker came in carrying a second wooden bucket.

"Prime stuff, gents," he chuckled. "Aged nearly fifteen minutes."

"That's ten minutes longer'n usual," said one of the poker players.

Kingston Henry threw down his cards and stumbled to his feet, steadying himself by gripping the rim of the barrel. He turned bleary eyes on Maury Duke.

"I say," he mumbled, "I say . . . I'd ought t' take some men an' hit that Texas bunch t'night. I got a pers'nal int'rest in one of 'em. . . ."

"I told you," growled Maury Duke, "things has changed. We can't just ride in and gun ever'body down. We'll have to burn 'em out. We'll ride under cover of the first snow. Won't be no way they can rebuild before spring. That's how long we got to run 'em off Box Elder Creek."

"Them gold pockets is awful damn skimpy fer a bonanza," said Vonnecker. "I'm startin' to wonder if it's worth all the hassle."

"What're you bitchin' about?" snarled Duke. "You're gettin' rich sellin' this god-awful whiskey at two bits a dipperful. Besides, these claims, once they're proved up, is cash money in our pockets."

"I'm layin' odds," said Vonnecker, "this jasper in Omaha ain't goin' to go on payin' the lot of us thirty an' found just to set on these claims and play poker. He finds out just how little gold they is, he won't care if we prove 'em up or not. And if they ain't enough gold in th' whole damn Sweetwater valley to bother with, then why fight to get our hands on that twenty-mile stretch north of Box Elder Creek? Them Texans have got the right idea. This whole blessed territory ain't fit for nothin' but growin' buffalo grass and raisin' cows."

"That ain't for you to decide," said Duke. "I been told them Texans got to go. Like I said, come the first snow, we'll fire them cabins on Box Elder Creek."

They were ten days on the trail and two hundred miles south of Fort Buford. The drive had been uneventful, and McCaleb believed it was too good to last. Right after supper he had words of caution for the outfit.

"I purely don't believe we'll make it through Sioux territory without some trouble. Now listen careful. If the Sioux hit us, don't go foggin' after them or you'll likely end up shot full of Shoshoni arrows. Let Goose and the Shoshoni take the lead."

"Just let 'em scatter the herd to hell an' gone, then," said Stoney.

"I'd rather spend a day roundin' up the herd than in burying some of you," said McCaleb. "Keep that in mind."

"It'll seem almighty unnatural," said Pen, "to just set back and let the herd run. We can cut loose with our rifles, can't we?"

"No," said McCaleb, "not unless you can tell a Shoshoni

from a Sioux in the dark. Except for Goose, none of us will do any shooting. Now, when we go after the herd, that's different. In daylight we can pick our targets, being dead sure they're Sioux."

It proved to be good advice. Two nights later, when clouds hid the pale quarter moon, the Sioux struck. They came shrieking into McCaleb's consciousness like a nightmare sprung to life. So strong were his instincts for survival, he almost violated his own order. He sprang out of his bedroll, finding it almost impossible to restrain himself. Men who survived on the frontier rarely did so by remaining passive amid the violence of it. The advice he'd given the others strong on his mind, he forced himself to remain calm. He counted four rapid shots from Goose's Winchester, and after a few seconds' interval, three more. The terrified bawling of the steers and the pounding of hoofs diminished until there again was silence.

"It don't seem right," said Pen, "the herd runnin' hell-bent-for-election and us settin' here lettin' 'em go."

"Contrary to what some folks think," said McCaleb, "there's not much else you *can* do. These pitch-dark Indian-provoked stampedes are all but impossible to head. One night in East Texas, I lost the best cow horse I ever owned, and almost died with him. We went headlong into an arroyo, and for all our efforts, we still didn't head the cattle."

"It's almighty quiet," said Stoney. "Wisht I had some hot coffee."

"I could use some myself," said McCaleb, "but I wouldn't swap my hair for it. In the dark, one wrong move can be your last."

"I purely hate not knowin' what's goin' on," said Jed. "I wisht them Injuns would ride in, since we can't ride out."

"I doubt we'll see them before daylight," said McCaleb, "and maybe not even then. I told Goose, if the Sioux jumped us, to stay on their trail. Rustlers—white men or red—go at it pretty much the same. They can't gather cows in the dark any better than we can. But they can scatter them from hell to breakfast, knowin' that even in daylight it'll take us a while to find them all. Meanwhile, they can grab a bunch and be gone."

"But you aim to put a kink in their tails," said Pen, chuckling, "by having Goose and the Shoshoni right there, come daylight."

"That's the idea," said McCaleb, "and I won't be surprised if the Sioux don't change their minds completely about wantin' our herd. Come first light, you'll see what I mean."

They rode out without breakfast as soon as the gray light of dawn permitted. Almost immediately, in the wake of the stampede, they found the bodies of three Sioux. One had died from a gunshot wound, and the other two by Shoshoni arrows.

"I reckon," said Jed, grinning at McCaleb, "you knowed what you was talkin' about. That's the kind of hombre I like to ride with."

To their satisfaction, they soon began finding remnants of the herd, two or three steers, sometimes a dozen, grazing peacefully. Near noon they sighted a small dust cloud to the south. It proved to be the remainder of the herd, or close to it. Trailing it came Goose and the Shoshoni. To a man, they were in high good humor.

"Get Sioux," grinned Goose. "Sioux no get cow."

The grisly scalps thonged about their middles—Goose had two and the Shoshoni at least one each—were mute testimony to the deadly effectiveness of their attack.

"My God," said Pen, in awe. "They must have killed them all!"

"I hope so," said McCaleb. "Dead men tell no tales. If there's one of them alive, I may be in big trouble."

11

One morning after breakfast, Brazos told Rebecca, Will, and Susannah about the situation at Kingston Henry's cabin, of his promise to take Rosalie and Penelope away, and of the gold nugget the child had given him.

"Brazos," cried Rebecca through a tearful smile, "God bless you! That's the most touching thing I've ever heard! Ever since that day at the store, I haven't been able to get that poor, unhappy child off my mind."

"If we go at all," said Brazos, "we'll be a while. I'll have to draw on my part of the stake, if everybody agrees. I don't feel right about this, sneaking out like a coyote while this bunch on the Sweetwater is a threat to us, but Rosalie won't have it any other way. Whatever happens here, she's convinced that Kingston Henry will back-shoot me first."

"She's right," said Susannah. "While they may come looking for us all, if this man's the brute he seems, then you'll be the one in constant danger. You can't avoid being shot in the back any more than Will could, unless you go away for a while. We want you to take the money you need and go. Don't we, Will?"

"If he can," said Will. "I'll never forget what the rest of you did for me after I was shot, and the work you put into this place while I was flat on my back in Omaha."

"Thanks," said Brazos, touched. He stared into his half-empty coffee cup, swallowing hard. Will had touched on the doubt that lay heavy on Brazos's own mind. Deep down he didn't believe they'd ever see Omaha, or even Cheyenne. He would make the effort for Rosalie's sake, but something told him this conflict with Kingston Henry would be resolved in Wyoming Territory, along the Sweetwater.

Monte busied himself in living up to Rebecca's prophecy. He began haunting the Shoshoni camp in a futile attempt to see Nania. He couldn't get her off his mind; in his memory she became more ravishing than ever. By the following Sunday—a week since their interrupted rendezvous—he was grasping at straws. Would she again attempt to meet him? He rode out after breakfast, but halted on the north bank of the Sweetwater, concealing himself among the box elders. This time he'd be sure he wasn't followed. It was only a matter of minutes until he sighted Brazos, but the surging anger diminished as Brazos continued west along the river. Still he waited, not sure that Brazos wouldn't double back under cover of the brush along the north bank. Finally he rode on, his impatience having gotten the better of him. Not really expecting to see her, he did. This time he controlled his eagerness, leading his horse into the thicket where she waited, half-hitching the reins to a cottonwood sapling.

"Nania," he said. "Nania."

She didn't immediately come to him. Instead she turned and, for what seemed an inordinately long time, looked in the direction he had come. But could he blame her? Finally satisfied he hadn't been followed, she turned to him with that taunting half smile. He shucked his hat, his pistol belt, and then sat down and removed his boots. Then, emulating her caution, he stood looking back toward the river. Satisfied, he turned and found she had peeled off the dress. He loosed his belt, stepped out of his Levi's and met her on equal terms. This time they were not disturbed.

* * *

Brazos rode along, his mind full of plans, silently blessing Rebecca, Will, and Susannah for their concern and support. But his joy was dashed on the rocks of disappointment when he reached the ridge above the cabin. The sheet wasn't there! He sighed. Not until this moment had he realized how much these visits had meant to him. There was a rustling of leaves and he whirled, his Colt cocked and ready.

"Brazos, it's me."

Penelope! He holstered his Colt, caught her slender wrists and lifted her up in front of him. He then jogged the horse over the ridge, out of sight of the cabin. Penelope sighed, mirroring his own disgust.

"He's drunk, Brazos. He was gone all week, but yesterday he came back. Mama sent me to tell you. She was afraid you . . . oh, I wish . . . I wish we could go . . . now."

"A week from Sunday," said Brazos. "No matter if he's here, drunk or sober, I'm taking you both with me. Be sure and tell your mama."

On September 12, without further incident, McCaleb's drive reached Fort Buford. Despite the stampede, they hadn't lost a steer! McCaleb left the herd in the hands of Goose and the Shoshoni. He took Pen, Jed, and Stoney with him, so that they might visit the sutler's store. He received the expected friendly welcome from Captain Sandoval.

"Bill Cody rode out a week after you did," said Sandoval. "Said tell you he'll see you in the spring. Where are your riders?"

"Three of them are at the store, and the others are with the herd. I doubt they'll come in; Indians don't like forts, for some reason."

"Indians? McCaleb, just when I'm halfway comfortable with you, you do something that just scares hell out of me. Do you have *any* idea what will happen in Washington if they discover you're taking Indians from Wyoming across Dakota Territory, for *any* reason?"

"Don't tell me," said McCaleb. "It'd likely keep me awake nights."

"Then I'll give you some advice. Take those Indians, whatever kind they are, back where you found them. I know you don't think highly of the Union army, McCaleb, but for better or worse, I'm part of it. In return for past favors, I know nothing about your having brought Indians on this trail drive, and I'll swear to that if I have to. But don't you ever put me in such a position again."

On September 13, McCaleb rode out of Fort Buford, and so began the long journey back to Box Elder Creek. The nights were already uncomfortably cold, and there was morning ice along the edges of the streams. They shivered in their blankets, risking a small fire at dawn only for the need of hot coffee. Winter was on a fast horse, the High Plains his destination. The chill west wind rustled through the final, falling leaves of autumn, and there was a feel of snow in the air.

Penelope's eyes haunting him, Brazos rode into the ranch an hour before dinner. He went to the cookhouse, straddled a stool, and was gloomily nursing a cup of coffee when Will joined him.

Will grinned. "Fast trip, and you look like you've been eating sour pickles. Get throwed out?"

"Might as well have," said Brazos morosely. "Kingston himself was there, sleeping off a drunk."

"Brazos, we've ridden a bunch of trails together, and I reckon you know I'll side you till Hell freezes, and then skate on the ice. I'd like to see this work out for you. If you want that woman, go get her. Or at least set the time a mite closer. Otherwise, you'll be three days away from October, and snow may be neck-deep. Omaha will be out of the question; you won't be able to get from here to Cheyenne. Alone, maybe, but not with a woman and a child."

Brazos said nothing, thinking. Slowly, uncertainty faded

and what had been temptation became resolution. As surely as Rebecca, Will, and Susannah had stood by him and his decision, so would Benton McCaleb. He grinned and slapped Will on the back.

"I'll ride back tomorrow," he said, "Kingston Henry or not. I'll take them away from there next Sunday!"

By then Salty had dinner ready. Rebecca and Susannah applauded his decision, and only the arrival of Monte Nance dampened their enthusiasm. His sour expression had been replaced with an equally obnoxious, self-satisfied smirk.

Brazos put aside his impatience and waited an extra day before riding back to the cabin on the Sweetwater. For Rosalie's sake, he would allow time to sleep off his drunk and depart. When he awoke he'd be sorely in need of some hair of the dog, and that meant a trip downriver. He hoped the brute wouldn't devote the week to drinking himself into another stupor and then spend the weekend at the cabin recovering. Wherever Kingston Henry was this next Sunday, at the cabin or not, drunk or sober, Brazos would take Rosalie and Penelope away. He didn't want to kill the bastard before their eyes, but if it was forced upon him, so be it.

Brazos had purposely gotten a late start, in case Henry's hangover had slowed his departure. He didn't see the familiar sheet, since Rosalie wasn't expecting him, nor did he see any sign of life around the cabin or barn. He had no way of knowing whether Kingston Henry was there or not. Leaving his horse on the ridge under cover of trees and brush, he made his way to the river. He was but a few yards from the rear of the cabin, and the only window was covered with a wooden shutter. There was a back door, but no porch and no steps. There was no outhouse, and sooner or later one of them had to head for the bushes. His patience had reached its limit when Penelope opened the leather-hinged door and looked out.

"Penelope," he called, as loud as he dared. "Centavo."

She came toward the river, and he thought she'd heard him, but obviously she had not. She squatted, and he got her attention only by stepping out of the thicket where she could see him.

"Brazos!" she cried joyfully. The river was shallow enough for her to splash across, and she did. He hunkered down, and she ran to him.

"Centavo, that water's too cold for wading. Besides, you promised your mama you wouldn't cross the river again."

"But you're over here! Where's your horse?"

"Up on the ridge. I didn't know if I could go in the house or not, so I waited for you to come out. Can I go in?"

"You can go in, but let's get your horse. The water is kind of cold."

He picketed his horse behind the cabin near the river. On the grassed-over bank there would be no tracks and the animal could graze. Rosalie met him at the door. He entered, Penelope roosting on his shoulder, and he did not waste words.

"We're leaving next Sunday. Can you ride astraddle?"

"Yes," she said, "but I thought—"

"I've changed my mind. I want you and Penelope away from here. It's a three-day ride to Cheyenne, and that's without drifted snow. It comes early in the high country, and we may already be too late; there's the feel of it in the air already."

"We'll be ready," she said softly. "Just take us far away."

Far down the Sweetwater, Maury Duke stood outside Vonnecker's tent and contemplated the threatening gray sky. Sleet pelted the tent like an unending fusillade of bird shot.

"She's gonna blow," predicted Vonnecker. "The boys ain't gonna like throwin' a torch party in this."

"They ain't gettin' paid to like it," growled Duke. "They're bein' paid to do it, and I'm almighty fed up with their gripes. Where the hell is that Kingston Henry? The big bastard's been pawin' the ground, wantin' to go after them Texans, and now he's not here when I need him."

"Rode out maybe two hours ago," said Vonnecker, "and didn't say nothing. He was in a rotten mood. 'Course that ain't nothin unusual for him. When you aimin' to ride?"

"Soon as it's dark enough or stormin' enough to cover us," said Duke.

McCaleb and his riders were two days on the trail, twenty miles south of the Little Missouri, when the weather changed dramatically. Goose jogged his horse alongside McCaleb's.

"Malo," he said, pointing to the ominous gray clouds. "Much *malo.*"

Although actual darkness was a good two hours away, they rode in the gray of twilight. Having already wintered in Colorado, McCaleb had some idea as to what to expect. The first storm of the season might blow itself out overnight or it might roar unabated for three days. In either case, they needed shelter. He pointed to Goose and then to the south. The Apache had anticipated the order, and without a word put his horse into a lope, heading south.

Supper was two hours away, but the storm lent all the effects of approaching darkness. Brazos sat on a stool staring into the fire, thinking of Rosalie and Penelope, sick at the thought of them being snowed in with a conscienceless brute like Kingston Henry. His only comfort lay in the possibility that Henry might remain downriver rather than face the fury of the impending storm. The wind moaned under the eaves, sending an occasional gust down the chimney, driving ashes, sparks, and smoke into the small room. Brazos pulled on his mackinaw, his gloves, and tied down his hat. He was uneasy, not quite understanding the why of what he felt compelled to do, but fully convinced of the need. From his saddlebag he took a tin of Winchester cartridges and stepped out into the wind.

The Indian camp appeared deserted. Their horses stood

dejectedly in the cottonwoods along the creek, tails to the wind. The tipis were half circled, Washakie's in the center. They all faced the south and the flaps were drawn. Through an open flap a friend entered without ceremony, but this was different. If he just walked in, he had the uneasy feeling he'd be violating some tribal custom.

"Washakie!"

The wind snatched his words and flung them away. He called again, with no response. He must attract their attention without actually entering the tipi. He felt along the outside until he found a lodge pole beneath the rough hide. With the butt of his Colt he rapped as hard as he could against the wooden pole. The hide flap was suddenly drawn back and he found himself facing the dark-eyed girl who had attracted Monte. She said nothing, nor did he. He stepped inside and she closed the flap.

Three Indians sat hunched around a small fire. Two of them remained as they were. Slowly Washakie lifted his head, his expressionless eyes meeting Brazos's. Silently Brazos handed him the tin of Winchester shells, and Washakie's reaction was what Brazos had expected and feared. The Shoshoni, without a word, extended to Brazos a pair of snowshoes, carefully woven from slender willow branches and heat-hardened. Washakie then resumed his head-down position before the fire, and the girl silently lifted the tipi flap for Brazos to depart. The visit was over, and so was their alliance with the Shoshoni, compliments of Monte Nance.

The shelter Goose found was adequate, but that was all. The high banks of an arroyo, clothed with pines, protected them from wind and snow. While the storm grew in intensity, they snaked in windblown trees for firewood. The Shoshoni, wary of the fire despite the storm, withdrew into the shadows and rolled in their blankets. There was little else to do. McCaleb lay with his head on his saddle, his eyes on the snow-laden pines leaning over their arroyo. They would be delayed in their return to Box Elder Creek, and despite Martin Sandoval's warning, he was thankful the ranch was under the watchful eyes of the Shoshoni.

Maury Duke was furious. Including himself, his raiding party consisted of but six men. The others were too drunk or too sick to ride. He suspected the shiftless bastards had planned it that way. Kingston Henry hadn't returned. He figured the drunken fool had passed out, lay somewhere in the snow freezing to death and decided he didn't give a damn. He would make do with what he had. Time was running out.

Unwilling to return to the loneliness of the cabin, Brazos went on to the cookhouse, immediately feeling better as he stepped into Salty's cheery domain. It was almost suppertime, and Rebecca stared morosely into her coffee cup. By the time Brazos had straddled a stool, Will and Rebecca had arrived. Nobody said anything. Rebecca, Will, and Susannah had their eyes on Brazos, and Brazos kept his eyes on the door. Finally Monte came in, stared at them, and asked a question he would soon regret.

"Why the long faces? Somebody dead?"

"Maybe," said Brazos grimly. He took the snowshoes from the floor and put them on the table. He then told them of his visit to the Shoshoni camp, and of Washakie's response.

"So he swapped you some snowshoes for a tin of shells," said Monte. "That wasn't much of a trade on your part."

Monte suddenly found himself halfway across the table, his wind cut off, the collar of his shirt caught in Brazos's fist. The ex-Ranger's eyes were cold, and his words colder still.

"Just when I think there's some hope for you, kid, you convince me I'm all wrong. Single-handed, you've left us at the mercy of that bunch on the Sweetwater. I doubt Washakie's boys will fight for us, and I'd not blame them if they didn't. Whether or not you continue as part of this outfit depends on Bent McCaleb. Was it all up to me, I'd buy your share, put you on a fast horse, and run you the hell out of here!"

He shoved Monte back across the table, the stool upended, and he whacked his head against the wall. White-faced, Monte stumbled to his feet, but Brazos's voice froze him in his tracks.

"Sit down. I've only started."

Monte righted the stool and sat down. Rebecca was biting her lower lip, her eyes downcast. Salty had started to the table but had withdrawn, still uncertainly holding the coffeepot.

"Go ahead, Salty," said Brazos, "and pour the coffee. We'll need it. Pour a cup for yourself and sit down. This includes you."

He waited until the old cook was seated before he began. Rebecca had recovered from the initial shock and had fixed her malevolent gaze on Monte. For all his bluster, his courage failed and his eyes couldn't meet hers.

"We're overdue for a visit from that bunch along the Sweetwater," said Brazos, "and I'm more concerned for our buildings than for the herd. Stay out of the cabins at night. We have a pretty good view of them all from here, so we'll keep watch from the cookhouse. Four of us—Salty, Will, Monte, and myself—will take turns walking the roofed dog trot from the cookhouse to the farthest cabin. Take your rifles, and at the first hint of trouble, fire a shot to alert the rest of us."

"You expect them to burn us out, then," said Rebecca.

"I expect them to try," said Brazos. "What better way to hurt us than by leaving us without shelter, with the worst of the winter yet to come? They'll expect to take us by surprise, catching us in the cabins, and that's why we won't be there. They'd like to fire the buildings, force us out and then cut us down."

"The Shoshoni won't help us, then," said Susannah.

"I don't know," said Brazos. "They might, and I hope they will, but we can't depend on them. We'll have to set up our defense like it all depends on us. Any more questions?"

"Yeah," snarled Monte. "Who elected you segundo?"

"So far," said Brazos, "nobody's complained except you. Let's put it to a vote. Anybody don't like takin' orders from me, put up your right hand."

Nobody lifted a hand. Monte started to, saw the futility of it, and said no more.

Kingston Henry was very much alive, as sober as he ever got, and the farthest thing from his mind was Maury Duke's raid. He had held his mule in the cottonwoods beyond the barn until Brazos had ridden away. Henry's eyes were a mix of cruelty and madness, and in his hands was a heavy, shot-loaded rawhide quirt. He had disposed of Mike Donnegal to get this woman, had not forced himself on her, and where had it gotten him? Too good for the likes of him, was she? He would go after the bastard she'd taken a fancy to and gut-shoot him, but first he would settle the score with her. He kneed his mule into a trot and rode to the cabin. He dismounted and stood there for a moment, slapping the heavy quirt against his thigh. He lumbered up the steps and kicked the door open. He grinned in anticipation at Rosalie's terrified face. She was going to pay.

12

Maury Duke had no illusions about actually getting close enough to fire the Six Bar buildings without discovery, blizzard or not. Days before, he had found a resinous pine log and had chopped it into foot-long lengths as thick as his wrist. They were heavy enough to throw and rich enough to burn. To be certain they did, he wrapped the ends with rags which, at the proper time, would be doused with coal oil.

A little snow had begun to mix with sleet when the six riders reined up within sight of the lighted cookhouse. Each man had a gunny sack in which he carried some of the pine torches. Duke had brought two gallons of coal oil, and one at a time he'd soaked the rag-wrapped ends of the resinous pine torches. When they were at last ready, he had some final instructions.

"Stallings, you take Frenchy, Balew and Neely and get behind the cabins. Drop some of them torches onto that shed roof where they'll be hardest to get to. Me and Vonnecker will cover the front and shoot anybody makin' a run for it, once the fire gets goin'. Once you got all your torches burnin', ride like hell, but not straight downriver. Split up and double back, in case somebody's of a mind to trail us."

Monte Nance had reached the cabin farthest from the cookhouse when the first firebrand was thrown. He fired one shot to alert the others and then ducked out from the sheltered run where firewood was stacked. Just as he rounded the corner of the last cabin, a slug thudded into the log wall just inches from his head. He dropped to one knee and blasted two shots at the muzzle flash. The pine torch on the roof cast an eerie glow, and the smell of coal oil was strong. A second rifle opened up to Monte's left, and slugs striking the log wall flung splinters into his face. He threw himself backward and rolled around the corner, out of the line of fire. No sooner had he scrambled to his feet when the first arrow caught him on the inside of his thigh. He stumbled against the cabin, felt the shock of the second arrow in his side, and knew no more.

Before the echo of Monte's shot died away, Brazos and Will had their rifles and were out the door.

"Rest of you stay put," shouted Brazos.

Will took cover at the corner of one cabin while Brazos ran to the next. They began firing at the muzzle flashes of those rifles they believed were attacking Monte's position. More torches were thrown, and to Rebecca and Susannah, the flames were terrifying.

"Damn it," shouted Rebecca, "I won't sit here and let them burn everything down around us! Salty, you stay here and keep your rifle handy. Me and Susannah are going after those torches. Come on, Susannah!"

Firewood had been stacked almost to the roof of the dog run behind the cabins, and it was on this flat, shingled roof the torches were being thrown. At the very end of the run, near the cookhouse, Rebecca climbed the stacked wood until her hands gripped the edge of the shingled roof. She got one leg up and gained enough leverage to hoist the rest of her body. Susannah then followed, and they began kicking the flaming torches to the ground.

Somewhere in the night there was a cry of mortal agony and a riderless horse galloped away. The attackers' rifles had gone silent, and without targets Will and Brazos held their fire. Some of the torches Rebecca and Susannah had kicked off the roof still burned, offering excellent targets of anybody venturing from cover.

"Looks like they've backed off," said Will. "Who's on the roof?"

"Santa Claus and his reindeer," said Rebecca.

"I told you to stay in the cookhouse," said Brazos. "You could have been shot dead by the light of those torches."

"We thought it was worth the risk," said Susannah. "We weren't of a mind to sit in the cookhouse and watch this whole place go up in flames."

"It's awful quiet," said Rebecca. "Where's Monte?"

"The shot came from down at the far end," said Will. "Cover me, Brazos, and I'll take a look. He might have been hit."

Will drew no fire. One by one the torches flickered out. Cautiously, Brazos made his way to where Will knelt by Monte Nance.

"He's hard hit," said Will. "That's a bad one in his side; it's almighty close to his vitals."

Unseen, unheard, the Shoshoni defenders slipped away. Washakie lingered a moment, his hard old eyes on the fallen Monte Nance. Finally he returned his bow to the quiver and departed as silently as he had come.

It was near midnight when Maury Duke finally reached Vonnecker's tent. Stallings and Vonnecker sat hunched over a small fire, nursing tin cups of whiskey.

"Took you long enough," said Vonnecker. "We got an almighty *big* crow to pick with you. We rode unsuspectin' into a hornet's nest, thanks to you. Stallings says Frenchy, Balew, an' Neely are dead, shot through with Injun arrows. There's gonna be hell to pay."

"I don't know nothin' about any Injuns," said Duke. "I didn't see 'em, so I ain't convinced."

"I am," snarled Stallings. "I saw the three of 'em go down with arrers in ther guts. You're likely to end up with some lead in *yours,* onct the rest of th' boys hears what you done to us."

"Them Injuns ain't got no business there," said Duke. "That's why they was put on a reservation, so's they wouldn't be scalpin' decent white folks. This kind of thing, in the hands of a gent lowdown enough to use it, could get them Texans in deep with the Federals."

And Maury Duke knew a man just low down enough to use it. It might be enough to get George Francis Train off his back.

Brazos and Will had carried Monte to the cookhouse and placed him facedown on one of the tables. McCaleb had seen to it that their medicine chest had plenty of laudanum for pain and iodine for disinfectant. Monte had been given a dose of the opiate, and snored raggedly.

"Salty," said Brazos, "take your rifle and mosey around outside. If you see anything that might be trouble, fire a shot. Me and Will are goin' to have our hands full for a while. Rebecca, you and Susannah ought not to be in here. This won't be pretty. Besides, we'll have to peel these britches off him."

"I'm staying," said Rebecca. "He's my brother."

"I'm not going off by myself," said Susannah stubbornly. "I'm part of this outfit and I can stand as much as any of you."

"All right, then," sighed Brazos. "Let's be done with it, Will."

The only thing Kingston Henry truly feared was hanging. It was a spector that had haunted his drunken dreams since he'd seen a man hanged by a miner's court in Denver in 1859. His crime had been the killing of a woman, a whore. That being the case, what chance did a man have who had killed not only a decent woman, but her child as well?

He fled the cabin as though all the demons from Hell pursued him, and stood leaning against the still-saddled mule, breathing hard. In his mind's eye he still saw that body dangling in the moonlight. His only chance, if he had a chance, was to run. But where? He was wanted in Omaha and Denver. Suppose he went to Montana? That wasn't far enough. The enormity of what he had done would force him to leave the territories altogether. He'd have to go to Oregon or maybe California.

He looked up at the threatening sky. It was a hell of a time to ride into the Big Horns, but he had no choice. He had jerky in his saddlebag and it would have to do until he could hole up. He went to the barn for his snowshoes, mounted up and rode north. Only a little sleet blew into his face, but there would be more snow. There had to be— to hide his tracks.

Brazos snapped off a third of the arrow's shaft, leaving just enough of its length to drive it on through the flesh and out the other side. He used the butt of his Colt for a hammer, and even in his drug-induced sleep, Monte flinched and groaned with every blow. Rebecca clenched her teeth to avoid crying out.

"Dear God," cried Susannah, "isn't there another way?"

"None that we know of," said Will. "Brazos tried to tell you this isn't something a woman should see. They've got to come out. I reckon there's been a few gents lived with barbs in 'em, but not the iron tips. Better to go on and die from the wound pronto than to hang on for a week and have gangrene kill you."

Salty came in, stamping the snow off his boots. He watched Brazos drive the arrow's barb through the last resisting flesh. Once the shaft of the arrow had been drawn through, the wound in Monte's side oozed fresh blood.

"He come out better'n them other three pilgrims," said Salty. "They all got arrers in their guts. Stone dead. Never seen any of 'em afore."

"The Shoshoni must have mistaken Monte for one of the attackers," said Rebecca.

"Mama," cried Penelope weakly. "Mama."

There was no answer. When Penelope moved, there was a sharp pain in her side, and she cried out. She found she could open only her left eye. The other was swollen shut. She licked her lips and there was the salty taste of blood. While her face felt hot, the rest of her was freezing. She found her dress had been ripped off and she was naked. She tried to move and again cried out. She hurt all over and her back burned like fire. Despite the pain, she sat up, and what she saw brought an involuntary cry of anguish and terror.

Rosalie lay on her back before the cold fireplace. Her clothes had been ripped from her body, all the more terrifying because it exposed the extent of her injury. The shot-loaded quirt had taken its toll. She had been brutally beaten, and her body was a mass of bloody welts. Blood had seeped from her lacerated back and had puddled on the floor around her. Penelope screamed and turned away from the terrible sight. For a while she lay still. Finally, she lifted her head. Surely it had all been a bad dream, a nightmare.

"Mama," she sobbed. "Mama."

She wept until no tears remained. She tried to rise and found she was unable to. Finally she rolled over, got on her hands and knees and crawled to Rosalie. Fearfully she took her mother's left hand, and to her horror the arm bent above the elbow. But before she could cry out, Rosalie groaned in pain. She was hurt, but she was alive! Penelope wept tears of thankfulness.

"Penelope," said Rosalie weakly. So swollen was her face, she couldn't open her eyes.

"I'm here, Mama."

"Are you . . . ?"

"I'm all right, Mama," she cried. "What can I . . . what should I do?"

"It's . . . so . . . cold," mumbled Rosalie. "The snow . . ."

Penelope grasped the rough edge of the table and dragged herself to her feet. Her legs trembled and she felt sick to her stomach. When the nausea had passed, she staggered into the bedroom and pulled a blanket from the bed. She covered Rosalie as best she could and then knelt beside her.

"Mama," she pleaded. "Mama."

But Rosalie spoke no more. Her face was hot to Penelope's touch. Her breathing seemed slow and painful.

"God," cried Penelope, "help us. Oh, please help us."

Once the iron arrow tips had been driven through, Brazos and Will disinfected the wounds with whiskey and again with iodine. Salty had been outside, and came in to warm himself.

"Almighty cold," he said. "Snow by mornin', if'n not sooner."

"I reckon I'll ride down the Sweetwater a ways," said Brazos, "before it snows out all the tracks. With the three dead and the two staked out with rifles, we're only accounting for five."

There would be more snow later, but now it was no more than hock deep. Brazos had lighted matches and examined the faces of the three dead men, finding that he knew none of them. It was unlikely that Kingston Henry, vindictive bastard that he obviously was, would have missed out on this attack. Once Brazos found their trail, he'd be looking for mule tracks.

Penelope opened the door, and as though in answer to her tearful prayer, a pale moon illuminated the snow-covered High Plains as far as she could see. She could hear the chuckling of the river, and it was as though a voice spoke to her.

"Brazos!" she cried. "I'll . . . I'll go to Brazos."

She had no idea how to reach him. She only knew that he always rode west along the Sweetwater and that he followed the river in the opposite direction when he left. There had been no supper and she had eaten nothing since breakfast. Her legs trembled and she almost fell as she tried to hurry. Her mother was terribly hurt, and she had no idea how far she must go or how long it would take to

get there. Rosalie had promised her new shoes. Someday.
The soles were worn through on her old ones, and having
no socks, she found some rags and bound her feet. It mattered not which of her calico dresses she wore. The thin
fabric would be no protection against the cold. Her only
coat was one of Rosalie's, the hem taken up to fit. Still, it
reached her feet. Once she had gotten into the heavy coat,
she discovered how severely she had been beaten. The
welts and cuts on her back and shoulders throbbed just
from the weight of the coat. Once more she knelt painfully
by Rosalie.

"Please be all right, Mama, until I can find Brazos. . . ."

Kingston Henry rode on, pausing only to rest the mule.
Looking back across the snow-covered plain he had traveled, he cursed. Even in the moonlight his trail was an
open book to anyone who chose to read it. His hands, toes,
and ears felt half frozen. Damn it, why had the snow
stopped? Again he thought of the man he'd seen hanged
for killing a woman. He could still see the shadowy figure
dangling in the wind, the knot tight under its left ear. But
now its contorted, agonized face had become his own.

Brazos continued along the south bank of the Sweetwater
for what he reckoned was five miles, and all he saw was
unbroken snow. Unless they had crossed the river and
come up the north bank, they'd been smart enough to
avoid the Sweetwater altogether. Concluding that he'd ridden far enough, he turned south. Unless he was totally
wrong, he would eventually find the trail he was seeking.
Just when he was about to turn back, convinced he had
miscalculated, he found it. Six riders, and unless he'd
swapped his mule for a horse, Kingston Henry wasn't
among them.

Brazos turned back toward the Sweetwater. He had
learned all he could, but for some reason he didn't quite
understand, he was uneasy. He had fully expected to find

Kingston Henry among the attackers. Why hadn't he
been? Had he gone on another drunk and been too hung
over to ride? He doubted it. When he reached the Sweetwater, he reined up his horse and sat there listening. For
what, he had no idea. Then, like the fulfillment of some
unspoken prophecy, came the far off, mournful baying of a
wolf. It died away, and the ensuing silence seemed all the
more ominous in its absence. It had come from somewhere
downriver. Something, whatever had been tugging at his
mind, got to him. He shucked his Henry, jacked a shell into
the chamber and turned his horse toward Kingston
Henry's lonely cabin.

Penelope stayed as near the river as she could, but the
greasewood and underbrush that had minimized the ac-
cumulation of snow made for difficult travel. Her hands,
feet, and ears hurt, and something within her skinny body
throbbed with every breath. Her head felt strange and she
was unable to hear out of her right ear. Suddenly there was
a sound that chilled her blood and stopped her dead in her
tracks. She had heard wolves bay before, but never so
close, and never while she was lost and at their mercy.
What was she to do? If she continued along the river, she
might walk right into them, and if she stayed where she
was, they would come to her. While she couldn't see them,
she knew they were near, and the chill that crept up her
spine had nothing to do with the cold.
    She stood there, her heart pounding, and for a terrifying
second saw their eyes. The pair of them were on the opposite bank of the river, stalking her! She struggled on, fearing to look for those fiendish eyes, fearing not to. There
was no feeling left in her feet. They felt clumsy, wooden,
and she fell. She was so sleepy. She lay there, no longer
feeling the cold. Perhaps if she rested a little.
    Suddenly conscious, uncertain as to how long she'd lain
there, she forced herself to get up and stumble on. She
thought she heard the rustling of leaves behind her, but
she was afraid to look. Half frozen, her body hurting from

the beating, she had no sense of direction. She could only follow the river, hoping she found Brazos before the wolves found her. It had begun to sleet, adding to her misery, the icy particles rattling into the dead leaves about her. She was so cold!

She stepped on a rotted log; it collapsed under her weight and again she fell, this time into the icy, swirling water of the river. The shock was terrible. She opened her mouth to cry out just as her head went under. No sooner did her head clear the surface than she was dragged down again. The current was swift, deep, and she felt it pulling her downstream. She frantically snatched at bushes and limbs along the bank, only to have them elude her grasp.

Suddenly she slammed into a root that slowed her enough that she got her trembling arms around the slender tree from which the root protruded. She struggled to her knees, the water up to her chin. She clung to the tree with all her failing strength. The sodden coat was dragging her down. She let go of the tree with her left hand and managed to free it from the sleeve of the coat. When she again got her left arm about the tree and turned loose with her right, the river did the rest. It snatched the coat away from her, and exhausted, she was able to climb out of the water.

"Please, God," she prayed aloud, "don't let the wolves find me. Let me rest . . . just a . . . little. . . ."

She was so tired, so sleepy, unaware of the falling snow and steadily dropping temperature. She was on her knees, and remained there weeping, not having the strength to rise to her feet. Finally her half-frozen, battered body could take no more, and she toppled forward on her face. No longer was she able to resist the cold, and the sodden dress she wore began to freeze to her body. But she was unaware of that or of anything. In the silent, deepening snow, she slept. . . .

On the farther side of the river, two great gray wolves loped along, seeking a point shallow enough that they might cross.

13

*B*razos rode warily, his Henry cocked and ready. The wolf's baying bothered him. One of the night riders he was seeking might lay wounded and bleeding, the blood accounting for the presence of the wolves. In the West, no man left another—however no-account—at the mercy of wolves. Often he paused, listening, but heard nothing. He paid particular attention to the temperament of his horse, knowing the animal would warn him if the huge gray predators came near. It happened as he rounded a bend in the river. When his horse reared, nickering in fear, it took his full attention to calm the animal. Only for a fleeting second did he see the two pairs of eyes, off to his right, across the river. By the time he had steadied the horse enough to fire, his targets had vanished. He continued along the river, wondering what had attracted the wolves.

The wind seemed colder than ever. His fingers, toes, and ears were already numb. The moon had been swallowed by a new mass of big gray clouds, and he found himself agreeing with Salty's prophecy. There would be more snow by morning, if not sooner. Suddenly his horse sidestepped. He half expected a blossom of muzzle flame from rifle or colt, but it didn't come. If it was a wounded man, he was beyond defending himself. He dismounted. Leading the horse, his rifle ready, he moved cautiously forward. Along the river the ground was deep in fallen leaves, and had his led horse not shied at the smell of blood, he might not have seen her.

Penelope lay on her side, her legs drawn up against the cold. She wore only her thin dress and one shoe. Fearfully, Brazos took her small wrist, seeking a pulse. He found it weak and irregular, but thank God it was there! He shrugged out of his mackinaw and spread it beside her. Gently as he could, he lifted her onto the coat and wrapped her in it. Her sodden dress had already frozen, and he could hear the crackle of ice as he moved her. Somehow she had fallen into the river and had been slowly but surely freezing to death! Could he save her?

He tried to mount his horse holding Penelope, but the twice-frightened animal was skittish. He led it until he found a windblown tree. Its trunk, several feet from the ground, allowed him to step into the saddle while holding the half-frozen girl. He hesitated only a moment, then kneed the horse into a lope toward Box Elder Creek. What had happened in that cabin to force Penelope into the cold and the darkness? He was afraid he knew. He had desperately wanted to ride on to the cabin, but that would have meant the death of Penelope, and he doubted he would have been in time to help Rosalie. He knew, with sickening certainty, that she was dead. He silently vowed to save Penelope if possible, and then do the one remaining thing he could for Rosalie. He would trail Kingston Henry to Canada if he must, and then kill the son of a bitch with his bare hands.

He wished he had pulled on his slicker as a windbreaker, but he'd forgotten it in his concern for Penelope. The north wind felt infinitely colder and more vicious, as though it sensed he was at its mercy. It seemed hours before he finally saw the cheerful light from the cookhouse door. He stumbled as he dismounted, almost falling with his burden, and left his reins trailing. He must yet ride to that lonely cabin, fearing what he would find, but knowing he must go.

They'd been watching for him. Salty stepped out of the

shadows and swung the door all the way back. The moment Brazos stepped inside, he heard Monte's labored breathing, but at least he was alive. That might be more than could be said for poor Penelope. He placed her on the other table and loosed the heavy mackinaw that protected her.

Seeing her in the light, Brazos was as shocked as the others. The entire right side of her face was a purple bruise. There was an ugly gash above her right eye from which blood still oozed. The warmth of Brazos's heavy coat had begun to thaw her frozen dress, water puddling on the table. But the worst was yet to come.

"I found her by the river," said Brazos. "God knows how long she was there, or what's been . . . done to her."

Rebecca wasted no time. She flung away the one shoe, unwound the rags from Penelope's feet and peeled off the calico dress. It was her only garment, and the hurt done to the thin little body froze them all into horrified silence. Salty slammed the butt of his Winchester against the floor. Penelope had been beaten from her shoulders to her knees. Some of the bloody welts began on her back and wrapped around her thin chest. Rebecca tried one wrist and then the other, seeking a pulse. There was none. She was so choked she couldn't speak, but there was no need. They read the grim news in the tears that wet her cheeks.

Brazos took one of the small wrists in his hands, unwilling to believe. Vainly he tried the other. Slowly he released it and buried his face in his hands.

"Centavo," he cried brokenly. "Centavo . . ."

His hat in his hands, he backed away, never taking his eyes from the small, still form on the table. In his eyes was a mix of grief and fury such as none of them had ever seen. When he finally spoke, his voice was as cold as the wind that moaned through the cottonwoods, as dead as the fallen leaves beneath them.

"Will, saddle me a fresh horse. I'll likely have a long ride. Salty, fix me a pack of grub. Enough for four days."

"I'd best go with you," said Will. "You'll need help . . . bringin' her in."

"I don't expect to bring her back," said Brazos. "Besides, with Monte down, you're needed here."

"I'll go with you," said Susannah. "I know what you're . . . expecting, but suppose she's . . . alive and badly hurt? You'll need a woman's help. Saddle me a horse, Will."

Shocked by this new tragedy, they hadn't noticed Rebecca leaving. She had gone to her cabin and found the small mirror she'd brought from East Texas. She placed the glass directly under Penelope's nose and they all watched as though she might perform a miracle. And she did! Quickly she knelt by the open fire, wiped the little glass on her sleeve and again held it under Penelope's nose.

"She's still alive, Brazos!" she cried. "Look!"

He was at her side in an instant. She wiped the glass clean, held it beneath Penelope's nostrils and then placed it in Brazos's trembling hands. He leaned close to the fire, and there it was! It was a tiny breath—a smear half the size of a two-bit piece—but she was alive! The spark might again become a flame! Almost reverently he placed the little mirror on the table and took both Rebecca's hands in his.

"Thank you, Rebecca," he said. "Please . . . do what you can for her."

Kingston Henry stopped to rest the mule, hopefully contemplating the mass of gray clouds that obscured the moon and most of the stars. While he wasn't sure how he knew, he knew for a certainty that he would be pursued, if only by the redheaded hombre who had visited the cabin while he'd been away. He let his mind roam back to the time he'd been forced to flee Denver to escape a lynch mob. Desperate, he'd first headed for the Bozeman trail, hopeful of reaching California, but had found the trail too crowded for him. Near Fort Phil Kearney he'd struck off to the west and had gotten lost in the Big Horn Mountains.

But it had been a blessing in disguise. He had holed up in a hard-to-find cave, surviving on snowshoe rabbits and other small game until he was sure his past wasn't going to catch up with him. He had then drifted back to Cheyenne and managed to get on with the railroad. He'd been a damn fool to let them shove him out of his strawboss job and stick him there on the Sweetwater, nursing a claim that wasn't even his. Now, if memory served him right, he could find that cave again. He need only follow the old Bozeman to where Kearney had stood and then ride due west. He could remain there until the snow hid his trail, and then make his way into the gold fields of Montana Territory. Once there, he could change his name and remain, or go on to California.

Brazos pushed his horse as hard as he dared. Whatever he found at the cabin, he would be going after Kingston Henry, and he must take the trail before snow covered it. Susannah kept pace, saying nothing. He believed she had the makings of a western woman, and he was glad for Will. When they reached the cabin, his hands were trembling and he was sick with dread at what he expected to find.

"I reckon you'd best wait," he said, "until I see . . . what's happened."

"No," said Susannah. "Whatever's been done to her, I'll have to see it. Putting it off won't make it any easier."

He found himself holding his breath as he mounted the steps. Silently he thanked God that Penelope had remembered to close the door. How long—if she was alive—had she lain in the cabin without warmth? Brazos eased open the door and lit a match, looking for the lamp. After the pitch-dark, it seemed unusually bright, and they turned to the blanket-wrapped figure lying on the floor. They could see only her face, but it was enough. It was a mass of purple and yellow bruises, and even from where Brazos stood, he could see the shine of matted blood in her dark hair. He waited, thankful for Susannah's presence. She had been dead right—he did need a woman there. She lifted the blanket and gasped.

"Is she . . . ?"

"I don't know," choked Susannah. "The poor woman's been beaten to death. If she's alive, it's a miracle."

She knelt and took Rosalie's wrist. Then she tried the other. Brazos held his breath in an agony of suspense. Susannah got to her feet, hands trembling.

"Brazos, she's alive, but not by much. Don't get your hopes too high, because, even for the terrible shape she's in, she may be hurt even worse inside. She may not survive the ride to the ranch."

"Please," said Brazos, "can you tell if she . . . did he . . . ?"

"No. She's been spared that, at least, but God knows what else may be wrong. Not being sure how or where she's hurt, it's a shame we have to move her. A broken rib could puncture a lung."

"Oh, God," sighed Brazos, "I know, but we can't stay here. I'll get another blanket or two, if I can find that many. She needs medicine, food, a warm bed, and somebody to look after her. She's made it this far; we'll have to gamble the rest of the way."

Rosalie was a far greater burden than Penelope had been, and there was simply no way to carry her other than in his arms. Brazos led his horse up next to the porch and finally managed to step into his saddle while holding the blanket-wrapped Rosalie.

"Susannah," he said, "will you . . . kind of . . . go through their things and take . . . what seems worth taking? Clothes, I mean. I don't aim for them to come back here."

Swiftly she gathered their belongings—pitifully few— and bundled them into a sheet. Brazos led out, Susannah following. Rosalie's slender body—light at first—grew heavier and heavier. His arms became leaden and he was on the brink of exhaustion when they finally reined up at the cookhouse. Will took the blanket-wrapped Rosalie from Brazos.

"Take her to my cabin, Will," said Rebecca.

"Penelope," choked Brazos. "How . . . ?"

"Holding on," said Rebecca. "She had no pulse because she was chilled to the bone and in the process of freezing to death. I built up a fire in my place and took her there. Do you want to see Penelope for a minute before we tend to her mother?"

Brazos knelt by the bunk, took one of the small hands in his and felt the blessed warmth. Her pulse—weakening as her body temperature had dropped—was now at least strong enough that he could feel it. Suddenly, like a miracle, she opened her one good eye.

"Brazos," she whispered through swollen lips, "I . . . found . . . you. . . ."

"Yes," he choked, "you found me."

"Will you . . . help my mama? She's hurt . . . awful bad. I had to . . . leave her."

"I went and got her, Centavo. She's here, and she'll be all right."

He got to his feet and stumbled to the door, praying he hadn't lied to her. Rebecca had spread blankets on the floor before the fire so they could see to Rosalie's hurts. Will eased her down and Susannah felt for her pulse. Brazos again held his breath.

"No weaker than it was," said Susannah. "She's been beaten unmercifully, but at least she isn't half frozen. Poor Penelope took almost as bad a beating, and might still have pneumonia from exposure."

"Please do for them whatever you can," said Brazos. "I reckon I waited too long. But there is one thing I can do for them, and I won't be back until it's finished."

Will followed Brazos out.

"Will," said Brazos, "if Bent gets back before I do, tell him . . . tell him I did what I had to do, and I'll be back when I can. How's Monte?"

"Only the good die young," said Will, chuckling. "That

little fool will likely have to be shot at the Resurrection. *Vaya con Dios, amigo.*"

Brazos had no trouble finding Kingston Henry's trail. It led due north, which made no sense unless Henry was quitting the territory. But what kind of fool lit out for the Big Horn Mountains with a blizzard almost certain? Having ties with the railroad, why hadn't Henry headed for Cheyenne and taken the next work train east? He could have lost himself in Omaha or Chicago, yet here he was leaving a trail across the snow-covered High Plains that a blind mule could follow. Then it all fell in place. He understood. Henry had broken with Maury Duke. That had to be it.

The question was, had he first had a falling out with Duke, or had he been forced to run as a result of what he had done to Rosalie and Penelope? It was the kind of crime that followed a man, so heinous that even Maury Duke's scruffy gang, given the chance, might have stretched Henry's neck.

Dawn broke gray and cold, and the promise of snow became reality. Susannah had spent the night in Rebecca's cabin, the two of them seeing to the hurts of Rosalie and Penelope. Will and Salty had rolled Monte Nance in a blanket and had taken him to the cabin next to Rebecca's. Armed with a pot of coffee and their rifles, they had kept watch from the cookhouse the rest of the night. Salty had breakfast ready long before first light. Will, Susannah, and Rebecca, weary and red-eyed, gathered at the table.

"Come on, Salty," said Rebecca, "and eat with us. You've had a hard night."

"Haven't we all?" said Susannah. "My God, I've never seen so much happen so fast. Will didn't tell me it would be like this when I hired on."

"Never a dull moment," said Will. "Next time there's a trail drive to Fort Buford, or anywhere else, I'm going on the drive and leave McCaleb here. I always get some sleep on the drive, even when there's a stampede."

"I wish Bent had been here," said Rebecca, "but I'll tell him the same thing I'm telling you. Shorthanded as we were, we held our own. But we'll have to share the credit with the Shoshoni. I don't know how many of the Sweetwater bunch came after us, but those three getting shot full of arrows sure made believers of the others. Which reminds me: what are we going to do with them? We can't just leave them lying dead behind our cabins."

"I reckon we owe them a burying," said Will, "but not during a snowstorm. I wouldn't expect you to bury me in frozen ground, with snow and sleet slapping you in the face."

"Susannah," said Rebecca, "we'd better take a walk around our hospital and be sure everybody's all right."

"I'm goin' to the Shoshoni camp," said Will.

There was no denying the Shoshoni had served them well, but the wounding of Monte Nance bothered Will. It was more than a warning; one of the wounds should have been mortal, and might yet be. Will reckoned he would be even less welcome at Washakie's tipi than Brazos had been, but he determined to at least make an effort. But the opportunity was gone, and so were the Shoshoni. The tipis might never have existed, and snow already covered the dead ashes of their lodge fires. Their rapidly fading trail led north, toward Powder River basin.

The storm became less intense during the night, and McCaleb pushed on at dawn. He expected more snow, but he wasn't of a mind to hold still and wait for it. They rode hard, taking shelter where they found it, doing without when they found none. They turned west, crossing into Wyoming Territory just south of the Powder, 125 miles north of Box Elder Creek. When they arose before dawn, they made a startling and disturbing discovery. Goose and the Shoshoni were gone!

"We'll saddle up and ride," said McCaleb. "They'll catch up to us."

They kept wary and anxious eyes on their back trail, but

the expected seven riders didn't show. Goose rode in alone. His explanation was brief.

"Injun go," he said, pointing west. "All Injun go."

Quickly he drew the story in the snow. Washakie's band had left Box Elder Creek and had camped near Powder River. McCaleb's Shoshoni escort had ridden away and joined them. Goose had trailed them, turning back once he had discovered where they were going.

"That beats all," said Jed. "How'd them six war whoops know Washakie's bunch was on the Powder?"

"I don't know," said McCaleb. "I'm more concerned with why they're camped on the Powder. We left them on Box Elder Creek, with the understanding they'd be there until we returned from Fort Buford."

"We'd best step up the pace," said Pen. "They'll need us at the ranch."

Snow began to fall in earnest, and Kingston Henry sighed with relief. A day of this, and even an Indian couldn't find him. But he didn't have a day. Reaching the foothills, he began his ascent into the Big Horns. Once he'd reached a promontory from which he could see much of the Big Horn basin, he couldn't resist a look at his back trail. While he believed he had eluded pursuit, he wanted reassurance. At first he saw nothing, and then his sigh of relief ran headlong into a knot of fear in his throat. Far away— four or five hours, maybe—there was a tiny moving dot bobbing across the snow-whitened expanse of Big Horn basin. A horse and rider! From the ashes of Kingston Henry's fear rose an insane fury. He would do what he should have done to start with. He tethered his mule in a cedar thicket, withdrew his rifle from its boot, and settled down behind some brush to wait.

Brazos reined up and dismounted. While he rested his horse, he stomped some feeling back into his half-frozen feet. Snow had begun to fall shortly after dawn, and the trail he'd been following was slowly but surely disappearing. But it didn't matter. Kingston Henry had a destination in mind, and it lay somewhere in the Big Horns. The man knew he was being followed, and Brazos no longer worried about finding Henry. Henry would find him, and only one of them would leave the Big Horns alive. He swung into the saddle and rode on. He *could* reach the foothills before dark, if he continued his present pace. He purposely slowed his horse to a walk. Now that he knew where the last hand would be played, there was no need for haste. He hadn't the slightest doubt that Henry was planning to greet him with a .44–40 slug. But there would be no moon, and darkness would become the equalizer. While he didn't relish the thought of them stalking one another in the snowy darkness, it was better than riding into a for-certain ambush. It evened the odds. No Texan asked or expected more than that.

Kingston Henry grew impatient. There was a pile of cigarette butts at his feet and he had shifted his huge bulk a hundred times, yet that cussed rider didn't seem any closer. Finally, in the gray of twilight—much more pronounced with continuing snow—it dawned on him. He stomped to his feet.

He had wasted most of the day, enjoying what he believed was an edge, only to have it snatched away by approaching darkness. His confidence ebbed. His adversary was not just some Texas cowboy with a mad on, but a man hunter of serious proportions. But he still held the advantage, because he was no stranger to these mountains. The higher one climbed, the more treacherous the trail! He turned the mule loose to graze, taking only his blankets, his saddlebags, and his Winchester.

Once it was dark, Brazos approached the foothills. He sensed that Henry had prior knowledge of the Big Horns. That being the case, the showdown would come at some higher elevation of Henry's choosing. He was sure of it when he found the mule. He unsaddled his horse, leaving the animal to seek shelter and graze among the cedars and spruce. He took the time to eat some cold beef and a couple of Salty's biscuits. He dared not burden himself unnecessarily. The air was thin already, and would become more so the higher he climbed. Reluctantly he wrapped his Henry in a blanket and left it with his saddle. He was going to need both hands. He would take only his Colt and his bowie knife. Unsure of the hazards ahead, he took the coiled lariat from his saddle and looped it over his shoulder.

Even in the darkness, he found Henry's trail in the otherwise unbroken snow. It was time for the snowshoes Washakie had given him, and he silently thanked the Shoshoni for the final favor. He set off up a slope that became steeper and steeper. He had but one advantage. Effective shooting downhill in *daylight* was difficult. Doing it by night, by sound, was virtually impossible. But that wasn't what Henry had in mind. The boulder came plummeting out of the darkness like a giant snowball, gaining momentum by the second. He was spared only because it struck a lesser stone and bounded over his head. He listened as it beat a path through the brush and trees below. Finally, except for the wind, there was only silence. Suddenly it was broken by a booming voice somewhere above him.

"Still down there, cowboy? They's plenny more where that 'un come from. Come an' git me, damn you!"

Slowly Brazos began moving to his right, away from the point of Henry's ascent. Obviously he had chosen the least hazardous way and he was expecting Brazos to follow. To do so would mean facing more boulders and possibly a fusillade of gunfire. The big man still had the edge. Familiar with the Big Horns, he had chosen a position of defense that would be difficult to breach.

Far above the treeline, Kingston Henry prepared to heave more boulders over the edge. He had chosen his position well. It was a half-moon ledge facing the east with a sheer drop at either end. In years past, a rock slide had torn away part of the ledge, and the resulting gap was the only logical access to Henry's position. Behind him the face of the mountain was almost straight up, so sheer that not even snow clung to it. He felt perfectly safe. Come first light, he could belly-down on the rim and kill this troublesome bastard without exposing himself.

Brazos rested often. The higher he climbed, the thinner and colder the air became. With his scarf he had tied his hat down, and the wind snatched at it with icy fingers. The snow had diminished to an occasional flurry. The clouds had thinned, and while there was no moon, the starlight against the white of the snow allowed Brazos to see what lay ahead. Once he had reached the point where he could climb no higher, he paused. He suspected the south end of this ledge would be just as inaccessible, so there was no point in back-tracking. Before he continued, he needed some movement from Henry. It wasn't long in coming. Henry sent another boulder crashing down the mountainside, and Brazos fixed his position. He was on the ledge above, and inaccessible as it seemed, there was another side to the mountain. Why couldn't he continue around it, climb higher, and come down from above Henry's position?

It proved difficult and hazardous. He moved only inches at a time, slipping repeatedly, saving himself by grabbing rock or bush. His knees were skinned and bleeding from contact with rocks beneath the snow. The wind still roared out of the west, and when he rounded the mountain, he was almost swept off his feet. By the stars he judged it had taken him more than two hours, and he still had to climb the mountain.

Kingston Henry had given in to a mix of impatience, fury, and frustration. He knew damn well he was being stalked, yet he hadn't the faintest idea where his pursuer was! He hadn't heard a sound! He no longer felt safe on this ledge. It now seemed as much a prison as though he'd heard the clang of the door behind him and stood looking through heavy iron bars. Despite the chill wind and the near-zero temperature, he was sweating. What was he going to do? He didn't even remember his last decent meal, and all he had in his saddlebag was a few strips of jerky. His eyes burned and his head ached for lack of sleep, but he dared not sleep. He couldn't even retreat into the small cave to escape the freezing wind, lest he be trapped there. He toyed with the notion of climbing back down the precipitous trail, finding his mule and making a run for it. Down the slope, in the starlight, against the white of the snow? He cursed himself for a fool. Suddenly there was a sound behind him! He whirled and fired. The lead struck the rock face and whanged off into the darkness.

Brazos waited awhile before throwing another stone. While he couldn't see Henry, he could see the edge of the bench, and he threw the next stone beyond the rim. It had the desired effect, seeming to have been dislodged by the clumsy foot of a man somewhere below. Henry cut loose with his Winchester, raking the slope as fast as he could shuck out the spent shells and pull the trigger. Brazos could hear him cursing.

Brazos's own patience was wearing thin. He had waited long enough. He looped one end of his lariat around a thin pinnacle of rock and tested it for strength. It seemed secure, but was the forty-foot lariat long enough? It would have to do. He threw one more stone, shortening the distance so that it fell barely beyond the rim on which Henry stood. It threw him into another frenzy of firing, and Brazos used that as cover to begin his descent. Just one dislodged stone.

Kingston Henry was sweating beneath his heavy shirt and long underwear. The Winchester was slippery in his sweating, trembling hands. He stalked from one end of his prison to the other, vainly seeking a target on the snowy slope beneath him.

Brazos silently gave thanks that the surface down which he crept faced the east and was steep enough that no snow had accumulated. It wouldn't take much to give him away. He was two-thirds of the way down when something slipped beneath his boot and clattered to the ledge below.

Henry whirled and fired at the sound. Brazos kicked away from the face of the mountain and let go of the lariat. He came down on his feet, bent his knees on impact and stumbled back against the rock down which he'd climbed. So suddenly had he appeared, Henry hadn't jacked a new shell into the chamber. He swung the rifle by its muzzle, aiming for Brazos's head. Brazos dropped and rolled clear, and the stock of the weapon splintered against the rock. Henry went for his pistol. From flat on his back Brazos fired, and the slug broke Henry's wrist just as he cleared leather. Henry made no move toward the fallen Colt, but drew his Bowie with his left hand.

"Shoot, you Texas bastard," he snarled, "'cause if you don't, I'll cut your gizzard out."

Brazos said nothing. Vivid in his mind's eyes was the bruised, bloody bodies of a helpless woman and a skinny little girl. He holstered his Colt and drew his Bowie. They circled, parried, Henry seeking to drive Brazos to the rock at his back. Brazos refused to be trapped, moving to his left. But he stumbled over Henry's broken Winchester. It was exactly the advantage the big man was seeking. His thrust slashed the left sleeve of Brazos' mackinaw from elbow to wrist, and his knee caught Brazos in the groin. Sick and off balance, he dropped his own Bowie and caught the massive wrist, halting a second thrust that would have gutted him. His only advantage was Henry's bloody, useless right hand. But he had the knife, and when they went down, Henry was on top. They were on the north end of the ledge. Brazos had moved laterally over this treacherous side of the mountain beneath where they were struggling, where a slip of the foot could have dropped him to the canyon far below. Now he was flat on his back, his head over the very edge, Henry trying to drive the big Bowie into his throat.

Brazos gripped Henry's wrist with both hands, but such was the man's brute strength, the knife inched closer and closer. Brazos arched his body, trying to throw Henry off, but the motion only slid him closer to that final, fatal drop.

Suddenly he freed his right hand and, mustering all his failing strength, smashed Henry in the nose with his fist. The pain was such that Henry involuntarily reared back. Brazos arched his body and, with the same motion, brought his right knee forward, catapulting Henry over the edge. Henry's scream of mortal terror melded briefly with the wind and then was no more. But for the wind, there was the silence that had prevailed in the Big Horns since the dawn of time.

Brazos inched away from the brink and for a while lay there exhausted, too weak to move farther. His left arm stung, and he found that the point of Henry's Bowie had gone beyond the sleeve of his heavy coat. It was almighty cold, and he was tempted to take Henry's blankets and get what sleep he could. But the wolves changed his mind. Somewhere to the north one bayed and was answered by another. Like buzzards, they always seemed to know. But it was a fitting end for Kingston Henry. Whatever was left of him.

However exhausted Brazos was, he dared not waste any time getting back to his horse, lest he end up afoot. With the baying of the wolves, the animal might already be rattling his hocks for the Sweetwater. He ejected the spent shell from his Colt, reloaded, and started down the mountain.

Again the wolf bayed, and it seemed a companion to the wind, coming from the farthermost reaches of the Big Horns. It was the eeriest, lonesomest sound he'd ever heard.

14

McCaleb and the rest of the outfit rode in Thursday, September 24, in the early afternoon. Rebecca, Will, and Susannah took turns explaining what had happened in his absence. He was told only that Monte had been wounded in the raid on the ranch. Rebecca took it upon herself to tell him the probable reason, once they were alone.

"I can't blame Washakie," said McCaleb. "It wasn't a good idea, them throwing in with us. I may have gotten them *and* us in more trouble than we can handle. I made the mistake of mentioning our Indian riders to Captain Sandoval, and now we're on shaky ground at Fort Buford. Thank God I *didn't* tell him that Goose and the Shsohoni wiped out a band of Sioux somewhere in Dakota Territory after the Sioux stampeded our herd. I'll be surprised if that bunch on the Sweetwater don't use the Shoshoni to account for their failure to burn us out. I look for them to put out the word that we lured a whole tribe of hostiles off the reservation and allowed them to murder innocent homesteaders."

"Perhaps bringing the Shoshoni here wasn't a good idea," said Rebecca, "but they saved us. That's why I feel so guilty. They stood by us, and we didn't do right by them. Now I have to tell you *why* I think they left, and why and how Monte was wounded."

He listened gravely until she finished and for a while he said nothing. She stood with her back to him, nervously clenching her hands. He got up, walked around to face her, and put his hands on her shoulders. He waited until her eyes met his before he spoke.

"Monte and I will talk. Brazos and Will have gone easy on him because he's your brother. So have I, but no more. We've taken plenty from him for your sake, and he's taken unfair advantage of us and of you. The next time he goes contrary to the best interests of the outfit, I'll tally up his share and boot him out. He's getting by this time only because our deal with the Shoshoni would have blown up anyway. But that doesn't change the fact that he went against Washakie's wishes and left me feeling guilty for the same reason you do. Do you understand?"

"Yes," she sighed, "and I agree. I've always stood up for him, even if he was in the wrong, but I can't do it anymore. I'll talk to him too, and I'll tell him I'm standing by your decision, whatever it is. And I will."

Just before dark Brazos rode in, leading a mule. There were no questions. Brazos was alive, and for a Texan that was testimony enough. While Brazos had a warm greeting for them all, there was something else on his mind, a question in his eyes. Without a word, Rebecca pointed to the cabin, and Brazos turned to it. There was a smile on every face when Penelope swung the door open and Brazos caught her up in his arms. Rosalie lay under blankets on one of the bunks. Her broken arm had been bound tight. The cuts and bruises were still evident, but she was alive! And she wore a smile!

"I'm so glad you're back," she sighed. "Did you—"

"No," said Brazos, "I didn't shoot him. He took a fall in the Big Horns."

"I'm glad," she said, "that . . . you didn't . . . that it . . . ended . . . like it did. Despite what he . . . did. . . ."

"Then we don't have to go away!" cried Penelope. "I

want to stay here. I want to ride a horse, milk the cows, learn to bake biscuits, shoot a gun—"

"Whoa," said Brazos. "There won't be anything for the rest of us to do."

"Someday, could I . . . have some boots? Some honest-to-goodness riding boots, like yours?"

"You have my promise," chuckled Brazos. "Now you sit still while me and your mama have us a talk."

He dragged up a stool and sat next to her bunk. He reached for her good hand. Despite her hurts—the yellow and purple bruises that still marred her face—she was beautiful to him. And there was no mistaking the happiness in her dark eyes.

"Penelope's right," she said. "We don't have to run away. There's nowhere I'd be happier than right here. But I know we're . . . taking one of your cabins . . . some of your riders. . . ."

"Jed and Stoney volunteered to spread their blankets in the cookhouse for the time being. Some of the outfit will soon be going to Texas for more cows. By the time they get back, we can have more cabins built. We'll need more room anyway, because we'll be hiring more riders. For right now, they all want you right where you are."

"They're all so nice," said Rosalie. "I didn't know there was so much kindness in all the world. When I'm able, I . . . I must do . . . something to earn my keep."

Brazos grinned. "I have something in mind, if you want the job."

"What is the job?" Penelope asked.

She didn't get an answer and she didn't understand their laughter, but they were all together and happy. That was all that mattered.

Benton McCaleb wasn't one to delay an unpleasant task. The day following his return, he spent a tense half hour with Monte Nance. It could go one of two ways. Monte could admit his mistake and yield to McCaleb's ultimatum, or he could hump his back and let his Nance pride make it unpleasant for them both. McCaleb did the talking, his eyes hard and unwavering. When he had finished, there were the same sparks in Monte's eyes he'd so often seen in Rebecca's. Slowly, Monte's anger faded and he grinned.

"You're a hard man, McCaleb, but by God, I wish my daddy had been just like you! You don't beat around the bush. I don't always like you, but I respect you."

Monte put out his hand and McCaleb took it, hoping the kid wouldn't backslide into some fool situation that would bring expulsion from the outfit down on his head.

Following McCaleb's set-to with Monte, he called the rest of the outfit together to hear his plans.

"Right after Christmas," said McCaleb, "soon as the weather permits, Will and Susannah will leave for Texas. Pen, Jed, Stoney, and Monte will be going, and Salty, you'll be taking the chuck wagon. Coming back, you'll be trailing up to five thousand steers, so you'll need to hire at least five more riders. Seven, if you can get them."

"But while we're gone," said Stoney, "that won't leave nobody here at the ranch but you, Brazos, and Goose."

"I'm coming to that," said McCaleb. "For the kind of spread we're building here, with trail drives into Dakota and Montana territories, we'll need twenty good riders. Before any of you leave for Texas, I aim to hire some riders. With the railroad, Abilene's become quite a cattle town, and I reckon I can find some Texas cowboys there needin' work. From Cheyenne, I can ride across the northeastern corner of Colorado and reach Abilene in a week. If all goes well, I ought to be back within two weeks with some hungry Texas cowboys. I aim to start in the morning. With Christmas comin' up in a couple of months, I reckon Salty ought to take the chuck wagon to Cheyenne and stock up. Brazos, why don't you ride with him?"

If nothing went wrong, it was four days to Cheyenne with the wagon. The makeshift road they'd cleared on the way in hadn't grown up enough to require more axe work, and that helped. It was a necessary trip in more ways than one.

It afforded McCaleb and Brazos an excellent chance to talk without interruption. McCaleb grinned when Brazos tossed him the gold nugget Penelope had taken from Kingston Henry.

"So that's why they don't want us on this end of the Sweetwater."

"I reckon you'll need this information now," said Brazos. "If Mr. Train gets us in Dutch because of our using the Shoshoni, you can always retaliate by having our friend Sam Colton publish the news and start a gold rush on the Sweetwater."

"The threat of one should be enough," said McCaleb. "Colton has a bad habit of letting his courage get in the way of his common sense. Just such a story could get him killed without helping us. We'll spend some time with Sam and let him talk, but not a word about gold on the Sweetwater. Not yet. By the way, what are you aimin' to get that little girl for Christmas? A doll?"

"Nope." Brazos grinned. "A pair of honest-to-goodness riding boots."

Late afternoon of the fourth day, they made camp just north of Cheyenne, on Lodge Pole Creek.

"I'll stay the night with you," said McCaleb, "and ride out for Abilene in the morning. I'd like to talk to Sam Colton tonight."

"While you're gone," said Brazos, "I aim to send Goose down the Sweetwater and maybe find out just how many men we're up against. If they keep hounding us, we'll have to go after them. There's a limit to how much of this scratchin' and clawin' I take before I start to bite back."

"I feel the same way," said McCaleb, "but for now, hold your fire, unless they strike first. Have Goose ride careful. Having their raid cut short by Shoshoni arrows, Duke's bunch might shoot an Indian on sight. Any Indian."

Just after dark, leaving Salty with the chuck wagon, McCaleb and Brazos rode into town. There was a light in Sam Colton's unimpressive little office, and they went in without knocking. Colton dragged his feet off the desk with a crash, almost upending the old swivel chair in which he sat.

"My God," Colton exclaimed, "am I glad to see you!"

"I reckon you've got some particular reason," said Mc-Caleb.

"You know damn well I have," said Colton. "Maury Duke showed up last Friday, claiming you sent out a band of hostile Indians and murdered three homesteaders. I asked for proof, something more than his word, and he stomped out. He fired off a wire to the papers in Omaha and Chicago, and my contact in Omaha's raising hell because I won't send him the story."

"Send it to him, then," said McCaleb. "Some night riders—six that we know of—rode in during a snowstorm and tried to burn us out. They made an attack on us, and three of them were killed. End of story."

"What about the Indians?"

"What Indians?" asked McCaleb innocently.

"You're saying there were no Indians?"

"I'm saying that's not the point," snapped McCaleb. "These bastards rode in throwing firebrands and shooting. We shot back, protecting our ranch and ourselves. Three of the attackers died. How they died, even if we chopped off their heads with axes, doesn't matter. What does matter is that they came after us. If you want to ask some questions, try these: what were those men doing on our claims, shooting at us and trying to burn our ranch buildings? Why are they determined to drive us away?"

"They're using talk about Indians, then," said Colton, "to try and get you in trouble with the Federals. Is that what you believe?"

"Don't you?"

"It had crossed my mind," said Colton, "but I can't say that. Damn it, McCaleb, I've got my own tail in a crack trying to keep yours out. What can I say in print?"

"Say this," said Brazos, "and it'll be the truth. There's not a hostile Indian within a hundred miles of our place. I helped bury the three men that died in the raid, and I can tell you there wasn't an arrow in any of them. Now if somebody wants proof, put him on a hoss and send him to the ranch. I'll personally put a shovel in his hands and show him where to dig."

"I can print that?"

"You can," said McCaleb, "and add this to it. Say that we know why this bunch along the Sweetwater wants rid of us. If there are more raids, they'll get a stronger dose of what they got the last time, and I'll personally release a story to the papers that'll blow the lid off the Sweetwater valley."

"My God," exclaimed Colton, "that's tough as whang leather!"

"I mean for it to be," said McCaleb. "Remember, you're printing my words, not yours. Don't put yourself out on a limb. This bunch isn't above riding in here and blowing your head off."

"You don't expect them to blow yours off?"

"I expect them to try," said McCaleb, "but I stomp my own snakes. Help me lure them out of their holes, but don't get bit."

They were almost back to the chuck wagon when McCaleb spoke.

"You made some tall claims, sayin' there were no arrows in those three hombres you and Will buried."

"With God as my witness, there wasn't," said Brazos with a grin. "Good old Will drove 'em on through, pulled 'em out and burned 'em all. Remember, his daddy's a fair to middlin' Texas lawyer, and some of it's rubbed off on Will. Said he wouldn't be a bit surprised if some Yankee blue bellies showed up with shovels, lookin' for those arrows."

McCaleb rode out before first light. Brazos and Salty were at Bullard's store when it opened for business.

"Salty," said Brazos, "you're the cook. You take care of the grub. I've got some other stuff to hunt for."

McCaleb might have been joking when he mentioned

Christmas, but Brazos was dead serious. He had enlisted the help of Rebecca and Susannah—secretly, of course—so that there might be a special holiday on Box Elder Creek. He would buy gifts for them all, and especially for Penelope. He doubted if she even knew what Christmas was, but after this she would. He topped it off with the boots she had asked for, and then bought a pair for Rosalie as well. He grinned to himself as he searched for something special for Goose. It was costing them, but not nearly as much as hiding out in Omaha would have. A lump rose in his throat when he remembered the first time he'd seen Penelope, and he bought an enormous supply of hard candy. He had found Rebecca and Susannah delightful accomplices. They had told him what to buy, but by grab, he would decide how much!

"I reckon," said Salty, "yer aimin' t' buy another wagon t' haul all that stuff. We got t' have grub fer that trip t' Texas."

"You also have to come right back through Cheyenne," said Brazos, "and you'll have an empty wagon. If you wasn't such an old grouch, I'd buy a Santa Claus suit and let you wear it Christmas day."

Brazos knew the old cook's weakness. He was forever feeding Penelope between meals, on the sly. While he seldom bought anything, even for himself, he had made an exception. He had bought a gift for Penelope.

Returning to Box Elder Creek, Brazos rode ahead, but always within sight of the chuck wagon. While the temperature dropped to near zero at night, the days remained fair. They reached Box Elder Creek on October 4.

The day following his return from Cheyenne, Brazos talked to Will, and the two of them spent some time with Goose. Brazos tore a page from a tablet, took a pencil and drew a sketch of their spread, of Box Elder Creek, and of the Sweetwater River to the west. He then tossed the gold nugget to Goose.

"*Oro,*" said Goose. "*Malo hombres.*"

"Numero malo hombres," said Brazos. He held up one finger, then two, finally extending them all.

Goose nodded. When he had ridden away, Will was the first to speak.

"I wish I'd known how to tell him to be careful without insulting him. If that bunch should catch him prowling around, they'll use him as an example to back up the foolish claims they've already made about us using hostile Indians."

"That's gospel," said Brazos. "I'd hate to think what might happen if they actually got their hands on Goose. I doubt that anything we could say or do would change anybody's mind. That Indian Affairs bunch in Washington wouldn't know a Lipan Apache from a Texas armadillo."

$\mathcal{M}$cCaleb found Abilene more interesting than Denver, although the Kansas town boasted only a few residences, barns, and stores. But the stockyards were alive with shuffling, bawling Texas longhorns, and a block west, surrounded by weed-grown vacant lots, stood the Drovers Cottage. It was the earliest and most famous of cattle-town hotels. Joe McCoy had built it in 1867, at a cost of $15,000, including lavish furnishings and an adjoining stable. The hotel was a wooden, boxlike structure, three stories high. It was forty by sixty feet, enclosing fifty spacious rooms, a bar, a restaurant, and a billiard room. The exterior was painted beige, and green-louvered shutters framed each of its windows. It fronted the railroad tracks, and there was a lengthy shaded veranda from which guests could watch trains arrive and depart. For the time and place, the Drovers Cottage was elegant. McCaleb took a room for the night.

Not being a drinking man, he disliked hanging around the saloons, but where else was he likely to find cowboys? There was simply nowhere else to go and nothing to do. He had seen everything Abilene had to offer within an hour, except the whorehouse. He picked three of the better saloons, and the Alamo was the most impressive. It had a forty-foot frontage on Texas Street, and was strung out for three times that distance along Cedar. There were two

entrances, the main one boasting three double-glass doors
that never closed. The bar was polished, brass-trimmed
mahogany, accented with brass rails and knee-high cuspi-
dors. Gambling tables offering faro, monte, and poker covered the entire floor. The Applejack and the Bull's Head
were considerably less impressive. There was a boardinghouse next to the Applejack, and he stopped to read a sign
that had been tacked to the front door:

> No more than five to a bed, and spurs must be
> took off.
> No razor grinders or tinkers on premises.
> No dogs allowed upstairs and no drunks in the
> kitchen.

Knowing no better place to begin, McCaleb pushed
through the batwings and into the Applejack. It was
crowded enough that the two bartenders didn't immediately spot him. He walked casually from one table to another, as though looking for someone. Cigar and cigarette
smoke hung like fog in the stale air, and brown splotches in
the sawdust attested to the total absence of spittoons. He
recognized at least two polished, professional gamblers.
No saloon was ever squalid enough to escape them.

He found the Bull's Head a little more to his liking, but
not much. The sawdust was cleaner and there were no
professional gamblers, but the patrons were anything but
Texas cowboys. Two tables had been pushed together, and
a dozen men sat slouched around a deck of cards and a
mess of bottles, empty or nearly so. They all wore Colts—
those with their backs to him, anyway—and most were tied
down. Bulges beneath their shirts at their middles attested
to the presence of second pistols. McCaleb waited until a
cowboy departed and followed him out. Once they were on
the boardwalk, McCaleb spoke.

"Pardner, I'm new in town. That dozen hombres camped
around that table, some of 'em look familiar. Got any idea
what outfit they're with?"

The stranger looked at him pityingly before he spoke.

"Friend, that's the Clary gang, what's left of 'em. Jack, Mitch, and Milo rode with Quantrell, and so did some of the others. The rest, so we hear, was with Bloody Bill Anderson. Hell's about to bust loose. Som'eres down the trail they stampeded somebody's herd, and two of the bunch, one of 'em brother Mitch, got strung up. The others, 'specially Milo and Jack, is layin' for the Texas outfit that done the hangin'. Was I you, I'd stay off the street and out of the saloons."

"No law, then," said McCaleb.

"Bible law. The law of the quick and the dead. You ain't quick, then you're dead."

McCaleb was returning to the Drovers Cottage when he witnessed the arrival of yet another herd of Texas cattle. He walked on down to the stockyards to watch the riders prod the steers into the pens. They wore a D-B connected brand, and McCaleb counted nine riders. The tenth—the trail boss or maybe the owner—had dismounted and stood next to the chuck wagon, talking to a Negro cook. McCaleb drew near and they became silent, watching him.

"I'm Benton McCaleb, Red River County, Texas."

"Dalt Bartholemew, from San Antone." He didn't offer his hand.

"I was with Goodnight on the first trail drive to Colorado," McCaleb said, "and more recently, some drives of my own, into Dakota Territory. I've never been through Indian Territory. Is it as bad as I've heard?"

"I've heard of you," said Bartholemew, relaxing a little. "Wasn't much Injun trouble. Damn rustlers. My boys strung up two of th' bastards. Th' others run like yellow coyotes."

"The Clary gang," said McCaleb, "and they're in the Bull's Head saloon, an even dozen of them. Word is, they're layin' for your outfit. One of the pair you hung was Mitch Clary."

"What's your stake in this?"

"Let's just say I don't like to see a Texas outfit walk into a den of sidewinders without warning," said McCaleb. "My business here is to try and hire riders for my spread in southern Wyoming. I'm of a mind to hire Texans, if I can. You aimin' to take all your riders home?"

"The Frenchies, the greasers, and the cook. The others, born an' bred Texans, just hired on for the drive. It's done."

Goose had ridden out long before dark, but darkness better suited his purpose. He reined up a dozen miles south and picketed his horse beneath a cottonwood in sight of the Sweetwater. It was pleasant for October, but come nightfall his buckskin shirt would not be sufficient. Not *all* white men's clothing was impractical; he fully appreciated the heavy mackinaw tied behind his saddle. He stretched out beneath the cottonwood on a carpet of dry leaves and chewed on a strip of jerky. He had enough of the tough, stringy beef to last seven suns. On his right hip, butt forward, he carried a Colt six-shooter, and a new seventeen-shot Winchester rode in his saddle boot. He had ammunition in plenty for both weapons, and on a rawhide thong around his neck was his treasured cuchilla. The big bowie hung down his back beneath the buckskin shirt, and he could have the lethal blade in either hand within seconds.

He pondered his mission. While he had become comfortable with some of the white man's ways, there were some he could not and would not accept. If the enemy attacked, burning and killing, then retaliation must be in like manner. The more unexpected and brutal, the better. There was no other way. Having seen the gold, Goose fully understood why the hombres along the river wanted McCaleb's outfit out of the eastern end of the Sweetwater valley. What he didn't understand was why, under cover of darkness, he couldn't slit their throats and be done with them. While he had some vague understanding as to the need of knowing the enemy's strength, what did it matter if there were ten or a hundred? Given the opportunity, he could dispatch them all, the darkness swallowing him before they knew of his presence. Except for those he rode with, white men were foolishly careless, placing little value on their lives. Perhaps it wasn't even worth counting coup on such men.

McCaleb had no trouble making the acquaintance of the five Texans. He waited until the herd had been tallied and penned, and he was there when Bartholemew gave each man his wages. Bartholemew told them McCaleb was seeking riders, but that was all. The rest was up to McCaleb.

"Come on," he said, once he had introduced himself and shook hands. "Supper's on me. I'm staying at the Drovers Cottage. It looks to have a better-than-average dining room. We can talk before and after we eat."

It was still early and they had the place practically to themselves. Once they had ordered their steaks and each had hot coffee, McCaleb spoke.

"Each of you tell me somethin' about yourselves. When you're done, I'll tell you about me, my outfit, and why I'm interested in you."

Laredo Perryman was a lanky young rider McCaleb judged to be a year or two shy of thirty. He had reddish-brown hair, brown eyes, and a ready grin. A scar trailed from the corner of his left eye to his jawbone. He seemed the self-appointed spokesman for the bunch, and took the lead.

"I'm from San Antone," he said. "Joined the Rangers when I was eighteen an' got starved out when Texas went broke. Spent near'bouts four years fightin' Injuns and outlaws, an' compared to that, trailin' cows is tame as grandma's quiltin' party. Me an' Charlie Tilghman was both there; he can tell you it was tough."

"I'm convinced," said McCaleb. "I was there myself. Charlie, are you kin to Bill Tilghman?"

"First cousin," said Charlie, "but I don't know if he'd claim me. Ain't much I can add to what Laredo's told you. I'm from south of San Antone too."

Tilghman was a wiry little man of not more than five-eight, and unless you were eyeball to eyeball with him, his gray eyes seemed as black as his hair. He reminded Mc-Caleb of Pendleton Rhodes, and like Pen, seemed to have some Indian in him. Since they had started clockwise around the table, McCaleb turned to the next man, Harley Irwin. Harley was an inch or two over six feet, with pale blue eyes and cornsilk-blond hair.

"I hail from Houston," he said. "Daddy never come home from the war, and Ma never got over that. The day I buried her, I pulled out for Galveston. Been to sea twice. Got shanghaied the first time and then went again on my own. I mostly fought pirates instead of Injuns and rustlers."

M. J. Cowley had deep brown eyes and wore a full black beard, similar to Charles Goodnight's. He reminded Mc-Caleb of Goodnight in other ways too. His arms and legs were like the trunks of trees, while there didn't seem to be an ounce of fat on him. He grinned and spoke.

"You don't want to know what the M. J. stands for. Just call me Cow. I'm from El Paso. My pa was at Goliad when we whupped Santa Ana. Might's well tell you I cashed in a gent in El Paso that wouldn't have it no other way an' was in bad need of it. His fam'ly owned the law an' more'n their share of everything else. I didn't have no choice. I shucked out, and I ain't been back."

McCaleb nodded and said nothing. It was a familiar story, and if the truth was known, might fit half the men in Texas. He turned to the fifth man, Benjamin "Badger" Waddell. He was maybe six feet, but seemed shorter and probably older than he actually was, because he was slightly stooped. His mild eyes were hazel and his hair was collar length and brown, matching his drooping moustache. His nose was flat, like it had been broken more than once.

"I'm just Badger," he said. "Nobody's ever called me anything else 'cept Ma, and she's dead. I started out prizefightin' in New Orleans. Done some wrasslin' too;

that's how I messed up my back. Reckoned I'd best give it up whilst I was ahead an' alive, so I took to wrasslin' cows."

McCaleb then told them of his own background up to and including the ranch on Box Elder Creek. But he didn't mention the possibility of gold on the Sweetwater. That could wait. Their food came and all conversation died until they had eaten. Laredo was the first to speak.

"You want riders with cow savvy that can pull a gun when there's a need for it. Men who'll fight for your outfit."

"That's it," said McCaleb. "If I'd hankered to be pushed around and told what to do, I'd have stayed in Texas with the carpetbaggers. I'm a peaceful man as long as I'm allowed to be. While I don't believe in startin' fights, I'm a believer in finishing them."

"That's kind of how we feel," said Charlie Tilghman. "I reckon you can say we finished one down the trail a ways. Bunch of rustlers stampeded our herd, and we strung two of 'em up. Damn shame we lost the others."

"You haven't lost them," said McCaleb. "There's an even dozen of them in the Bull's Head saloon. The Clary gang, from what I've heard, and one of the hoot owls you strung up was Mitch Clary. His brothers, Milo and Jack, aim to get even."

"Well, now," said Laredo, "that kind of throws a different light on the situation. You hirin' us before or after we show that bunch the error of their ways?"

"You're hired as of right now," said McCaleb, "if that suits you. Does it?"

"Depends on you," said Laredo, "and how big of a hurry you're in. Me, I purely refuse to slope out of here until I've accommodated them boys in the Bull's Head. Elsewise, there might be a misunderstanding. Somebody might get the idea I'm scared of them."

"Can't say I blame you," said McCaleb with a grin. "I've heard of misunderstandings like that. How do the rest of you feel?"

"Well," said Badger, "he didn't do the hangin' by his

lonesome. Anybody wantin' to fight with him is goin' to
end up fightin' with me. I'll side my friends to Hell an'
back. I ain't a man for trouble, but I'll die before I run, and
I'll gut-shoot any peckerwood that accuses me of it."

Loud and without reservation the others agreed. They
were exactly the kind of men McCaleb wanted, and when
they quieted, he spoke.

"In the morning, be ready to ride. I expect the Clarys
will be waiting."

"We'll get some beds for the night," said Laredo, "and
after that, a bath. Then maybe we'll give the Clarys a
chance to open the ball."

The first stars were out when Goose dismounted and made
his way to the cabin that had been Kingston Henry's. He
had left his horse distant enough so that the animal
wouldn't encourage a nicker from an unseen horse in the
log barn. If the cabin was deserted—and it seemed to be—
it followed that the barn would be empty as well. The
cabin's several windows were shuttered. He avoided the
steps, approaching the door from one end of the shallow
front porch. Standing to one side of the door, Goose
kicked it open. The cabin yielded nothing. Goose returned
to his horse, continuing downriver.

Maury Duke, Irv Vonnecker, and four other men sat
around the fire before Vonnecker's tent. Duke listened
sourly to their griping.

"I'm givin' it till spring," growled Vonnecker, "and then
I'm lightin' a shuck back to civilization. I don't care diddly
what Mister Big in Omaha thinks. He ain't settin' out here
on the backside of nowhere in the wind and the cold. This
ain't gonna be no bonanza, for the same reason Cherry
Creek wasn't. Th' gold's too spotty. Sure, there's a few
decent nuggets, but damn few. Just like it was on Cherry
Creek in 'fifty-eight. They built a town around a diggin's
that ended up payin' a man seventy cents a day."

"He's talkin' sense, Duke," said another man. "What if

the gold does play out? We was to be paid for provin' up these claims. They ain't gonna be worth a damn if there ain't no gold."

Cautiously, Duke put down his tin cup and reached for his Colt.

"Quiet," he hissed. "Somebody's out there!"

Goose froze and waited. While he didn't understand all their words, the tone of Duke's voice—edged with caution —told him much. Slowly he backed away, lest his foot dislodge another stone. He had been clumsy as a squaw! He returned to his horse and rode on, crossing the Sweetwater to the north bank.

"Get your horses," said Duke. "I still think somebody's scoutin' us. We got nothin' better to do, and I say let's ride downriver to Tanner's place. If there's anybody ahead of us, them hounds of his will sound off."

Goose reined up, uneasy. He lived and rode with white men, but the old ways, the ways of his people, were still part of him. Omens, bad medicine, manifested themselves in many ways. Such as the untimely rattle of a stone in the quiet of the night. Turning treacherous, the wind shifted, coming from the northeast. Sound traveled far at night, and it might betray those who pursued him. But it would also betray him to the unknown enemy somewhere ahead, his own movement riding the wind. The rattling stone. The shifting wind. Bad medicine. Despite his misgivings, he kneed his horse forward, only to be brought up short by a new sound. Somewhere ahead, even against the wind, there was the ominous baying of hounds.

"I told you!" shouted Duke excitedly. "There was somebody sneakin' around. Tanner's hounds have scented him. Fan out! Some of you cross the river, and cut him down when he runs for it!"

Goose wheeled his horse and guided the animal into the river. It was his only chance to evade the eager noses of the dogs. But that was a lesser danger. The baying of the approaching hounds would alert the six men who had gathered before the tent. He had no doubt they were coming. While the river was shallow enough not to impede his progress, there was no way of lessening the noise. It would draw them to him.

"He's in the river!" a voice shouted. "Gun him down!"

Slugs cut the overhanging willows. Goose flattened himself on the neck of his horse and sent the animal scrambling up the north bank, only to be met with a new burst of firing. They were boxing him from the north and the south while the hounds approached from behind! A slug stung the horse and the animal reared, nickering in pain. Goose had but one chance. He snatched his Winchester from the boot, dropped to the ground and slapped the horse on the rump. They would know at the ranch that his medicine had gone bad when the horse returned. If the horse survived the continuing gunfire.

Stoney was up before daylight, taking a necessary trip outside, when he found the blood-smeared, riderless horse.

"Dear God," cried Rebecca, "they've killed Goose!"

"Dead or alive," said Brazos grimly, "we're going after him. Pen, Jed, and Stoney, you'll ride with me. Bring an extra horse for Goose."

16

*T*he Drovers Cottage offered hot water and clean towels, but McCaleb doubted his new hands would avail themselves to the convenience. While they might have preferred a hotel bath, shying away from the town's barbershop and bathhouse might have been taken as an act of cowardice. But this Clary gang was only a temporary inconvenience. These five Texans were men with the bark on, armed and capable of defending themselves, but many a good man had been shot in the back from the darkness. They took second-floor rooms, and McCaleb was waiting for them when they returned to the lobby.

"Too early for bed," said McCaleb. "Mind if I mosey along with you?"

It was his way of siding them without seeming to, and they all knew it. It was a subtle thing. The quickest way to insult a Texan was to imply that he couldn't stand up to and overcome any adversary that walked, crawled, or flew.

"Come on," said Laredo. "Once we're cleaned up, barbered, and lookin' as close to human as we're likely to, we'll have us a look at this Alamo saloon."

"I'm comin' back here," said Harley Irwin, "and beat Cow at billiards. He's the only cowboy in Texas that ever lost his whole damn pile at the billiard table."

"I ain't quite figgered out how you're doin' it," said Cow,

"but you got to be cheatin'. Someday I'll get a handle on it an' have to gut-shoot you."

Once they were bathed and had their "ears lowered," they were quite an impressive bunch. Like most cowboys, they wore their hair short.

"Where I come from," said Badger, "nobody trusted a feller with hair down over his ears. Years back, when folks was more tolerant an' foolish, they didn't always hang cow thieves. They'd just whack off the upper third of his ear so's everbody knowed he was a thief. Them as had their ears cut took to wearin' their hair long, so's nobody knowed they'd been caught stealin'. I knowed one ol' boy that was caught twice, an' each time, they lopped off one of his ears. He allus wore his hair long to cover 'em. Third time they caught him with a runnin' iron, they hung the bastard. Plumb reformed him. He never stole another cow."

Two abreast, they walked the several blocks to the Bull's Head saloon.

"There's a back door," said McCaleb. "Want me to cover you from there?"

"I'd be obliged," said Laredo. "Badger, you and Charlie go with him. Pull your irons as you need to, but let me take the lead."

McCaleb waited until Laredo stepped through the bat-wings at the front before entering at the back. Badger and Charlie were right behind him. The Clarys, whether by reputation or presence, had all but emptied the Bull's Head. The four men at the bar hastily moved to the farthest end from the Clary table. The bartender froze, bottle half tilted over an empty glass. The Clary table was still a mess of empty and near empty bottles, but the playing cards were no longer in evidence. Laredo spoke.

"You Clarys listen up. Down the trail a ways, a bunch of thievin', lowdown coyotes stampeded our herd, the D-B connected. We hung two of the scurvy bastards, and we got the word the rest of the gang aims to do something about it. You men, besides the Clarys, are you ready to die over a Clary grudge?"

Laredo paused for effect. He continued in the dead silence.

"In the morning, at dawn, we'll meet you by the tracks, beyond the water tank. If there's a man among you wantin' satisfaction, with the guts to face me, let that man be there. My boys will side me, and any man pullin' his iron out of order won't ever do it again. If you don't show in the morning, all bets are off. We'll gun you down whenever and wherever we find you."

One of the gang laughed, and the glass in his hand exploded in his face. Laredo holstered his Colt. Nobody else laughed or made a sound. Laredo backed out of the saloon; McCaleb, Badger, and Charlie eased out the back door; and they all met on the boardwalk in front of the place.

Goose had been pistol-whipped, and it was near dawn before he became aware of his surroundings. The cabin was dark, its floor dirt, and when he moved there was the rattle of chains. He was in leg irons. From the short chain restricting his ankles, there was a longer one, its other end anchored to the log wall. His hands had been bound behind him with wet rawhide, and it had cut into his flesh as the thongs dried. He heard voices.

"We should of killed the bastard," growled Vonnecker. "He shot Tanner, killed one of the hounds, an' near'bout gutted Manson with that bowie. He won't live to see daylight."

"Just be damn glad you didn't kill him," said Duke. "This Indian's goin' to Omaha, and he's goin' there alive. We're tryin' to get them Texans in trouble with the Federals for mistreating Indians, and then we show up with a dead one. Smart, Vonnecker. Real smart."

"Maybe smarter than you," snapped Vonnecker. "This ain't no ordinary Injun. He was totin' a new Colt six-shooter, a new Winchester, and wearin' a white man's coat.

He's part of that Texas outfit. When his hoss shows up without him, you think that ain't gonna bring the others on the run?"

"Let 'em come," said Duke. "Just be waitin' with your guns. Time they get here, I'll be well on my way to the railroad. I'll have this Indian on the train and headed for Omaha before they know where he is. This story'll fit what the papers have already printed. They'll eat this up!"

With Pen leading an extra horse for Goose, they rode hard, knowing that if the Indian still lived, seconds might count. When they reined up to rest the horses, Brazos spoke.

"One of these hombres has a still and a makeshift saloon in a tent. I reckon they'll have cabins or tents strung out for miles along the river. We don't know how far Goose rode before they caught him, so we've got a job ahead of us. They'll expect us to trail him, and may set up an ambush."

"Let's just grab one of these gents," said Stoney. "I'd bet my saddle Pen can persuade him to tell us what they done with Goose."

"First we find that tent saloon," said Brazos. "There's bound to be some of 'em gathered there."

"Let me do the honors," said Pen. "Remember, I'm part Injun myself. I'll snatch us one of these *buzardos,* and he'll sing like a mockingbird."

The wind was out of the northwest and soon brought them the smell of wood smoke and of cooking meat. They reined up and dismounted. Lifting his hand in silent farewell, Pen faded into an oak thicket. In less than an hour he was back. A man stumbled ahead of him, hands bound behind his back, Pen's bandanna stuffed in his mouth.

"Found this jigger at the still," said Pen. He took his Bowie and cut the captive's bonds, then removed the gag. Brazos, Jed, and Stoney waited.

"Mister," said Pen softly, "we're lookin' for an Indian friend of ours; what's been done with him?"

"Go to hell," snarled Vonnecker. "If I knew, I wouldn't tell you."

"It's you that'll be goin' to hell if you don't tell me," said Pen. "I don't carry this *cuchilla* to pick my teeth."

When Vonnecker said nothing, Pen took a fistful of the man's shirt and hoisted him to his toes. Like a surgeon, with the point of the Bowie he made an incision from Vonnecker's whiskered chin to his Adam's apple. Blood dripped on Pen's fist, and Vonnecker eyed it in fascinated horror. Despite the near-zero temperature, sweat beaded his face.

"Talk," said Pen, "or you get the full Injun treatment. I'll drop your britches and whack off some parts you'd purely hate to lose."

"No," choked Vonnecker. "I'll—I'll talk."

Pen let go of Vonnecker's shirt but kept the Bowie at the man's throat. Vonnecker swallowed hard and spoke.

"They're takin' him . . . Duke took him . . . to th' railroad. Aims to . . . to . . . take him to Omaha."

"Duke and who else," Brazos demanded, "and how long have they been gone?"

"Duke an' three others," said Vonnecker. "Left before first light."

"He must know when the train's comin'," said Stoney.

"Tell us," said Pen. "When is the train going to be there, and where along the line will they wait for it?"

"I dunno," cried Vonnecker desperately. "Duke never tells us nothin'. I heard him say somethin' about Bridger Pass once, but that's all. Honest to God, I don't know nothin' else."

"I reckon he ain't smart enough to lie," said Pen. "Why don't I slit his throat so's he don't tell that we've been here?"

"Turn him loose," said Brazos. "I want them to know we've been here."

Pen backed away, and Brazos faced the still trembling Vonnecker.

"Mister," said Brazos, "it's goin' to be downright unhealthy along the Sweetwater from here on. If we ever have to come here again—for any reason—don't you be here. When we ride out of here, don't you even think of comin' after us. You do, and it'll be your last ride. *Comprender?*"

Without a word, Vonnecker stumbled away.

"Mount up," said Brazos, "and let's ride. We have to catch a train."

Brazos tried to remember the Union Pacific route from the railroad map on Sam Colton's wall. The rails actually passed a dozen miles to the north of Bridger Pass, paralleling the old Overland Stage route. This long northern curve, just before the tracks crossed the North Platte River, would be the closest point at which Duke could board a train. The man had ridden the returning work train into Cheyenne often enough that he must have some idea when the train would reach the curve above Bridger Pass. The train, pulling flat cars laden with rails and ties, usually passed through Cheyenne during the night and returned the following day. How long Duke must wait—and how much time they had—depended on where end-of-track was and how long it took the train to return. Brazos estimated they had at least a seventy-mile ride, and that Duke had more than an hour's start.

There was no opportunity for Goose to escape. The chain hadn't been long enough for them to use the leg irons, but once Goose was mounted, Duke had taken a length of rope and bound his ankles together under the belly of the horse. Again they rawhided his hands behind his back. There was a rider to his right and another to his left, each with a lariat looped about his saddle horn and the other end knotted about the Apache's neck. Maury Duke and the fourth rider brought up the rear, each armed with a rifle.

Goose rode with a heavy heart. He knew he had been kept alive for some reason, and from the direction they took, he suspected their destination was the endless road on which the iron horse ran. He knew, having spent a night in the Santa Fe jail, that white men had prisons, and he believed the iron horse would deliver him to such a place. He had little hope that his horse had returned to the ranch. If it had, long before his friends discovered where he had been taken, the iron horse would have taken him far beyond their reach. Better he should die. If he made a break, kicked the horse into a run, they might be forced to shoot him.

Making good on Laredo's promise, McCaleb and his five new riders left the hotel at the gray of first light. They walked away from town, beyond the water tank, and waited for a while alongside the empty railroad track.

"I wanted to put this grudge fight behind us," said Laredo, "but I should have known they wouldn't have the guts to face us."

"I ain't fussy," said Cow. "We can kill th' bastards just as quick out on th' plains as we could have here at th' depot."

"Not if they cut us down from ambush," said Harley.

"They'll have an edge," said McCaleb, "only if they're ahead of us. I'd say we're in for a storm. From the look of those thunderheads, when it hits us, there may be rain for the rest of the day. We'll wait for the storm, and then we'll ride out. This bunch of coyotes won't know the direction we're taking. Even if they figure that out, shootin' in a driving rain will be tough. We'll ride hard, gaining as many miles as we can, while the storm covers us. When the storm lets up, if this pack of damn fools is still thinkin' of an ambush, still trailin' us, then we'll have a surprise for them."

"McCaleb," said Laredo, "I'm goin' to like working for you. You still think like a Ranger, and out here, that keeps a man alive."

Pausing to rest the horses, Brazos told the others of his thoughts.

"They won't expect us this close behind them, but they'll be watching their back trail. We'll have to ride farther east and double back. Last thing we want is a standoff. They'll just kill Goose."

"If they're smart," said Pen, "they'll pick an open stretch of track so's it's nigh impossible to catch them by surprise."

"I doubt we'll overtake them before they're aboard the train," Brazos said, "and that's another reason we're bearing to the east. I want to get ahead of that train, and even if they beat us there, I've got one more ace to play."

"Can't be much farther," said Stoney. "We still have time."

Almost immediately he was proven wrong. Somewhere to the west of them there was the low, mournful whistle of a locomotive.

Maury Duke had chosen a straight stretch of track that would allow the engineer plenty of time to stop. The trainmen resented his flagging them down, and he took sadistic pleasure in doing so. Within sight of the track, Duke reined up and turned to his men.

"Palmer, once the train gets here, you'll take the horses back to camp. Burke, you and Devins will ride the caboose with this Indian. I'll be in the cab with the engineer, keepin' an eye on the track ahead. I won't rest easy until we're past Cheyenne."

"Why can't Burke or Devins take the horses back?" growled Palmer. "I got as much right to go to Omaha as they have. I been stuck in this god-forsaken country fer months."

"Damn it," bawled Duke, "I said take the horses back to camp!"

There was an uneasy silence. More and more they had begun to question his authority. Duke turned his back on them and missed the look that passed between Burke and Devins. Palmer had booted his rifle, and his right hand rested just inches above the butt of his Colt. But the tension was broken by the whistle of the oncoming train.

17

*B*razos reined up. Despite the nearness of the train, they had to rest the horses. The others drew up abreast of him.

"We ain't gonna catch 'em before they stop the train," said Jed. "You'd best play that last ace."

"I aim to," said Brazos. "We're close to where the railroad crosses the Medicine Bow Mountains. There should be an almighty steep grade where a trotting horse can keep ahead of the train, and it's got to slow down for what I'm plannin' to do. We're going to find us a cut bank along that upgrade where me, Jed, and Stoney can drop off on that train. Pen, you stay with the horses, and once the train's past, follow us. Jed, you and Stoney will take opposite ends of that caboose and get the drop on Duke's men. If they force it, shoot. Once we're over the hump and on the downgrade, when there's enough slack in the coupling, I aim to free that caboose from the rest of the train. Once we reach the bottom of the grade, the train will pull away from us. That'll be time enough for Pen to get to us with our horses and for us to ride out before they find the caboose missing and backtrack. Once the train arrives, I'm countin' on Duke sending all their horses back to camp, leaving them no way to follow us. Now let's ride!"

Maury Duke stood on the track waving his hat, and for a horrified moment he thought the engineer wasn't going to stop. Duke was about to run for his life when the big loco-motive began to slow. The man had purposely baited him, and Duke was furious. The engineer put his head out the cab window and Duke had to shout to make himself heard above the hissing and chuffing of the locomotive.

"We're going to Omaha with you," he yelled.

"Peterson, the brakeman, is in the caboose," shouted the engineer, without a sign of enthusiasm or friendliness. "There ain't room for five more."

"Just three," shouted Duke. "Two of my boys and the Indian. I'll ride up front with you."

"Regulations say you ain't allowed in the cab," snapped the engineer.

"This says I am," snarled Duke, jacking a shell into the chamber of his Winchester. "Now, you back off, or I can arrange to make this your last run. Burke, you and Devins get that Indian into the caboose and put the irons on him."

Rifle under his arm, Duke caught the stanchion and hoisted himself up the iron-runged ladder into the cab. Their lariats still around Goose's neck, Burke and Devins led him past half a dozen empty flat cars to the caboose.

The whistle sounded, much closer. The brush-shrouded cut bank was there, but the grade wasn't nearly as steep as Brazos had hoped for. But it would have to do. Time had run out. The engineer had taken advantage of a long, flat stretch of track to build a head of steam for the climb up the western flank of the Medicine Bow mountain range. Brazos, Jed, and Stoney stood poised on the brink of the cut as the train roared closer and closer. Each knew the odds. Miscalculation could cost Goose his life, and they might break their necks to boot.

"I'll drop on the next-to-last flatcar ahead of the ca-boose," said Brazos. "Stoney, you and Jed jump when the last flatcar's under you. That'll bring you down on top of the caboose. Good luck."

Brazos came down on the rough oak floorboards of the second flatcar ahead of the caboose. He held his breath as

Jed and Stoney made their leap, almost too late. The iron railing encircling the roof of the caboose was all that saved them.

The grade became more intense, and the train's momentum lessened. Jed and Stoney, recovering their wind, had swung down the iron ladders at either end of the caboose. Jed grinned at Brazos. Colt in hand, he opened the door and stepped inside. Stoney came in the door at the opposite end. There was a small cast-iron stove near the rear of the caboose and a hard bench ran along either wall. Goose lay on the floor. Devins sat on one bench and Burke on the other. Peterson, the brakeman, sat on the bench with Devins, but as far away as he could get.

"Don't nobody move," warned Jed.

Burke's Winchester was cocked and ready, but he wasn't fast enough. Stoney put a .44 slug in his shoulder and Burke's shot blasted a hole through the roof of the caboose. Devins slowly lifted his hands.

"Put the rifles down," said Stoney. "Then take them pistols out and drop 'em at your feet. Do it slow."

Burke had already dropped his Winchester. He clutched his right shoulder with his left hand, blood dripping through his fingers. Slowly he reached his left hand to the butt of his Colt and dropped the weapon at his feet. Devins followed. Peterson's face was chalk-white and his raised hands trembled.

"I ain't got a gun," he stammered. "I'm just the brakeman."

"See that you go on just bein' the brakeman," said Jed. "Now one of you cough up the key to them leg irons and let the Indian loose."

Nobody moved. Jed's Colt spoke once, and the lobe of Devins's left ear vanished, leaving a bloody smear.

"I ain't got the key!" he squalled.

Jed turned to the cowering Burke.

"Then it must be you," he said. "You got maybe ten seconds before I put some lead in your other shoulder."

"I can't," whined Burke. "Duke will kill me."

"I'll kill you if you don't," snapped Jed.

Burke eased his bloody left hand into his pocket and came out with the key. Jed wagged his Colt at Devins.

"Take the key and unlock them irons. When you've done that, free his hands. Move!"

Freed, Goose rolled away and got shakily to his feet. He retrieved the Colt and Winchester, his own, which Devins had dropped. He slammed Devins against the wall, removing his Bowie from the man's belt. Meanwhile, the train had begun its descent, the downgrade taking the pressure off the iron couplings. Brazos stood between the empty flat and the caboose, struggling with the huge iron coupling pin that would separate the cars. Suddenly it gave, and the caboose continued as part of the train only because of gravity and the downgrade. Once the track leveled, the caboose would be left behind. Brazos stepped through the door into the caboose.

"We got a few minutes," he said, "before this thing slows down enough to let us off. These gents are so almighty fond of leg irons, let's give 'em a dose of what they gave Goose. You boys get down on the floor. We're goin' to send you to Omaha in style."

Jed and Stoney kept their Colts handy. Brazos locked one of the manacles to Burke's left ankle and wrapped the chain around the iron leg of the bench, which was a solid piece of iron extending up from the floor. He then locked the second manacle to Devins's right ankle. Neither man could pass beneath the squat iron bench. The caboose began to slow.

"The train's left us," said Stoney.

"Let's go, then," said Brazos. "Sooner or later they'll discover their caboose is gone. They can back up and get it, but Duke can't come after us without horses."

"Here comes ol' Pen with ours," said Jed, chuckling.

"Gents," said Pen admiringly, when he had reined up a few minutes later, "that was as slick a piece of work as I ever seen. Welcome home, *Ganos.*"

* * *

When the storm roared in, McCaleb led out. The rain came down in blinding gray torrents. Looking back, McCaleb could barely see the rider behind him. They stopped only to rest the horses. It was late afternoon before the rain began to slack. On his way to Abilene, a day west of the town, McCaleb had crossed a creek that had eaten deep into the plain, leaving overhanging banks. The stream was now a roaring brown torrent, but beneath the west bank there was an almost flat outcropping of rock. It was shelter, although the lapping water was only inches away.

"This ledge may be underwater before long," said Mc-Caleb, "but it'll get us out of the wind and give us a chance to eat. If there's anything that'll burn, let's brew some coffee. We'll have to douse the fire before dark."

"Might as well call it a day," said Laredo. "Even them damn fool Clarys won't ride in the dark."

"We'll keep watch in pairs," said McCaleb, "so we can all get some sleep. Come first light, we'll have a look at our back trail."

There was excitement on Box Elder Creek when Goose returned. Penelope ran to the Apache and caught up one of his hands. Goose was uncomfortable with all the attention. He could stand anything except somebody fussing over him. Rosalie was up and about. So was Monte. He seemed let down because so much had happened without him. The second day after their return, Will had a suggestion.

"We'd ought not to waste these fair days. When Bent shows up with more riders, we'll be needin' more cabins. I say let's get 'em started now."

Maury Duke was furious. When they had discovered the caboose missing, and the reason for it, the trainmen had laughed at him. It had been a real temptation to shoot them. Instead, he contented himself with abusing Burke and Devins. Since there was no longer any reason for them to go to Omaha, they quit the train at Cheyenne. Or Maury

Duke did. The trainmen had to find a blacksmith to free the unfortunate Burke and Devins, for Jed had kept the key to the leg irons. The train was delayed in Cheyenne for nearly two hours, attracting attention all the while. A normal stop was but a few minutes, long enough to water the thirsty engine. Sam Colton talked to the work train's crew while Maury Duke ground his teeth in frustration and anger. He hated Sam Colton anyway, because the newspaperman hadn't been gullible enough to swallow the lies Duke had fed the other papers. Now Colton, damn him, was grinning at Duke, and it was almost more than he could stand. But the worst was yet to come. Finally freed from their prison, he was confronted by Burke and Devins.

"By God," snarled the wounded Burke, "I wouldn't spend another day, not even another hour, with you, for all the damn land in Wyoming."

"Me neither," growled Devins, "and if I don't see some hard cash pronto, I'll spill my guts to anybody that'll listen, startin' with this Sam Colton."

Duke would have loved nothing more than to have gut-shot the both of them, but they had attracted too much attention, and his angry confrontation with them had been witnessed by too many people, including Sam Colton. To prevent a total collapse of his shaky empire, he was forced to go to the bank and withdraw two thousand dollars from his own account. It was money lost to him. George Francis Train didn't pay for failure.

18

The new day dawned clear, the October sun warm. The Kansas plains were virtually flat, and McCaleb had to ride several miles before finding a rise from which he could observe their back trail. At first he saw nothing but the early morning haze. Then a tiny speck appeared and was gone again. He waited for it to appear a second time, and when it did, he wheeled his horse and rode back to his outfit.

"One rider," McCaleb told them, "but the others will be near enough to hear a shot. We've got to eliminate that advance rider without shooting him. I can do it, unless one of you prefer the honor."

"Charlie Tilghman's mostly Injun," said Laredo. "Charlie, find you a good place along the back trail, and kill that *pelado*. Do it quiet."

"A lobo wolf couldn't have tracked us through that storm," said Harley. "They got to be ridin' blind; they left a man in town to see what direction we took."

"Long as they've got their advance man's tracks ahead of them," said McCaleb, "they won't expect us. Somewhere beyond where Charlie waylays him, we'll set up an ambush and gun down the rest of them."

Jack Clary saw nothing ahead but trackless plain. When he approached an oak thicket, his eyes swept it but saw noth-

ing to arouse his suspicion. He skirted it, and the only
warning he had was the hiss of a lariat. Before he could
wheel his horse, the loop dropped over his shoulders, pin-
ning the upraised barrel of his Winchester. The rope went
taut and Jack Clary was dragged from his saddle, landing
flat on his back with a bone-jarring thud. The last thing he
saw was the swiftly descending blade of Tilghman's Bowie.

Riding wide, careful to leave Jack Clary's solitary set of
tracks undisturbed, McCaleb and his riders rode a mile
beyond the thicket where Tilghman had waylaid Jack
Clary. They found a "wet weather" stream where the water
had already subsided to a trickle. Its eastern bank was
chest high on a man, and it was from here they would
ambush the outlaws. When the riders finally appeared,
there were only eight, and they rode two abreast.

"They lost three men," said Badger. "Our little party at
th' saloon wasn't all for nothin'."

"Wait till they're within forty to fifty yards," said Laredo.

They hunkered down behind the creek bank, and when
Laredo gave the sign, they raised their rifles and began
firing. Four riders went down with the first volley. The others frantically wheeled their horses and lit out back the way
they had come. But the fire was deadly, and McCaleb's
outfit emptied two more saddles.

"Let's git our horses," shouted Cow, "an' ride down
them last two!"

"They're not worth the killing of our horses," said
Laredo. "They won't be bothering us. Let's ride; we've got
work in Wyoming!"

McCaleb and his five riders rode into Cheyenne on October 19, 1868.

"No hotel yet," said McCaleb, "but there's a boardinghouse. It's late in the day, so we'll stay the night. It's a
chance to grain our horses and get ourselves a couple of
hot meals before riding on to the ranch. There's some business I need to take care of too."

The "business" was Sam Colton, and McCaleb walked into the shabby little office unannounced. Colton again had his feet on his desk, and removed them in his usual clumsy manner.

"You never give a man any warning, do you, McCaleb?"

"Didn't know you needed any," said McCaleb, grinning. "You had your feet on that desk when I last saw you two weeks ago. You haven't moved since then?"

"Once or twice." He chuckled, his good humor returning. "I wasn't looking to see you so soon. Not after what you pulled last week."

"I left for Abilene the morning after I last saw you," said McCaleb, "and I just got back. What am I supposed to have done now?"

With obvious relish, Colton repeated the story the trainmen had told him. He chuckled delightedly as he recounted Duke's exasperation and fury when the entire town became aware that a pair of Duke's men were chained in the caboose.

McCaleb chuckled. "Sounds like a slick piece of work, but it didn't have to be us. You charge everything that happens around here to me."

"You Texans have a style all your own, McCaleb. I admire men with guts. But you've made some powerful enemies. They're going to put you on the outs with the Federals, and you'll end up fighting with their weapons, not yours. Do you think they care a damn about the well-being of the Indians? They're just using the Indian situation to build a gallows to hang you. In just a few days, Ulysses S. Grant will be elected president of the United States. I think, once he takes office and the people behind him take the reins, you, my friend, are going to be in trouble."

"I've done nothing to justify that kind of attention," said McCaleb. "You say Grant's going to be president, but somebody else will be running the country, and it's this 'somebody else' that's comin' down on me."

"That's it," said Colton. "Grant's a nice enough fellow, and a hero of sorts, but that's all. He's on the ticket not because he's qualified, but because he can be manipulated and led. I know you're just a cowboy, McCaleb, and maybe you don't fully understand the uniqueness of your situation. You have, in your own way, put the hurt on some high-ups who are engaged in defrauding the United States of America. They're prepared to destroy you before you destroy them. While I've respected your need for secrecy, I know there's some connection between the situation in the Sweetwater valley and the Credit Mobilier. I have no facts, but I have my suspicions."

McCaleb had been standing. He sat on one corner of Colton's desk and kicked the toe of his boot against Colton's swivel chair. Making up his mind, he spoke.

"Sam, when it's time to tell the secret of Sweetwater valley, you'll be the first to get the story. Right now, it's my ace in the hole. I think it can serve two purposes. First, I intend to use it to counter any moves the Federals make in regards to this Indian situation. Before I'm done, I aim to go after this tall dog in the brass collar and force him out of the Sweetwater valley and off those claims along the Sweetwater River."

"McCaleb," said Colton, grinning, "I've never met another man like you. You honest-to-God believe you can fight the Federals and win. The hell of it is, you've got me believing it too."

McCaleb purposely took his new riders to Bullard's store and bought a supply of ammunition they didn't really need. Word would get around. They rode out of Cheyenne at noon, armed with Colts and repeating rifles, Texans all. They reached Box Elder Creek on October 21, to find that three new cabins were all but completed. Suppertime found both the long tables full.

"This place," said Salty with satisfaction, "is fin'lly takin' on th' look of an honest-t'-God cow ranch."

"It's about all the ranch we can handle," said McCaleb, "once we get a new herd from Texas in the spring. Soon as Will and his riders return with the herd, I aim to take a drive into the gold fields of Montana Territory. That'll empty our range, except for the steers comin' from Texas."

Once Maury Duke had paid off Burke and Devins, and was satisfied they'd left town, he got a horse and saddle at the livery and rode back to the Sweetwater. How had that Texas outfit gotten on his trail so fast? Somebody had talked, and he'd give them hell for that. But Duke had a surprise awaiting him. Vonnecker's old tent was still there, its patched gray bulk seeming more forlorn than ever. The fire was long dead. The old carpetbag in which Vonnecker had kept his few belongings was gone, and so was Vonnecker. His rage diluted by unease, Duke rode on downriver to Tanner's place. He found Tanner limping around in a foul mood, his wounded thigh still unhealed.

"I dunno where Vonnecker went," he said irritably, "an' I purely don't give a damn. I just wisht he'd of offered me a chanct to of rode with 'im."

"Where's Palmer?"

"How'n hell should I know?" snarled Tanner. "Some no-account Injun kilt one of my dogs, an' near kilt me. I'm stuck here a hunnert miles from th' nearest doc, an' you expect me t' wet nurse this miserable outfit whilst you ride off t' Omaha."

Duke rode away in disgust. He had trusted Vonnecker. He didn't seem the kind to just ride out, not without demanding money. Even Burke and Devins had that much sand. His next thought was so startling, he reined up his horse and just sat there mulling it over, not wanting to accept it. The money Duke had in the bank was what Train had paid him. Not daring to redeem so much gold, Duke had stashed it beneath a stone in his fireplace. Vonnecker, the bastard, had known it was somewhere in the cabin. His mind in a turmoil of fear and fury, Maury Duke kicked his horse into a gallop.

McCaleb, knowing the fair weather wouldn't last, put the final days of October to good use.

"The snow's coming," he said, "and we can't have too much firewood. We're all going to become woodcutters as long as the weather holds."

They saw or heard nothing more of Maury Duke or his men, but McCaleb took no chances. From dusk to dawn he kept a pair of sentries on watch. The second day of November, they were engulfed in a blizzard that lasted four days. The longhorns huddled along Box Elder Creek, their tails to the wind.

"Come summer," said McCaleb, "we're going into the valleys where the grass is belly deep to a horse and cut hay for winter feeding. Fifteen hundred head, which is what we have now, wouldn't wipe us out if we lost them all. But next winter there may be three times that many."

"That calls for wagons and hay sheds," said Will.

"Some of us will ride to Cheyenne in the spring," said McCaleb, "and get a couple of wagons. Those of you who are going to Texas this winter will get to spend next summer here, cutting hay and putting up some sheds."

"You purely know how to take the joy out of a trip to Texas," said Jed, sighing.

Since Will Elliot was to be in charge of the trip to Texas and the drive back to Wyoming, McCaleb left it to him as to when they would depart. But one blizzard followed another, and the temperature hovered near zero. Existing snow froze, and was deepened almost daily until mid-December.

"We'll spend Christmas right here," said Will, "and with the first break in the weather, we'll go."

It was bitter cold. To everybody's surprise and relief, Goose finally shared a cabin with Monte, compromising by ignoring the bunk and sleeping on the floor. Brazos rode out, accompanied by Penelope, and cut a young fir. Using horseshoe nails, Brazos put feet on it, and they made a place for the tree in the cookhouse. On Christmas eve the sky cleared. It was eerily beautiful, with the stars and a pale quarter moon looking down on an endless expanse of unbroken snow. In the warmth and cheer of the cook-house, they gathered around the unadorned tree and sang the old songs, fondly and dimly remembered from child-hood.

When they arose on that Christmas day, 1868, the wind seemed almost warm and the sky was a cloudless blue. Although they had five new riders, Brazos had foreseen that and had bought accordingly. There were gifts for each of them, and an abundance for Penelope. The gift Salty had bought turned out to be a tiny golden heart on a slen-der chain. She embarrassed the old cook with a hug, and immediately stomped into her new boots. She clomped about, as Laredo put it, "like an old cow on a wooden bridge."

The clear days and nights continued. The temperature rose, and on the last day of December, Will and Susannah led out. Salty followed with the chuck wagon. Behind him rode Monte, Pen, Jed, and Stoney. The return to Texas had begun. In the spring they would head the herd, five thou-sand strong, north to Fort Dodge, to Ogallala, to Chey-enne. Along the Western trail.

When Will and his outfit had gone, McCaleb went to the cookhouse for a cup of coffee. It seemed strangely empty without Salty. Rebecca and Rosalie came in. Rebecca spoke.

"You sent Salty to Texas, leaving us without a cook, so we took things into our own hands. This is Salty's replace-ment, with his blessing."

"It's something I can do, something I want to do," said Rosalie. "This is the first real home I've ever had, and I want to do my share."

McCaleb grinned. "Welcome home. You can start to-day."

19

*M*aury Duke knew Vonnecker and Palmer had taken his gold, as surely as if he'd witnessed them ransacking his cabin. He also knew that catching up to them would be virtually impossible. He might search for weeks, even months, without a trace of them. Meanwhile, the rest of his "homesteaders" might vamoose in his absence. He fought away his anger, forcing his crafty mind to think logically. Train had warned him specifically not to stir up trouble until after Grant had been elected, until forces friendly to Train had taken control of government.

He had five months, then, in which nothing was expected of him except to lay low. He could do that, simply by redoubling his efforts and stripping the Sweetwater of whatever gold remained in the time left to him. If he continued to drive the men—and himself—hard enough, he could build another stake. But Vonnecker had been right about one thing: this was no bonanza worthy of acquiring the entire Sweetwater valley. The gold was spotty, with long stretches of the river yielding only sand and gravel. It was a truth he might use in pushing his partners in crime all the harder. He would convince them they were on a collision course with Train's deadline. And death. He wouldn't have to lie, he thought gloomily. It was God's truth, something he was rarely able to use to his benefit. In the little time left, he must recoup his stake and somehow get beyond the vindictive reach of George Francis Train.

Will and his riders were five days reaching Cheyenne, one disadvantage of taking the chuck wagon. They drew up north of town in the late afternoon.

"Salty," said Will, "we'll stock the chuck wagon tomorrow. I'll need to take some money from the bank, and I'll save that until we're ready to leave. For right now, the rest of you stick close to camp. I'd as soon the town didn't know we're here. I'm riding in so's I can look at some maps, but I won't go until after dark."

Will and Susannah rode into Cheyenne and, following Brazos's advice, went to Sam Colton's office. Colton answered Will's knock.

Colton grinned. "I haven't met you, but I know you. You're the gent that took a ride in Mr. Train's private coach and then carried off the handsomest schoolmarm the town ever had."

"Brazos told me you have some maps," said Will. "We're going to Texas by way of Ogallala and Fort Dodge, and I want some idea as to the distance."

"You're welcome to look at what I have, but the railroad maps won't help you much, once you leave their right-of-way. The surveyors say it's a hundred sixty miles from here to Ogallala."

Will took the known distances from the maps of Kansas and Texas, and used them to estimate the unknowns. There was no way to determine distance within Indian Territory, but fortunately they only had to cross the western end, at the panhandle. He thanked Colton for the use of the maps, and they rode quietly out of town.

"How far?" asked Susannah.

"Taking it from Box Elder Creek to San Antone," said Will, "if we have to go that far south, I'd put it at eleven hundred miles."

* * *

Will waited until the following afternoon before taking his saddlebags to the bank for the gold. Susannah accompanied him. Despite his precautions, the withdrawal didn't go unnoticed. A bearded man stood across the street and watched them ride away. A knife scar had puckered the right corner of his mouth into a lopsided grin, and he wore twin Colts in a buscadero rig. He waited until he was sure of the direction Will and Susannah were riding. He then mounted his horse and followed.

"Will," said Susannah, "that man—"

"Don't look back," said Will. "We'll be seeing him somewhere along the trail, and I'd as soon he didn't know we're expectin' him. He's the kind who'll have some friends with him."

"Lord," sighed Susannah, "we're not even out of Wyoming, and there's trouble following us already. Is it *always* like this?"

"Damn near," said Will. "Once we buy the herd, we'll likely have to fight to hold it. Not sorry you came along, are you?"

"No, but I guess I . . . didn't know very much about it. I thought we just bought the cows, pointed them the way we wanted them to go, and—"

Will laughed.

"Be serious, Will. That man's following us because of the gold, and you've just said he won't be alone."

"Neither will *we,* my dear. We have five fair-to-middlin' gun hands, includin' me, and I have a spare Colt you can use."

The others were waiting, prepared to leave. They had accompanied Salty to Bullard's and had seen to their own needs. Will told them of the bearded stranger who had followed them.

"We'll bed down here," said Will. "If there's a problem, I'd as soon be done with it. We'll douse the fire after supper. Salty, you stay in the wagon and keep your gun handy. The rest of us will spread our blankets, but we won't be in them."

They positioned their bedrolls, saddles, and hats around the chuck wagon, and beneath a moonless, starlit sky, it appeared the outfit was sleeping.

"We'll let them make the first move," said Will, "and then we'll fire at their muzzle flashes."

Will kept them together, lest they become separated in the dark and end up shooting at each other. They waited until past midnight. Just when Will had begun to think they weren't going to show, they did. There was a faint but unmistakable snick of a pistol being cocked.

"Fire!" shouted a voice.

There was an instant thunder of rifles and Colts. There was a matching thunder as Will and the outfit began firing at muzzle flashes. Just as suddenly as it had begun, there was silence. Susannah leaned against Will, and he felt her trembling. The muzzle of her Colt was warm against his arm.

"Is . . . is it over?" she asked in a whisper.

"Maybe," said Will.

By feel, he shucked the spent shells from his Colt and reloaded. With his pistol in hand, he walked among the fallen men, nudging them with his foot. The fourth and last groaned.

"Mister," said a pain-racked voice, "I'm . . . gut-shot. Cain't you do . . . nothin' . . . fer me?"

Will fired once and the voice was silenced.

"What are we going to . . . do with them?" Susannah asked. "We can't just . . . leave them here. Can we?"

"We can," said Will, "and we're going to. We only did to them what they planned to do to us. Salty, hitch up the team, and the rest of you saddle up. We're going to put some miles behind us before daylight. Sound travels far at night. Soon as it's light enough to see, there'll be somebody nosin' out here to see what all the shooting was about, and I don't aim to be here to answer any questions."

* * *

It was an easy 160 miles to Ogallala, even with the chuck wagon slowing them down. They followed the Union Pacific tracks, making twenty miles a day.

"This is too easy," said Stoney. "We'll likely end up axe-clearin' a wagon road from Ogallala to Fort Dodge. How far is it, anyway?"

"I figure it at two hundred thirty miles south of Ogallala," said Will, "maybe two hundred fifty."

On January 15, 1869, they reached Ogallala. Turning south, only flat, grassy prairie stretched as far as they could see.

"My God," said Pen, "if Kansas is even close to this, it'll be a trail driver's dream. Look at that grass!"

"From the maps I've seen," said Will, "it's maybe eighty miles from here to the Republican River. Once we cross it, we ought to be within two hundred thirty miles of Fort Dodge."

On the first day of February, they reined up on the north bank of the Arkansas River.

"Fort Dodge is somewhere east of here," said Will. "If there's a town, it'll be between here and the fort."

The "town" proved to be a lone building housing a general store and saloon.

"My God," cried Susannah, aghast. "Is that it?"

"I reckon," said Will. "Someday, when the railroad gets here, this will be a cattle town. It's less than three hundred miles from Red River. For now, we'll pass up the store and go on to the fort. I want to talk to the commander. Maybe he can tell us what to expect in Indian Territory."

They came upon an Indian camp, a dozen lodges, maybe three-quarters of a mile north of the river. Six Indians sat their spotted ponies in silence and watched the Texans pass.

"Osage," said Pen.

"They're so far away," said Susannah, "how can you tell?"

"This Injun can read," said Pen, chuckling. "The government moved them here. Saw it in a Denver newspaper once."

"Don't tell her it was that time we was in the Denver jail," said Jed. "It'll hurt our reputation."

"Don't tell her McCaleb was in there with us either," said Stoney, "or it'll hurt his reputation maybe more than ours."

"I don't think anybody in this outfit's got enough reputation to be concerned about," said Susannah. "Why were you in jail?"

"You don't want to know," said Will. "They were all guilty as sin, and it cost us a bunch to get them out. Since there's nothing here but Fort Dodge, we shouldn't have any trouble, unless we fight the army."

He was wrong.

Will spent an hour at Fort Dodge with Lieutenant Harper, the post commander.

"Most of the Indian trouble," said Harper, "has been to the east of us. As the railroad moves west, that will change, but for now, most of the Texas herds are being trailed to Abilene."

"Since we're not sure what to expect from the Indians," said Will, "what about outlaws?"

"Sorry," said Harper, "but I have no facts for you. There's very little outlaw activity within the territory itself, because there are no whites to prey on, except other outlaws. Renegades, probably the remnants of the Quantrill and Anderson gangs, do their sacking and killing elsewhere, and then vanish into the territory. You'll be crossing the part of the panhandle they call the Cherokee Strip. Traveling south, there's a good chance you'll make it unmolested, but returning with a herd may be a different story. How large a herd do you have in mind?"

"Five thousand head," said Will.

The lieutenant whistled long and low. "You don't have enough riders or guns," he said.

"I aim to have more of both," said Will, "when I start the drive."

"If I'm any judge," said Harper, "you'll need them. Good luck."

The store was an enormous structure with a shake roof. Behind the store was an open-sided shed, beneath which were stacks of buffalo hides, rawhided into crude bales. Literally surrounding the store, already bleached white by the elements, were mounds of bones. Buffalo bones, stacked higher than the flat, false-fronted roof of the store.

"We don't need supplies," said Susannah. "Why are we even stopping here?"

"Maybe I can pick up some information from the buffalo hunters and bone pickers," said Will. "There's a dozen horses tied alongside the store."

"With all them horses," said Monte, "must be a saloon in there."

"If there is," said Will, "stay out of it."

Trotting along behind them was a half-starved yellow hound. So poor was the unfortunate animal, it appeared to have been skinned, all the flesh rendered from its bones and the hide stretched over the skeleton. The dog stopped short of the door, watching with hopeful eyes as they entered. He knew better than to follow. He well remembered having been beaten within an inch of his life for earlier trespasses.

There was a saloon in the rear of the store, consisting of a makeshift bar and five tables, four of them occupied. Rough, bearded men—buffalo hunters and skinners—drank from tin cups. There was coarse laughter and the slap of playing cards. No bottles were in evidence. The brew was dispensed directly from bungholed barrels. Suddenly one of the cardplayers discovered Susannah. He slapped his cards down on the table and lurched drunkenly to his feet.

"Damn my eyes!" he bawled, "if it ain't a she-male wearin' britches!"

In their haste, the four of them upended the table, sending tin cups clattering to the floor. From out of nowhere the barkeep produced a sawed-off shotgun. His voice had the volume of a steamboat whistle.

"Siddown," he bellowed, "an' Thacker, you watch your mouth. There's a lady in the store. Th' first one o' you heathen bastards that makes a move t'wards her, I'll cut him down like a yellow coyote."

Will steered Susannah away from the saloon area, and Salty bought dried apples to replenish their supply. But Thacker had followed them, stalking up to Monte, who was hefting a pair of silver-mounted Colts.

"Well, bless my soul," he sneered, "a reg'lar two-gun man!"

"Thacker!" It was the barkeep with the steamboat whistle voice and the sawed-off scattergun.

"I ain't botherin' th' bi—th' lady, Garrett."

"I don't want you botherin' *nobody*. Now git back to th' bar, or just git out. Th' choice is yours."

Thacker wanted to argue, but not with a sawed-off. He shambled toward the back of the store and the bar. Monte returned the pistols to their pegs and joined Pen, Jed, and Stoney, who had discovered a big hoop of cheese. He cut himself a hunk the size of his doubled fists. Will had seen Thacker approach Monte. More than a dozen men, most of them drunk, all of them probably of Thacker's caliber, knew Susannah was in the store. It was time for Will and his outfit to ride on. Salty and Susannah followed him to the counter where their four comrades were eating the cheese they had bought.

"Let's go," said Will. "I don't like the looks of this bunch."

Will and the rest of the outfit were almost to the chuck wagon when Will discovered Monte wasn't with them. He looked back, and Monte was hunkered down near the door, feeding cheese to the hungry, grateful old hound. Out the door stumbled Thacker. Missing the bottom step, he almost fell. The dog yelped in fear, and Thacker savagely kicked the scrawny animal in the head. Stunned, it fell, whining. Still hunkered down, Monte came up swinging, burying his fist in Thacker's big belly. When the wind went out of Thacker and he doubled up, Monte brought up his right knee. It connected with Thacker's bearded chin and slammed him against the wall with a force that seemed to shake the building. He slid to a sitting position, his head down, breathing hard. Finally he looked at Monte until his bleary eyes focused, and then he went for his gun. He found himself looking into the deadly muzzle of Monte's Colt, and releasing his own weapon, allowed it to slip back into its holster.

None of the rest of the outfit had made a move. It had been Monte's play, and to Will's way of thinking, he had handled himself exceptionally well. Monte holstered his Colt and then did something that marked him as either the biggest damn fool or the bravest man Will Elliot had ever seen. He turned his back on the drunken, vindictive Thacker! Will and the rest of the outfit could only watch it happen, for Monte was between them and the bearded gunman. None of them, not even Monte himself, knew from whence came the warning. Monte Nance, sometimes immature, sometimes foolish, had the intuition and the reflexes of a gunfighter. Those who had witnessed it, even Will Elliot, swore that Thacker had his pistol drawn and cocked before Monte drew. He fired only once. Thacker's slug plowed into the dirt at his feet, and again he slammed into the wall. He sank to the ground, and this time he didn't rise. Blood quickly darkened the front of his shirt. For a long minute Monte stood there, his Colt ready, his eyes hard and cold. Nobody wished to take up the fight. This time Monte backed away from the store, not turning his back until Jed and Stoney stepped forward to cover him. In silence they returned to the chuck wagon. They wouldn't be spending the night here. Monte shucked the empty shell and reloaded his Colt. Whatever else he was, Monte Nance was a man.

"Hitch up and saddle up," said Will.

Killing a troublemaker didn't always resolve a fight. The

man's friends might decide to take it up after they became drunk enough. They reached a creek that spilled off from the Arkansas and followed it south. When it was too dark for them to travel farther, they made camp and ate a cold supper, washing it down with creek water. Fire drew enemies, red and white, like a beacon. Normally, without a fire, they would take to their blankets early, but not this night. They might yet have visitors. They listened, and when the alien sound came, each man quietly drew his Colt. But they had nothing to fear from their visitor. As though sensing his danger, the dog whined.

The dog dropped to his belly in a show of humility and beat the ground with his tail in a frenzy of excitement.

Pen chuckled. "It looks like Monte's become a daddy."

"Well, hell," said Monte, embarrassed, "he was hungry and needin' a friend. I know the feelin'."

Nobody laughed. Without a word, Salty went to the wagon, got some cold biscuits, and fed the dog. They moved out at dawn, the gaunt old hound trotting behind the chuck wagon. Indian Territory lay ahead.

20

*I*t was a hard winter in the high country. Twice they lost cows to the wolves, and McCaleb led an unsuccessful wolf hunt into the Big Horn basin. They were snowed in until mid-March, when the weather finally broke.

"It's time for another trip to town," said McCaleb. "This might be a good time to bring in those hay wagons and some tools. I'll need two men who can handle teams."

"That'll be me an' Cow," said Badger. "We done more'n our share of bull whackin'. Mules ain't no trouble atall."

Skies were still clear, but the temperature had again dropped to near zero by the time they reached Cheyenne. McCaleb got them rooms for the night at the boarding-house and made arrangements to pick up the wagons the following day.

"Stay out of the saloons," he warned Cow and Badger.

McCaleb stepped in unannounced, and found Sam Colton with a newspaper spread out on his desk. The lamp's flame had been turned too high and was beginning to smoke the globe.

"My God," groaned Colton, rolling his eyes in mock horror. "McCaleb's in town; hell's going to bust loose tonight."

"I'm gettin' the idea this is a mighty dull place when I'm not around."

"Not necessarily," said Colton. "When it comes to facing up to trouble, the rest of your outfit's about as sudden as you. One of your boys, the one you took to Omaha in Train's private coach, was in here the week after Christmas. He studied some of my maps, rode out, and next day, a few miles south, four hombres were found shot dead. The sheriff's still wondering if there's some connection."

"Sounds like outlaws," said McCaleb. "Has the sheriff wondered long enough and strong enough to look through his wanted posters?"

"He has," said Colton, "and two of the dead men had records. Wanted for robbery and murder. But the sheriff still wants to talk to whoever cut 'em down."

"He's barking up the wrong tree," said McCaleb. "What else has happened since I was here?"

"I told you Grant was going to be elected, and he was. He's taken office, and I was just reading of some of his appointments. Disappointing."

Before entering Indian Territory, Will paused for a day to shoe their horses and mules. Jed and Stoney were especially adept at paring the hoof and fitting the shoe. It was a disagreeable task, made more so by Salty's off-side mule, which didn't want to be reshod. They took him first, and the rest were easy. Once across the Cherokee Strip, they traveled south along the extreme western border of Indian Territory. The hound still trotted along behind the chuck wagon, and they called him "Dodge." He quickly made friends with Salty.

"He's smarter than he looks," said Monte. "He knows who cooks the grub."

Will kept a written record of each day's travel, of every water hole and stream. On February 15 they forded the Red and made camp on Texas soil. A week later they were in Palo Pinto County, just south of old Fort Belknap, on the Brazos River. It was here that McCaleb's original outfit had joined Charles Goodnight's drive to Colorado, taking part in the blazing of the historic Goodnight trail.*

"Tomorrow," said Will, "we'll split up and ride to outlying ranches and towns. We need to know who has two-year-olds to sell, and the going price. Once we're sure of the herd, we can take a few days to visit family and friends."

"When are we startin' the drive back to Wyoming?" Jed asked.

"Mid-March," said Will, "if we can buy and trail-brand the herd by then."

"If you don't hire all the new riders before we get home," said Stoney, "we might bring along a couple of ol' boys we rode with 'fore the war. That is, if they made it back alive."

"If they can ride, rope, and shoot," said Will, "bring them."

Will and Susannah rode to Mineral Wells, since that was where Will's parents lived. Susannah, never having met them, was nervous.

"They don't know I exist," she said. "Suppose they don't like me?"

"Too bad," said Will, "but they'll be tickled to death. I'm such an ugly galoot, I think they expected me to end up with an Injun squaw; likely a fat one, with buckteeth severe enough to eat roasting ears through a picket fence."

"I hope I'm not too much of a disappointment, since I'm not fat and don't have buckteeth."

"I'd have to count you a notch or two above a squaw," said Will. "You can ride, you're learnin' to rope, you can cook, and you're downright easy on the eyes. Most squaws ain't worth a damn beyond scrapin' hides and a romp in the blankets."

"I suppose," said Susannah, her voice cooling to a noticeable degree, "you've romped with your share of them."

"Nary a one," said Will, chuckling. "I learned to scrape

* Trail Drive series #1—*The Goodnight Trail*

my own hides, and who wants to take on a full-time woman who's no account for anything but a romp in the blankets?"

Will's family seemed surprised and pleased with Susannah. He left her with them and went about the business of contacting ranchers who might have steers to sell. The asking price was eight dollars for steers and five for cows. Will offered seven for steers, in gold, and wasn't once refused.

"Some of us been talkin' about puttin' us together a trail herd," said one rancher, "but we ain't had the money fer decent hosses an' grub. That's why we're sellin' to you at your price, just to get our hands on some honest-to-God cash money."

Bring together enough ten-cow Texas ranchers, thought Will, and sooner or later they'd get a herd to market. Soon the trails and the markets would become glutted. The lush graze would be gone, and someday the trail drive itself. It would flourish and die in his lifetime, thought Will morosely, and already he was mourning its passing.

Old Josh Olson had been in charge of the depot at Cheyenne ever since Grenville Dodge had created the town as a division point for the Union Pacific. The railroad provided him a place to sleep and paid him enough to survive. When he became dissatisfied with his lot, he reminded himself of the times when he had lacked even these basics. For whatever it was worth, he was the man in charge. Since the railroad hadn't been completed, there was no legitimate mail delivery. The brakeman brought whatever there was, passed it along to old Josh, and he held it at the depot until whoever it belonged to came looking for it. Days and weeks passed, with nothing but the Omaha and Chicago newspapers Sam Colton received. So on that April morning, April Fool's Day, Josh could scarcely believe it when there actually was a letter. It was addressed to Benton McCaleb, Cheyenne, Wyoming. Josh knew a lot about McCaleb. He had taken vicious pleasure in Maury Duke's gunmen being chained in the caboose, and that was owed to McCaleb's Texas outfit. Josh examined the letter more closely. It had a printed address, and had been sent from Washington, from the Secretary of War! Josh Olson believed nothing good ever took place in Washington. There had been no lasting peace with the Indians, land granted the railroads had fallen into the hands of greedy speculators, and the most brazen swindle in the history of the world had taken place through the Credit Mobilier. The country was going to hell, pure and simple, with Washington greasing the skids. Josh had no obligation beyond holding the letter until it was called for, but suppose McCaleb had no idea it was there? He had the uneasy feeling McCaleb needed that letter. While the man was the avowed enemy of Maury Duke, he had friends. One of them was Sam Colton. Taking the letter, he headed for Colton's office.

"Josh," said Colton, "don't mention this letter to anybody. They're setting McCaleb up for a fall. Somehow I'll get it to him. Thanks."

It took Sam Colton the better part of three days to reach Box Elder Creek. When he finally did, he simply fell off the horse. The animal wandered on to the barn, and Charlie Tilghman and Harley Irwin found Colton stumbling along the creek. They helped him to the cookhouse. Unable to sit, he slid to the floor with a sigh and lay there with his eyes closed.

"Sam," said McCaleb, "you look a mite used up. What's the occasion?"

With a groan, Colton moved just enough to get the crumpled letter out of his pocket. By now everybody, including Rosalie and Penelope, were there. Silently, McCaleb opened the envelope and unfolded the single sheet. There were but two sentences:

You have been cited for violation of Federal law on two counts: the first, for using Indians in the commission of a crime, and the second, for encouraging their violation of the treaty of 1868. Your hearing has been scheduled for July 12, 1869, and your presence is compulsory.

John A. Rawlins, Secretary of War.

Rebecca took the letter from McCaleb and the others gathered around her to read it. They were silent, with unasked questions and worry in their eyes. But McCaleb had no answers. He needed to talk to Sam Colton.

"Some of you help Sam to a bunk," he said.

Colton rested until suppertime. After the meal he went to McCaleb's cabin to talk. Rebecca turned questioning eyes to McCaleb.

"Sit down," he said. "You're entitled to hear this."

Colton read the letter twice before he commented.

"Diplomatic of them," he said, "referring to it as a hearing."

"More like a trial, then," said McCaleb.

"Not even that. First paragraph gives them away. You've been 'cited' for violation of federal law. 'Accused' is one thing, and 'cited' is another. They're ready to nail you to the cross, and this 'hearing' is a means of getting you there for the occasion."

"Then don't go!" cried Rebecca.

"He'll have to," said Colton, "unless this thing is defused before the day of the hearing. You told me you have a hole card, McCaleb. It's time to play it."

"You're right, Sam," said McCaleb. "I owe you for getting this letter to me. What I'm about to tell you must be kept in confidence until I play out my hand. Then you can use the information as you see fit. Once you've heard what I'm about to tell you, you'll understand my need for silence. Agreed?"

"Agreed," said Colton.

McCaleb told him of the apparent discovery of gold on the Sweetwater, and of Train's scheme to gain control of the Sweetwater valley. First, by taking over government grants along the Union Pacific right-of-way, and second, by hiring Maury Duke's gang to homestead the land along the river itself.

"So you intend to trade your silence for a withdrawal of federal charges?"

"Something like that," said McCaleb. "Have I any choice?"

"I suppose not," said Colton, "but a bluff's only good until somebody calls it. Suppose they do?"

"Then they'll discover I'm not bluffing. The Sweetwater land grab ought to revive interest in Train's Credit Mobilier. With two full-blown scandals on its hands, the government should have plenty to keep it busy without hounding me."

"There's a weak link in your chain," said Colton. "How can you tie the Sweetwater land grab in with the Credit Mobilier fraud?"

"No certainty that I can," said McCaleb, "but from what I know about newspapers, I expect them to tie it all up in one neat package for me."

"Thanks," said Colton dryly, "but such a crusade takes time, and you only have three months, my friend. Can you apply enough pressure in the time that you have, to kill this so-called hearing set for July twelfth?"

"I aim to try," said McCaleb. "I'm going directly to Ulysses S. Grant."

"It's a bold plan, but you can't just walk in off the street and confront the president. How do you expect to get to Grant with this elaborate piece of blackmail?"

"I'll need your help," said McCaleb, grinning.

"You want a cellmate for Leavenworth, don't you?"

"Not that kind of help," said McCaleb. "The railroad's going to be completed before the end of May, somewhere in Utah. When the rails meet, Grant will be there. I need to know when they aim to have the ceremony, and when Grant's train will reach Omaha."

"McCaleb," said Colton incredulously, "except for Grant's private coach, that whole damn train's going to be loaded with soldiers for the ceremony. If the train stops at Omaha at all, it'll be just long enough to take on water. You won't be allowed even close to it."

"Sam," said McCaleb, "you just get me the time of the ceremony in Utah and the time Grant's train will reach Omaha. I'll take it from there."

"McCaleb, if you pull this off, it will have been worth the devilish ride to warn you. If you fail, I'll send you a newspaper subscription to Leavenworth, although I doubt they'll allow you anything to read while you're in solitary."

"Thanks," said McCaleb, "but if I fail, you can come to the hanging."

Sam Colton spent two days at the ranch before he felt capable of the ride back to Cheyenne.

"Give me a week," he said, "and I'll have the information you need."

McCaleb waited ten days, until April 15, and he went alone. It was after dark when he approached Colton's office.

"They'll actually join the rails on May eighth," said Colton, "but to allow time for the dignitaries to arrive, they'll drive the ceremonial spike on the tenth. Grant's train will be in Omaha early on May ninth. There'll be a two-hour layover, and Grant will speak at the depot. But like I told you, except for the president's private coach and a press car, the rest of the train will be loaded with Federal troops."

"A press car?"

"There'll be reporters from every major newspaper in the country," said Colton. "The railroad's providing a special coach for them."

21

$\mathcal{W}$ithin three days Will had commitments for more than five thousand steers. He bought as few as ten head and as many as five hundred. One of the young down-at-the-heels cowboys who sold him ten steers became the first new rider to hire on for the drive to Wyoming.

"It's taken me three months," said Poke Shambler, "to drag them steers out of the brush, riskin' my hair ever' day. Do you know, for ever' cow in them Trinity brakes, they's ten Comanche?"

"I believe you," said Will with a grin. "That's where we got our first herd, and we had to fight our way out."

Shambler had his horse, his saddle, and the clothes that he wore.

"I got shot up some in th' war," he said. "I can't walk straight, but I can shoot straight. I can rope an' ride with the best of 'em."

He was thin and lanky, over six feet, with gray eyes and dark hair. He had told Will he was twenty-five, but he looked older. The age was in his eyes and the patch of gray at each temple. He wore a tied-down Colt on his left hip, its well-worn butt reversed.

"Once I got back to Texas," he said, "I reckoned I'd never leave again, but things ain't th' same. I ain't sure they ever will be again. I see I got to ride some diff'rent trails. Maybe this trail to Wyoming will be a good one."

Monte returned from Weatherford with the promise of more steers if they were needed. Riding with him was a pair of grinning Mexicans. Emilio and Donato Vasquez had been part of Charles Goodnight's outfit the last time Will had seen them. They had proven themselves capable hands, and with their fluent Spanish, had been helpful in communicating with Goose.

"They left Goodnight for a spell and went home," said Monte. "Now they need work."

They hadn't changed at all, as far as Will could tell. There was but a year's difference in their ages. Will shook their hands and welcomed them to the outfit. He had enjoyed their company while he, Brazos, and McCaleb had trailed with Goodnight. Emilio had cooked for Goodnight's outfit and was better than average. They both played guitar and sang the old songs in flowing, graceful Spanish.

Pen, Jed, and Stoney had ridden downriver, south of Fort Worth. They returned without any measurable success.

"You were dead right, Will," said Pen. "The Comanches are still raisin' hell down there. Some of the folks we talked to have had their herds stampeded and stolen. Damn Injuns have started gettin' picky. They're runnin' off herds, takin' the steers and leaving everything else. One day we'll meet an outfit on the trail and all the riders will be Comanche, driving their own herd to market."

"Goodnight must have gathered farther south for his last herd," said Will. "We've already had the promise of enough steers. More than enough, in fact, and we have three new riders. Why don't you gents take a couple of weeks to visit your friends and kin? We can use three or four more good riders, if you can find them. You know the kind of men we want. Another thing, I want you to take some money along and keep an eye out for some good cow horses. We're going to need a remuda."

Once Will had hired enough hands for the branding to proceed without him, he set about building a horse remuda. They needed fifteen extra mounts, and he had no idea if Pen, Jed, and Stoney would be successful in their hunt. Poke Shambler and the Vasquez boys would each need a pair of extra mounts. So would Will, Monte, Pen, Jed, Stoney, and the extra riders yet to be hired.

On a trail drive, every rider needed at least three dependable horses, with some extras available, should one of the first-line broncs be killed or become lame. With Poke Shambler's help, Will found two good cow horses, and bought three more from hard-up temporary hands hired for the branding. March 15 came and went with no sign of Pen, Jed, and Stoney. Suppose the home call was too strong and he never saw them again? But they rode in two days later, accompanied by two other riders and leading eight horses.

"Sorry we're late," said Pen, "but we had to ride all over Hell and South Texas to find these horses. We reckoned they'd be worth the extra time. We spent all but ten dollars of your money."

Thirty dollars a horse! Will sighed. Times were changing.

"We found them ol' boys I was tellin' you about." Jed grinned. "They're broke an' needin' work. This gent with th' red hair is Theodore Dulaney. He's got a standin' offer to gut-shoot anybody that don't call him Red. He's got freckles all over his carcass—even his eyeballs—an' likely other parts he'd not want mentioned. This other ugly jasper is Holton Nettles. 'Cept for his mama, ever'body calls him Holt."

Both men stood well over six feet, and both wore tied-down Colts. Red's eyes were green and his hair reddish-orange. Holt had blue-black hair and black eyes that said one of his parents had been Indian. Both men shook Will's hand, and he liked the way they looked him in the eye. He liked the looks of them, although he knew little about them except that they had been to war. Each had been man enough to return, and that said it all.

March 19, Will rode back to Mineral Wells for Susannah. In the few days she'd been there, she had endeared herself to his family, and they to her. The parting was more painful than he'd imagined. To his surprise, he found that Susannah had acquired an enormous load of things, including a goose-down feather bed, handmade quilts, and a generations-old chest of German silverware.

"Please, Mama," he begged, "no more. We'll have to buy a pack mule. This is a trail drive, and there's a thousand-mile ride ahead of us. We're not goin' away forever. I promise you we'll be back, and next time I'll bring a wagon."

They rode out, their horses so overloaded they might have been a pair of itinerant peddlers.

"I reckon you had a nice visit," said Will.

"I did." She smiled. "You never told me your middle name was Rupert."

"You tell that to anybody," he said grimly, "and I'll get me a squaw to bunk with, and put you to scraping hides."

They moved out the herd, 5,200 strong, on March 20, 1869. The chuck wagon took the lead, the old yellow hound trotting alongside. The first days were the hardest, until the longhorns accepted the routine.

"We'll make do with two nighthawks," Will told them, "unless there's threat of a storm, Indians, or outlaws. We could have used two or three more good riders, but we'll have to get by with what we have. When you sleep, don't shuck anything but your hat. If they get spooked and run, you won't have time to grab anything else."

The third night out, a spring storm struck. There was a minimum of thunder and lightning and plenty of rain. They rode for three hours, circling the nervous herd until the thunder and lightning died away. The rain continued for the rest of the night and all the following day. It rattled into their tin plates while they ate, and diluted the hot black coffee they drank. They slept in wet clothes, in wet blankets, on wet, muddy ground.

"I suppose," sighed Susannah, "when you've been rained on for two days, you can't get any wetter."

"That's what you think," said Will, chuckling. "After all

this rain, wait'll we get to Doan's Crossing and you see the Red."

"That's gospel," said Poke Shambler. "I won't be surprised t' see backwater for half a mile off'n each bank. She'll be runnin' full an' more."

"If it's that bad," said Susannah, "how can we get ourselves, the herd, and the chuck wagon across?"

"We can't," said Will. "We'll be stuck until the water goes down. Longhorns won't ford a river when they can't see the other bank."

"Ain't that the truth," said Red Dulaney. "I've seen 'em balk when th' sun was in their eyes an' th' river wasn't knee deep."

"This storm blew out of the west," said Pen. "She might have been pouring for a week out there, all of it finding its way back to the Red."

It was a prophetic statement. They found the Red River a raging torrent of muddy water that had overrun its banks and conquered new territory.

"Wait here in the office," Colton told McCaleb. "It's early enough for Josh to still be at the depot. Maybe I can at least find out if he's willing to get you on a train to Omaha."

Olson had his back to the wall, his chair reared up on its hind legs.

"Josh," said Colton, "I got that letter to McCaleb. It was important, and he sends you his thanks. Are you good for one more favor?"

"Maybe," said Olson cautiously. "What is it?"

"McCaleb needs to be in Omaha by May ninth. Can you get him on one of the returning work trains?"

"This got anything to do with that Injun he took away from Maury Duke?"

"It has," said Colton, "but I can't tell you about it now. I know the rails are going to meet soon. Can you get McCaleb to Omaha on one of the last work trains?"

"If he don't mind gettin' there early, like on May seventh. That'll be th' last work train before the rails meet."

The day after McCaleb left Cheyenne, Maury Duke rode in. He went to the depot. Sam Colton waited until Duke had left, and then headed for the depot himself. He found Josh frowning over a yellow sheet of paper.

"He didn't stay long," said Colton. "What did he want?"

"Sent a wire," said Josh.

Colton reached for the paper and Josh withdrew it.

"You ain't supposed to read other folks' telegrams."

"I'm a newspaperman," said Colton. "If I could get my hands on it, I'd steam open President Grant's mail."

Josh slid the sheet across the counter, and Colton read the one perplexing word. It asked a question: "When?" The telegram was addressed to S. J. Pauley, Omaha.

"He's stingy with words," said Colton. "Has he done this before?"

"Yeah," said Josh, "time or two, an' never anything that makes sense. He done it back in September. All it said was 'Three. Ours.' Sent it to this same S. J. Pauley."

"Any answer?"

"Two words," said Josh. "It was a day of a month."

"If he gets an answer to this one, let me know what it says."

"I'd be violatin' comp'ny policy," said Josh. "Th' railroad could fire me, kick me out, an' I'd have no place to sleep."

"You can sleep on my desk," said Colton.

They waited three days before the backwater receded enough for the Red River to appear fordable. Clouds had rolled in from the west and there was the feel of rain in the air. Long before it reached them, it would be swelling the Red. Will had a decision to make.

"We'll cross the chuck wagon first," he said.

They cut cottonwood logs and lashed one on each side of the wagon. Once it was in deep enough to float, Salty cracked his whip and the mules surged into the current. Jed and Stoney swam their horses alongside, upriver, with lariats lashed to the front and rear of the wagon. Even with the log floats, the angry Red might capsize it. Dodge, the yellow hound, sat calmly on the wagon seat beside Salty. They sat their saddles on the south bank, watching the chuck wagon safely across. Jed and Stoney loosed the wagon from its log floats, waving their hats in triumph as Salty sent the team scrambling out of the muddy Red.

"This is an almighty big herd," said Will. "I'm tempted to split it and make two crossings."

"Ain't more'n two hours of light," said Poke Shambler. "Not that much if that storm keeps a-comin'. I say let's take 'em all across an' be done with it."

"I'm for that," said Red Dulaney. "I'd like t' have time t' dry out 'fore I get wet again. Just run th' leaders in, swat th' follerers into a lope, an' where can they go but to th' other bank?"

It made sense in theory but became a disaster in practice. Red's words would come back to haunt him.

"We'll take them all at once, then," said Will, "soon as Jed and Stoney get back across."

It began as perfectly as any crossing Will had ever seen. Stoney, Jed, Will, and Poke Shambler flanked the herd on the upriver side. Emilio and Donato Vasquez, Red Dulaney, and Holt Nettles rode the downriver flank. Pen, Monte, and Susannah were at drag, swatting the stragglers and screeching like Comanches. Almost imperceptibly the Red had begun to rise. Suddenly, between the farther bank and the swimming lead steers, a grotesque tree stump bobbed to the surface of the rushing water. Bleached white, it had the appearance of some kind of devil's head, its long, gnarled roots looking like a cluster of horns. Bawling in terror, the lead steers turned downriver to escape the thing, doubling back toward the south bank.

"Let them go!" shouted Will. "Save yourselves!"

But his voice was lost in the fury of the stampede. He could only watch it happen. Faintly, as though from a distance, he could hear gunfire as the downriver flankers tried valiantly to turn the milling herd. Finally they gave it up, swimming their horses toward the south bank. Will gritted his teeth as he lost sight of them in the plunging, struggling mass of steers. Emilio and Donato scrambled their horses out of the muddy red water safely, followed by Red Dulaney. But the fourth horse was riderless. Holt Nettles had been lost in the turbulent waters of Red River, amid the bawling, stampeding longhorns.

Maury Duke spent the afternoon in a saloon, waiting for an answer to his telegram. When he reached the depot, Josh Olson handed him a yellow sheet of paper on which he had written "June first." Duke shoved the paper carelessly into his pocket, suppressing his satisfaction. This fitted perfectly into his plans. He was to return to Omaha on June first to learn his next move. However, he thought smugly, he already knew his next move, and this rich bastard in Omaha had obligingly given him an extra month in which to make it. He grinned to himself. Just when he had believed the gold was played out, they'd found the richest deposit of all. The hell of it was, this richest, most lucrative find was considerably east of Kingston Henry's old cabin, uncomfortably close to the ranch on Box Elder Creek. He was now faced with the unpleasant possibility that the richest pocket of all might lie along the eastern end of the Sweetwater. From the western boundary of the Six Bar holdings all the way to the North Platte River, the Sweetwater paralleled Box Elder Creek.

Duke believed when he went to Omaha on June first—if he went—that he'd be given orders to gun those Texans down. He needed them out of the way, but if he waited for permission from Omaha, he would forfeit this newly discovered gold. George Francis Train would force him into an accounting before he could complete his stake and get safely away. No, he must dispose of that bunch on Box Elder ahead of schedule, grab what gold he could, and then travel fast enough and far enough that Train couldn't find him.

But it was more than just the gold. Maury Duke had a score to settle with that high-and-mighty bastard who had taken Susannah Cody away from him. Marriage had been the furthest thing from his mind. She had been too good for him, and he had known it. Still, he could have had his fun if Will Elliot hadn't stolen her away. She was used goods now, but that didn't matter to Duke. While he didn't really want her, he aimed to have her. For a while, anyway. He was a spoiler. It would be far more satisfying to steal her away and violate her than to just kill the bastard who'd married her.

Will Elliot had never seen anything like it. Before reaching the river bank from which they'd started, the first several hundred head of steers were pulled downriver. Five hundred yards below where they should have left the water, they stumbled out on the north bank. Despite the tragic loss of Holt Nettles, the riders plunged back into the Red, shouting, shooting, and swinging lariats. A second bunch of leaders was pushed across, climbing out on the north bank where they should have. The rest of the herd followed. When the herd had crossed, the riders gathered on the north bank, looking downriver. Monte, Pen, and Susannah hadn't witnessed the tragedy of the crossing and were just learning of it.

"We must find him!" cried Susannah. "Even if he's . . . dead . . . he deserves better than this."

"I agree," said Will, "but it'll be dark in a few minutes. We'll have to wait until morning. We'll take tomorrow and look for him."

But in their grief they'd forgotten the impending storm. During the night it broke in all its fury. By dawn they had to move the camp and the herd to escape the rising backwater from the Red. In the first gray light, in the driving rain, Will saw a solitary figure on the river bank staring into the roiling muddy water. He wasn't surprised when he found out it was Red Dulaney. Will stood there with him, at a loss for words. It was Red who finally spoke.

"We was at Shiloh," he said. "Closest thing to Hell I ever want to see. I had my hoss shot out from under me, and it was Holt who come back for me. Before we got out of it, his own hoss was shot. I was hard hit. He took me on his back, an' if I wasn't a believer in God 'fore that, I was after. If I knowed how, I . . . I'd ask th' same God that saw us through that battle . . . to be kind . . . to Holt. I ain't got th' right t' ask anything for myself, 'cause it was me . . . that didn't want t' split th' herd. . . ."

"I made the decision, Red," said Will. "It wasn't your fault."

The storm passed and they waited another day for some of the water to recede. Will divided the outfit and they rode downriver for miles, searching north and south banks of the Red. They found only Holt's battered hat. Will gathered them on the bank of the river. His voice breaking, he read the Twenty-third Psalm from a small bible. Then they rode out, pushing the herd into Indian Territory.

Maury Duke took to watching the ranch on Box Elder Creek. He had an old spyglass, and he watched until he knew exactly how many men were there. He was aware, from what he'd learned in Cheyenne, that there were new riders. What he didn't know was what had become of the others. Where was Susannah? He soon discovered that Rosalie and Penelope were there, and that explained the disappearance of Kingston Henry. He watched the red-headed Texan go into the cabin where the woman and the kid lived. So that's how it was. It might be information he could use.

The loss of Holt Nettles pulled the outfit together, made them stronger, more determined. Day after day, without complaint, Susannah rode drag, the dirtiest, lowliest position on a trail drive. Their first five days in Indian Territory were a disaster. There was a storm and a stampede every night. When the weather finally broke and the herd calmed, they had been seventy hours without sleep, their food limited to what they could eat in the saddle.

"We'll rest a day," said Will. "We've made so little progress in the last five, one more won't matter."

22

"*T*hank God the storms have let up," said Susannah. "I'd forgotten what it was like to wear dry clothes and sleep in dry blankets."

The storm-bred stampedes had been bad enough, but the worst was yet to come. Two-thirds of the way across Indian Territory, on a clear, moonless night, something spooked the herd. Monte, Red Dulaney, and Poke Shambler were nighthawking, and when the longhorns lit out to the south, the riders were at the opposite side. The brutes stampeded right through camp, one of them smashing headlong into the chuck wagon. The jangle of pots and pans could be heard above the roar of the stampede. Will's horse nickered and reared as he swung into the saddle. In the starlight he could see riderless horses, and he swore. The damn longhorns had snagged the horse remuda and were taking it with them. The herd was strung out, running like hell wouldn't have it. Will slowed his horse. There was no point in killing the animal when there was no hope of heading the stampede. They would have to wait until morning.

With each passing day, Rebecca became more concerned about McCaleb's daring confrontation with President Grant. Four years ago a popular president had been shot down. Rebecca feared any move toward Grant, threatening or not, might result in McCaleb being riddled with lead from Union soldiers. At best, he might be hanged or put to death before a firing squad. While she tried not to burden him with her fears, he knew. The night before he left for Omaha, he awakened to find her lying wide-eyed beside him. She said nothing, but when he touched her cheek, the tears were there.

The last returning work train reached Cheyenne just before sundown on May 6. McCaleb had waited in Sam Colton's office until they had heard the whistle of the approaching locomotive. It would stop just long enough to take on water. McCaleb got to his feet.

"Thanks, Sam," he said. He offered his hand, and Colton took it.

"Good luck, McCaleb," said the newspaperman, serious for once. "If any man ever deserved to win, it's you. Just for pure guts, if nothing else."

McCaleb walked alone to the depot and found the old ticket agent expecting him.

He grinned. "Josh, our first meeting was a mite strained. I'll try and do better this time."

"You done what you had to," said Josh.

They stepped out of the depot as the engine hissed to a stop beside the water tank. The train consisted, as usual, of flatcars and a caboose. The brakeman swung down the iron ladder and came to meet them. Josh spoke.

"Peterson, this is McCaleb. It was his boys that grabbed that Injun from right under Maury Duke's nose an' left them two jaspers chained in the caboose. McCaleb needs t' get t' Omaha, and I don't see no reason why he can't ride with you. If anybody says anything, then you can lay th' blame on me."

"Won't be no trouble." Peterson grinned. "It'll be near mornin' when we get there, but still dark. Come on and get aboard."

The quality of the ride hadn't improved since McCaleb's first trip to Omaha. He found it impossible to doze in the rocking, jouncing caboose, but he pretended to. Peterson was overly friendly, overly inquisitive, and McCaleb spent the first several hours evading his questions. If any of his plan went sour, the less known of him, the better. By the time they finally reached Omaha, he was thinking he could have brought three good horses, ridden them in relays, and beaten the train in both comfort and speed. It was still two hours until daylight when he thanked Peterson and climbed down from the caboose.

Omaha had grown to the extent that there was an all-night café near the depot, and McCaleb headed for it. He didn't want to check into a hotel at such an hour, because it would plant him firmly in some desk clerk's memory. There was nobody in the café but a bleary-eyed old-timer who had the look of a stove-up cowboy. He wondered if there was a cook anywhere on the frontier, from the Pedernales to the Powder, who hadn't once been a rider and felt less a man because he was no longer able. Wordlessly the old man slid a mug of hot black coffee down the counter. If McCaleb wanted anything else, he'd have to ask for it. He did.

"Fry me half a dozen eggs, some potatoes, and ham. Steak, if you don't have the ham."

He left the café with time on his hands, twenty-four hours in which to do nothing. He was exhausted as a result of the all-night ride in the caboose. He purposely passed up the better hotels, and headed for a less imposing one called the Nebraska House. Nobody was at the desk, and a single lamp burned on a small table near the foot of the stairs. Beside the lamp, in a lobby chair, sat a buckskin-clad man reading a newspaper. Before McCaleb could retreat, Buffalo Bill Cody was on his feet, the light of recognition strong in his eyes. As much as McCaleb liked and admired the scout, this was the worst possible time and place to encounter him.

"Well, God bless me," exclaimed Cody with a grin. "Benton McCaleb. It's almighty refreshin' to meet a frontiersman in this town. It's gettin' so damn civilized, ain't nobody here but gover'ment fat cats and Yankees. Is Will and Susy with you?"

"They're somewhere between Texas and Wyoming with a herd of steers," said McCaleb. "Susannah wanted to meet Will's folks, so I let him go back for another trail drive. I thought you were comin' out to the ranch for a spell?"

"I am," said Cody, "but I let myself get talked into goin' to some god-forsaken place in Utah for the joining of the rails. I reckoned I'd get done with that, come back to Cheyenne, and ride up to your place. For now, I'm stuck here until tomorrow mornin' with nothin' to do. Thank God you're in town. Let's go somewhere and eat and talk."

"I've just had breakfast," said McCaleb, "but I can always stand some more coffee."

McCaleb allowed Cody to do most of the talking. His mind was busy considering and rejecting explanations as to why he was in Omaha. He was caught on the painful horns of a dilemma. He had tried to avoid attracting attention to himself. Now he was stuck with one of the best-known frontiersmen in the west, and the man would be a passenger on the very damn train where he himself planned a showdown with the president of the United States!

Will returned to what was left of their camp, and slowly the others rode in to join him. The longhorn that had crashed into the chuck wagon was dead, and even by starlight they could see the wagon's right rear wheel was damaged.

"Get what sleep you can," Will told them. "Come first light, we've got some hard ridin' ahead of us."

North of the Powder, in Big Horn basin, Washakie's band had gone in search of buffalo. It was the start of the third day of a fruitless quest, and Washakie called the hunters together.

"The buffalo are few," he said, "but we must have one. We have need of the hide."

Nania's time had come, and his decision, painful as it

had been, had been made. Tribal custom must be honored. The child—with Nania's dark hair and cheekbones, and the cursed blue eyes of the white man—was already three days old. His eyes strayed to the silent Nania and his heart was heavy. He was sure the gods were angry, that being the reason for their not having killed a single buffalo. Further delay would only anger them all the more. The sun vanished beyond the Rockies and a cooling breeze crept down from the Big Horns. Still the hunting party did not return.

It was two hours past dawn when the hunters rode in. Three ponies bore the buffalo meat and a fourth the green hides. Silently the squaws unloaded the meat, covering it with two of the hides. Later it would be cut into thin slivers and smoked, but that must wait. Washakie said nothing; the squaws knew their duty. The place—two miles down-river—had already been chosen. Two squaws, bearing one of the buffalo hides, began their slow walk. Nania, carrying the child, silently followed. Behind her walked two more squaws. Washakie watched them until they passed from his sight around a bend in the river. The chosen place was a flat stone ledge that would reflect the heat of the sun, and upon it the squaws spread the green buffalo hide, hair side up. One of them nodded to Nania and she lay down on it, the fretful child beside her. A bone cup was passed to her and she drank its bitter contents. Slowly, carefully, they wound the hide about her and the child until they were covered. So that there could be no escape, around the pathetic bundle they wrapped heavy rawhide thongs, tying the ends. Finished, without a backward look, the squaws walked away. The merciless sun rose higher and grew hotter. The green hide began to shrink, growing tighter. The cry of the child grew faint and ceased. There was no sound except the unheard song of a mockingbird and the sigh of the wind in the cottonwoods along the Powder River.

In the cool of the night the wolves came, but the cruel sun had turned the hide cocoon hard as stone. Frustrated, the gray predators went away. The following day at sun-down, Washakie rode his pony along the river until he came within sight of the wrinkled, sun-drawn buffalo hide. His day, and that of the buffalo, were gone. Slowly he rode away, leaving Nania and her blue-eyed child to sleep forever in the loneliness of Powder River basin.

The moment of truth arrived all too soon for McCaleb.

"Now that the track's done," said Cody, "there won't be any more work trains through Cheyenne, and it'll be a while before there's any passenger trains. I can get you on this special train, the Golden Spike Express, as far as Cheyenne. But it's due out of here at eight in the morning."

"I might not be ready—" McCaleb began.

"It's a hell of a ways from here to Cheyenne," said Cody, "and God only knows when there'll be another train. I'll tell them you're a friend of mine, and I'll be responsible for you."

There it was. McCaleb sighed. Lies, however useful they seemed at the moment, never worked. He would have to take Cody into his confidence.

"Bill, I'm in trouble. Long before that train reaches Cheyenne, I may be in even more trouble, but it's a chance I have to take. I won't risk you putting your neck in the same noose, my friend."

"I'm no stranger to trouble," said Cody. "Let's go back to my room so's we can talk in private. I don't trust towns."

McCaleb began by allowing Cody to read the letter that had prompted this mission of desperation. He then explained his protective arrangement with Washakie and the aborted attempt by night riders to fire the ranch while he was away.

"I got more respect for a back-shootin' killer," Cody snorted, "than a hypocrite. They don't care a damn about the Indians. Somebody's out to get you, and he's usin' his so-called concern for the Indians for an excuse. Do they have any proof Indians was involved?"

"Only the word of those who escaped, I reckon. Brazos went out afterward and found their trail in the snow. Five men attacked the ranch, and three were killed. So their proof is only the word of the two who escaped."

"So it's your word against somebody else's," said Cody.

"That's it," McCaleb replied, "but this 'somebody else' stands tall enough in Washington to get me tried and convicted without me even knowin' about it. That letter don't say anything about a trial. It says I've been 'cited for violation of Federal law.' That means I've been convicted already, and if I'm fool enough to show up on July twelfth, they'll skin me, scrape my hide, and peg it out to dry."

"Much as I hate to," said the old scout, "I got to agree with you. But you're not a man to give up without a fight, McCaleb. I'll help you if I can. You wouldn't have told me this much if you didn't aim to tell me the rest. Ride on."

Cody listened silently until McCaleb finished. When he spoke, it was matter-of-factly, without judgment.

"I can get you on the train, but I don't have enough pull to get you to the president. He'll have a private coach, and you can count on it bein' guarded. Grant has his faults, but a lack of guts ain't one of 'em. Once you're in there, you'll have to convince him you've got a club big enough to deal him some hurt. He's got to believe your silence is worth the price you're askin'. I hope it is."

"So do I," said McCaleb. "It'll be a long walk to Cheyenne, especially with Yankee lead in me."

23

"*O*ur luck ain't all bad," said Pen. "We recovered all the horses. We can spare some cows, but not horses."

Will sighed. After five days of daylight-to-dark searching, they were still missing a hundred head of steers.

"If we can get through Indian Territory with no more loss than that," said Will, "let's count our blessings and move on."

Come dawn, they turned the herd north toward Fort Dodge.

For some reason nobody seemed able to determine, Grant's train was late. Ten o'clock came and went. So did most of the people who had gathered at the depot. Bill Cody grinned.

"That's in your favor, McCaleb. It'll be dark long before the train gets to Cheyenne, and that's what you need. You've got to get into the president's car, lay your threat on Grant, and get out alive. Right under the noses of a bunch of newspaper folks and Yankee soldiers. Just about as tricky as sneakin' daylight past a rooster."

"Bill Cody, you're a man to ride the river with. If this goes sour, after you getting me on the train, they'll peg your hide to the ground alongside mine. You don't have to do this. You have no stake in it."

"The hell I don't!" said Cody hotly. "You're a frontiersman who's been set up for a fall. That, and I consider you a friend of mine. That's stake enough. You need somebody to side you, somebody to tell your story, if his excellency decides you're bluffing. There's a far greater risk, my friend, than simply having Grant laugh in your face. Lincoln was shot just four years ago. If you're caught even close to the president's coach, you'll be shot dead, no questions asked."

It was the undeniable truth. McCaleb said nothing. He looked around at the diminishing crowd. The town had risen to the occasion as best it could, erecting a speaker's platform near the track. Valiant attempts had been made to conceal the rough lumber with red, white, and blue banners. McCaleb thought the white looked suspiciously like the muslin sheets from somebody's bed. He wasn't sure about the origin of the blue, but the red reminded him of some gaudy drapes he'd once seen in a New Orleans bawdy house. His thoughts were interrupted by a ragged cheer from the faithful few who hadn't given up on the train. Far to the east there was a dirty smudge on the blue of the sky. Bill Cody hauled out a pocket watch as big as a cow camp biscuit.

"Quarter past noon." He chuckled. "The railroad's first passenger train is four hours an' fifteen minutes late. We're payin' seventy million for this. Reckon how much more it would of cost to get this iron buggy here on time?"

"From what I've learned about some of the railroad's habits," said McCaleb, "probably another seventy million."

The locomotive hissed to a stop alongside the water tank. The fireman immediately climbed atop the tender, reaching for the dangling rope that would lower the tank's spout to the engine's thirsty boilers. This was a full-fledged passenger train. There were four coaches. The first three were maroon and gray, while the fourth was a solid, gleaming black. At the rear of it was an observation platform, encircled with an iron railing that glistened gold in the noonday sun. Before the door of the coach stood a Union soldier in dress blue uniform, his rifle at port arms. When the door behind him opened, he stepped aside. A half-bald little man wearing a blue pinstripe suit and thick glasses emerged. He was abrupt and to the point.

"The president's speech has been canceled. However, he will greet you briefly while the locomotive takes on water."

He disappeared through the door, and McCaleb shifted his attention to the other coaches. Several civilians exited the car directly ahead of Grant's, and McCaleb sighed with relief. That meant the soldiers—except for probable guards at each end of Grant's coach—would be in the first two cars. The newspapermen, then, were riding directly ahead of the presidential coach. The soldier guard came to attention as Grant stepped out the door. He wore a dark suit, a red-striped tie, and a flat-crowned straw hat. There was some polite hand clapping, a cheer or two, and then an expectant silence. Some of the earlier spectators had returned.

"Folks," said Grant apologetically, "we're considerably behind schedule, so I'm forced to limit my remarks. Perhaps as we return, we can stop for a longer visit."

With that he was gone. There were some boos, hissing, and catcalls. A conductor stepped down from the third coach and stood looking around.

"He's likely looking for me," said Cody. "Come on."

That proved to be the case. The conductor, however, was reluctant to allow McCaleb on the train. Cody got angry.

"Damn it, this man's a friend of mine. If he's not welcome, then neither am I. I've put myself to considerable trouble to attend this hog killin' in Utah. Now, you either make room for my friend as far as Cheyenne, or you can go on without me."

McCaleb was uncomfortable among the newspapermen. Some of them stared at him and Cody with unconcealed amusement. Cody chuckled.

"I reckon we stand out like a pair of ganders in a hen yard."

"I reckon we do," said McCaleb grimly. It was exactly the kind of situation he'd sought to avoid.

Without further trouble, Will and the outfit moved into southern Kansas, bedding down the herd on the south bank of the Arkansas.

"Bein' as how we're this close to th' store," said Salty, "they's some things we could use."

"I expect there is," said Will, "but is there anything we can't do without until we get to Cheyenne?"

"I reckon not," said Salty, "if'n you kin live without dried apple pie."

"We'll gamble on it," said Will.

Except for occasional amused looks and whispers, Cody and McCaleb were ignored by the occupants of the press car. Those who had brought bottles began passing them around. They grew so rowdy at times, McCaleb couldn't hear the clicking of the wheels over coupling joints. Midway in the car was a small stove in which a fire roared. The railroad had thoughtfully provided a keg of water, a two-gallon blue granite coffeepot, and an ample supply of ground coffee. They had already emptied the pot, and a second boiling was under way. The air was blue with a fog of tobacco smoke. McCaleb fanned himself with his hat. Finally he got up.

"I'd as soon ride the roof of this damn coach," he growled. "It's hot in here as the Llano Estacado in July. I need some air."

He headed for the door, Cody following. They stepped out onto an observation platform. The iron railing that partially encircled it was divided in the middle to permit access to a similar area at the end of the adjoining car. McCaleb leaned across the interval and tried the door at the end of the presidential coach. It was locked. Even with the rush of the wind in their ears, it was less noisy than inside the coach.

"They ain't goin' to unlock that door without a damn good reason," said Cody.

"I aim to give them one," said McCaleb, "if that car has a stove with a fire going. It's near suppertime. You still got that newspaper?"

Cody passed it to him.

"I'm going up there and stuff this down the flue," said McCaleb. "I'll have just about enough time to get down before somebody opens this door to either get some air or find out what's blocking the flue."

"There's a door at the other end," said Cody. "You're almighty sure they'll use this one."

"Anybody climbing to the roof won't have any choice," said McCaleb. "There's no ladder at the other end. At least there wasn't when the train left Omaha. You can go back inside and not become involved in this."

"I wouldn't miss it for half ownership in the Union Pacific. Besides, you're goin' to need somebody to unstop that flue if you're aiming to spend some time in that coach. You'd best get goin', before that bunch in the press car sobers up enough to wonder what we're doin' out here."

McCaleb pulled a leather thong from his pocket and tied down his hat. He reached the top of the presidential coach, easing himself onto the catwalk on his hands and knees. With the snakelike curves, the swaying of the train, and the bumpy irregularity of the track, he dared not risk standing. He reached the protruding stove flue, found it warm to the touch and grinned to himself. It was a skimpy newspaper, but the flue wasn't large. Quickly he descended the ladder, positioning himself against the wall next to the locked door of the presidential coach. He didn't have long to wait. When the door swung open, a Union soldier stepped out. McCaleb got an arm around his throat, cut off his wind, and with the muzzle of his Colt, hit him just hard enough.

"There'll be another one, Bill, when this one doesn't get the job done. I'll take care of him, and drag them back inside, out of sight. Once I've grabbed the second one, cat-foot it up the ladder and unstop that flue. I'll be inside by then. One of these blue bellies will have a key to that door. Tie these old boys so's they can't get loose, lock that door from the inside, and wait there for me. If you know any prayers, say them."

Again he positioned himself by the door. Again it opened and a second Union soldier appeared.

"Howell," he bawled, "where are you? What's—"

McCaleb caught him around the throat and silenced him with a swift blow of the Colt's muzzle. Swiftly Cody ascended the ladder as McCaleb dragged the two unconscious men into the presidential coach. He closed the door behind him and advanced to the door ahead. He drew his Colt, turned the knob, and confronted the president of the United States.

24

*F*ollowing a hard winter, spring came early to the high country. The cows driven from Texas as part of the original herd brought the Bar Six its first natural increase. More than a hundred calves.

"They're so pretty," cried Penelope. "Why do they have to grow up into big old ugly cows and be eaten?"

Except for branding the calves and guarding against wolves, there was little to do at the ranch. Taking Goose with him, Brazos rode west along the Sweetwater. While they hadn't seen hide nor hair of Maury Duke's bunch, Brazos still expected trouble from them. He believed McCaleb was right about one thing: Duke had been told to pull in his horns until after July 12. However McCaleb's daring confrontation came out, they needed some idea as to what was going on in Duke's camp. To that end, Brazos determined to scout the Sweetwater regularly. To vary the routine and relieve boredom, he sent a different pair of riders each time.

"Stay out of sight," Brazos told them. "When McCaleb returns, we'll have some idea as to how to handle them."

One thing they learned immediately. The gold seekers had long since moved eastward past Kingston Henry's old cabin. They were within a few miles of the Bar Six western boundary.

* * *

The balding little man who had introduced the president in Omaha sat there gasping like a fish out of water. Grant's expression didn't change. If he was afraid, there was no evidence of it.

"Mr. President," said McCaleb, "I have to talk to you."

"I'll talk to no man who conducts his business with a loaded pistol," said Grant. "I'll see you in Leavenworth for this."

"Maybe," said McCaleb, "but I'll take some of your congressmen with me. You have nothing to fear from me. I'm asking only for you to hear me out."

He holstered the Colt.

"What have you done with my sentries? The soldiers?"

"In the outer room," said McCaleb. "They're unhurt except for sore heads. Now will you listen to me?"

"Have I any choice?"

"You do," said McCaleb, "but like I told you, you won't like it. Is there anybody in that room behind you?"

"No," said Grant. "There was a soldier at each end; no one else."

"In that case," said McCaleb, pointing to the bald little man, "you can wait out there."

The presidential aide seemed eager to follow McCaleb's order, but Grant stopped him.

"Mr. Elkins is one of my private secretaries. He handles much of my communication with the Congress. If what you're about to tell me involves one or more congressmen, it will be to your advantage to have Mr. Elkins present."

"Sit down, Elkins," said McCaleb.

Elkins sat, a little less frightened now. McCaleb dug out the crumpled letter and passed it to Grant. He read it swiftly and handed it to Elkins. Grant sighed and finally spoke.

"You're McCaleb, then. You've gotten yourself in trouble and you expect me to get you out of it. I presume you're prepared to give me some good reasons why I should, are you not?"

"I am," said McCaleb. "Since Mr. Elkins is all that close

to Congress, why don't you ask him if what I'm about to tell you is true?"

Swiftly he presented his case, using facts supplied him by Sam Colton and the land office to implicate George Francis Train in the land grab in the Sweetwater valley.

"I can't be the conscience of the nation, Mr. President. If the Congress is satisfied, allowing one man to swallow up a third of Wyoming Territory, then so be it. But I'm not satisfied, because that same man is trying to run me out. He's using his money, his position, and your office to do it. Now you get him out of the Sweetwater valley, or I promise you, every newspaper in this nation is going to get the same facts I've just handed you. Even if I have to tell the story from a cell in Leavenworth."

For a long moment there was only the clicking of wheels over uneven iron rails. Elkins's face paled. When Grant finally spoke, it was with a poorly restrained fury. He spoke not to McCaleb, but to Elkins.

"Mr. Elkins, is this true?"

"I, ah . . . I'm afraid it . . . it is, sir. Most of it. It goes back to . . . well, to Mr. Lincoln's time. He . . . it was he who . . . commissioned Oakes Ames to build the . . . the railroad . . . whatever the cost. Mr. Ames is . . . you know his stature in the Congress—"

"Damn his stature in the Congress!" roared Grant. "I didn't seek this office; it was forced upon me. Two months of it, by God, and already I'm having to answer for everything except the cracking of the Liberty Bell. Elkins, once we reach a stop where there's a telegraph key, send a wire to Rawlins. I want him in my office the minute I return to Washington."

It was more than McCaleb had hoped for. He moved toward the door through which he had entered. In a near normal voice, Grant spoke.

"I'll keep this letter, Mr. McCaleb. I'm not sure how much of this I can undo, insofar as the seizing of public lands is concerned, but I can kill this so-called hearing and spare you further harassment. From Washington, anyhow. I expect you can handle it on a local level."

Reaching the door, McCaleb paused. He removed his hat, turned to the president and put out his hand. Grant took it, and while he didn't permit himself a smile, the show of respect touched him. Their eyes met, and it was an experience McCaleb never forgot. He stepped out the door and closed it behind him. Bill Cody was waiting.

"My God," he whispered, "what took you so long? I thought he was maybe court-martialing you on the spot."

"I met a friend," said McCaleb, "and I had trouble getting away."

"What about these soldiers?"

"Leave them be," said McCaleb. "They'll be attended to. Now let's get back to that rolling saloon, before some of that bunch comes looking for us."

Will continued a three-man night watch from dusk to dawn, and none of them drew an easy breath until they crossed into southern Nebraska. Once they reached the Union Pacific tracks, they turned west, following the cleared right-of-way.

"Can you imagine what these critters would do," said Red, chuckling, "if one of them trains showed up sudden an' cut loose with its whistle?"

"They wouldn't quit running until they hit Indian Territory," said Jed.

"East and west tracks have been joined by now," said Will, "but it's a little soon for regular trains. But we'll play it safe. We won't bed down the herd anywhere near the track. All of you listen close from here on to Cheyenne. If you even think you hear a whistle, run these brutes into the brush and away from the track."

The train reached Cheyenne at four o'clock in the morning, and to the surprise of McCaleb and Cody, the town was wide awake. Despite the hour, Grant rewarded their patience by greeting them from the rear of the presidential coach. Elkins had gone immediately to the depot, and McCaleb was elated. He believed the little man was following Grant's instructions and was sending a telegram to Rawlins. Sam Colton would find out later. McCaleb stepped down from the coach, followed by Bill Cody, and found the grinning Colton waiting.

"Sam," said McCaleb, "this is Bill Cody. Buffalo Bill Cody. He was kind enough to get me a seat on the train."

"I've heard a lot about you," said Colton. "I'd like to do a story on you, when it's convenient."

"It ain't convenient now," said Cody. "I'm just stretching my legs and gettin' some fresh air. I got to ride this iron bronc plumb to Utah for the joining of the rails."

"Then we'll talk on the way," said Colton. "I'm a newspaperman, and I've been promised a seat."

"You can have mine," said McCaleb, "but I'm not sure you'll be welcome unless you've got a bottle."

"McCaleb," said Cody, "why don't you stay in town tonight? Soon as this marryin' of the east and west has took place in Utah, I'm comin' right back here. Then I'll ride with you to the ranch for that visit I been promisin'."

"Do that, McCaleb," urged Colton. "I want to talk to you, and I won't have time now. We'll be back either late tonight or early tomorrow."

"On one condition," said McCaleb. "One of the president's men is sending a telegram to Washington. When you get back, I want to know who it was sent to and what it said."

Colton grinned. "You'd have made a hell of a newspaperman. We'll see you tomorrow."

The engineer blew a warning blast on the whistle, and the conductor looked impatiently at his watch. Reluctantly Cody followed Sam Colton up the steps to the press car. McCaleb watched the train vanish into the darkness, soon to begin its climb into the Rockies. He found old Josh Olson standing on the depot steps.

"Did you have a good trip, McCaleb?"

"Far better than I expected. I appreciate what you did

for me. Lock your door and come along. I'll buy your breakfast."

Will and his outfit reached Cheyenne on May 24, 1869. They bypassed the town, bedding down the herd on Lodge Pole Creek, half a dozen miles north.

"We'll rest here a day," said Will. "We could all use some clean clothes and some barbering. Tomorrow you can take turns riding into town. Tonight I have some business to take care of."

There was no moon. Waiting until good dark, Will took Susannah with him and rode in to talk to Sam Colton. He would have news of McCaleb. The grinning newspaperman met them at the door. Without a word, he took a sheet of yellow paper from a desk drawer. Will read the telegram, Susannah crowding close. It was addressed to Benton McCaleb, Cheyenne, Wyoming. There was a very brief message. It read:

> Disregard letter. July 12 hearing canceled.
> John A. Rawlins

Laughing and crying, Susannah threw her arms around Will. He just stood there, his grin matching Colton's. Sam recovered first.

"If McCaleb told me he could walk on water, I'd believe him. But you haven't seen anything yet. Even McCaleb doesn't know about this, because it happened after he and Bill Cody left for the ranch."

"Uncle Bill's here!" cried Susannah.

"Yes," said Colton. "He had been invited to the meeting of the rails, and managed to get McCaleb on the train in Omaha. I'm a member of the press, so I had an invitation to the ceremony. Cody persuaded McCaleb to spend the night here so they could ride to the ranch together. I joined Cody in the press car. We were there for the ceremony and were back in Cheyenne later that same night.

My God, I never dreamed I'd travel at such speed! There were times when we reached forty miles an hour!"

"Enough of that," said Will impatiently. "Besides the telegram from Washington, what happened after McCaleb and Cody rode out?"

"Maury Duke showed up and started a ruckus at the bank. He claimed the bank had cheated him. Musgrove closed his account, gave him his money, and the sheriff made him leave. I managed to learn what the fight was about. The fifteenth of every month, there's been a bank draft sent from Omaha and deposited in Duke's account. Well, this month it didn't come, and that's what Duke was raising hell about. When they kicked him out of the bank, he went to the telegraph office and sent a telegram to Omaha. S. J. Pauley. All it said was 'confirm June first.' He waited three days and didn't get an answer. Josh checked with the operator in Omaha, and the wire was never picked up. He also found that the office rented under Pauley's name had been closed. Josh said Maury Duke acted damn strange when he got that wire. He just mounted up and rode out of town. Following a hunch, I wired my newspaper contact in Omaha and asked for an update on the Credit Mobilier story. Half the papers in the country have been howling for a congressional investigation, so my request wasn't unusual. Now this is barely ten days after McCaleb's appeal to the president. My informant says George Francis Train has sold all his Credit Mobilier stock and is no longer associated with the Union Pacific in any way. All his considerable holdings in Omaha are to be liquidated. He has departed on a trip around the world. He issued a brief statement claiming other interests, one of which is another bid for the presidency in 'seventy-two.'"

"President Train." Will grinned. "What are his chances?"

"Not nearly as good as last time. In 'sixty-eight the Democrats wouldn't even accept him as a candidate, and he had thirty million dollars."

"Thank God he's gone," said Susannah. "Our troubles in the Sweetwater valley are over."

"Not necessarily," said Will. "Even if Train's backing out of the land grab, that doesn't mean Duke's bunch has. I expect we'll still end up in a fight with them."

"That's about the way I see it," said Colton. "Now that there's no deal with Train, no sharing, I expect those 'homesteaders' will hang on till hell freezes. When you deliver this news to McCaleb, tell him I still want to break the story of the discovery of gold on the Sweetwater. I promised to hold off until he made his play. He's drawn to an inside straight and taken the pot; now I need to hear from him."

"Brazos will be riding in," said Will, "just as soon as we get there with the herd. I'll see that McCaleb sends you some word, either to hold off awhile longer, or go ahead. It'll be his decision, but now that Duke's lost his Washington influence, I don't see how it can hurt us."

"In a way it will," said Colton. "Once word gets out that there's gold along the Sweetwater, the valley will be swarming with miners. There'll be so many of them, your outfit will be lost in the crowd."

"You're right," said Will, "and I'm not sure I'll like that any better than having Duke's bunch there. We settled here because it was unspoiled. Overrun it with placer mining and it'll never be the same."

"Only if it's a bonanza," said Colton. "Remember, Duke's gang obviously has been bankrolled by George Train. However little gold there was, they *still* got paid. Now they're on their own and we've got a railroad. Give it a week after I break the story. Mr. Duke and his boys will have more company than they ever dreamed of. Just tell McCaleb this: turn me loose with this story, and I'll water down the soup. Duke and his bunch will have two choices. They can be satisfied with the land on which they've filed, or they can get out. The land grab is over."

"Now that the railroad's finished," said Susannah,

"when will there be a passenger train to Omaha? Brazos is planning to go there around the first of June."

"The first train is supposed to run tomorrow," said Colton. "Why don't you stay until then and take McCaleb an Omaha newspaper? It'll have the full story on Train, probably with a lot more detail than I was sent by telegraph."

"Will, let's do it," said Susannah. "We're not that far from the ranch. It'll be worth the wait, just to see Bent McCaleb's face when he reads it. Besides, I need some time in town to buy some special things for Rosalie and Penelope. I promised Rebecca."

"I'd kind of like to read the full story on Train myself," said Will. "McCaleb needs to know about this as soon as possible. Now that Duke and his bunch has been cut loose, they may take to back-shooting us."

"All the more reason to break that story," said Colton.

Maury Duke rode out of Cheyenne in a blind fury, not caring where his horse took him. Before he cut loose from Train, he'd counted on one more check. It was getting so a man couldn't depend on anything or anybody, he thought glumly. Just when he had been about to double-cross Train, the back-shooting bastard had double-crossed him. That had been bad enough, but he was consumed with curiosity as to who or what had forced Train to cut and run. How did it affect him? Once his irrational fury subsided and he began weighing his alternatives, he decided Train had done him a favor. Now that he didn't have to take his stake and run, fearing retribution once his treachery was discovered, he could remain in the Sweetwater valley until all the gold was his. Of course he'd have to give up half of it to the men who spent their days slogging around in the Sweetwater River, but there might be a way around that. By the time they'd picked the river clean, he would come up with a scheme to divert their share of the gold into his own pockets.

But he had a more immediate problem. He intended to follow the Sweetwater all the way to its confluence with the

North Platte. That would take him across the claims of that bunch of Texans along Box Elder Creek. Train, with all his cautions, was out of it. What was to stop Maury Duke and his men from riding in and killing them all? They could then search the creek at their leisure and scatter to the four winds before anybody was the wiser. He vowed to scout the ranch daily until Susannah returned. True, it would mean more fighting men once the rest of the outfit returned, but what did he care? He could still outnumber them two to one, and the girl, despite her being married and lost to him forever, had become an obsession. He rode on, his evil heart aflame with anticipation.

25

$\mathcal{W}$ill and his riders completed the drive to Box Elder Creek without incident. Since they'd been away for six months, Susannah had taken the time in Cheyenne to buy special provisions for a homecoming celebration. She and Salty had bought smoked hams, smoked and tinned fish, tinned fruits and vegetables, and a big basket of fresh eggs. Will helped Salty loose a crate that was lashed to the rear of the chuck wagon. In it was a rooster and a dozen noisy hens Salty had found and bought.

"The wolves and coyotes will love them," said McCaleb.

"For fresh eggs," said Rebecca, "I'll personally shoot every damn wolf and coyote in Wyoming."

Monte's hound had been lagging behind, and when he finally plodded into the yard, Penelope lost interest in the chickens and adopted him. It was a gala evening of good food, good humor, and a sense of belonging. Bill Cody had made himself at home, and the new riders from Texas were made welcome. It wasn't until long after supper that McCaleb, Brazos, and Will had a chance to talk. Will told them what Sam Colton had learned about Train's departure.

"This changes things considerable," said Brazos, "Duke bein' on his own. We've been scoutin' the Sweetwater nearly every day, and we've accounted for thirty riders so far. They're advancing along the Sweetwater toward us. I think we ought to go after them and not wait for them to come after us."

"I'm of the same mind," said McCaleb. "I'd planned to take a drive into Montana, but I can't take half the outfit away when we're already outnumbered."

"Sam Colton has the right idea," said Will. "Turn him loose with that story on the discovery of gold, and Duke's bunch will be overrun. They're already off their homesteaded property and onto public land."

"I've already talked to Rosie," said Brazos, "and we won't leave the rest of you to face this showdown with Duke's men."

"Brazos," said McCaleb, "you can save that trip to Omaha for later. For now, take Rosalie to Cheyenne and the two of you stand up before a preacher. Then you can bring her back here and move into that cabin with her."

Maury Duke found his men enthusiastically receptive to the idea of stripping the remaining gold from the Sweetwater valley. Without fear of retribution hanging over their heads, they'd be in no hurry to leave, and if they stayed, that bunch of Texans on Box Elder Creek had to go. He would kill two birds with one stone, staging it all so that he could steal Susannah from under their noses during the attack.

Duke began spying on the ranch, and just a week following his return from Cheyenne, he spotted the approaching herd. He noted with satisfaction that Susannah was back, and after the long drive, he reckoned it was unlikely that she'd be leaving again soon. On the other hand, with another herd of steers, plus what they already had, there might be another trail drive north. He had learned of the several drives to Fort Buford. Such a drive now would again split the outfit, almost surely leaving Susannah at the ranch. The day after the arrival of the new herd, he watched Brazos and Rosalie ride out.

* * *

"It's the first time I ever left Penelope," worried Rosalie. "I hope she'll be all right."

"She'll be fine," said Brazos, "but the dog, the rooster, and the hens won't be worth a damn. She'll feed them six times a day, and spoil the lot of them."

"I'm glad they were there to distract her. I was afraid she'd throw a fit to come with us. I'll miss her, but I . . . I wanted this first night or two . . . just for us."

"So did I," said Brazos, "so I had a talk with her. I promised her we'd take the train to Omaha, maybe in the fall. I also promised I'd bring her anything she wanted from Cheyenne, if she'd let us have this time to ourselves."

"You'll spoil her. I'm afraid for you to tell me what she asked for."

"She says all she wants is a daddy. I promised her one."

Including himself, McCaleb had sixteen riders. Brazos and Rosalie would be gone probably a week, and allowing Colton time to get out the paper, it might be two weeks or longer before the story produced any results. Too long for them to just wait and do nothing. When Brazos and Rosalie were gone, McCaleb called the outfit together.

"Gents," he said, "I know any man of you would rather cross the Staked Plains on foot, in the dead of summer and without water, than endure what I'm about to suggest, but it's got to be done. For the next couple of weeks, we will be cutting hay."

Their agonized groans lived up to his every expectation. A cowboy would spend sixteen hours in the saddle and never complain. But ground him with a hay fork in his hands and he'd moan like he'd sold his soul to the devil and the evil one had just shown up to collect. While Goose accepted many of the white man's ways, he drew the line at anything that left him afoot with a tool in his hands. Goose was left to ride where he saw fit, a Winchester under his arm, ever wary of intruders.

"We work like dogs while he sets his saddle," complained Monte. "How come that no-account Injun never does any of the dirty work?"

McCaleb chuckled. "It's in his contract. The Injun treaty signed at Fort Laramie in 'sixty-eight forbids it."

They built open-sided hay sheds, roofing them with cedar shakes.

"The time will come," said McCaleb, "when cattlemen will be forced to plant hay for winter feeding. That, or risk losing everything to a hard winter. I don't aim for that to happen to us."

Cheyenne was a two-day journey, and Brazos and Rosalie rode in at sundown on the second day. The town already reflected the influence of the railroad. Several new businesses had sprung up, one of them a hotel.

"We'll get us a room there," said Brazos, "but there's something else we need to do first."

"I can't think beyond getting off this horse," said Rosalie wearily. "I hate to disappoint you, but I may spend the night leaning against a wall. I'm not sure I'll ever sit down again, or want to."

"We'll leave our horses at the livery," said Brazos, "and walk. That'll help. Then we'll give McCaleb's message to Sam Colton and have him take us to a preacher. Once we're in our room, I'll get you a tub of hot water and you can soak some of the misery out."

"It would be just our luck for this town not to have a preacher."

"Susannah says there's at least one. She came here to teach school and was living here when she met Will. We're going to put her talents to use. When we finally get to Omaha, we'll take a list Susannah's making up and buy the books she'll need for Penelope's schooling. I reckon it'll come as a considerable shock to her, but she's got more ahead than riding horses and roping cows."

"Brazos Gifford," she cried, "you're so much more than

just a cowboy. I'm never sure what you're going to do next."

"This once you can," said Brazos, "after that parson makes it legal."

She didn't even blush.

"I'm going to thoroughly enjoy publishing this next issue," said Colton. "You tell McCaleb I'll send copies of it east, including Omaha and Chicago. Ma'am, you look like I *felt* after my ride to Box Elder Creek. We'd better get you to that preacher, while you can still make it."

The ceremony was brief. Colton served as best man and brashly kissed the bride before she knew what was coming.

"Colton," Brazos said, "don't you ever do that again."

They found the hotel a little rough around the edges. While there was a bathtub, Brazos had to carry the hot water from the kitchen to the second floor. Rosalie collapsed across the bed and Brazos dragged off her boots. She struggled to her feet and Brazos looked at her uncertainly.

"Since this is our . . . my, uh . . . Damn it, do you want me to take a walk so's you can take your bath?"

"Not unless you plan to get yourself another room for the night. You'll just have to see me at my worst, all sweaty and blistered. Besides, I need you to scrub my back."

"Yes, ma'am," said Brazos. "Anything else I can do for you?"

"Whatever you're of a mind to," she said roguishly. "Use your cowboy imagination. I'm just blistered, not crippled."

It was time for the attack, Duke decided. He had waited, expecting another trail drive that would split the outfit and lessen resistance, but saw no sign of it. He assembled his men.

"Two more months," he said, "and we're into another winter in this godforsaken country. We play our cards right and we can be out of here before snow flies. That means gettin' rid of the Texans at the eastern end of the valley. Is everybody with me?"

"Not me," said a voice. "I ain't forgot that last raid of yours."

"Then ride out, Adams, and don't come back. Any more of you that feels the way he does, mount up and ride with him. Otherwise, be here at midnight tomorrow night."

They drifted away, and he realized they weren't wholeheartedly with him. They were weighing the risk against the possible remaining gold. This time they'd be up against sixteen fighting Texans. In his mind's eye he could see the Texans fighting like demons, while his own halfhearted band turned tail and ran like frightened coyotes. But the sound of approaching horses startled him into awareness, and he moved cautiously to the door. They had considered the risk, he thought sourly, and some of them were riding back to weasel out. But it was far worse. He eased open the door, his hand on the butt of his Colt, and was greeted by a cold, familiar voice from the darkness.

"Drop your hand away from that gun."

"Burke?"

"Yeah," said Burke with an evil chuckle. "Devins is here too, an' we got some friends with us."

"Damn you," snarled Duke, "I paid the two of you to quit the territory."

"Oh, we did," chuckled Burke, "an' our word's just as good as yours. We rode out, but we didn't promise to stay out, did we, Devins?"

"Naw," said Devins. "How could we? We still got claims here, all legal an' honest. We come back 'cause we seen in th' paper where th' tall hog at th' trough ain't there no more. We got ever' right to them claims."

"Damn right," said Burke. "Now that the word's out, gold fever will spread like a prairie fire."

"You double-crossing bastards!" bawled Duke. "You put out the word on the gold?"

"You don't know, do you?" Burke chuckled. "Th' story come out in that piddly little paper in Cheyenne. I got it with me. Now ever' paper in the country's talkin' about gold in the Sweetwater valley."

Duke leaned against the doorjamb, breathing hard. If they told the truth, their showing up wouldn't make a particle of difference. The valley would soon be alive with men. There was only one thing in his favor. Maybe he could enlist these fools in his attack on the Texans.

"Step down and come in," said Duke, as calmly as he could. "I'd like to see that paper."

He turned back into the cabin and lit a lamp.

Cautiously, Burke and Devins stepped into the room. Behind them stood two bearded strangers with cold eyes and tied-down Colts, as vicious a pair of lobo wolves as Duke had ever seen.

"This is Hogan an' Eford," said Burke. "They filed on a couple of th' quarter sections th' other side of Kingston Henry's old cabin."

"Looks like some sticky-fingered bastards has been workin' our claims," growled Hogan. "I reckon somebody's owin' us. Mebbe you."

"Nobody owes you a damn thing," snarled Duke. "Until you filed on it, if you filed on it, it was public land." He turned to Burke. "Where's that paper you said you had?"

Burke dragged it out of his hip pocket and handed it over. It was all there. It sickened Duke after a few paragraphs and he could read no more. Mutely he returned the paper to Burke.

"We ain't told nobody nothin'," said Burke. "You can see that. Likely them cowboys figgered it out an' spilled th' beans."

"We're going after that bunch of Texans tomorrow night," said Duke. "The richest pockets of gold are at the eastern end of the valley, and not only are they settin' on it, they're on patented land."

"Texans bleed just like ever'body else," said Hogan. "They won't need no land if'n they're dead."

"You got the idea," said Duke, "and I got a plan. We ride out tomorrow at midnight."

* * *

After four days in Cheyenne, Brazos and Rosalie returned to a good-natured hoorawing from the outfit and an emotional reception from Penelope. McCaleb read the story Colton had published and immediately got the outfit together.

"Once they're aware of this," he said, "they'll strike. They won't have anything to lose. They'll only have a little time to prospect this end of the valley, and they can't do that with us here. They might fire our buildings or stampede the herd to draw us out, so we're going to eliminate the possibility of that. Until this is finished, every man of us will roll his blankets outside. Keep your horses saddled and don't shuck anything but your hat. We'll nighthawk in four watches, four riders at a time. When we sleep, we'll throw our blankets in a kind of skirmish line. When you go on watch, the man you relieve will take your place. We're going to handle this so that the surprise will be theirs, not ours. We'll have two outriders, and I'm leaving that to our Injuns. Pen, you'll ride until midnight. Goose will relieve you and ride until dawn. You'll take your positions three miles east, riding a swath from a mile north of the Sweetwater to four miles south of it. At first sign of their approach, light a shuck back here and alert the rest of us. Those of you on watch with the herd, stay there. We mustn't allow them to penetrate our line of defense. By keeping them out in front of us, we can shoot anything that moves. Any questions?"

"That's as good a defense as I ever saw or heard tell of," said Red. "Was you by any chance with Forrest or Mosby?"

McCaleb chuckled. "Better than that. I fought the Kiowa, the Comanche, and border outlaws with the Rangers."

They took their supper well before dark. Salty, although he didn't show a light, kept the coffee hot. For security's sake, Rebecca and Susannah spent their nights in Brazos's larger cabin, with Rosalie and Penelope. It became a time of waiting, but McCaleb didn't believe they'd have to wait for long. He was right.

Maury Duke was in a rotten mood. Including himself, Burke, Devins, and their pair of hardcase friends, he had but twenty-five men. That meant a dozen of his own bunch, damn them, had laid out on him. With that in mind, he spoke to the rest.

"We're missin' some men. Them as ain't willin' to fight with the rest of us, way I see it, have folded and pulled out of the game. If they're still around tomorrow, we'll give 'em a choice: live somewhere else or be planted here permanent. Any questions before we ride?"

"Yeah," said a disgruntled voice. "Th' soup's already too thin t' suit me, an' now you brung in four more jaspers fer a dip in th' pot. Where'n hell has Burke an' Devins been fer all this time?"

"Duke'll explain it to you," said Devins, chuckling. "It was all his idee, me an' Burke takin' a trip. Hogan an' Eford are pards of ours, an' they filed their claims in Cheyenne, all legal an' proper. You don't like it, I reckon they'll set you straight."

"We don't need nobody talkin' fer us," growled Hogan. "Me an' Eford, we do our own talkin' an' our own killin'. Anybody callin' us?"

"Back off, damn it!" bawled Duke. "Fightin' amongst yourselves won't put gold in your pokes. As for Burke, Devins, Hogan, and Eford, they're willing to fight for the gold, so that entitles them to share whatever there is. Them of you with a mad on, save it for the fight. Now let's ride!"

By the stars, it was after midnight when Will awakened McCaleb.

"Goose just rode in," said Will. "They're coming. Twenty-five of them."

"Pull one of the riders away from the herd, take Goose, and the three of you watch the valley where our hay sheds are. They'll have some diversion in mind to pull us out of the cabins. You see anybody heading for the hay sheds, it won't be any of our riders. Shoot to kill."

26

Maury Duke reined up two miles west of the Six Bar ranch.

"We're goin' to get close to the cabins as we can," he said. "When they come out, we cut them down."

"Ain't he the smart one?" said Devins sarcastically. "We'll just ask 'em polite to come out an' be shot."

Duke continued, ignoring the interruption and the insult.

"Kincer, I want you and Slick to work your way north, cross the river, and get into that valley where they been cuttin' hay. Set fire to as many haystacks as you can. Tinker, you and Williams get as close as you can to that herd of cows. Soon as you see the flames from the burning hay, cut loose with your rifles and stampede the herd. That'll stir up enough of a commotion to bring them running, and then we'll shoot them down. Get goin'."

They rode out without complaint, so quickly that Duke suspicioned they were eager to avoid the fight.

"The rest of us will fan out and move within rifle range," said Duke. "Soon as you got a target, shoot. Now let's ride."

But there was no fire and no stampede. McCaleb's skirmish line had been established a mile west of the ranch and threw a protective oval of defenders around the perimeter. The four men Duke had delegated never got to their destinations. Duke led his men into the very teeth of the ambush. The moment the attackers rode out of the shadow of the protective trees and into the dim starlight, the Six Bar riders cut loose with their rifles.

"Come on!" shouted Will. "The hay don't need us. The outfit does."

He kicked his horse into a run, Goose and Stoney close behind. They splashed across the Sweetwater and ran headlong into four of Duke's riders. Warned by the shooting, they had forgotten about firing the hay and starting a stampede. They sought only to escape. Certain that the mounted men were none of his own, Will shot the leader out of the saddle. Frantically the others wheeled their horses and lit out down the river. Goose and Stoney had begun firing, but the three had vanished into the shadows beneath the cottonwoods.

"Hold your fire," shouted Will. "Let 'em go."

He turned his horse south. They were safely between the ranch buildings and their own line of defense, but Will reined up well to the rear of the line. He dismounted, Goose and Stoney following.

"On foot from here," said Will. "We're not supposed to be here. We go riding in and we're likely to get shot by our own men."

The first volley cut down Duke's horse, and it was all that saved him. Men to his right and left pitched out of their saddles, their frightened horses galloping hell-bent in the direction they'd come. Duke snatched the flying reins of one of them and got his foot in the stirrup. He hunched low on the horse's neck and let the animal run. They caught up to another horse just as the rider, hard hit, was flung out of the saddle into the path of Duke's mount. The horse shied and reared. Duke fought it to a trembling standstill. Before he could ride on, the wounded man on the ground spoke in a pain-racked voice.

"Help . . . me. I'm hard . . . hit. . . ."

"Burke?"

"Duke . . . it was . . . a trap. You . . . you led us

. . . into a trap, you bastard. Help . . . me . . . I . . . I'm . . . gut-shot. . . ."

"No help for you then," said Duke callously. "Adios, Burke."

"Run," gritted Burke weakly. "You yellow . . . bellied . . . son of a bitch . . ."

By the time Will, Goose, and Stoney reached the line, the firing had all but ceased.

"Hold your fire!" shouted McCaleb.

"No pursuit, then," said Will.

"No," said McCaleb. "If they have the guts, they could ambush us. We got enough of them, I think, to make believers of the rest. Come morning, we'll see how many men this fool stunt cost them. Then we'll ride downriver and have a serious talk with anybody brash enough to stick around."

"We ran into four of them," said Will. "On their way to stampede the herd, I reckon. Three of them got away. Lit a shuck downriver."

Slowly the outfit came together. McCaleb called their names and everybody answered except Goose.

"Out there taking scalps," said Brazos.

"Pen," said Monte, "you're Injun too. How come you ain't takin' scalps?"

"I ain't that much Injun," said Pen.

"We're all alive, then," said McCaleb. "Anybody hurt?"

"I run into a stubbed-off dead limb," said Harley. "Cut a turrible gash across my jaw."

"Sorry to hear it," said McCaleb dryly. "We'll bury you alongside the Sweetwater."

"There's a horse coming," said Pen.

The horse approached from the direction of the ranch. It slowed from a gallop to a trot.

"That's far enough," said McCaleb, "until we know who you are."

"It's me!" cried Rebecca.

McCaleb helped her down.

"Was any of us hurt?" she asked fearfully.

"Just Harley," said McCaleb. "He was fatally slashed by a tree limb."

"You'll have to get shot between the eyes, Harley," she said, "to get any sympathy from this bunch. Ride back with me and I'll patch you up."

"I told all of you to stay inside," said McCaleb. "What are you doing here, anyhow?"

"Well, hell's bells," she snapped, "it sounded like a war going on, and then it all just stopped. We didn't know if you'd killed all of them or if they'd killed all of you. You could have sent somebody to . . . to tell us that nobody was hurt. Brazos, I wish you'd ride back with me. Rosalie's worried and poor Penelope's having conniption fits. Rosalie had to whip her to keep her from trying to come with me."

"We'll all ride in," said McCaleb. "Will, ride out and check on the herd. Tell the boys everything's under control and that the watch goes on as usual. When Goose comes in, I'll have him ride the area for the rest of the night so the rest of you can get some sleep. I don't expect any more visitors, but we won't gamble on it.

"Go on and get some sleep," McCaleb told Rebecca. "I need to talk to Goose, and I want to know how effective our ambush was."

"How many of them are . . . dead?"

"Seven," said McCaleb.

"Then come in with me. I've spent too many nights here alone while you were somewhere else. I'll light the lamp. Goose will know you'll want to hear from him."

McCaleb sank down wearily on a stool. He was exhausted.

"I'm sorry I was cross with you," she said, "but Penelope went wild. If Brazos was . . . had been . . . killed . . . I believe we'd have been able to bury the child with him. She would have died of a broken heart, literally."

"I'm as envious of him as I am glad for him," said McCaleb. "Me and Will both got hitched before he did, and he's already got a young'un old enough to cry over him. Can't we do something to remedy that?"

"Not with you sleeping in the brush minus only your hat and leaving me here while you're away on trail drives. Where is Goose, anyway?"

"Taking scalps, I reckon."

"Dear God, I thought . . . I'd hoped . . . he had become civilized enough to . . . not do that anymore."

It was characteristic of Goose that there wasn't a sound to announce his arrival. There came a soft rap on the door. Once, twice, a pause, and then a third time. McCaleb stood to the side of the door.

"Ganos?" he inquired.

"Ganos," came the reply. *"Tejano* Injun."

McCaleb chuckled. Pen had begun calling Goose "Texas Indian," and the term had amused the Apache.

"I'll talk to him outside," said McCaleb, "unless you'd like to see his latest collection of scalps."

"My God, no!" Rebecca shuddered.

Goose smelled of sweat and blood. There was a muted clanking of metal and jingle of buckles as he lowered his load of Colts and pistol belts to the ground.

"Much gun," said Goose. "Much shell."

McCaleb grinned. While the Apache was still barbaric in some ways, he was becoming more practical in others. While it wouldn't have occurred to him to rifle the pockets of the dead men, he had collected their weapons and ammunition. That was something he could relate to.

"Muerto, Goose. *Muerto hombres?"*

"Uno, dos, dos, dos," said Goose. *"Muerto."*

Seven dead. It was more than McCaleb had expected, and it was all Goose could tell him. The identities of the men wouldn't matter unless one of them was Maury Duke. They would know, come first light. He left Goose to continue his scouting, gathered up the pile of weapons and belts and gently kicked the door with the toe of his boot. Rebecca opened it and he entered, depositing his load on the floor.

"What on earth?" she said.

"Chalk up one for Goose." McCaleb chuckled. "You haven't cured him of taking scalps, but he's becoming more materialistic."

"How many . . . dead?"

"Seven that Goose was able to find. There may be more, but we won't find them in the dark. We're not more than three hours away from first light. We'd better get to bed."

"I'll never be able to sleep."

"Who said anything about sleeping?" said McCaleb. "Put out the lamp."

Maury Duke rode recklessly, with but a single thought in mind. He must take what gold he had and run for it. He didn't know how many of his men had survived. But he did know that, given the chance, any one of them would gut-shoot him and consider it a privilege. That created a real problem. Where was he to go? Cheyenne was the only town closer than Denver, and either or both of them might be crawling with men who would shoot on sight. He felt no remorse for those who had died, lavishing all his pity upon himself. He cursed the Six Bar outfit, George Francis Train, and perverse fate. He had been dealt a busted flush when he had deserved an inside straight.

Well before reaching his cabin, he dismounted and half-hitched his horse to a box elder sapling. He wouldn't put it past a man of them, having gotten there ahead of him, to gun him down from the shadows. It was exactly what he would have done. He reached the cabin and, standing to one side of the door, kicked it open. Satisfied he was alone, without a light, he removed a section of log from the wall above his bunk. He let out a sigh of relief when he found the two leather pokes still there. His life had gone to hell so totally and so rapidly, he had half expected they would be gone. He shoved the piece of log back in place. He wouldn't make it easy for them. Finding the cabin deserted, they wouldn't know he hadn't died in the ambush. He took fiendish pleasure in the possibility some of them

would waste a day or two in a futile search for his gold. Of
necessity, he began planning his escape. He had dismissed
Cheyenne and Denver, and that left him but one choice.
Swiftly he gathered his provisions into a blanket, topping it
off with a frying pan and coffeepot. He pulled the door
shut behind him and returned to his horse. If anybody
wanted him badly enough to trail him, he would make it as
difficult as possible. He rode his horse into the Sweetwater
and didn't leave it until the water became too deep. From
there he rode north. Toward the Big Horn Mountains.

At dawn, following the ambush, McCaleb took eight men,
including Goose, to verify the dead. They rode in ever-
widening half circles until they had covered an area extending almost three miles from their western boundary.
Even in the dark Goose had been remarkably thorough.
For all their searching, they found only the seven bodies he
had reported. Seeing them in daylight, Goose quickly veri-
fied what McCaleb had expected. Maury Duke had escaped. Some of the new riders, viewing the ghastly
remains, turned away. They didn't appreciate Goose's
handiwork.

"My God," said Red Dulaney, "whatever else these
gents was, they was white men. Does he always take
scalps?"

"Only from them as he don't like," said McCaleb. "Stay
on the good side of him."

Two of the night riders had lost more than their scalps.
Goose had gotten creative, and even McCaleb was re-
pulsed. Brazos laughed.

"You don't recognize these two hombres, but Goose did.
They, along with Maury Duke, tried to take him to Omaha
in chains. Sam Colton said Duke paid them off and ran
them out of the territory. Their tough luck that they came
back."

"Break out the shovels," said McCaleb. "Let's plant
these coyotes and be done with it. Then we'll ride downriver and see if any of that bunch is still around."

* * *

Maury Duke hunched over a small fire in Big Horn basin, eating beans from the frying pan and drinking coffee from the pot. The three days and nights since the disaster at Box Elder Creek hadn't improved his disposition a particle. The more he thought about it, the more he thirsted for vengeance. First, there was the gold that remained in the portion of the river that crossed Six Bar land. Then there was the gold in the pokes of the thirty men who had been part of his scheme. He hadn't had time to devise a means of getting his hands on that, and now he never would. Second, after the loss of the gold he might have stolen, was his planned abduction of Susannah. Finally, he decided his hate was stronger than his greed, and he set his devious mind to work on a means of getting even. He would steal Susannah away, take his pleasure with her, and be gone, maybe to California. He would stalk them like a lobo wolf. Sooner or later there would be another trail drive, and the outfit would again be divided. But trail drive or not, the girl had to come out of that cabin sometime, for some reason. When she did, Maury Duke would be waiting.

McCaleb took six men with him and they rode the Sweetwater west as far as its confluence with the Green. They found nine men still in possession of their homesteads, and each denied having taken part in the raid. McCaleb left them with a warning and the assurance he wanted no more trouble. When they returned to the ranch, he called the outfit together.

"It's time to get on with the business of buying and selling cows," he said. "I figure we've got maybe ten weeks before the first snow. I'm a mite unsure as to whether we ought to take that drive to Montana this late in the summer. Do any of you know anything about the territory or what we might encounter there?"

"I do," said Bill Cody, "but I'm not part of your outfit."

"You don't have to be," said McCaleb. "As a scout, not a man here is your equal, except maybe Goose. Montana will be as new to him as it will be to the rest of us. Any information you'll share with us will be appreciated."

"In 'sixty-seven," said Cody, "right after the railroad built the town of Cheyenne, I scouted for some army brass and we traveled from Cheyenne to Miles City, in eastern Montana Territory. It's maybe four hundred miles as the crow flies. From here, about three hundred. Plenty of water, but no bad rivers to cross. Trouble is, there ain't been much gold found in the eastern part. The gold fields kind of fan out around Virginia City for maybe a hundred and fifty miles. You'd have to drive west for maybe two hundred miles after you get to Miles City. That is, if you're shootin' for the gold fields."

"What we're looking at is a six hundred mile drive," said McCaleb.

"Not if you can make a deal to your likin' in Miles City," said Cody. "I ain't sayin' you can't. But I've heard you talk of goin' to the gold fields, and that's the best market. Findin' gold always kicks the price of everything higher than a buck-jumpin' bronc's back."

"Uncle Bill," said Susannah, "you know so much about the country, why don't you go along on this drive?"

"Can't," said Cody. "The damn army won't leave me alone, girl. I let them talk me into another contract. I wouldn't do it, 'cept I get to feelin' sorry for 'em. Them West Point boys is full of book-learnin' but no common sense or sense of direction. Put 'em out here in the wilds, and they can't find their hind quarters with both hands and a coal oil lantern."

"I'm going to ask you a hard question, Bill," said McCaleb, "and I want you to give me the answer straight. From what you know of Montana, should I trail a herd there now or wait until spring? If you were doing it, what would *you* do?"

"I'd go in the spring," said Cody, "and instead of takin' a thousand head, I'd take two thousand. You can do that, because you'll have all summer to pick your market. Go now, and you'll have to take the first offer to get out ahead of the snow. Go in the spring, sell your herd, and spend a couple of months huntin' wild hosses. My God, there's broomtails on that Montana range that'll make the best cow ponies you'll ever lay a saddle on."

"Suppose we did wait for spring," said Jed. "Could we hunt some of them wild ponies after the herd's sold?"

"I don't see why not," said McCaleb. "We're short on horses now."

"Great," said Monte, "but what'll we do the rest of the summer?"

"Cut hay," said McCaleb, to a chorus of groans.

27

"**B**razos," said McCaleb, "since we're holding off until spring on the drive to Montana, this would be a good time for your visit to Omaha. That is, if you still aim to go."

"I reckon there won't be a better time. I haven't told Rosalie or Penelope yet, but I aim to see about legally givin' Penelope my name. There's a lawyer in Cheyenne, but Sam Colton don't think too well of him. I don't trust any of 'em as far as I could walk on water, but I reckon I'll need one for this."

"Do it, man!" McCaleb urged. "Penelope's worth it. I've never envied you before, but I do now. If I was in your boots, I'd swap all I own for her, if that's what it took."

"I'll talk to Rosie, then. If it suits her, then we'll go."

Bill Cody had enjoyed his stay, but he was getting restless. One morning early in July he told McCaleb what was on his mind.

"August tenth, Bent, I'm due at Fort Sill, Indian Territory. I'd thought about takin' you on a huntin' trip into the Big Horns, but I've kind of changed my mind. I don't know when I'm liable to get back this way, and Susannah bein' so partial to me, I'd like to give her somethin' to remember. Somethin' that will mean lots more to her than a huntin' trip would mean to us. I aim to take her and Will to the very top of the Big Horns, ten thousand feet above sea level. It's a peak called Bald Mountain, and there's a kind of plateau, once you've gone as high as you can go. And there's the Medicine Wheel. It's so old, even the Indians don't know who built it or why. In all my scouting, I've never seen anything like it, and I . . . I reckon I just want to share somethin' with Susannah that means a lot to me."

"I don't blame you, Bill," said McCaleb. "What you have in mind sounds more interesting than a hunting trip. I'd like to see that myself, but with Will and Brazos away, I'd feel better if I was here. The outfit don't like cuttin' that tall grass for winter feed. I'd feel guilty, sentencing them to it and then running out on them."

"I reckon it's my fault you'll be needin' that extra feed. Holdin' off until spring on your Montana drive leaves you with all them extra steers to see through the winter. In the high country you never know when winter'll come early and stay late, so you got to be ready."

McCaleb waited until he could talk to Will alone.

"Why don't you take Goose along on that ride into the Big Horns? He's not worth a damn for cutting hay. The outfit likes Bill Cody, and if they think he wants Goose along, it won't look so much like I'm lettin' Goose off easy."

"Which you are," said Will, grinning.

"Maybe, but like I keep telling Rebecca, the more civilized he becomes, the less useful he'll be to us. It's his way to believe anything less than scouting, fighting, and hunting is squaw work. He's found trail driving an acceptable fourth duty because it includes all the elements of the first three."

"We'll get you off the hook," said Will, "and take him with us. He likes Bill Cody anyway. Since we're ranching practically at the foot of the Big Horns, it won't hurt Goose to have some knowledge of them. The same goes for me."

Goose stubbornly rode his favorite horse, although Cody chose mules for himself, Will, and Susannah. They took a pack mule with enough provisions for two weeks. The same morning they rode out for the Big Horns, Brazos, Rosalie, and Penelope left for Cheyenne. From there they would take the train to Omaha.

Maury Duke had ridden back at night and scrounged enough food from the deserted cabins along the Sweetwater to keep him alive. The rest of them seemed to have left as hurriedly as he had, taking little or nothing with them. It was the only crumb of good luck that had fallen to him. He had lost count of the days he had watched the Six Bar ranch without even seeing his quarry at all. He had begun to suspect she had slipped out under cover of darkness and was gone. His impatience was running neck and neck with his hate when he finally observed the two parties preparing to ride out. He was elated, finding Susannah's group mounted on mules, for mountainous trails and such terrain would better suit his devious purpose. His elation, soaring when only three men accompanied Susannah, suffered an earth-shaking fall when he discovered one of those riders was the hated Indian. But Duke believed he had one small advantage. Since he didn't know for sure where they were going, he could only follow. They had no reason to suspect pursuit. There were times when it was neck meat or nothing, he thought, and he might get close enough to back-shoot the Indian. He decided he hated the Indian most of all. Chained, without a weapon, without hope, Goose had not been afraid of Maury Duke. In those Indian eyes there had been only contempt. A foreboding chill crept up Duke's spine, diminishing his savage anticipation of killing the Indian. He wiped his sweaty palms on his Levi's and rode north, toward Big Horn basin.

The outfit had finished the first day of the resumed cutting of hay. They washed off the sweat and dirt in Box Elder Creek, gobbled the supper Salty had ready, and made for their bunks. McCaleb, Charlie Tilghman, and Badger Waddell were night riding the third watch, beginning at midnight. McCaleb tugged off his boots and groaned in relief.

"You can see why they all hate this," said Rebecca.

"My God, yes," said McCaleb. "The very worst day I ever spent on a trail drive was like a Sunday afternoon tea party, compared to this."

"What about the night the herd stampeded and you ended up in an arroyo with your dead horse on top of you? When me and Goodnight found you, there was water up to your nose, and rising."

"That's the only exception." McCaleb grinned weakly. "They wait until it's my turn with the scythe and they work like demons to keep ahead of my cutting. They stand there leaning on their hay forks, aimin' them damnable grins at me. I was a fool for not leavin' one of them in charge of this. Then we could have gone with Bill Cody, Will, and Susannah."

"I'd have enjoyed that. Bent, how much must we make —how far do we go before we settle down and enjoy some of it? If the market in Montana is right, we could have half a million dollars on the hoof right now. But Susannah heard you and Will talking about bringing still another herd from Texas next spring. How, when you'll need riders for the drive into Montana? If half the outfit goes with you and the rest to Texas, who will take care of things here?"

"I wish you'd waited until another time to get into all this," said McCaleb. "I'm preparing for the day—and we'll live to see it—when the trail drives will be done forever and there'll be no open range. I have plans for that half million too, God granting that it's there. Once this gold fever runs its course, all or most of these homesteads to the west of us will be abandoned. Every one has permanent water, bordered on the north by the Sweetwater River. I aim to buy as many of those acres as we're able to afford. Instead of the single ranch we now have, there'll be a string of them, all held together by our own Texas brand. I aim to change it to the Lone Star Brand. There'll be a ranch for Will, Brazos, Monte, and even Goose, if he ever becomes that civilized. For some of our other riders with the ambition, I'm thinkin' of at least a workin' partnership.

The railroad is just four days' drive, and it'll take our cows as far east or west as there's a call for them. Then there are the markets in Idaho, Montana, and Dakota. We're years away from connecting railroad lines, but we're eleven hundred miles closer to these markets than Texas cattlemen."

He paused. She said nothing and he continued.

"I reckon I was with Charlie Goodnight too long. He has dreams of an empire built on Texas cattle. So do I, but like you just pointed out, when does a man stop makin' money just for the sake of makin' money? I'd like to share my empire with those who helped make it possible, those with the guts to side me while we fought outlaws, Indians, and the odds. Sure, if we bring another herd from Texas in the spring, we'll need more riders, but I aim for at least a thousand head to be cows. With enough cows, good natural increase, and the range we need, our drives will be only to the markets we can't get to by the rails."

He said no more. He sat with his hands folded, his eyes on his sock feet. She went to him, knelt down and looked up into his face.

"Benton McCaleb, I admire Charles Goodnight, but I've never thought of you as his imitator. You're man enough to cast your own shadow, equal to or greater than his. The Lone Star Brand! I like it. We're in Wyoming, but it sets us apart. So let's *do* bring that herd from Texas in the spring and buy the extra range we'll need. I'll be with you every step of the way. For now, we'd best get to bed. It's only four hours until the nighthawk has to fly."

He got up and made his way wearily toward the bed.

"Whoa," she said. "You've slept in the brush too long. Get out of the dirty clothes. Socks too. Even Goodnight has to take his britches off once in a while."

"How do you know? Like you said, I've only got four hours. Will it be worth it?"

"Why don't you try it and find out?"

*   *   *

"Penelope'd never been on a horse in her life," said Rosalie, "until we came here. We're talking about a hundred mile ride. I'm just not sure."

"I am," said Penelope. "Brazos, I want my own horse."

She played them one against the other, and she always had more success with Brazos. He looked at Rosalie, and she nodded.

"We'll slow the pace some," said Brazos, "so you don't kill yourself, but it's time you learned a valuable lesson, young lady. Riding around here is one thing, but taking a hundred mile journey is another. If you ride a horse to Cheyenne, you're riding him back. Even if you have to stand up to eat, and sleep on your belly."

"I'll ride him," said Penelope defiantly, "if I have to stand up to eat and sleep on my belly the rest of my life."

The first day they covered twenty-five miles. Penelope all but fell from the horse. She got down on her knees for supper, and Brazos winked at Rosalie. Penelope wasn't going to give Brazos the satisfaction of seeing her stand to eat. He didn't watch her to see how she managed to sleep. When they came to the end of the second day, she humbly asked Brazos to help her off the horse, and when they resumed the journey next morning, he helped her back into the saddle. But Penelope was game, and Brazos tried to spare her some of the misery. A two-day ride stretched into three, and they didn't reach Cheyenne until well after dark. There wouldn't be another train until the following morning. They left the horses at the livery, walking to the hotel. Penelope walked spraddle-legged and slow. Brazos took a room for Penelope and another for Rosalie and himself.

"Now," said Brazos, "let's find a place to eat."

"I'm not hungry," said Penelope.

"Just stay in your room, then," said Brazos, "and lock your door."

Brazos and Rosalie found a newly opened café and had supper there.

"You were her knight in shining armor," said Rosalie

with a smile, "but I think your armor's beginning to tar-
nish."

"I expect it is," said Brazos with a grin. "Her bottom's
got to be as raw as fresh-killed beef. We'll stop at the store
for some sulfur salve."

Brazos knocked on the door, and it was a while before
Penelope got to it.

"We brought you some salve," said Brazos. "Want me to
daub it on?"

"No, thank you," she said grimly. "I can manage." She
closed the door.

"No, you can't," said Rosalie. "Penelope, you open that
door."

She opened it just far enough to get her head out.

"Centavo," said Brazos, "you let her in to doctor you.
Just remember, however sore your tail is, you're riding that
horse back to the ranch. Besides, you can't stand up from
here to Omaha."

Without a word she stepped back, allowing Rosalie to
enter. Brazos waited in their room until Rosalie returned.

"She's a mess," said Rosalie. "In even worse shape than
I was."

"She could have ridden with one of us, or took turns,"
said Brazos, "so it's her own fault. It's time she learned
that always having your own way ain't always the best way."

The seats in the passenger coach weren't all that uncomfortable, but for a dime there were extra cushions available. Brazos got one for Penelope and she thanked him
politely. It was dusky dark when they reached Omaha, and
even in a town of its considerable size, the arrival of the
train was an event. The depot was larger than the one in
Cheyenne, and next to the telegrapher's station was a small
waiting room with a single bench, one window, and a
Franklin stove. Among the spectators was a tall man wearing a flat-crowned gambler's hat, gray striped pants, white
ruffled shirt, and a black string tie. He sported a thigh-tied,
pearl-handled Colt. Rosalie felt his eyes upon her the moment they stepped down from the train and she stifled a

gasp. Brazos was helping Penelope down and didn't notice. The stranger's eyes went to Penelope and back to Rosalie. Her heart pounded and she felt faint. He was heavier, ten years older, but she knew him and he knew her. A specter from her dead past had come to life, and she was afraid.

Bill Cody knew exactly where he was going, but he sent Goose to scout ahead. It was a show of respect on Cody's part that wasn't lost on Goose.

"You know where we're going," said Susannah, "but you haven't said how far. Why not?"

"Scared to," said Cody, "until we was on the way. I reckoned you'd back out if you knowed it was a two hundred mile ride."

"Don't think I'm tough enough, do you? Well, I just rode back from Texas on a trail drive. Eleven hundred miles."

"Maybe I shouldn't have told him you rode part of the way *to* Texas in the chuck wagon," said Will.

Susannah turned her sheepish grin on Cody, and he slapped his thigh with his flop-brimmed hat and laughed.

"I'm anxious to see this Medicine Wheel," said Will. "It must be something else, luring a frontiersman like you back for another look."

"It is," said Cody, "and it's somethin' you got to experience for yourself. It's a feeling you get, like all the wisdom and mystery of the ages is within reach if you could somehow understand what it's tryin' to tell you. I want to see how it affects Goose."

Goose waited for them on the crest of the next hill and they followed him to a secluded campsite in the valley below. They unsaddled beside a willow-lined creek and Will unloaded the pack mule. The sun slipped nearer the jagged backbone of the towering Rockies, but it was still an hour away from good dark. Goose unsaddled and picketed his horse. Without a word he vanished upstream in the greenery that lined the creek.

"I expect we'll have fish for supper," said Will.

* * *

Maury Duke spent his first day on their trail cussing his luck. The hated Indian had devoted all his time to scouting ahead, as he likely would for the rest of the trip. Gone was any hope Duke had of back-shooting him. He now faced a new danger. The Indian would be far enough ahead and on a high enough elevation that he might become aware of a rider on the back trail. He could circle back, lay his own ambush, and Duke could ride into it headlong. Trail a man long enough and some intuition seems to warn him of the pursuit. Duke had experienced that himself, and it had to be strong in an Indian. Somehow he must force them to pursue him, and there was but one way. If he took Susannah, they would have no choice. When they came, Maury Duke would greet them. On his terms.

For their stay in Omaha, Bill Cody had recommended the Union Hotel, and Brazos checked them into it. There were three floors, but their rooms were on the first, near the rear entrance. There was a dining room. Each table wore a red-and-white checked cloth, and every chair was upholstered in matching red. First they went to their rooms. While Brazos unlocked Penelope's door, Rosalie looked down the hall. He stood in the lobby, his thumbs hooked in his belt. Seeing her watching, he turned away, sidled across the lobby and out the front door. Rosalie leaned against the wall, her heart pounding. Brazos took her trembling hands in his.

"What's wrong?"

"Tired," she mumbled. "Just awfully tired."

They had supper in the hotel dining room, and it was a silent meal. Afterward, Rosalie couldn't remember what she had eaten. She pretended to sleep until Brazos was snoring. For a while she could hear the jangle of a piano. Somewhere a woman laughed, and Rosalie envied her. Far into the night she lay there, and when she finally slept, it was only long enough for her fears to clothe themselves as horrifying nightmares. Brazos shook her awake and held her close until she stopped trembling. Fearing a return of the nightmares, she forced herself to remain awake for the rest of the night.

"While you're getting ready for breakfast," said Brazos, "I'm goin' to the lobby for a newspaper. I'll get Penelope up on my way back."

Hurriedly she got up and bolted the door behind him. There was a big white porcelain pitcher of water and a matching white basin. She washed her feverish face, found her comb and tried to do something with her hair. The rattling of the door so upset her that she dropped the comb and almost upset the pitcher.

"Who . . . is it?"

"Me," said Brazos irritably. "Who do you reckon?"

She fumbled at the bolt and finally got the door open.

"Why did you bolt the door? I only went down the hall."

"Where's Penelope?" she mumbled.

"Asleep, I reckon. You'll have to get her. With my luck, I'd walk in on her jaybird naked. She's down on me enough already."

They made it through breakfast, the only favorable aspect being that Penelope's hurts had begun to heal and her appetite had returned.

"Centavo," said Brazos, "there's a circus in town. Would you like to go?"

"I don't know. I've never been to one. But I'd like to do something."

"Then we'll go this evening," said Brazos, "after I track down this lawyer."

"Brazos," said Rosalie, "I don't feel well. I have some fever, I think. Can't we wait until tomorrow to see him?"

"I reckon we can. But I'll go loco sittin' in this hotel. Do you think you ought to see a doc?"

"No. Why don't you take Penelope to the circus, to see the town or something. Maybe you can find this lawyer and set a time for us tomorrow. I'll stay here and rest. I didn't get much sleep last night."

She bolted the door behind them and sat there wringing

her hands, at a loss as to what she should do. There came a soft knock on the door and she jumped. It couldn't be Brazos. Not so soon. The knock was repeated.

"Who is it?" she asked tremulously.

"Desk clerk," said a voice. "Message for you."

Something had happened to Brazos and Penelope! She sprang to the door and fumbled the bolt loose. She opened the door a crack, and with a startled gasp tried to close it, but his boot was in the way.

"I saw them leave," he said softly. "Let me in or you'll be sorry."

She stumbled away from the door as though her mind had no control over her body. He stepped into the room, closing the door after him.

"Well, now," he said with an unpleasant chuckle, "ain't you growed up into a nice piece of baggage? Wasn't sure it was you gettin' off that train till I saw the kid. Three or four years more an' she'll look like you did, back when we had our roll in th' hay."

"Get out of here," she whispered. "My . . . my husband will kill you!"

"Your husband? Yeah, sure," he chuckled. "Your husband. Just like I was. I've gunned down three men, an' I just as easy can make it four. We didn't have but a week 'fore your old daddy caught up to you. I reckoned that was enough till I saw you get off that train. You done changed my mind, girl, an' I'm takin' up where we left off."

"No!" she cried desperately. "No!"

"Babe, what Jack Kirby wants, Jack Kirby takes!"

Like a striking rattler, his hand jumped to the collar of her blouse. The buttons popped off and the fabric ripped. He licked his lips and she saw the lust in his eyes.

"Jack, please. Not here. Please don't ruin everything. Tell me where I . . . I can find you, and I'll . . . I'll come. Tonight. Late tonight."

"You ain't forgot how it was, have you?"

"No," she said, "I haven't forgotten . . . anything. I

. . . I promise. I'll come to you tonight, and . . . you'll get what you . . . deserve. I promise. . . ."

"You stand me up," he gritted, "an' I'll kill that redhead you got follerin' you around. Then maybe I'll grab that young'un for a spell. Just a mite young, but that didn't slow you down none."

"Leave them alone, Jack. Please. I'll go . . . wherever you say. Where?"

"Nebraska House. Room twenty-two, on th' second floor. Come in th' back door. If you ain't there tonight, then I'll be here in th' mornin'. I had you once, an' if you know what's good for you, I'll have you a'gin."

He stepped into the hall, closing the door after him. Frantically she shot the bolt and stumbled to the bed. She buried her face in the covers and sobbed until no tears remained. Finally she got up, removed the ruined blouse and donned another. Again she washed her face. Then she went to the dresser and got the little purse Brazos had bought for her in Cheyenne. She counted her money. Twenty dollars. Would it be enough? She had no idea when Brazos and Penelope might return. She eased open the door and looked down the long hall toward the lobby. She saw nobody, and the rear entrance was but a few feet away. She quietly locked her door and exited the hotel into the alley behind it. Kirby might be watching the front door, and she was equally fearful of being seen by Brazos and Penelope before finishing what she had set out to do.

She found a store and wandered from one display to another until she located what she sought.

"Do you need some help, ma'am?" a clerk inquired.

"Yes," said Rosalie. "I need a gun. A . . . a pistol."

It was near dawn of their second day on the trail when Will suddenly sat up, wide awake.

"Where are you going?"

"To the bushes," said Susannah, "and don't ask me what for."

"Want me to go with you, just so you'll feel protected?"

"No. I'll be within a few yards of camp. Besides, we just woke up Uncle Bill, and Goose is around somewhere."

Goose had been upstream fishing. Just seconds after Susannah crossed the creek into the brush, the Apache showed up with a string of trout. When Susannah screamed, he dropped the fish and hit the creek in a run. Will and Cody were right behind him. Beyond the creek the brush thinned out and there was little else but tall buffalo grass to the top of the hill. Forty yards up the rise, Maury Duke had his left arm tight around Susannah's throat. With his right hand he held a Colt to her head.

"Drop your guns!" shouted Duke.

They had no choice. Cody dropped his Winchester to the grass at his feet. Will carefully lifted his Colt from the holster and dropped it. But Goose had kept his Colt.

"I'm givin' that heathen bastard to th' count of three!" shouted Duke.

"Ganos," said Will quietly.

Goose understood. Reluctantly he loosed the Colt and it fell at his feet.

"Now," exulted Duke with an insane cackle, "walk toward me until I tell you to stop. Move!"

Slowly they began walking, Goose in the lead. To a man they knew what was coming. He would bring them within range of his Colt, and without mercy gun them down.

28

*B*razos found the lawyer, a man named Hicks, and set a time for the three of them to meet with him the following day. By the time they left his office, Penelope had begun to warm to Brazos again. They heard the far-off whistle of the approaching train and she turned to him.

"Can we go watch the train come in?"

"Why not?" said Brazos.

They found a stack of cross-ties, climbed to the top and hung their feet off. She leaned forward, cocking her head like an inquisitive bird so she could see his face.

"Thank you for getting the salve for me," she said. "It helped."

"You're welcome. I'm glad it helped."

When the train had arrived, they went to a confectionery shop and had ice cream.

"The circus won't start until two o'clock," said Brazos. "Why don't we go back to the hotel and see how your mama's feeling?"

They found Rosalie awake, dressed, and waiting for them.

"I slept some," she said, "and feel better. I'll go with you to the circus."

"That's far enough," said Duke. "Don't come any closer."

Will and Cody halted, but Goose didn't.

"One more step, Injun, and she dies. Now turn around, all of you. Put your backs to me."

Even Susannah knew what he had in mind. There was but one chance, and she took it. She went limp, as though in a faint, slipping out of Duke's encircling arm. Frantically he tried to renew his grasp on her. It bought them only seconds, but it was all the edge Goose needed. He launched himself into a dive as Duke fired; the slug went high. When Goose's hands touched the ground, he used them as springs, turned a somersault and came down on his feet facing Maury Duke. He was but an arm's length away, and in his left hand he gripped his Bowie, a gleaming *cuchillo* with a foot-long blade.

It was an unnerving sight, and the very shock of it delayed Duke's reaction. Goose caught his right wrist, forcing the muzzle of the Colt upward, Duke's final shot blasting harmlessly into the blue Wyoming sky. With an upward thrust of his lethal left hand, the Apache buried the Bowie to the hilt in Duke's belly. His agonized groan faded to a whimper; it was the last sound he would ever utter. For a few seconds he seemed to hang there, like a worm impaled on a hook. Then, with a shove, Goose freed his Bowie, allowing the lifeless Duke to collapse like a bundle of old rags. For the space of a heartbeat Goose lifted his eyes, and in them his three companions saw nothing human. He was all savage, bidding them leave. Will led Susannah away, and Cody followed, none of them looking back. Grasping Duke's hair, Goose lifted the body off the ground. Of all the scalps he had taken, Comanche included, he would value this one the most.

The circus was a small one, and they left early, returning to the hotel. Rosalie's mood had dragged them all down. Thunderheads were rolling in from the west, and sometime during the night there would be a storm. After a silent supper, they retired for the night. Rosalie seemed to fall asleep quickly. Too quickly, Brazos thought. She was allowing him time to get to sleep, so her lying awake wouldn't disturb him. He began breathing easily, producing some believable snores, waiting. Thunder rumbled closer. Rosalie moved, the springs creaked, and she froze. Brazos continued snoring, and she tried again. This time she made it, and he could see her pale body as she peeled off her gown. He could hear the rustle of clothes. Lightning flashed, and in its brief flicker through the window he saw her moving toward the door. He longed to call out to her, to stop this, but then he still wouldn't know what was troubling her.

Once she was in the hall and had softly closed the door, he rolled out, got into his clothes and grabbed his boots. He was virtually certain she wouldn't go through the lobby, and the alley behind the hotel would be pitch-black. Once outside the door, he stomped into his boots and began looking for her. Far down the alley, a ray of light shone through a window, and he saw her pass in front of it. He hurried after her, and reaching the next cross street, she turned toward the railroad. He could think of nothing along that street except a pair of saloons, a bawdy house, and a hotel Bill Cody had told him to avoid. Her destination had to be the hotel. But why? He didn't want to know, but he had to know. The front of the hotel faced the street he was on, so he ducked between a pair of vacant buildings to the alley. There had been enough rain to muddy the ground. He slipped, almost fell, but reached the alley in time to see her enter the back door of the hotel.

The hall smelled of dust and mildew. Against her skin, the pistol felt cold, ominous. She unbuttoned her dress, removed the gun from her waistband and cocked it. On trembling legs she ascended the stairs and found her end of the hall so dark she couldn't read the numbers on the doors. But he had been listening for her. On her left a door opened slightly. Quickly she thrust her hands behind her.

"In here," he said.

Reluctantly Rosalie entered. Except for boots and hat, Kirby was fully dressed. He got up off the bed and she edged away from him. He went to the door, kicked it shut and turned to face her. Kirby found himself looking into the muzzle of a cocked pistol. She held the weapon with both hands but was unable to steady it.

"So that's how it is," he said.

"That's how it is," she said. "Jack, for the first time in my miserable life, I've done something right. I don't care what you think of me. I have a good man who wants me for all time, not just for a night or two. I won't let you hurt him. You have a choice. You can leave me . . . us alone, or I'll kill you."

"Turned into a regular wampus kitty with claws, ain't you? Well, nobody bluffs Jack Kirby. Give me the gun."

"I'm not bluffing, Jack. I'll shoot."

"You ain't got the guts."

He took a step toward her and she fired. The slug caught him high in the chest and he faltered. Then, snarling like a wounded animal, he came for her. She fired again, lower down. He stumbled backward, knees buckling, and fell on his back. She froze. The pistol slipped from her hands, and she stared in fascinated horror as blood crimsoned the front of his shirt.

The hotel had two floors and maybe two dozen rooms. But once she went into one, Brazos not knowing which one, there might as well be a hundred. A low-burning bracket lamp hung at each end of the hall, with darkness and shadows in between. He saw nobody and heard nothing except the patter of rain as the storm grew in intensity. On the stairs to the second floor, third step up, he found a bit of fresh mud. When he reached the second floor, he found the lamp at his end of the hall had guttered out and he was barely able to see the wooden floor. There was a narrow band of light under the second door on his left, and he moved toward it, listening. The walls were thin enough that he could hear voices, but he was unable to understand the words. The voices ceased, and the shot that followed seemed inordinately loud in the silence. He had his back to the wall beside the door and his hand on the knob when the second shot came. While he had no idea what he was buying into, the time for caution was past. He turned the knob, the door swung open, and the first thing he saw was the bloodied body of the man on the floor. Rosalie stood there as though chiseled from stone. On the faded carpet at her feet lay a pistol.

Goose returned to camp leading Duke's horse. It was a roan, a handsome animal, and it was all that interested the Apache. He handed Duke's saddlebags to Will. Cody had made coffee, and Susannah gripped her tin cup with both of her still-trembling hands. Will emptied the saddlebags on a blanket. Among the few personal items was a brown envelope and two buckskin pouches. Will opened the envelope first and spread out the contents. There was a bank statement and fifty $100 bills. Finally Will emptied the buckskin pouches, the pile of gold nuggets shining bright in the morning sun.

"Maybe ten thousand in gold," said Will, "and all that's left of Maury Duke. Not nearly enough, for what it cost him."

"Susannah," said Cody, "maybe we'd better forget this trip for now. This ain't the kind of day you'll want to remember."

"No," said Susannah, "I want to go on." She poured herself another cup of strong black coffee. "Maybe it sounds cold-blooded, but I do want to remember this day. This was the man who shot Will in the back and took Goose away in chains. It was a fitting end for him, and he got what he deserved."

"Will," said Cody, "you got yourself a western woman! I reckon this climb to the top of the world will be good medicine for us all. Let's ride!"

Brazos stepped into the room, closed and bolted the door. Then he took Rosalie's pistol, a Colt .31 caliber, and stuck it under his belt. There wasn't much time. Theirs was a

time and place where few people stood on ceremony. They
had but a few seconds, a minute or two at most, before
somebody broke down the door. He already could hear the
thud of boots on the wooden stairs. There was a single
window, and their only way out was the fire escape. It consisted of a rope, one end of which was knotted to the leg of
the iron bed. Rosalie still hadn't uttered a word. Brazos
tried the window and it seemed stuck, lifting only a little.
He got his back to it, gripped its bottom edge with both
hands and heaved. It went up with an ear-piercing shriek,
and the storm-bred wind whipped rain into the room. He
flung the loose end of the rope out the window just as
there came a pounding on the door. Rosalie stared dumbly
at him. He grabbed her by the shoulders and shook her
without result. He picked her up bodily, sat her on the
windowsill and slapped her hard. The clamor in the hall
and the pounding on the door grew louder. For the first
time she seemed aware of their predicament, and he saw
the terror in her eyes.

"Rosalie," he said as calmly as he could, "we have to get
out of here. It's only a few feet to the ground. You'll have
to take this rope and let yourself down."

She only clenched her hands into fists and sat there
trembling. There was more commotion in the hall as somebody put a shoulder to the door. The sound jolted her back
to reality and her eyes met his.

"Damn it, Rosalie, take hold of that rope and get out
that window. Move!"

The urgency in his voice got to her, and she took the
rope with both hands. He thrust her bodily into the rainswept darkness, and she had nowhere to go but down.
Even if she lost her grip and fell, it was still the better of
their two choices. He went out the window feet first, belly
down over the sill, and slid down the rope. Rosalie sat on
the muddy ground. He helped her to her feet and she
seemed all right. Brazos hurried her alongside the hotel to
the alley behind it. Once they were away from the building,
the force of the wind and rain almost swept them off their

feet. The alley was pitch-black, without so much as a lighted window. Rosalie slipped and Brazos caught her. He plunged on, half dragging her. The rain became more intense, and he kept to the darkest streets. It was hard going, but their only hope. Just being seen on such a night at the height of such a storm was enough to arouse suspicion. Finally they reached the alley that ran behind the Union Hotel, and Brazos paused. Exhausted, Rosalie clung to him; even amid the fury of the storm he could hear her labored breathing.

There was a small roofed landing at the hotel's rear entrance and it was in total darkness. The bracket lamps had fallen victim to the wind and blowing rain. When they reached the landing, Brazos paused again. While he begrudged the time it would take, there was a final precaution they dared not ignore. He backed Rosalie against the wall for support, and one after the other, removed her muddy boots. Quickly he tugged off his own, eased open the door and pushed her into the hall ahead of him. At least they would leave no muddy footprints on the stairs. This was where Brazos most feared discovery. Two lamps burned in the hall, and the lighted lobby was at the farther end of it. Quietly he unlocked their door, shoved Rosalie into the room and locked the door behind them. He felt his way to the bed and to the lamp on the table beside it. Next to the lamp were matches. He struck one, lighted the lamp, and turned the flame as low as he could without it going out. Rosalie sat on the bed, saying nothing.

"Rosalie," said Brazos, "get out of those wet clothes."

She wouldn't look at him. Just when he was doubting she was going to respond at all, she got up and slowly began removing her sodden clothes. Her teeth were chattering. Brazos took a blanket from the bed and wrapped her in it. She sank down on the bed. He dragged up the only chair in the room and sat facing her.

"You have some explaining to do," he said. "You can start by tellin' me who he was and why you shot him."

* * *

"Northwestern Wyoming," said Bill Cody, "is mostly just one big mesa with saddlebacks dividin' the peaks. There's the Tetons, the Wind Rivers, the Absarokas, and the Big Horns. The very least of 'em is six thousand feet above sea level."

They sat around the fire drinking coffee. Tomorrow they would begin their ascent into the Big Horns.

"The Columbia, Colorado, and Missouri rivers all have their beginnings right here in these mountains," said Cody.

"I thought you were joking when you told us to bring coats," Susannah said. "Now I wish I'd brought a heavier one."

"Wait'll we get to Bald Mountain," said Cody. "There'll be ice."

"I'll have to see that," said Susannah. "Ice in July?"

"In July," chuckled Cody, "an' it'll still be there come August."

"It's the most unspoiled country I've ever seen," said Will.

"We owe that to the Indians," said Cody. "White men ain't got a hold of it yet. Fremont was here in 1840, but few white men have seen what you're goin' to see tomorrow. It's like it was when th' Almighty created it. Most whites never got any deeper into Wyoming than the Bozeman trail, thank God."

They camped on the last saddleback before starting the climb up Bald Mountain. There were several hours of daylight left, but Cody insisted they stop for the night.

"We start at sunup," he said, "and return here before sundown. We don't want to stay the night at the top. For one thing, it'll be twenty degrees colder. And then there's the Medicine Wheel. Indians, although they don't know where it came from or why it's there, say it's big medicine. They say that after sundown the voices of the old ones can be heard in the sigh of the wind."

"That's spooky," said Susannah.

"Some laugh and call it Injun superstition," said Cody, "but I don't. It's some kind of presence, but it ain't hostile.

You just feel a kind of reverence, like walkin' into a church. You'll understand when we get there."

Slowly but surely, Brazos dragged the story out of her.

"I was afraid he'd kill you," she sobbed.

"I reckon if you'd had a little more confidence in me, none of this would have happened. Where'd you get the gun?"

"At a . . . a store up the street. Why?"

"It's a Colt pocket pistol. Mostly a gambler's gun. They don't sell many of them. Once they dig the slugs out of Kirby, it won't take an hour for the sheriff or town marshal to start lookin' for people who own these guns."

"Then we'll get rid of it!"

"That's the worst possible thing we could do," said Brazos. "You might as well confess."

"Let's get away from here!" she cried. "Let's take the train tomorrow!"

"That's the next worst possible thing we could do. The sheriff will be almighty interested in anybody that's in a hurry to leave town."

"Then what am I—are we—going to do?" she cried.

"We'll have to bluff it out. I doubt we were seen leaving that hotel. Just pray that nobody saw either of us entering it."

"Brazos," she cried, "if they—anybody—questions me, I . . . I know I'll break down. I . . . I'm guilty. I feel like . . . like the devil's just waiting to get his hands on me. I feel just awful. I killed a man."

Brazos took her by the shoulders and made her face him.

"Are you *sorry* you did it?"

"Yes, I . . . no . . . I . . ."

"Are you sorry you did it?"

"No, damn it, no!" she virtually shouted. "He was trash. Sorry, lowdown trash. He ruined me once and was going to do it again. I gave him what he deserved, and I'm not sorry. I'm only sorry I got myself—us—in this mess."

"You're going to have to get us out of it," said Brazos, "and you can't do it standin' up to your ears in guilt. Come morning, if anybody's got any questions about that pistol, you're going to have some answers ready. Fill that pan with water and clean the mud off our boots while I clean this Colt. Then we'll have to spread out our clothes and hope they'll dry by morning."

"Brazos," she asked tremulously, "how do you feel . . . about me . . . after this?"

"No different. I understand why you did it. I've had to shoot some hombres that wouldn't settle for anything less. I reckon this coyote got a dose of lead poisonin' he was sorely in need of, but it wasn't your place to give it to him. The Book says a wife obeys her husband. Next time you get a notion to take the bit in your teeth and run the other way, remember that. You've squared it with me, but you're not out of it by a jugful. I'll side you, but it's your play, and you can win. Just dig down and come up with some of the nerve that took you to that hotel room with a pistol."

Setting out on the last leg of the journey, they came to an enormous rock formation in the rough shape of a V that rose to a height of probably a hundred fifty feet.

"Somebody named it Steamboat Rock," said Cody. "God only knows why. Looks about as much like a steamboat as a Conestoga wagon, to me."

Just before they began the ascent of Bald Mountain, they came upon a mountain meadow. It stretched perhaps a mile along a saddleback and it was a veritable Garden of Eden. The slopes were clothed with pine, spruce, fir, and cedar, while every other available patch of earth boasted a profusion of flowering plants. Clusters of blooms clung to the spires of Indian paintbrush. There was the mingled blue of gentians, harebells, blue and purple lupines, and tangles of wild rose.

"My God," cried Susannah in awe, "I didn't know there was this much beauty in all the world. I could look at it forever."

"You can spend some more time with it on the way down," said Cody. "Let's go on to the top of old Baldy. Wait'll you see the view from up there."

Near the top of the mountain they dismounted and led their mules. The clear, cold air pricked their lungs like thousands of needles and they had to stop often. They were now above all the other peaks, and Cody pointed to the east.

"See that sort of black smudge over yonder? That's the Black Hills, Dakota Territory. It's two hundred miles away."

They came upon an outcropping that might have been stone, but it was cold to the touch and looked like dark glass.

"Ice," said Cody.

"Where is the top of this mountain?" cried Susannah.

"You're on it," chuckled Cody. "We're less than a mile from the Medicine Wheel."

"Take a breather," said Will. "We've lost Goose. I'd better check."

He found Goose at the very edge of the plateau. He had picketed his horses and sat on a rock outcropping staring into the far distance.

"*Ganos!*" shouted Will.

Goose looked at him, and Will beckoned. Goose shook his head. Exasperated, Will descended farther and again appealed to the Apache.

"*Ninguno,*" said Goose. "*Espectro. Viejo espectros hablar. Malo medicina. Ninguno molestar.*"

Nothing Will could say or do had any effect. Clearly Goose intended to remain where he was until they returned. Will made his way back to where Cody and Susannah waited.

"He's down yonder a ways," said Will. "He's picketed his horses and he won't budge. He says the old spirits speak, that it's bad medicine to molest them."

"It's got to him," said Cody, "and he don't even know about the Medicine Wheel."

"I'm not sure I want to know about it either," said Susannah, "if it can cast that kind of spell. Suppose he's right? What if we fall off this mountain on the way down?"

"Well, I aim to see it," said Will. "I want somethin' out of this climb."

"Don't be put out with Goose," said Cody. "Indians have a reverence for old ways that we rarely understand or appreciate."

Distraught as Rosalie had been the night before, she had recovered to a surprising degree by the time they arose for breakfast. Their clothes had dried and could be packed away. The mud had been cleaned from their boots and Brazos had freshly oiled the leather. More importantly, the Colt pocket pistol had been cleaned and Rosalie carried it in the little bag that contained her personal items.

"Pay more attention to Penelope," said Brazos. "She picked up on your mood yesterday and knew somethin' was wrong. This ain't the time for any of us to look like we had sour pickles for breakfast."

The three of them went to the hotel dining room and enjoyed their cheeriest meal since their arrival. And that's where the sheriff found them.

29

*T*he top of the mountain leveled off into a grassy plateau, and it was here that at some ancient time the
Medicine Wheel had been laid. None of the stones were
larger than a man could lift, and they had been placed side
by side in a nearly perfect circle.

"I paced it off," said Cody. "It's maybe seventy feet
across and two hundred and fifty feet around it."

There was a hub of stones at the center of the wheel.
Radiating from the hub were twenty-eight spokes connected to the rim. Each spoke was carefully constructed of
stones. At six points around the rim of the wheel, there was
a stone mound just slightly smaller than the hub. Each was
built like a crude armchair, with one side left open. Five of
them had the open side facing the wheel's hub. The sixth
faced outward toward the east. At the center of the wheel,
atop the hub, rested a bleached buffalo skull, its sightless
eye sockets facing the rising sun.

"It's hard to believe the Indians know nothing about
this," said Will. "It has to have figured into some religious
ceremony. I'd bet my hat the stone seat facing the sun was
reserved for the medicine man."

"The Indians claim it was here when they first came to
the Big Horns," said Cody. "It had to have been built
sometime after the great flood, so it could be nearly four
thousand years old."

"The buffalo skull is facing east," said Susannah. "What could it mean?"

"Who knows?" said Cody. "If I was guessin', I'd say they included the sun and the buffalo in their ceremony. The sun made the grass grow, the buffalo fed on the grass, and the Indians depended on the buffalo."

"I can understand how all this could affect Goose," said Susannah, "but he doesn't even know it's up here."

"He knows," said Will, "and he's afraid of it. Maybe the old ones have reached out across the centuries and told him things we don't know. Maybe he knows the secret of it. There is a mystery here, a feeling that gets to you."

"I don't blame Goose," said Susannah. "I'd not want to be here after sundown. I almost believe we could see them in the moonlight, sitting in those stone seats, and I wouldn't be surprised to hear their voices in the wind."

"That's the feelin' I got," said Cody, "first time I was here. It's somethin' from the past that I wanted you to see. The world's goin' to hell in a hand basket, girl. The time's comin' when folks won't care about the old times and the old ways."

They found Goose on the way down, and he seemed awed. Clearly, the Apache hadn't expected them to return. They descended in silence, each of them half expecting to hear ghostly voices in the sigh of the rising wind.

Brazos stood up. The sheriff doffed his hat to Rosalie and Penelope.

"I'm John Biggers, sheriff in these parts."

"Brazos Gifford. This is Rosalie and Penelope. Drag up a chair and set."

The sheriff seemed uncomfortable. It was his play. Brazos said nothing more and Biggers cleared his throat.

"Sorry t' bother you folks, but there ain't no good way t' do this. Had a man killed last night. Shot with a .31-caliber pistol. Fact is, I tried to think of somebody that had one, an' couldn't. First thing this mornin', I made the rounds of th' stores an' found nobody could remember sellin' such a gun till yesterday. You bein' a stranger, ma'am, an' a pretty lady t' boot, you was remembered. So I got t' ask you t' show me th' pistol."

Brazos held his breath and Penelope's eyes got big as Rosalie opened her bag and removed the Colt. She passed it to the sheriff with a steady hand and he examined it. He placed it on the table before Rosalie.

"No shells?"

"I have some," said Rosalie, "but I'm saving them until we get back to the ranch. I need to practice. I'm afraid I'd shoot myself."

"Ranching, huh? Whereabouts?"

"Southern Wyoming," said Rosalie. "Just north of Cheyenne. Everybody at the ranch has a gun except me."

"I don't," said Penelope.

It broke the tension and they all laughed. The sheriff looked across the table at Brazos.

"Pretty young lady you got," he said. "Don't take after you none, does she?"

"Not a bit," said Brazos, grinning. "We've been blessed."

The sheriff chuckled in appreciation. Finally, with a sigh, he got to his feet and put on his hat. He seemed more at ease.

"My apologies, ma'am, for botherin' you. I ain't got much t' go on, so I can't overlook nothin'. This feller was a gambler. Still had his money on him. He'd been here a week, an' he's trimmed some folks. Bartenders say he was mighty good with the cards. Maybe too good, judgin' from last night."

When he was gone, Rosalie sighed. Penelope could contain her curiosity no longer.

"Mama, when did you—"

"Yesterday morning," said Rosalie. "It's just like the gun Rebecca has, and Bullard's in Cheyenne didn't have one."

"We have less than an hour to get ready and over to the lawyer's office," said Brazos. "Centavo, are you ready to become a Gifford?"

"I've wanted to be one since the first time I saw you," said Penelope.

"Me too," said Rosalie.

It was Sunday afternoon in mid-July when Will, Susannah, Goose, and Bill Cody rode into the ranch. They headed for the cookhouse, except for Goose, the rest of the outfit following.

"What'n hell's goin' on?" growled Salty. "It ain't suppertime."

They all ignored him. Will dropped Maury Duke's saddlebags on one of the tables, and when they quieted, he told them the story.

"The money and the gold belongs to you and Goose," said McCaleb.

"Goose wanted only the horse," said Will. "Put the rest in the pot with our stake toward that next Texas herd. Brazos, how was the visit to Omaha?"

"Fine," said Brazos. "Got me another Gifford."

"Mama bought a pistol," said the newest Gifford, "and the sheriff thought she shot a gambler with it."

Fall brought their first snow and a new calf crop. Each was branded with a perfect star on its left hip. The Lone Star Brand. McCaleb, after his understanding with Rebecca, had gone ahead with their plans.

"I can't wait for Charlie Goodnight to hear about this," said Brazos. "It'll equal or better anything he's got goin' in Colorado. Since we're bringin' another herd from Texas, it ain't too early to decide who'll be bossin' the drive. Made any decisions, Bent?"

"No," said McCaleb. "Only a recommendation. I want yours and Will's feelings. Then we'll reach a decision. This next Texas drive will be lots tougher, because it'll be a mixed herd. Goodnight always hated driving a mixed herd, but I can't see driving steers all the way from Texas when we can raise them right here through natural increase. For that we need cows. One day these trails we're blazing will be glutted with herds and the graze will be gone."

"With that in mind," said Will, "why not make this a sixty-forty mix? If we bring five thousand head, let two thousand of them be cows. With what we have, that'll give us twenty-five hundred."

"I'll buy that," said Brazos. "Two thousand won't slow the drive any more than a thousand. When we started, we had no home range and we needed the fast money the steers would bring. Now we not only have a range, but a chance to add to it. We also got enough of a stake to see us through some hard times. We ought to come out of this Montana drive with more than enough to pay for another Texas herd, without even touching our stake."

"Back to the Montana drive," said McCaleb. "Some of the outfit will have to stay here at the ranch. Montana Territory is unknown to us, and I'd want at least seven riders. That means the lucky hombre trailing the herd from Texas will have to do as Will did last time, and hire more riders."

"Will brought in the last herd," said Brazos, "and you'll be trailing a herd to Montana, so I reckon that lucky hombre will be me."

"It won't have to be either of you," said McCaleb, "depending on what you think of what I'm about to suggest. I'd like for Pendleton Rhodes to boss this Texas drive. Since we'll be hiring more riders, some of our old-timers deserve something better than thirty a month and found. I'm thinking we ought to offer working partnerships to some of them who have served us as faithfully as Pen has."

"He could boss the drive," said Will. "Next to Goose, he's the best I've ever seen on the trail. He'll be takin' a saddlebag of gold coin with him. We'll be trusting him with that and trusting his judgment in hiring of new hands."

"I'm prepared to do that," said McCaleb. "Brazos?"

"I'm satisfied with him," said Brazos. "The kind of empire we're looking at, we'll be needin' good men who'll ride and fight for the brand. Let Pen be the first. It'll give the others something to shoot for."

"He gets my vote, then," said Will. "How about Monte and Rebecca?"

"Rebecca stands with me," said McCaleb. "Monte's still more interested in the drives than he is in the ranch, but it'll be a while before he bosses one. If ever."

"There's Goose," said Brazos. "He deserves something more, but what?"

"The kind of spread we're aimin' for," said McCaleb, "will need good cow horses. An almighty lot of them. Is there a rider in this outfit with more of a passion for horses than Goose? I'm thinking of our own horse ranch, with Goose handling and gentling the horses. He'll always be valuable to us on trail drives, but he can become even more valuable to us here."

They found Pen Rhodes ready and willing to trail a new herd from Texas.

"Let me take just four riders," said Pen. "I know I can get eight more, if I have to hire some of my Injun kin."

"Long as they can rope, ride, and shoot," said McCaleb. "Who do you aim to take with you?"

"Red Dulaney, Poke Shambler, and the Vasquez boys. Emilio used to cook for Goodnight. He can do the same for us."

"Good thinking," said McCaleb. "Salty just got back from Texas and he's rarin' to go on the drive to Montana."

"For grub on the way there," said Pen, "we can take a pack mule. Won't be that many of us to feed, and it won't slow us down like a wagon would. Comin' back, though, we'll have a dozen riders. Do you reckon we can afford to go to Fort Worth and buy a chuck wagon? They can be had for seventy-five dollars. Not more than a hundred."

"I reckon we can afford that," said McCaleb. "Eventually we'll have a big enough outfit to keep two trail drives goin', so why not have two good chuck wagons? Is there anything else?"

"It'll be the dead of winter here," said Pen, "and not much to do, so I'd like to start in mid-November. We'll need some time to find some good riders for an outfit and some good horses for our remuda. Might take us a while to build a herd, if we aim to do it at last year's prices."

Penelope had an unpleasant surprise. While in Omaha, Brazos had found and bought the books recommended by Susannah. Every morning after breakfast Penelope had school.

"I don't need any of this to ride, rope, and shoot," she said.

"Oh, but you do," said Brazos, "because you're not gettin' into that until you master this. You can't chouse cows proper until you're smarter than they are."

When Pen and his outfit rode out on November 15, there was snow in the high country, but not enough to be a problem. Will had advised them not to stop at Fort Dodge, so they took two pack mules. The provisions would be equally divided. Beneath them, attached to the frames of the pack saddles, Pen had secured a series of leather pouches in which the gold was to be concealed. Only by unpacking the mules and removing the pack saddles could it be found. McCaleb and the riders remaining at the ranch watched them ride out.

"Pen's cautious," said McCaleb. "He'll make it."

"He's got more going for him than I had," said Will. "I kept a log of every water hole, river, and landmark from here to Fort Belknap, and he's got a copy of it. That, along with that half-Injun head of his, and he's got a powerful edge."

The first week in December, between blizzards, McCaleb decided it was time for a trip to Cheyenne. Christmas was coming, and they needed supplies for the winter. Salty drove the chuck wagon, McCaleb and Rebecca following.

"I can't believe we're actually going somewhere together," said Rebecca. "Since we got more riders, you're always off with some of them."

"I thought that was the idea behind all these trail drives," said McCaleb, "to hire more riders, so you could have it a little easier."

"I'd planned on you being with me, and us taking it easier together, but it's not working out. I reckon I'll have to go on the trail drives again."

"I can just hear folks talking," said McCaleb. "They'll say, 'My God, that McCaleb's a cheap bastard. All them cows, money, land from the Platte to Green River, and he's still got his pore old wore out wife ridin' drag.'"

His droll humor always got to her. She laughed, but it trailed off into a sigh. While she shared his dream of empire, it was costing her more than she had expected to pay.

Cheyenne was a railroad town, but without Train opposing him, McCaleb had begun making friends. He had a line of credit at Bullard's, and Musgrove at the bank seemed genuinely glad to see him.

"Take your time," McCaleb told Rebecca. "We'll stay the night. I want to visit with Sam Colton awhile, and have a talk with Malcolm Walker at the land office."

Colton was reared back in his chair, his feet on the desk.

"Well, Sam," said McCaleb, "I see you're doin' what you do best."

"Nothing else to do. What happened to the gold rush?"

"Nobody reads your paper, Sam."

"You could be right." Colton grinned ruefully. "But I know of some who did. Remember those two hired guns that ended up chained in the caboose after they grabbed your Indian? They came back, brought two other men with them, bought horses and rode out."

"Their mistake," said McCaleb. "They played out their string. So did Maury Duke."

"Damn it, McCaleb, you'd deny food to a starving man. Tell me the rest of it."

McCaleb did.

"My God," said Colton admiringly, "I ought to just follow you around and write dime novels from your experiences. Trouble is, everybody would think I was just making it up."

Reaching the land office, McCaleb confronted Malcolm Walker with a direct question.

"Walker, how are chances of me buyin' some of the abandoned claims along the Sweetwater?"

"Once we're sure they're abandoned," said Walker, "I don't see why not. I'll send an inquiry to Washington. I believe there's a waiting period of a year without activity before you can claim abandonment."

"Got any idea what it might cost?"

"Twenty-five cents to a dollar an acre," said Walker, "depending on its location. There's so much land in Wyoming, you might get it at a lower price; as many acres as you can afford to buy."

They rode out of Cheyenne, the wagon loaded to the bows with supplies and gifts for Christmas. McCaleb's mind was roaming the Sweetwater, where a man might buy a hundred square miles of grassland, 64,000 acres, for $16,000. In his mind's eye he could see cattle roaming from the North Platte to Green River, each with a star burned on its left hip. The Lone Star Brand!

They were at the ranch before Rebecca got around to reading the Omaha newspaper she'd bought at Bullard's. They were all congregated in the cookhouse, just minutes away from supper, when Rebecca held up the newspaper and shrieked.

"Train's in jail! He's in jail in England!"

There was only a paragraph or two. Rebecca read it aloud. Train, on a trip around the world, had gotten no farther than England. He had taken sides in the continuing war between England and Ireland, speaking out for the Irish. He had been sentenced to a year in prison.

It was March before there was even a hint of spring, and that was early for the High Plains. McCaleb sent Salty,

Badger, and Cow to Cheyenne for supplies they needed for the trail drive into Montana Territory.

"This is a rotten thing to say," Rebecca told McCaleb, "but I have a bad feeling about this drive. Have you decided who's going with you?"

"Yes," said McCaleb. "I'm taking Salty, Goose, Brazos, Monte, Charlie, Laredo, and Harley. I realize Montana's unknown territory, but so was Dakota. Maybe you're right, havin' this bad feeling, but however it turns out, I aim to get on with it. I'm ready to ride."

$\mathcal{B}$y the first week in April the grass had begun to green, and McCaleb judged it was time to go. Rebecca had her misgivings about the drive, and Penelope added to their unease by clinging to Brazos as though she never expected to see him again. But on April 10, 1870, McCaleb gave the order:

"Move 'em out!"

Goose led out, followed by Salty's chuck wagon. McCaleb and Charlie rode drag, swinging doubled lariats against the flanks of stragglers, keeping the herd bunched. Brazos and Monte flanked them on the right, Laredo and Harley on the left. Until the two thousand big Texas steers got used to trailing, it would be hell on everybody, especially the flank riders. The first day's drive was a nightmare. By the time they reached the North Platte River, the day was done. So were the riders.

"I doubt we've made more'n ten miles," said Laredo, "but my carcass says we've done a hundred."

"We'll give 'em the night to settle down," said McCaleb. "Tomorrow will have to be better. I don't expect much, the first day on the trail."

The second day was a marked improvement over the first. McCaleb judged they had made twenty miles.

"Talkin' to Bill Cody," said Charlie Tilghman, "I got the impression the Sioux Indians ain't above jumpin' their reservation in Dakota and sashayin' back into their old Wyoming hunting grounds."

"I expect he's right," said McCaleb. "We had a fight with some of them on our last drive to Fort Buford, but we crossed their reservation."

"If Goose finds any sign," said Laredo, "let's show 'em some Texas hospitality and call on them before they call on us."

"I'll agree to that," said Brazos, "as long as we're sure they're laying for us. This used to be their hunting grounds, before they were sent to the reservation. Let's don't ambush an honest hunting party."

"Somebody," said Monte sarcastically, "is goin' to have to figger out if they're a huntin' party, or if they're aimin' to take our scalps and the herd. Who's sharp enough to do that? You, maybe?"

His words struck sparks from Brazos's green eyes. When he spoke, his voice was dangerously quiet.

"I reckon I got more savvy for it than some short horn just three years out of Missouri."

"I'm bossing this drive," said McCaleb. "If and when the time comes, that will be my decision. If I give an order that's strong against any man's religion, then he's welcome to saddle up and ride. South."

While he spoke to the outfit, his eyes were on Monte Nance. Monte just turned and stalked into the gathering darkness. Maybe this was what bothered Rebecca, McCaleb thought. The kid was quick as forked lightning with a Colt, and had all the elements of a full-fledged gunfighter.

Their third night on the trail a spring storm came roaring out of the west. Every man was in the saddle, circling the nervous herd. They pulled on their slickers and tied down their hats with rawhide thongs. Lightning did a zigzag dance across the western horizon, and thunder rumbled closer. Gray sheets of rain rode a violent, screaming wind. Steers bawled their unease as lightning transformed the entire world into a huge flickering ball of fire. Finally, directly overhead, lightning illuminated the storm-swept landscape in a blaze of blinding light. The herd didn't wait for the earthshaking clap of thunder. They were off and running, back the way they'd come.

Every rider kicked his horse into a run, and the horses, as skittish as the steers, needed no urging. The earth trembled as the impact of eight thousand hooves competed with the crash of thunder. Slowly they gained on the lead steers. McCaleb's bay, his favorite cutting horse, knew what was expected of him. Once they were neck and neck with one of the lead steers, the bay drove a shoulder into the brute. The steer stumbled, raking a running mate with a horn. On the far side other riders had gotten ahead of the charging herd. Slowly but surely the lead steers were turned west and then north, bending the strung-out herd into a crude horseshoe. Finally the charging mass doubled back on itself, the outer steers still running, while those in the center climbed over one another in blind panic. The worst of the storm had passed, but the rain continued. Slowly the outfit came together, singing out as McCaleb called their names. Every man was accounted for. It was a hard night, the rain continuing until dawn. But a hot breakfast, clear skies, and a warm sun lifted their spirits. They covered a good twenty miles, and the night that followed was as peaceful as the previous one had been hectic.

The morning of their fifth day on the trail, McCaleb had sent Goose to scout ahead. But Goose reported no Indian sign, and they spent another quiet night. But the following day McCaleb's caution was justified. Goose rode in before the sun was noon-high.

"Sioux come," said Goose. He extended both hands, fingers spread, and fisted them. He then extended two more fingers.

"A dozen Sioux," said McCaleb. "Brazos, you and Laredo come with Goose and me. We'll ride out to meet them. Rest of you, stay with the herd and watch our back trail. While these twelve get our attention, a second bunch could sneak up from behind and stampede the herd from here to yonder."

Goose trotted his horse forward, McCaleb, Brazos, and Laredo following. They reined up, watching the Sioux approach in a column of twos. Turning to McCaleb, Goose pointed to himself.

"Habla?"

McCaleb nodded. Goose intended to communicate with them through sign. The Sioux all rode spotted ponies, and except for knives, appeared unarmed. They all wore leggings, moccasins, and several wore sleeveless buckskin shirts. Being unfamiliar with the tribe, McCaleb had no idea which of them might be a chief or medicine man. A dozen yards shy of them, Goose reined up. Their spokesman would identify himself. The Sioux drew up and one of their number trotted his horse to meet Goose. He raised his right hand, palm out, as a sign of peace. Goose had initially offered no such sign, but now he did so. Not a word passed between them. Goose had his back to McCaleb, so he sidestepped his horse until he could see the Sioux response to Goose's signs. The Indian's hands moved swiftly, and McCaleb caught only one response that seemed to answer a question. The Sioux spread both hands, extending all his fingers. He then dropped his hands, indicating the conversation was over. McCaleb, Brazos, and Laredo hooked their thumbs in their belts near their holstered Colts as Goose wheeled his horse and trotted back to them. Goose reined up, extended his hands and spread all his fingers.

"Want cow," he said.

"Give cow?" McCaleb lifted his eyebrows in question.

"Ninguno," said Goose. *"Ninguno."*

McCaleb nodded and Goose rode back to deliver the answer to the Sioux. While McCaleb didn't understand their language, facial expression knew no such barrier, and he believed the Sioux were surprised at his refusal. For a long, hard minute they glared at McCaleb before turning their horses and riding away.

"We'll be seein' that bunch again," said Laredo, "and they'll likely bring along a couple of dozen friends just to make it interestin'."

"Maybe," said McCaleb, "but maybe not. Goose knows the Indian mind. Give them ten cows today and tomorrow they'll want twenty. Or fifty. I won't be bled dry. Indians respect courage. They know there's just eight of us, includin' Salty, while we don't know how many of them we're facing. It's a calculated risk. They can either call our bluff or decide that our medicine's too powerful and leave us alone. We're not exactly holdin' aces, but it's not quite a busted flush either."

Pendleton Rhodes breathed a huge sigh of relief. They had reached Doan's Crossing, had forded the Red, and were safely in Texas. Now all he had to do was hire an outfit, buy a herd, brand it, and get that five thousand steers and cows back to southern Wyoming.

"Gents," he said, "it's two weeks until Christmas. I'd like to visit my kin, but while I'm there, I aim to be looking for some good horses and good riders. I'd like for the rest of you to do the same. This worked for Will and it should for us. I'm giving each of you a hundred and fifty dollars. Thirty of that is wages for the trip down here. The rest is for horses. Remember, there'll be thirteen or more of us goin' back, so we'll need a good remuda. Soon as I return from Waco, I'll go to Fort Worth for the chuck wagon and pitch camp on the Brazos, just south of old Fort Belknap. I'll expect all of you to meet me there no later than the last day of December."

The second watch didn't take over until midnight, but Mc-Caleb found himself unable to sleep. He got up and found Goose, Charlie, and Brazos waiting at the chuck wagon.

"If they're comin'," said Brazos, "it'll be just before dawn."

"That's about what I expect," said McCaleb, "but they won't be taking us by surprise."

When the second watch took over, McCaleb paused for a word with Monte, Laredo, and Harley. McCaleb and his men circled the herd, two riding clockwise, two counter-clockwise. With the darkest hour approaching, every man strained his ears, seeking some warning that death approached on spotted ponies. When the first gray of approaching dawn touched the sky, McCaleb sighed in relief.

"I can't believe we're getting out of this without at least a stampede," said Brazos. "I'd have bet, since they didn't get any cows, that they'd be sure to get even."

"They still might," said McCaleb. "We'll have to be just as careful tonight and for the next several nights as we were last night. Unless something or somebody has changed their minds, they'll come after us."

But the danger was past, and before the day was over they learned the reason. When Goose returned from his daily scout, he had news, but not of the Sioux.

"Soldados," said Goose.

McCaleb rode ahead to the soldier camp. Ten miles north, beside a creek, he found a company of blue coats from Fort Buford. The officer in charge was Captain Martin Sandoval and he was in a far more genial mood than when McCaleb had last seen him. McCaleb grinned.

"Have some of your boys escaped, Captain?"

"McCaleb," sighed Sandoval, "just be thankful all you have to keep up with is a bunch of wild cows. When I took command at Buford, they didn't tell me I'd have to police all of Dakota Territory and Wyoming as well."

"They tried to shake us down for some cows yesterday," said McCaleb, "and we expected them back last night. I reckon we owe you one."

They bedded down the herd near the soldiers' camp, and McCaleb invited them to supper. Salty outdid himself with fried ham, beans, sourdough biscuits, and dried apple pie.

"Magnificent meal," said Sandoval, lighting his pipe. "A man never truly appreciates good food until he's eaten field rations for a week."

"We parted on somewhat of a sour note last time," said

McCaleb. "What are conditions at Buford insofar as the sale of beef is concerned?"

"I suppose I overreacted a bit. But I was new at the post, there less than a month. It was—and still is—a volatile situation. Frankly, I had more than I could say grace over without having any wild cards thrown into the game. Having to explain the Shoshoni on the Sioux Reservation would have finished me. Having said that, let me say this: you'll always be welcome at the fort, as long as you don't cross the Sioux Reservation to get there. Trail your herd north, just as you're doing this one, staying in eastern Wyoming. When you reach the Missouri, follow it east to the fort."

"We'll do that," said McCaleb. "When we return from Montana, if there's time before snow flies, we'll take another herd to Fort Buford. Maybe we'll bid on the beef contracts. When are they to be let?"

"Bids are taken in August," said Sandoval. "I'll put in a word for you. Wilson McKendree has the contract now, and he's driving all the way from Texas. He's been told, however, not to drive across the Sioux Reservation, but to turn northeast at Ogallala and go around it. It seems he's consistently violating that order, because the detour is costing him time and money. His beef contract will be renewed over my dead body."

"We can get to you without setting foot on the reservation," McCaleb said, "but I'm not sure I can get there in time to bid."

"Write out your bid and I'll take it with me. I'll see that it's in the pot on time. Just be there with a thousand head before first snow."

McCaleb grinned. "I wouldn't want you breaking any rules."

"Oh, perish the thought. I just bend them a mite when it suits my purpose. You taught me that in Waco."

"Sandoval," chuckled McCaleb, "there's hope for you. When your tour of duty's done, get out and come to southern Wyoming. I'll teach you to chase cows instead of Indians. The pay's better and the cows won't scalp you."

"Don't tempt me." Sandoval grinned. "I might desert."

Irv Vonnecker hadn't once regretted taking Maury Duke's gold and fleeing the Sweetwater valley. Cheyenne or Denver would have been too obvious, so he had endured the long, hard ride to Miles City, Montana Territory.

"Mr. Vonnecker?"

Vonnecker got up from his plush chair and opened the door. One of his housemen handed him a thick roll of bills from his gambling tables. When he had closed and locked the door, Vonnecker turned to the big iron safe. He twirled the combination dial, swung back the heavy door and added the money to his growing pile. With four thousand of his own, plus what he'd stolen from Duke, he had quickly become a prominent and respected figure in Miles City. Nobody gave a damn where you got your money, he thought smugly, as long as you had it. He owned the Gilded Lily, the fanciest saloon in town, and had secretly acquired an interest in the bank. In Vonnecker's devious mind, the end always justified the means. He had stolen and killed before, and a lot less profitably.

31

"*M*ove 'em out!" shouted Pendleton Rhodes.

March 2, 1870, the herd, 5,050 head, began the eleven hundred mile journey to southern Wyoming. It had been the most difficult task of Pen Rhodes's life. Finding good cow horses hadn't been easy, and they were working with a short remuda. More and more ranchers were driving their own herds to market and were themselves in need of good cow horses. With the demand for steers increasing and the supply decreasing, prices had risen from eight dollars a head to ten. Forced to rely on his own judgment, Pen bought 2,550 steers and 2,500 cows. McCaleb had been dead right. With ever-increasing Texas cattle prices, their future depended on natural increase.

Having reported the presence of the Union soldiers, Goose took the trail of the Sioux. Well-aware of the presence of the troops, the wily Indians had veered north in a half circle to evade the cavalry. Then they had simply ridden east to the reservation in western Dakota Territory.

"Mission accomplished," said Captain Sandoval, "for whatever it's worth. They'll loiter on the reservation until we return to the fort and then just ride out again. But it should buy you enough time to get into Montana Territory."

When they reached the Missouri, Sandoval and his troops turned east toward Fort Buford.

"We still have some daylight," said McCaleb. "Let's see if this bunch has enough trail savvy to cross the river this late in the day. We'll take the chuck wagon across last."

"Give it a few more minutes," said Charlie Tilghman. "Wait for the sun to drop behind that cloud bank. They still may see their ugly mugs in the water, but at least the sun won't reflect in their eyes."

The herd crossed easily and they followed with the chuck wagon.

"Bed 'em down," said McCaleb. "I won't leave good water and good grass this close to sundown."

They drove twenty miles the following day, only to have an early evening thunderstorm stampede most of the herd south. They ended up grazing along the north bank of the Missouri.

"We might as well of spent yesterday and last night here," said Harley, "because here we are."

They had three days of uninterrupted good weather, and from McCaleb's figuring, were within a hundred miles of Miles City, Montana. They had just bedded down the herd for the night when Goose, without a word, mounted and rode out.

"Somebody's coming," said McCaleb. "Smell the dust?"

"Can't," said Harley. "Bein' on drag all day, I couldn't smell it if you laid me belly down and shoved my face into it."

Goose returned at sundown.

"Injun come," he said. "Crow. Hunt horse." He held up five fingers, then two.

They rode in from the west on spotted ponies, leading nine haltered, half-gentled broncs. Some of them would make good cow horses, McCaleb judged. The Crow, buckskin-clad, impressed him favorably. He was downwind from them and all he could smell was horse sweat. At a sign from Goose, they dismounted and picketed their horses. Goose turned to McCaleb.

"Eat," he said. "Crow want eat."

Salty glared at Goose. Indians had prodigious appetites, a trait all tribes seemed to share. They ate as though they'd never seen food before and never expected to see it again. McCaleb nudged Brazos.

"This is going to be an experience," he said.

And it was. Salty always made enough dried apple pies for every man to have several. This time, to be safe, he made two dozen. The Crow wolfed them all down and waited expectantly for more.

"My God," said Laredo, "I'm glad we had pie. That bought me enough time to grab some biscuits and beans. There won't be any seconds tonight."

"Seconds, hell," snarled Monte. "I ain't had firsts yet."

"This is almighty strange country," said Brazos, chuckling. "The locusts walk on their hind legs and ride spotted horses."

"Was I t' have a choice," snapped Salty, "I'd as soon fight th' bastards as feed 'em."

"They'll likely be gone by morning," said McCaleb, "and tonight we're going to be more concerned with our horses than the cattle. From what I've heard, the Crow is a notorious horse thief, and is not particular. He'll steal from other tribes, from whites, and from his friends."

"That," growled Monte, "after eatin' our grub, the ungrateful sons. Once they settle down, let's gut-shoot them in their blankets and take their horses."

McCaleb turned on him and his voice was deadly soft.

"I said watch them. Nothing more."

Having eaten, the Crow distanced themselves from the cow camp. They rode out before dawn, taking only their horses.

"Nothin' keeps a man honest," observed Harley, "like bein' watched by another gent who's got a loaded gun handy."

"They're ridin' southeast," said Laredo. "This time tomorrow, some of the Sioux may be wonderin' what happened to their horses."

* * *

The three outlaws sat their horses in silence. Each had his hands bound behind his back and each had a noose knotted beneath his left ear. Pen Rhodes spoke, lifting his hand.

"Do any of you have last words?"

The trio remained silent.

"Let's be done with it, then," said Pen.

He dropped his hand, and in a single motion, Red, Poke, and Donato slapped the rumps of the three horses. The men swung free, kicked for a few seconds, and were still.

"We should of run down th' rest of 'em," said Poke.

"We're not the cavalry," said Pen. "Let's hope this will be enough to keep the others at a distance."

Deep in Indian territory, they rounded up their scattered herd and again pointed them north, toward Fort Dodge.

On May 4, without the loss of a steer, they bedded down the herd half a dozen miles south of Miles City, Montana.

"In the morning," said McCaleb, "I'll ride in and see if there's a chance we can sell all or part of the herd here."

"We're needin' grub," said Salty. "Them Crows picked us clean."

"Come with me, then," said McCaleb, "and load up. Couple more of you can come, if you'd like. Those staying with the herd can ride in for a while after we return. We'll be here tonight and tomorrow night."

Charlie, Laredo, Harley, and Goose remained with the herd. Monte had offered to help Salty load the chuck wagon. Since he might be negotiating the sale of the herd, McCaleb wanted Brazos there. Reaching town, they separated, Salty and Monte seeking a trading post or general store.

"I reckon you got some idea," said Brazos, "as to our bottom figure?"

"Thirty dollars a head. We can go on to the gold fields if we have to, or even to Fort Benton. But if there's a market here, so much the better. We're only a three week drive from the ranch."

Every town of size had a livestock dealer, and Miles City was no exception. There were three horses in the corral but not a sign of a cow. On a board that hung above the barn door, somebody had painted SWEDE OLIPHANT, PROP. Oliphant was a big man gone to fat, bald, with a stub of cigar clenched in his teeth. His back was to the wall, his chair resting on its hind legs, and he stayed where he was.

"We got two thousand big Texas steers south of town," said McCaleb.

"How much?"

"Thirty," said McCaleb.

"Average?"

"Thousand to twelve hundred," said McCaleb.

"I'll have a look at 'em. If they're as good as you say, I'll take five hundred."

"We'll be here until the day after tomorrow," said Mc-Caleb. "Know of anybody else who might be interested?"

"Not around here. Your best bet would be Fort Benton an' the gold camps. Outfit from Oregon brought in fifteen hundred head last fall. Sold a buyer at Fort Benton a thousand and th' rest at th' minin' camps. There's a new diggings on Flat Willow Creek, hundred an' fifty mile west of here."

"The buyer at Fort Benton," said McCaleb. "Do you know who he is?"

"Feller named Raymond Dantzler. You could telegraph him."

"Thanks," said McCaleb. He and Brazos had reached the door before Oliphant spoke again.

"Five hundred for me. I'll let you know for sure 'fore th' day's done."

They were on the boardwalk when Brazos spoke.

"That might not be a bad idea, telegraphing this gent. It's got to be as far from here to Fort Benton as it is from the ranch to here."

"By my figuring," said McCaleb, "it's close to three hundred miles from here to Benton. Too long a drive without some assurance we have a sale. Let's find the telegraph office."

At the rear of the Gilded Lily, Vonnecker had furnished a large private room with enough tables and chairs to seat two dozen men. Half that number, rough, bearded, armed, sat there smoking and nursing their drinks while Vonnecker talked.

"Get out there on Flat Willow Creek and stake claims. Get as close to the richer claims as you can. Then, when somebody quits his claim, you can step in and take over. Got any questions?"

"Yeah," said a hard voice, "why would an hombre with a rich claim just up an' quit?"

"He might be dead," said Vonnecker. "There's all kinds of accidents that can happen around a mining camp."

They laughed, banging their shot glasses on the tables. The merriment was cut short by a pistol shot from the front of the saloon. Glasses fell and chairs clattered as they sprang to their feet.

"Sit down!" bawled Vonnecker. "I don't want any of you seen leaving here. Don't make a move until I get back."

He dashed out into the hall and collided with a bartender.

"What is it?" snapped Vonnecker. "What's happened?"

"Mullins," stammered the bartender. "Mullins is dead. Them two drifters seen him bottom-dealin', shot him dead and robbed him. They're holed up across th' street in th' billiard hall."

"Damn," snarled Vonnecker. "How much money did they take?"

"Th' winnings from Mullins's table. Upwards of a thousand dollars."

"Get the sheriff," said Vonnecker.

*   *   *

McCaleb and Brazos, after leaving the telegraph office, returned to the store to find Salty loading the chuck wagon by himself.

"Monte came along to help you," said McCaleb. "Where is he?"

"How'n hell do I know?" snapped Salty. "There was a shot somewheres up th' street, an' he took off toward it."

Suddenly there were three shots, and within seconds two more. By the time McCaleb and Brazos reached the billiard parlor, the bloodied body of the sheriff was stretched out on the boardwalk. A crowd had gathered, and Mc-Caleb nudged a white-aproned bartender.

"What's goin' on?"

"Pair of drifters robbed an' killed a gambler in the Gilded Lily. They holed up in th' billiard parlor, an' when th' sheriff thought they was goin' to surrender, they cut him down. Now there's some young fool, stranger in town, that's behind th' buildin', sneakin' in th' back door."

McCaleb looked at Brazos and found Brazos looking at him. They knew who that "young fool" was. Wordlessly they ran for the alley, only to be brought up short by four rapid shots. There were two more, and then only silence. It was over.

Monte Nance limped out, his Colt still in his hand. The left side of his shirt was bloody from a shoulder wound, and the slug he'd taken in his right thigh had bloodied his Levi's to the knee.

"Let's git him to th' doc!" somebody shouted.

Monte was caught up by four men and carried away. McCaleb and Brazos followed the throng to the doctor's house and waited until Monte had been carried inside. Some of the crowd was about to follow when something more astounding drew them away. The bartender McCaleb had talked to had remained at the billiard parlor, and now he arrived, breathless.

"The kid drilled both them drifters," he shouted, "and

them layin' for him! He got 'em with a shot apiece, in the head!"

There was a virtual human stampede as the curious lit out to see the gory remains of the men Monte had shot.

"Well, by God," growled Brazos, "if that don't beat the goose a-gobblin'. He jumps in a fight that's none of his business, gets himself shot, and he's right in the middle of a trail drive. What are we gonna do with him?"

"Leave him here," said McCaleb grimly, "until we've sold the herd. We can pick him up on the way back, unless he manages to get himself shot dead between now and then. Come on, we might as well make arrangements for the doc to put him up somewhere until he heals."

They returned to the store, helped Salty finish loading the wagon, and the three of them returned to camp. They found Swede Oliphant had driven out in a buckboard.

"I'll take five hundred," said Oliphant. "They're prime, and I wish I could take 'em all. Next time you bring a herd, see me 'fore you make any deals. I'll have th' pens ready tomorrow morning. We'll go to th' bank an' get your money."

When the buyer had gone, McCaleb explained to the rest of the outfit what Monte had done. He concluded with a warning.

"Stay out of trouble in town. By that, I mean gun trouble. We're already shorthanded, and this drive is far from finished."

"We're mostly wantin' to visit a bathhouse and barbershop," said Laredo, "but we can go two at a time. We all go, and that leaves just you and Brazos with the herd."

"Ganos no go," said Goose.

McCaleb, Brazos, and Goose remained with the herd, and in the late afternoon they had an unexpected visitor. He was a big, bearded man with friendly brown eyes, and he rode a mule. He wore flat-heeled boots and the rough garb of a miner.

"Step down," McCaleb invited.

"I'm Daniel Gantry and I've got a claim on Flat Willow Creek. Oliphant told me you've got beef to sell. There's upwards of a hundred of us there on Flat Willow, and my God, we're tired of beans and rank bacon. We crave meat! If we all pitch in and buy five hundred steers, will you bring them to us?"

"Count on it. I'm Benton McCaleb. This redheaded hombre is Brazos Gifford, one of my pardners. That's Salty and Goose by the chuck wagon. Rest of the outfit's in town. How do we find your diggings?"

"It's right at a hundred and fifty miles west of here. If you start within the next couple of days, I'll ride back with you."

"We'll move out the day after tomorrow," said McCaleb, "and we'll be startin' early. Why don't you ride out tomorrow night and bunk with us?"

"Thanks," said Gantry. "I'll do that."

On their way to the bank the following morning, McCaleb and Brazos stopped at the telegraph office. Dantzler's telegraphed response was brief and to the point:

Deliver one thousand head. Payment on arrival.
                                        Raymond Dantzler

Swede Oliphant was waiting at the bank and introduced them to Otis Jernigan, the banker. But McCaleb wasn't impressed with the man's expensive blue serge suit and his mane of flowing white hair. The banker's eyes were bloodshot and his face a mass of broken blood vessels, the mark of a hard-drinking man. Then, from the inner sanctum that concealed the vault, stepped another man, more eloquently dressed than Jernigan. Brazos got hastily to his feet and turned away.

"I'm goin' outside, Bent."

McCaleb said nothing, eyeing the stranger more carefully. The bank wasn't all that large. What had this man been doing in or near the vault?

"McCaleb," said Jernigan, "this is Mr. Vonnecker, one of our most prominent and respected citizens." He then turned to Vonnecker. "Mr. McCaleb has brought in a herd of Texas steers, and Mr. Oliphant has bought five hundred head."

That got Vonnecker's attention, and he looked at Mc-Caleb with new interest.

"How many more do you have?" he asked.

"Fifteen hundred head," said McCaleb, "but they're spoken for."

"I'll better their offer by five dollars a head."

"No," said McCaleb, "I've given my word. Now, Mr. Jernigan, if you don't mind, let's get on with this. I have other things to do."

Vonnecker walked away without a word, and Jernigan looked worriedly after him. McCaleb decided he neither liked nor trusted either of them. He and Oliphant parted company outside the bank. McCaleb said nothing, waiting for Brazos to speak.

"He's one of Maury Duke's men, Bent."

"His name's Vonnecker," said McCaleb. "At least that's what he's using here. What do you know about him?"

"He had that makeshift tent saloon on the Sweetwater. Pen grabbed him and threatened to cut his gizzard out if he didn't tell us what Duke had done with Goose. He didn't have the sand to face Duke after spilling his guts, so he hauled out and come here."

"He offered to buy the rest of the herd at five dollars a head more than our best price," said McCaleb. "When I refused, he glared at me like I was bein' measured for a coffin. He's scared the bejabbers out of Jernigan and fancies himself a bull of the woods."

"I wouldn't sell to him at *any* price. Whatever he was into on the Sweetwater was nothing compared to this. That slippery coyote's got plans for this town, and I'd bet my saddle they're of no benefit to anybody but him."

"He's got some kind of hold on Jernigan," said Mc-

Caleb, "but none on us. I expect we'll be selling beef here again, but not to him."

One room in the doctor's house had been set aside for recuperating patients, and they found Monte Nance stretched out on one of the beds. He received them in sullen silence. Obviously he expected a reprimand and was building a head of steam for his response. McCaleb fooled him.

"We've just sold five hundred head, Monte. We're taking another five hundred to Flat Willow Creek, and the rest to Fort Benton. We're moving out in the morning."

He placed ten double eagles on the table beside the bed.

"That should hold you until we return. Anything else, before we go?"

"No," said Monte, refusing to look at him. "Nothin' else."

Brazos contained himself until they were outside, and then he laughed.

"He had a hell of a mad on, and you didn't give him a chance to use it."

"He's used to bein' scolded like Rebecca's little brother," said McCaleb, "but no more. Let's go."

Irv Vonnecker wasn't accustomed to being refused. While he could have turned a good profit on the herd, the loss didn't bother him; the fact that for all his money and position, he had been turned down, did. He returned to the Gilded Lily and nodded to one of his men who sat nursing a drink. When they reached Vonnecker's office, he locked the door behind them.

"Carp, I have a job for you. You'll need some help. Figure on ten men besides yourself. Interested?"

"Maybe. What's in it fer me?"

"Fifteen thousand in gold, if you handle it right."

"How many you want killed an' who are they?"

"Some Texas cowboys. The steers are mine. The gold's yours. They've just left the bank with it."

*   *   *

Despite Brazos's hasty departure from the bank, Vonnecker had recognized him and the old hatred had flared up. The redheaded bastard had humiliated him, threatened him. Now he would die, along with his uppity friends.

32

Leading a pack mule, Dan Gantry rode into McCaleb's camp at sundown. After supper they gathered around the chuck wagon and listened as the young miner told them about the Montana gold fields.

"Grub, or the lack of it, is the biggest problem," said Gantry. "No way to keep fresh meat, except on the hoof. Last fall, some ranchers from Oregon brought in a herd, but it didn't help us none because it was sold to speculators. They bought it on the hoof and sold it by the pound, so we still ended up eatin' bacon and beans."

"Had any trouble with Indians?" McCaleb asked.

"Only where our livestock is concerned," said Gantry. "This is mostly Crow country. They seem to get their enjoys out of taking our horses and mules instead of our scalps. I suppose we should be grateful."

"Maybe they're mule eaters," said Brazos. "Some tribes prefer mule to beef or buffalo."

"That reminds me," said Gantry. "I'd heard there was buffalo here, yet we haven't seen a one."

"You probably won't," said McCaleb. "They're moving east, away from the gold camps, and that accounts for the lessening of Indian trouble. Indians follow the buffalo."

They arose early, ate their breakfast in the dark, and had the herd moving in the first gray light of dawn. Gantry rode the point position with McCaleb, while Goose scouted ahead. When they bedded down for the night, McCaleb estimated they'd covered twenty miles.

When Carp left Vonnecker's office, he had no trouble spotting McCaleb and Brazos. He watched them ride south and that was all he needed to know. Vonnecker had said they had fifteen thousand in gold. Carp briefly toyed with the idea of just getting ahead of these two, ambushing them and taking the gold. But then he'd have to quit the territory to escape Vonnecker's wrath, and he hadn't that many places to which he could run. In most of the more civilized territories to the east, there was a price on his head. Besides an endless supply of liquor, he was enjoying a life of considerable ease in Vonnecker's employ. He began making the rounds of the other saloons, seeking the men he needed.

Despite Gantry's assurance of little or no Indian trouble, McCaleb didn't relax his guard. Nighthawking continued as usual. Their second night on the trail, deep into the second watch, Goose heard something. His search revealed nothing. But the next morning, instead of scouting ahead, the Apache circled the camp and scouted their back trail. When he caught up with the herd, he beckoned to McCaleb. Brazos caught the gesture and trotted his horse alongside McCaleb's.

"Trouble?"

"I don't know," said McCaleb. "Goose has found something he thinks we ought to see. Come on; the herd's behaving itself."

Goose led them through the valley in which they'd spent the previous night and over the crest of the hill beyond. There, they dismounted and followed the Apache into a thicket where two horses had been picketed.

"Shod horses," said McCaleb. "White men."

Goose pointed to the tracks, to himself, and then to the east. McCaleb shook his head. The trail would lead to

Miles City, where it would be lost in a conglomeration of other tracks. Following it would be a waste of time. They mounted and rode back to the herd.

"From now on," said McCaleb, "we're going to be prepared for an attack. These are white men and they're after the gold we're carrying."

"Somebody put them on to us," said Brazos. "Was it Oliphant, Jernigan, or Vonnecker?"

"Maybe none of them," said McCaleb. "Gantry knew about the sale after talking to Oliphant. He showed up mighty convenient. For that matter, when we drove five hundred steers into Oliphant's pens, the whole town knew about the sale. They'd only have to think one step beyond that to figure that we'd be collecting some money before we pulled out."

"I don't believe it's Oliphant or Gantry," said Brazos. "It's one of those sneaking coyotes at the bank."

"I hope you're right," said McCaleb, "but just in case Gantry is mixed up in this, I don't want him knowing we suspect anything. Let's get this over and done with. Get the word to the rest of the outfit so they'll be ready. I want you, Laredo, and Goose on the second watch with me. I'll put Goose on our back trail from midnight until dawn. I aim to spread my blankets close to Gantry. When I leave for the second watch, I want Charlie Tilghman to take my place. I believe Gantry's leveling with us, but we're in no position to gamble."

McCaleb looked at Goose and the Apache nodded. He had understood the significance of the tracks and knew they were in danger of an attack. He had only waited for McCaleb to confirm the action he had expected them to take. When they caught up to the herd, Brazos quietly passed the word to the rest of the outfit. Nothing was said to Gantry. If he made a wrong move, he would be under McCaleb's or Tilghman's gun.

Just after dark, the third day after the drive had left Miles City, Carp gathered his men just west of town. He had ignored Vonnecker and had picked only nine men. After all, he reasoned, these Texans pulled on their britches one leg at a time just like everybody else, and when shot, they'd bleed. Why hire more men than he needed? They were a nondescript bunch, armed with rifles, pistols, and Bowie knives. Carp had managed to keep them out of the saloons, so they were reasonably sober, a new and strange experience for some of them.

"There's eight men," said Carp, "includin' some miner that's tagging along. We'll wait till after midnight, when they've settled down, before we hit 'em. I want 'em shot dead, to th' last man."

"Ain't scairt of them Tejanos, are ye, Carp?"

"Damn right I am," said Carp. "Why do you think we're goin' after 'em in the dead of night? I ain't seen one yet that wouldn't spit in the devil's eye an' draw on some bastard that already had the drop."

They bedded down the herd as usual, and after supper Charles Tilghman and Harley Irwin began the first watch. If Dan Gantry noticed anything amiss, he didn't show it. Brazos and Laredo took to their blankets early. Goose had simply disappeared after supper. McCaleb nursed a third cup of coffee, waiting for Gantry. Finally the solitude got the best of Gantry and he spoke.

"If it's any of my business, where will you be going after you leave Flat Willow Creek?"

"Fort Benton," said McCaleb.

Again the silence grew long. Gantry got to his feet and stretched.

"Not much to do after dark. I might as well turn in."

"What I aim to do," said McCaleb, "soon as I finish this coffee."

McCaleb waited a decent interval and then spread his own blankets near enough to be aware of any movement from Gantry. He had no intention of sleeping, and he suspected that Brazos and Laredo were equally wide awake. Time meant nothing to Goose when an enemy threatened.

Already the Apache was somewhere on their back trail, awaiting the men who would be coming. McCaleb lay there watching the stars. Those same stars he had shared with Rebecca in the Trinity River brakes of East Texas. It seemed so long ago. He was lost in his thoughts when that sixth sense that had kept him alive again got to him. He sensed rather than saw Gantry move. He eased his Colt from its holster and sat up.

"Gantry!"

"Got a cramp in my leg. I need to stand on it."

"Stand, then," said McCaleb, "but don't go wandering around in the dark. It makes my outfit nervous. You could end up with a knife in your gut."

"Sorry. I wasn't thinking."

There was no further movement. Charles Tilghman swapped places with McCaleb at midnight, and he found Laredo and Brazos already with the herd.

"Almighty quiet," said Brazos. "Heard you challenge Gantry."

"He settled down," said McCaleb. "I don't think he's involved in this."

"I hope not," said Laredo. "He's a likable gent. Besides, if he's not straight, we're taking these steers all the way to Flat Willow Creek for nothing."

By the stars it was near three o'clock when Goose stepped out of the shadows. McCaleb reined up and they waited until Brazos and Laredo had circled the herd and joined them. Only then did Goose speak.

"*Hombres* come," he said, holding up both hands in the starlight.

"Ten of them," said McCaleb. "Not bad odds, since we're expecting them. Wait here until I get the others and we'll go welcome them."

He got to Harley first, and when he reached Tilghman, he found Charlie awake. Words were unnecessary.

"What is it?" Gantry was awake too.

"Company's coming," said McCaleb.

"Indians?"

"Worse. White men. Thieves."

"I'll help. What do you want me to do?"

"This is not your fight," said McCaleb.

"I think it is," said Gantry. "Five hundred of these steers are going to Flat Willow Creek to feed us next winter. I won't set here and see them stolen from under my nose. Besides, they may kill us all first."

"If I'm any judge," said McCaleb, "that's exactly what they have in mind. Don't need ten men to stampede the herd. Come on."

Gantry got his rifle and followed. Goose led them almost two miles before they dismounted and hid themselves in a heavily wooded area. It joined a treeless clearing which was devoid of cover.

"Fan out in a line," said McCaleb, "but don't fire until I challenge them. Then shoot to kill."

McCaleb found Gantry sticking close to him, and for all his brave talk, he seemed uneasy.

"How do you know they'll come this way?" Gantry asked in a whisper.

"Goose has a feel for this," said McCaleb. "Anyway, this is far enough from our camp that they'll still be bunched. You've never done this before, have you?"

"Frankly, no," said Gantry, "and I can see how I might be forced to at any time. I guess I need to know if I have the guts to do it."

"More common sense than guts," said McCaleb. "Once you know an attack is coming, choose the field of battle that leaves your enemy at the greatest disadvantage. Like that open plain this bunch will have to cross, leaving them at our mercy. When you're fighting at night—and that's when most attacks take place—force your enemy to shoot first. Regardless how dark it is, there's a muzzle flash for you to shoot at. But keep this in mind: the other man can fire at *your* muzzle flash too, so make your first shots count."

They settled down to wait. In the small hours of the morning the most insignificant sound seemed inordinately loud. The chink of a horse's hoof on a stone could be heard for half a mile. McCaleb heard the approaching riders long before they entered the clearing. He waited until he could see the shadowy forms of men and horses in the starlight, and then he challenged them.

"Drop your guns! You're covered!"

There was a moment of shocked silence and then all hell broke loose. Slugs whipped through the branches of trees and slammed into the trunks of pines. McCaleb was belly down, raking the clearing with fire from his Henry. A few yards to his right he could hear the roar of Gantry's Winchester. Horses reared and screamed, and there was the clatter of retreating hoofbeats as some of the attackers gave up the fight and ran for it. Even in the starlight, McCaleb could see that some of the galloping horses were riderless. Just as suddenly as it began, it was over.

"Lone Star," McCaleb called cautiously, "make your way back to the horses."

There was sudden movement to his right and he cocked the Henry.

"It's me," said Gantry softly.

By the time they reached the picketed horses, everybody was there except Goose, and McCaleb knew where he was.

"Mount up," said McCaleb. "Goose will bring us a count of the dead."

Goose rode in before first light, while they were having breakfast. He raised his right hand, all fingers extended, then made a fist and extended two more fingers.

"Seven out of ten," said Brazos. "In the dark, that's good shootin'."

"That's good shootin' *anytime,*" said Harley.

Gantry said nothing. His eyes were on the grisly thing at Goose's feet. It was a hairy, bloody bundle tied with a rawhide thong.

"What is . . . that?" Gantry asked.

"Scalps," said Brazos. "Goose has got plumb civilized. Only scalps them that's tryin' to kill him."

Carp rode into Miles City two hours after daylight, entering the Gilded Lily through the back door. He stumbled into Vonnecker's office without knocking. His left ear was encrusted with blood from a head wound, and his right arm hung limp, bloodied from shoulder to elbow. Vonnecker looked up.

"What in hell happened to you?"

"You double-crossin' bastard," snarled Carp, "somebody told 'em we was comin'. They was layin' for us an' we got shot to doll rags. Ever'body shot dead 'cept Jessup, Turk, an' me. You set me up!"

"Get out of here," said Vonnecker, "and stay out. You're through."

The drive reached Flat Willow Creek without further trouble, and their arrival created a furor. Word spread rapidly along the creek, and miners dropped whatever they were doing and came to see the herd. It was here that Dan Gantry took over and lived up to his promise.

"Boys," he said, after he'd shouted them to silence, "we got a chance to eat steak this winter instead of beans. Who wants steak?"

There was an enthusiastic uproar as miners clanged their gold pans with their fists and the butts of their Colts. When the din subsided, Gantry continued.

"These men brought a herd of steers all the way from Wyoming. I promised we'd take five hundred of them. Now there's at least seventy-five of us. Is there a man here who's so tight he won't lay down two hundred dollars to eat steak all winter? That's fresh meat for a year!"

McCaleb and the outfit looked on in amazement as the miners lined up and, one at a time, Gantry used a scale to weigh out their dust. Finally they were through, and Gantry approached McCaleb with a grin.

"There were more of them than I figured on. Just take

that as a bonus. If this strike holds out, maybe we can do business with you again."

They left Flat Willow Creek on May 15, bound for Fort Benton.

"Even with the poor map that I have," said McCaleb, "I'd say we're within a hundred and fifty miles of Benton. About the same distance from here to Fort Benton as it was from Miles City to here."

Without further incident they reached Fort Benton eight days later. McCaleb and Brazos rode in to meet Raymond Dantzler. The man was near seven feet tall, heavy, with cold blue eyes.

"If you'll write me a bill of sale," he said, "I'll write you a check."

"We prefer gold," said McCaleb.

"Sorry, but that won't be possible. The check will be drawn on the bank in Miles City. You'll be returning there, won't you?"

They had little choice. It was accept Dantzler's check or seek another market. McCaleb had promised Martin Sandoval he'd bring another herd to Fort Buford before first snow, and this was no time to wander aimlessly around Montana Territory.

"I reckon," said Brazos ruefully, "we could have just driven that bunch of steers on to Fort Buford."

"I thought of that," said McCaleb, "but it's a good five hundred miles. Without stampedes, outlaws, or Indians, that's a month away. We can't hunt wild horses with a thousand steers on our hands, and we're honestly in need of some good saddle stock."

"You're right," said Brazos, "but I'd as soon have took Confederate scrip as a check on that Miles City bank."

"I'm uneasy about that myself. We'll go there first, dispose of this check, and then plan our wild horse hunt."

"There's Monte," said Brazos. "The kid's got all the earmarks of a fiddle-foot gunslinger. He's got his old daddy's bad judgment, and a fast gun to back it up."

"We'll hold his stake until he's grown up enough and has sense enough to claim it, but I'm done with trying to keep his tail out of the fire. This last incident may have brought him to a fork in the trail. We'll see."

33

May 24, 1870. On the Arkansas, near Fort Dodge, Kansas.

"According to Will's log," said Pen, "we're just a little more than six hundred miles from Box Elder Creek."

"We'll be there by July fourth," said Poke Shambler, "if there's no storms, no stampedes, an' we don't have to stop an' hang some more thieves."

"Yeah," chuckled Red Dulancy. "We had some ham, we could have ham and eggs. If we had some eggs."

Before leaving Fort Benton, McCaleb spoke to Captain Herndon, the post commander, about Montana's wild horse herds.

"We're wanting to catch some wild horses," said Mc-Caleb. "You patrol the area; have any of your men seen the herds?"

"Not lately," said Herndon. "The Indians, the Crow, tell us the herds have drifted northeasterly. That would put them somewhere north of Miles City, up toward the Canadian border."

McCaleb called the outfit together.

"We might as well return to Miles City," he said, "and plan from there. That'll give us a chance to rid ourselves of this check written on the Miles City bank. Then, before we go horse hunting or anywhere else, we'll need to replenish our supplies. Right, Salty?"

"We'll be on short rations 'fore we ever git to Miles City," said Salty.

They started each day when it was barely light enough to see, stopping only when darkness caught up with them. They were four days on the trail, when the Indians rode into their camp. It was just before supper.

"My God," groaned Salty, remembering the last bunch. "Ten of 'em!"

But these Indians were different, more aloof, and they hadn't come for supper. Three of the ten were women, one of them a young girl. McCaleb decided she was barely seventeen, if that. Her dark eyes were on Goose as the Apache conversed in sign with the leader of the band. Everybody, especially Salty, sighed with relief when they rode away. Only the girl looked back. Goose watched them out of sight as they followed the creek. In the gathering darkness their fire was a tiny dot of light. They had made their own camp half a mile downstream. Goose told them nothing. Finally, after they had eaten, McCaleb asked him.

"Ganos," he asked, pointing downstream, "Crow?"

"Crow," said Goose. "Hunt horse."

Goose vanished after supper, which wasn't unusual. McCaleb never put the Apache on a specific watch, because he was *always* on his guard. When danger threatened, he never slept until it had been met and conquered. The Crow were gone before first light. Not encumbered with a chuck wagon, they kept well ahead of McCaleb's outfit. They caused no trouble, and none of the Lone Star riders saw them again. They saw only an occasional unshod hoofprint and the ashes of old fires. Two days west of Miles City, McCaleb veered to the south and they saw no further sign of the Crow.

"That fits what Captain Herndon told me," said McCaleb. "They're going where he suggested we go."

"If all the wild horses have gone to the northeastern corner of the territory," said Brazos, "and all the Indians are following, it's likely to get almighty crowded by the time we get there."

"I've heard there are thousands of horses," said Mc-Caleb. "Even the Crow can't catch them all. Besides, we can't handle more than a dozen, if that many. They can't be driven, so they'll have to be gentled before we go anywhere. That'll take some time, and I think we'll let Goose do it his way. Ride a horse into the ground, and you end up with a broken-spirited nag that's not worth shooting."

They picketed their horse remuda along a creek just west of Miles City. Brazos and McCaleb rode in first, accompanied by Salty with the chuck wagon. Leaving Salty at the store, they rode on to the bank. To their total surprise, they found Irv Vonnecker at the front desk and there was no sign of Jernigan. Vonnecker looked up, found Brazos glaring directly at him, and turned back to the papers on the desk.

"We've got business with Jernigan," said McCaleb. "Where is he?"

"Mr. Jernigan decided to retire. For his health. Whatever business you have with this bank, I'll handle."

"Fine," said McCaleb, dropping the check on the desk.

Vonnecker looked at it, turned it over and looked at the back, and then took one of the ledgers from a shelf behind his desk. He made a show of carefully thumbing through the pages. He stopped, studied a particular page and frowned.

"Sorry, McCaleb, I can't cash this."

"You'd better have a damn good reason," said McCaleb grimly.

"I have," said Vonnecker with a half smile. "There's not enough money in the account to cover it."

"You thieving coyote!" bawled Brazos. He was halfway across the desk when McCaleb stopped him.

"So the account's short," said McCaleb. "By how much?"

"Five hundred and twenty dollars."

"It's three hundred miles to Fort Benton," said Mc-

Caleb, "and I'm not going there on the strength of what *you* say. We'll accept what's in the account and consider the check paid."

"I couldn't do that," said Vonnecker smugly. "It wouldn't be legal."

"Legal?" shouted Brazos. "When has that ever concerned you?"

Vonnecker said nothing, but got to his feet, dismissing them.

"Hold it," said McCaleb. "We're not done with you."

"The answer is still no."

"Suppose another five hundred and twenty dollars is put into that account," said McCaleb. "Then you could honor this check, couldn't you?"

"Certainly," said Vonnecker, with a frown.

McCaleb opened the saddlebag at his feet and dipped out a double handful of double eagles into his hat. Carefully he stacked twenty-six of them before Vonnecker.

"Consider this a deposit to Mr. Dantzler's account," said McCaleb, "and since there's enough to cover this check, cash it. I want gold."

"Why, ah, I don't know—"

"Gold," said McCaleb. "Now!"

McCaleb was on his feet, leaning across the desk. His eyes were cold, like blue ice, and to Vonnecker he looked ten feet tall. Hastily he got up and went to the vault.

They left Vonnecker glaring after them and stepped out onto the boardwalk. Brazos was breathing hard. He spoke.

"That lying, thieving skunk just cheated us out of five hundred dollars. I don't believe that account was short unless he shorted it."

"Neither do I," said McCaleb. "If Dantzler planned to sucker us, he'd have gone for it all. We were taken, but what choice did we have? Somewhere down the road, Mr. Vonnecker's going to pay. With interest."

They rode back to the store where they'd left Salty, dismounted and half-hitched their horses to the rail.

"Bent," said Brazos. "Across the street."

Across the street was the sheriff's office. Monte Nance stood in the doorway, the evening sun reflecting off the silver star pinned to his shirt. They waited as he crossed the dusty street, still limping slightly. Just short of the board-walk he stopped, leaning on the hitching rail.

"The town insisted I take the job," he said defiantly. "Mayor Vonnecker offered me a hundred dollars a month."

McCaleb said nothing. Brazos exploded.

"*Mayor* Vonnecker? Why, that thieving bastard just cheated us at the bank! He's one of Maury Duke's men, straight off the Sweetwater!"

Monte paled. Without a word he turned and limped back across the street.

"Well, if that don't rip the rag off the bush," snorted Brazos. "Bent, we can't let him do this fool thing."

"What do you suggest we do? Hog-tie him and tote him back to Wyoming, belly down over his saddle?"

"Aw hell," groaned Brazos, "I don't know. How can a man grow up everywhere 'cept between his ears?"

They went on into the store looking for Salty. Tacked to one of the log walls was a sign announcing a Fourth of July festival that included a horse race, among other things.

"I'd like to see that," said Brazos, "if we're still here."

The storekeeper overheard.

"Mayor Vonnecker's got two hosses runnin', an' they'll be hard to beat. Ever' gambler an' ever' Injun in th' terri-tory will be here."

"How long a race?" Brazos asked.

"Quarter mile," said the storekeeper.

They helped Salty load the chuck wagon and they all returned to camp.

"The rest of you can ride into town," said McCaleb, "but don't start anything you can't finish today. We leave early in the morning."

Goose almost never went to town if he had any choice, and it came as a surprise when he mounted and rode off with Harley, Laredo, and Charlie.

"I reckon this is the day for surprises," said McCaleb. "I just hope if there's any ahead, they're more pleasant than what we've had so far."

When the riders returned from town, there was no evidence that Goose had bought anything except some saddlebags. Though nobody had any idea why he wanted them or what they contained, it seemed the Apache had moved a step closer to civilization.

Monte Nance tugged off his boots and stretched out on his hotel bed. Had Vonnecker been part of Maury Duke's gang? There had been a ring of truth in Brazos's words, and while McCaleb had said nothing, Monte had seen the disappointment—or maybe disgust—in his eyes. Monte's room was on the second floor of the town's only hotel. There was a saloon on either side of it and a third across the street. There would be a horse race, a barbecue, and a street dance on July 4, and he dreaded that. Every damn Indian, outlaw, and troublemaker in the territory would be there. There would be drinking, gambling, maybe killing. There would be nobody, nothing, standing in the way except Monte Nance and his gun. Below, in the saloons, pianos jangled, one as out of tune as the other. Women laughed, men cursed, and in the midst of it all there was the sound of breaking glass. Bottles? Windows? Maybe both. Somebody pounded on his door. He sighed, sat up and reached for his boots.

Goose led out and they were riding before first light, heading north. The second day, Goose guided them slightly to the east, and at sundown they drew up beside a creek where there were ashes of an old fire. McCaleb suspected they were following that same band of Crow that had visited their camp. Once the Indians discovered them and learned their intentions, there might be trouble. But he knew Goose well enough to rely on his judgment. The Apache wouldn't lead them into anything he couldn't get them out of.

"I've never hunted wild broncs," said Laredo, "but I've talked to gents that have. Mostly they just rode the herd down and roped as many as they could. When a man roped one, he'd just ride it to a standstill."

"I don't hold with that," said McCaleb. "Do that, and from the very start you've got a horse that's scared to death of you. Somewhere there'll be a canyon where the herd comes to drink. All the better if it's a box canyon, but I doubt we'll be that lucky. The herds usually water late at night, and contrary to what some believe, they're usually led by a wise old mare, not a stallion. Once we find a canyon that can become a trap, it's up to us to build barriers that can be raised once the horses are inside."

"You've hunted wild broncs before," said Charlie Tilghman.

"No," said McCaleb, "but I've seen it done. When I was maybe eight years old, my daddy and me went with some friendly Indians on a hunt. That's when there were still wild horse herds in East Texas. That's how the Comanche did it. In a fight, they're the 'bastardos' Goose calls them. But they're horse Indians and they know their horses."

Four days out of Miles City they caught up to the band of Crow. Less than a mile beyond their own camp they could see the winking eye of another fire. After supper Goose rode to the Indian camp, and when he returned, his new saddlebags were missing. Goose summed up his meeting with the Crow in just one sentence.

"Crow hunt horse, *Tejanos* hunt horse. *Mañana.*"

It was barely light enough to see when they followed Goose to a steep-sided canyon through which a creek ran. The Crow were already at work building a brush fence that could be quickly put in place across the mouth of the canyon. They paid no attention to the Texans. The women were nowhere in sight.

"First time in all my born days," said Brazos, "that I actually saw Indians working. I didn't know they could do anything but take scalps and kill buffalo."

"I think they aim for us to build the brush and log fence

at the other end of the canyon," said McCaleb. "This is the most important, where the herd enters. All we have to do is block the other end with a solid fence."

"In other words," said Laredo, "they don't trust us to do this end and do it right."

McCaleb grinned. "That's what it amounts to. Now I'm curious as to how we'll divide the catch. *Ganos?*"

Goose jogged his horse over to McCaleb's.

"Wild horse," said McCaleb. "What Crow want?"

"Spotted horse," said Goose.

"Damn the luck," said Brazos, "I was hopin' I could take Penelope one of them spotted ponies."

"We catch enough," said McCaleb, "the Crow won't be able to handle them all. Get with Goose and tell him you want one for Penelope. Bloodthirsty heathen he may be, but he's got a soft spot for her."

They got busy and built a brush and log fence at the far end of the canyon. Several of the Crow came, observed their handiwork and rode away. Goose led them far from the canyon, and after supper mounted his horse.

"Stay," he said, riding back in the direction from which they'd come.

"They purely don't have much confidence in us," said Brazos.

"We'd best not push our luck," said McCaleb. "This canyon may be the only decent horse trap in eastern Montana. Goose seems to have worked out some kind of deal with the Crow. Does anybody know what he had in those saddlebags?"

"Could have been anything from plug tobacco to six-shooters," said Laredo. "He was still in the store when the rest of us left for the billiard parlor."

Goose rode into the Crow camp, dismounted, and joined the men around a small fire. There were no tipis and the women were not present, but dark eyes observed Goose from the shadows. There was a faint glow on the horizon. There would be a full moon, and they must take their positions before it lighted the plains. The Crow mounted their horses and rode out, Goose following. Two miles south of the canyon they picketed their horses lest they nicker and warn the approaching wild ones.

Upon reaching the mouth of the canyon, they split up, four of the Crow crossing to the other side. Once their quarry was trapped, they would raise barriers quickly from both sides. Not a word was spoken and not a sound was made. The full moon rose, a silver globe that cast a spectral glow across the earth. The first sound was so slight it might have existed only in the imagination. But no! There it was again. Finally, in the moonlight, they saw the trailwise old black mare approaching the mouth of the canyon. For a long minute she stood there, keening the down-canyon breeze like a wolf. Then she half turned toward the waiting herd, the sound that came from her throat not quite a nicker. It was more of a rumble. And the others came. Some were spotted. The rest were sorrels, bays, duns, chestnuts, browns, blacks, grays, and grullas. A gray stallion brought up the rear, nipping the flanks of the stragglers.

Three-quarters of the way down the canyon, a stream cascaded out of the upper wall, forming a pool at its base. It was here that the horses came to drink. When the animals reached the water, it was time to raise the barricade. Swiftly they worked, dragging logs and brush into place. Although upwind from them, the stallion scented danger and sounded a warning whistle. But it was too late. Goose and three of the Crow trotted along the canyon wall to the farther end. They would spend the night there, reinforcing the log and brush wall with their presence. Soon the captives would exhaust themselves trying to climb the unscalable canyon walls. Tomorrow their education would begin.

Goose rode into the camp at dawn. McCaleb and the rest of the outfit followed him back to the canyon. They reined up on the canyon wall, and the scene below all but took their breath away.

"There must be forty horses down there," cried Brazos, "and look at that big gray!"

"My God," said Laredo in awe. "They're cow horses, every one. I'll bet there ain't a one of 'em under fourteen hands."

They were stocky animals, deep-muscled and sturdy-legged. They all had deep chests, low withers, and powerful hindquarters. Their necks were thick, their heads broad and short. Already the Crow had begun working with some of the spotted horses. Once they roped a horse, they would work patiently until the animal was ready for a halter. Mc-Caleb could see their lips moving as they talked "horse talk." It seemed their goal was to talk to the horse until he was ready for their touch. By then he had learned he wasn't going to be hurt.

"They'll be a month gentling one horse," said Brazos. "We don't have that much time."

"They'll have theirs gentled and be gone before we are," said McCaleb. "We're going to watch Goose and learn from him, so let's get down there and get started. *Ganos?*"

He pointed toward the horses below, and Goose nodded. They picketed their horses where they could graze and made their way to the barricaded mouth of the canyon. They climbed over the brush and logs, Goose carrying only his lariat and a saddle blanket.

"These Injuns don't use a snubbing post," said Harley. "How in thunder can they rope a wild bronc and stay on their feet?"

"I don't know," said McCaleb. "Let's see how Goose does it."

The captives retreated before them. Goose had his eye on a big gray. The horse flattened his ears and back-stepped, his eyes on the Indian. When he had his back to the canyon wall and could go no farther, Goose cast his loop. With the first touch of the rope, the horse screamed and reared. He towered over Goose, his hooves poised for a death blow, but the Apache didn't move. Instead he spoke to the horse in guttural tones that sounded like "hoh, hoh, hoh." The gray brought his lethal hoofs to earth and stood there trembling, staring at this man who didn't fear him. His curiosity got the best of him and he lifted his flattened ears. He actually seemed to listen as Goose continued his meaningless talk. Suddenly he placed his hand on the gray's withers and the startled horse backstepped into the canyon wall. Time after time Goose repeated the process until the gray no longer flinched at his touch. Not only had the hand not harmed him, it had a strangely soothing effect. Goose unfolded the sweaty saddle blanket and again the horse backed away. It took more than two hours and dozens of failed attempts, but the blanket finally rested on the gray's broad back. It remained there until Goose removed it. By sundown he was able to place his loop loosely around the gray's neck and the animal followed him willingly out of the canyon.

"My God," said Laredo, "we've been here since daylight without grub or water. I'm not sure I believe what I'd swear I've been seein'."

"He's not finished," said McCaleb. "It'll be a week or more before the gray's ready for the saddle, but once he's with our remuda, he'll settle down and we can control him. He's gentled enough so that he's no longer afraid."

"I wouldn't have missed that for a hundred dollars," said Harley, "but there's somethin' botherin' me. Can I do that without gettin' my liver and lights stomped out?"

All of them, even McCaleb, had the same misgivings, but the appeal of the horses was strong, and they envied the affection the gray horse developed for Goose. They ended up with eighteen horses, including a spotted mare for Penelope. They endured three weeks of the most trying and frustrating toil any of them had ever experienced. McCaleb, Brazos, Harley, Laredo, and Charlie managed to gentle ten of the horses. Goose tamed the rest of them, and every evening they watched him work with the gray. He would stand next to the horse, his arms across its broad back, lifting his feet off the ground. It became accustomed to his weight, and none of them ever forgot the first time

Goose rode the horse. He used no halter, no rope, no saddle. Only a saddle blanket. They whooped and hollered until they were hoarse as Goose galloped the gray across the prairie, wheeled him and galloped back.

"That horse," laughed Laredo, "can turn on a nickel and give you change. Put him in a race, and I'd bet everything I own and all I could borrow."

"We're just a week away from the Fourth of July," said Brazos. "Since we've been here this long, let's go back to Miles City and let this big gray take that race away from both of Vonnecker's nags."

"That's up to Goose," said McCaleb. "It's his horse."

"Ganos," said Brazos, pointing to the gray, *"carrera,* much gamble."

Goose grinned. *"Bueno.* Much gamble."

They whooped and hollered some more, pounding him on the back in their enthusiasm, forgetting he was Indian. Whatever he had been, he was now one of them, and he had become civilized enough to enjoy it.

The rest of the outfit never learned that they owed the success of the wild horse hunt to those saddlebags Goose had brought. Simple gifts for the Crow, mostly rock candy and tobacco. . . .

34

With their previous remuda and the newly gentled broncs, they had almost more horses than they could handle. McCaleb arranged with Swede Oliphant to use his livestock barn and cattle pens while they were in Miles City.

"Feed them a bait of grain while they're here," said Mc-Caleb. "We'll settle with you when we're ready to leave."

The wisdom of putting up their horses at Oliphant's soon became apparent. Indians were everywhere, awaiting the festivities, most notably the horse race. Every merchant in town had contributed to the pot, and there was a $500 prize. Vonnecker's horses, a black and a bay, were previous winners, and according to rumor he had more than $5,000 bet on them.

"This is goin' to be some hell of a race," said Laredo. "Every Indian in Montana must be here, and they've all got horses to enter."

It came as no surprise when McCaleb discovered that the band of Crow with whom they'd shared the wild broncs were there for the festivities. More than once he saw Goose with the young girl. He saw Monte Nance almost daily, but the new sheriff pointedly ignored him. Once he saw Jernigan stumble out of a saloon and stagger along the boardwalk. He was tempted to ask the old man about Dantzler's "short" account, but decided it would accomplish nothing. There was a growing list in the hotel lobby of those who had entered the horse race and the names of their mounts. They hadn't even bothered with Indian names, just penciling in "Injun rider." That's how Goose was listed, but somebody had written "Gray Goose" for the name of the horse. McCaleb had advanced everybody in the outfit a hundred dollars. Some of them, Salty included, had added to that, betting it all on Goose and the big gray. With Goose being considered just another "Injun rider," the odds against him were enormous. The day before the race, McCaleb made the rounds of the saloons, listening to talk, watching bets being placed. Vonnecker's horses were the favorites, with twenty-to-one odds on the rest.

"If Goose takes this," said Brazos, "we may end up with Vonnecker's bank and saloon. At the least, we'll shake him down for ten times what he took from us."

McCaleb and Brazos rode down to the Yellowstone River. The water was at midsummer low, and the river bottom was long enough, wide enough, and flat enough to accommodate the many riders who had entered the race. White flags already flew at starting and finish lines.

It was near sundown on July 3 when the first of the Texas steers reached the ranch on Box Elder Creek. Grinning, bearded, and dirty, Pen Rhodes swung out of the saddle and took Will Elliot's hand.

Emilio Vasquez drew the chuck wagon up next to the barn and unhitched the mules. Donato, Red, and Poke rode up, grimy, bearded, and grinning.

"Got some new riders you'll want to meet," said Pen. "Where's McCaleb?"

"Still in Montana, I reckon," said Will. "The girls are all startin' to worry, but I expect this wild horse hunt is taking more time than we thought it would. Get these critters on our range and bring the new riders along to the cookhouse."

* * *

July 4 dawned clear, and although the race didn't begin until two o'clock, most of the Indian riders already had their horses somewhere near the track. Along the south bank, across from the track, smoke rose from a hundred fires. Swede Oliphant was in a café having breakfast. McCaleb kicked back a chair and sat down.

"I'll kind of be glad when this is over and done," said Oliphant. "It ain't a nice thing to say, but I ain't never seen this many Injuns in one place at one time that there wasn't trouble. Not to say it's always th' fault of the Injuns. There'll be more money changin' hands today than this town sees in a year."

"It would have been a good day to close all the saloons."

"You kiddin'? Anybody suggestin' that would of been gut-shot just on general principles. It's th' saloons that's put up most of the money for th' prize. Naturally they aim to make it back ten times over."

"Even if everybody gets liquored up and somebody gets killed."

"That's just the way it is," said Oliphant. "Kind of goes with th' territory. You can't have a doin's like this without some risk."

A black mare jogged past the café, a young boy in the saddle. The mare had four white stockings and a white blaze on its face.

"Unusual," said McCaleb. "They usually have two or three stockings, but seldom four. Is that one going to run?"

"Yeah," said Oliphant. "That's Dancing Molly. Willie Benteen ridin' her. His daddy, old Jubal, is th' town drunk. He claims the horse, but left to him, it'd starve to death. Th' kid raised it from a colt. It's got th' looks but it ain't got th' blood. It ain't got a prayer, but th' kid's proud of it. When you're twelve years old, you need somethin' to look up to, an' he sure as hell ain't got nothin' else."

Monte Nance came in, sat down at another table and ordered coffee. He made it a point not to look at McCaleb. Oliphant seemed aware of the strain between them. He looked at Monte with a kind of half grin.

"Best keep your gun handy, Sheriff. When all this bunch gets drunk, gambles away their money an' ends up with a mad on, this town'll be Hell with th' lid off an' all th' fires lit."

Monte glared at them as though he suspected McCaleb had put Oliphant up to taunting him. McCaleb said nothing and his look was steady, unwavering. Monte gulped his coffee, got up and walked out. Oliphant looked at McCaleb. When he spoke, he was dead serious.

"Th' kid's drove his ducks to a bad market. He's th' third sheriff in less'n a year."

McCaleb didn't need to ask what had become of the others. The second he had seen bleeding and dying. It wasn't difficult to imagine the first one suffering a similar fate. He purely hated having to ride back to the ranch without Monte. Knowing her brother, Rebecca would understand, but it wouldn't lessen her pain.

By one o'clock everything and everybody was ready. They spent an impatient hour slaking their thirst in the saloons, placing final bets or just wandering about town. Goose was already near the starting line and the gray horse was ready. Although the animal readily accepted a saddle, Goose had chosen to ride without one. While it would spare the horse the extra weight, McCaleb suspected an ulterior motive. None of the other Indian riders were using saddles. Goose was furthering the illusion that he was just another "Injun rider," not to be taken seriously. If Goose, being Indian, actually won the race, all hell was likely to break loose. With that in mind, he went looking for Brazos and shared his misgivings.

"Find the rest of the outfit," said McCaleb, "and join me near the finish line. Goose may need us."

Few wished to witness the start of the race, but everybody seemed to want to see the finish. A few had binoculars or telescopes, and the many who didn't were envious. McCaleb had an old glass that had seen him through the Rangers, and he used it now, finding Goose at the starting line. There was a total of fifty riders, and the Apache was near the middle of the long line. Finally it was time. Mc-Caleb didn't even hear the starting gun. He knew the race had started only because he could see the running horses through the glass. Both Vonnecker's horses were to the right of Goose, while Willie Benteen's Dancing Molly was to his left. Several of the Indian ponies took an early lead, the rest in hot pursuit, boxing both Vonnecker's riders. In an attempt to break loose, the black shouldered into an Indian horse. The spotted horse began to buck jump, and a dozen others, including Vonnecker's black, collided with it. They went down in a neighing, screaming tangle. Vonnecker's bay, frightened by the spectacle, did some bucking of its own. The rider was dumped on the track and run over by another horse. The bay lit out for the Yellowstone, splashed across to the south bank and stood looking back at all the confusion. Goose trotted the gray across the finish line and the horse wasn't even sweating. Dancing Molly finished second.

Interest in the finish had become secondary. Many of those who had gathered at the finish line were now on their way to the opposite end of the track to better view the disaster on the track. Willie Benteen reined up the black and dismounted. A big man came stomping out of the crowd and headed for Willie. But Jubal Benteen ignored Willie. He had a heavy, shot-filled quirt, and swinging it as hard as he could, he struck the black mare across her nose. The animal screamed, jerked the reins from Willie's hand and ran. Goose moved with the speed of a striking rattler. He tore the quirt from the big man's hand. Swinging it as hard as he could, he opened a bloody gash on Benteen's cheek from eye to jawbone. Benteen screamed and collapsed in the dust, but his fury overcame his pain. He went for his gun, but his hand froze in midair. He found himself looking into the muzzle of a Colt, rock-steady in the Indian's left hand. Few of them liked Benteen. They knew what he was, but however no-account, he was still a white man. An Indian didn't draw on a white man, whatever the provocation, and live to tell about it. A dozen men moved toward Goose, their hands on their guns. But they paused. The Indian wasn't alone. McCaleb and Brazos stood to his left, Charlie and Laredo to his right. Their thumbs were hooked in their belts just inches away from holstered Colts. Directly behind Goose stood Harley Irwin with a Winchester.

"He's part of my outfit," said McCaleb quietly. "You saw what happened. He did what needed doing. You're not taking him unless you take us all, and somebody's going to die."

Muttering, they backed away. They managed to escape further embarrassment when the bunch from the other end of the track arrived, whooping and hollering. At the head of the crowd was Vonnecker, and behind him were his two riders, bloody, bruised, and limping. Swede Oliphant was there, saying nothing. Vonnecker was trailed by some of the other saloon owners, and none of them looked happy. Everybody talked or shouted at once.

"Quiet!" bawled McCaleb. *"Everybody just shut up!"*

"You can't tell me to shut up!" squalled Vonnecker.

"I can and you will," said McCaleb, "or I'll silence you with a pistol barrel alongside your skull. Now Oliphant, why don't you explain what this uproar's all about?"

"I'll try," said Oliphant. "Vonnecker claims the race was fixed, that one of the Injun riders purposely caused that tangle so's your man could win. He's demanding that the race be run again, between his horses and the gray the Indian was riding."

"You're entitled to no such thing, Vonnecker," said McCaleb. "I was watching through a glass and it was one of *your* riders that shouldered into an Indian pony and caused all this."

"Nobody else saw it," shouted Vonnecker. "These damn Indians all stick together when they go up against a white man."

He was telling the crowd what they wanted to hear.

There was but one way out and Goose took it. He walked up to Vonnecker, his dark eyes sparking fire. Everybody froze, and for the first time that day there was utter, uninterrupted silence. Goose spoke softly, but they heard every word.

"Ganos lose, you take." He pointed to the gray horse.

It was exactly what the crowd wanted to hear. Goose was betting his horse against Vonnecker's, forcing Vonnecker to match his bet. Vonnecker swallowed hard, hesitating. Like a pack of wolves turning on a wounded comrade, they jumped Vonnecker.

"The Indian's got sand, Vonnecker," somebody shouted. "Where's yours?"

"You wanted another race," bawled another. "Now put up or shut up. Th' Injun's already won. You don't match his bet, the finish stands."

"All right," growled Vonnecker with poor grace, "I'll match your bet. You win, you take my horse. I win, I take yours."

The crowd went crazy. More bets were placed. Goose mounted the gray and rode back to the starting line. Somebody had caught Vonnecker's horses, and neither seemed any the worse for their experience. Despite their cuts and bruises, Vonnecker's riders insisted on riding the second race. When they were mounted and in position next to Goose, the starting gun was fired and the second race was under way. The black and the bay seemed eager to redeem themselves for their ignominious behavior in the first race and took an immediate lead. Their riders, determined to maintain that lead to the finish, began using their quirts. Goose kept the gray at an even, lazy pace, neither losing nor gaining. For the first two-thirds of the race, he was a full two lengths behind. Then Goose did a curious thing. He leaned far out on the gray's neck and, with the help of the glass, McCaleb could see his lips moving. The gray's ears went up and he put his belly to the ground like a running wolf. From there on it was no contest. They shot past Vonnecker's horses and crossed the finish line two full lengths ahead.

"Let's hear it for the Indian!" shouted a voice.

They surrounded Goose, whooping and yelling, and embarrassed as he was by the attention, he was unable to escape. Somebody snatched away the reins of the two horses and brought them to Goose. But McCaleb was looking at Irv Vonnecker, and there was murder in the man's eyes. He had twice been humiliated, and had lost literally thousands of dollars in bets. While Goose was being mobbed by men wanting to shake his hand, Vonnecker was surrounded by men waiting to collect their bets.

"We'll be pulling out in the morning," McCaleb told Oliphant. "We've been here too long already. I'm supposed to deliver a herd to Dakota Territory before snow flies. I'll plan on bringin' you some more steers next spring."

The street dance was well-attended. Lanterns flickered in the July darkness and every saloon in town was roaring. For music there was a fiddle, a banjo, and a mouth harp. While one old-timer sawed the fiddle, another beat straws to keep time.

"My God," said Harley Irwin, "winnin' at twenty-to-one odds! I never had so much money in my life!"

Things had turned out too well, thought McCaleb, except for Monte. He returned to camp and listened to them crow over the Apache's victory and their enormous winnings.

"Goose lit out after the race," said McCaleb. "Any of you seen him?"

"Yeah," said Harley. "He went over to that Crow camp on the other side of the Yellowstone. Them Injuns think he's a rich man, winnin' them hosses and all that money. Lord, he put up five times as much as the rest of us."

McCaleb was up before good daylight. After breakfast they turned south, stopping in Miles City just long enough to get their horses from Oliphant and for a last word with

Monte. McCaleb wasn't looking forward to that. Brazos went with him, not because he wanted to, but because he felt sorry for McCaleb. Leaving Charlie, Laredo, Harley, and Salty at Oliphant's, McCaleb and Brazos went to the sheriff's office. Monte didn't seem especially pleased to see them.

"We're pulling out, Monte," said McCaleb. "You have money due you, if you need it. Do you?"

"No," said Monte. "I . . . tell Rebecca—"

"She knows," said McCaleb. "She knew when you rode out the last time."

Monte swallowed hard. Brazos put out his hand, and Monte took it. He turned to McCaleb and saw only sadness in the man's face. There was no malice, no anger. Monte took the hand McCaleb offered. McCaleb spoke.

"Good luck, Monte. You have a stake in Wyoming, when you're ready for it."

Without another word he turned away, Brazos following. Monte watched them out of sight, and he had never felt so alone in all his life.

"One more thing," said McCaleb. "Goose. Go on back to Oliphant's and I'll join you there. I want to check out that Crow camp."

The bank of the Yellowstone was deserted, only the ashes of old fires attesting to those who had been there. While there were numerous trails and many led horses, only two of them were shod—those that Goose had won. The trail led to the northeast. The Crow were gone, and Goose with them.

"I'm going to miss Goose more than Monte," said Brazos. "At least he's got a reason, that young Indian girl making eyes at him."

McCaleb still watched their back trail, but after the third day, even he gave up. Their horses, even the newly gentled, trailed well, and they were soon in northern Wyoming.

They were six days out of Miles City. It was past sundown and they had picketed the horses near a small creek where the grass was good. Suddenly there were hoofbeats. Three horses.

"Two riders," said Brazos, "comin' along our back trail."

Goose rode the gray horse and led the bay. The Crow girl with the dark eyes rode the black. Goose dismounted and nodded toward the girl.

"Belleza," he said.

It was all the introduction he offered, but for now it was enough.

It had been easy for Monte Nance to ignore McCaleb as long as he was in Miles City. Once the outfit was gone, he found his mind drifting back to those days in East Texas, on the Trinity River. He had been a snot-nosed kid the first time he'd seen McCaleb. He had drawn on the Texan, and McCaleb could have killed him instead of nicking his shoulder. McCaleb had given him hell. But only when he had behaved, as Brazos put it, like "a Missouri short horn." He recalled the old days in Missouri when York Nance, his old mule-rustling daddy, had drifted from pillar to post. For the first time in his life he had had a home, somewhere he belonged. What was he doing here, breaking up fights between drunks and jumping every time Vonnecker pulled his string? On the fifth day after the outfit pulled out, he made his decision. He walked into Vonnecker's saloon office without knocking. He took the star from his shirt and dropped it on the desk.

"I'm done," he said.

"I see," said Vonnecker. "Don't have the sand, do you?"

"I don't need sand to be a flunky. Or even brains."

"So when things get tough, you run out."

"Yeah," said Monte, "like you ran from the Sweetwater."

The ugly look in Vonnecker's eyes should have warned Monte, but his mind was far away, on Box Elder Creek, in southern Wyoming. He had turned, started for the door, when Vonnecker cocked the Colt. The click of the hammer jolted Monte back to reality, and he hit the floor, drawing as he went down. Vonnecker's first shot splintered the door, and the second one blasted into the floor at his feet. Monte had rolled to his left and put two slugs into Vonnecker's belly, just above his belt buckle. Vonnecker sagged against the wall, hung there until his knees buckled, and slid down to the floor. Without a backward glance, Monte left the office and slipped out the back door. He went to the livery, saddled his horse, and rode south.

For three days after her arrival, Belleza cooked her own meals over a separate fire. Salty saw her as a challenge, and finally won her over with his dried apple pie. Goose was helpful, and slowly the girl began to trust them. She developed a real affection for Salty.

"Injuns is all alike," said Salty. "They ain't too diff'rent from Texas cowboys. Take care of their bellies, an' ever'thing else'll work out."

They'd been on the trail ten days when Monte rode in. He was unshaven and dirty. Wearily he dismounted and turned to McCaleb.

"I thought about what you said, Bent. About my stake. If you don't mind havin' a damn fool around, one that sometimes don't know what he wants, I'd like to go home."

"Welcome," said McCaleb with a grin. "Man's got a right to make a fool of himself, long as he don't let it become permanent."

"You won't be bunking with Goose anymore," said Brazos. "He's done gone and improved his status. With some help from this little gal, he might even prefer a bed to the floor. By the way, how did Mayor Vonnecker like it when you pulled out?"

"He didn't," said Monte. "Tried to shoot me in the back, so I gut-shot him. I might not be able to go back to Miles City with you next year."

"Kid," said Brazos, "I'm sorry I ever called you a Missouri short horn. You may be a damn fool at times, but you're a damn fool Texan!"

* * *

They were an outfit, triumphant, Texans all. In the Sweetwater valley, from the Platte River to the Green, they would build a High Plains empire, never forgetting their Texas heritage. Theirs would be the Lone Star Brand.

EPILOGUE

*G*eorge Francis Train, with all his millions, came out of the Credit Mobilier disaster without a scratch. The scandal, when it finally broke in 1872, shook America. Oakes Ames, given the mandate by President Lincoln to build the railroad, was censured by Congress. The nation had spent $70 million to build a $50-million railroad.

George Francis Train tried again for the presidency in 1872, and the following year he ran for the dictatorship of the United States.

Train set off on a trip around the world. Reaching Britain, he took a stand for Irish independence, and spent many months in an English jail. He was finally freed, and was promptly jailed in France, after joining the revolutionists. Two weeks later he was freed and kicked out of France. Train was a staunch supporter of women's suffrage, and contributed $15,000 to Susan B. Anthony.

Victoria Woodhull, a nineteenth-century crusader for free love, had been arrested on charges of obscenity. Through a newspaper he founded, Train so vigorously fought for her that he was also jailed for obscenity. Despite Train's protests, his lawyers got him acquitted through a plea of insanity. But the verdict tied up most of his wealth for the rest of his life. George Francis Train died in 1904, in a cheap New York hotel.

William F. (Buffalo Bill) Cody, following his days of buffalo shooting, Indian fighting, and scouting, found his true calling. He began a flamboyant outdoor melodrama he called "The Wild West," which took him to Broadway and eventually to Europe. Cody, a town in northwestern Wyoming, is named for him.

The Medicine Wheel, its origin unknown, is located atop Bald Mountain, a few miles southwest of Sheridan, Wyoming.

The discovery of gold in the Sweetwater valley created some excitement, but not for long. Pockets of gold were few and far between, and the valley again became cattle country.

HERE IS AN EXCERPT FROM *THE CHISHOLM TRAIL*—BOOK 3 IN RALPH COMPTON'S EXCITING WESTERN SERIES:

The nights continued peaceful, leading Ten more and more to expect a daytime attack while they were on the trail. They were a few miles south of the Red River crossing when the Comanches struck. Ten was half a dozen miles ahead of the herd, and with the wind from the northwest, the dust warned him of approaching riders long before he saw them.

He first sighted the Comanches as they emerged from a brushy draw. They rode in a column of twos, trotting their horses. Ten watched as long as as he dared, not wishing to stampede the herd unless the odds were otherwise insurmountable. Clear of the draw, the mounted Comanches bunched, and Ten had his answer. He kicked his horse into a run, riding south toward the oncoming herd. He pulled his Henry and fired three quick shots. Even with the wind against them, the Comanches were close enough to hear his warning shots. They would be after him within seconds, but there was no help for it. It would take time for the drag riders to get the herd running. Even against the wind, he heard Charlie Two Hats repeat his three shots. Almost immediately, there was the distant thunder of rifles, and the drag riders began forcing the herd to run.

Ten slowed his horse, looking back. He must bait the trap, allowing the pursuing Comanches to see him. He rode one of the blacks they'd gotten from Maynard Herndon, and from here on, his very life would depend on the valiant horse. If the maneuver was to be successful, he would have to lure the attackers into the teeth of the stampede. But he also must avoid being caught in the stampede himself. Once the herd began to run, they might overrun the flank riders, bearing down on him like a living avalanche of destruction. However they ran, his only chance lay in riding around the thundering herd at right or left flank.

When he saw the charging herd coming, it was even more massed, presenting an even wider front than he'd feared. Some of the longhorns from the middle and tag end of the herd had broken ranks, had swerved around, and were following the leaders. Coming at him on the run was an unbroken line of wild Texas longhorns a mile wide! It was time to get out of their path—if he could. He wheeled his black to the east, riding hard. But without warning, the earth seemed to give away beneath them. The running horse screamed, stumbled, and Ten left the saddle. He rolled, barely escaping being crushed by the falling horse. Dazed, he got to his knees. The black had staggered to its feet just in time for a Comanche arrow to graze its flank. Nickering in fear, the black galloped away. Ten eyed the oncoming herd, and he saw no escape. Then, far to his left, from among the charging longhorns, came a buckskin-clad Indian rider. The task he had chosen was impossible, but on he came! Soon he was ahead of the herd, and he wheeled his horse directly across its path. But the attacking Comanches, seeking to escape the oncoming herd, had followed Ten. Now they found themselves within range of this oncoming rider, and loosed a barrage of arrows at him. Ten's would-be rescuer rode all the harder, and in response to the Comanche arrows, pulled his Henry and began firing. But the arrows were many, and one of them found its mark. Ten saw the rider flinch as the arrow caught him in the right side. But still he rode, and now he was close enough for Ten to recognize the grinning face of Sashavado!

The Cherokee circled Ten, wheeled his horse, and gave Ten his hand. Ten pulled himself up behind Sashavado, and the Indian kicked the weary horse into a run. The animal's flanks were wet, and Ten could hear it blowing. There were no more arrows. Ten looked back, and the Comanches had given up everything except getting out of the path of the herd. Despite Sashavado's hard riding, and the supreme efforts of his horse, they were caught up in part of the stampede. But they were near the outer edge, on the left flank, and Sashavado allowed the horse to lope along with the slowing longhorns. The stampede had lost its momentum, but so had the attack by the Comanches.

Once free of the herd, Ten dropped off the weary horse. Sashavado reined up, but when he tried to dismount, he fell. Ten caught the Indian, easing him to the ground. The arrow had gone in just above his waistband, and he looked hard hit. Charlie Two Hats, Marty, and Priscilla reined up, and quit their saddles on the run. Priscilla's face went white as she saw the arrow in Sashavado's side. Charlie Two Hats said nothing.

"Marty," said Ten, "bring me a horse, and a fresh one for Sashavado. You and me are takin' him back to Fort Worth. There'll be a doc at the fort, and they'll have medicine."

"Dear God," cried Priscilla, "he's hurt. How can he ride?"

"Sashavado ride," gritted the Indian.

Marty returned with a horse for Ten, and a fresh one for Sashavado. Ten spoke to Charlie Two Hats.

"Charlie, the rest of you begin rounding up the herd. Move them to the nearest water and graze, and bed them down. Keep everybody on watch, just in case those Comanches have another go at us. Me and Marty will be back when Sashavado's been taken care of, and after I've reported this attack to Captain Fanning."

"There's nobody left with the herd," said Priscilla, "except Wes, Chris, and Lou. The Cherokees have gone after the Comanches."

Ten looked at Two Hats, and the Indian shrugged.

"Cow no run," said Two Hats. "Comanche run. Kill Comanche, catch cow."

It was Indian logic. Ten nodded. The herd was moving north, and had slowed to barely a walk. Many of the longhorns had stopped to graze. Two Hats' riders wouldn't pursue the Comanches too far. The Cherokees were far outnumbered, and smart enough not to ride into an ambush. Ten turned to Priscilla.

"Find Wes, Chris, and Lou," he said, "and stay with them until I return."

THE CHISHOLM TRAIL—NOW AVAILABLE FROM ST. MARTIN'S PAPERBACKS!